THE WRITE ROMANT

PRESENT

WINTER TALES

STORIES TO WARM YOUR HEART

A CHARITY ANTHOLOGY IN AID OF

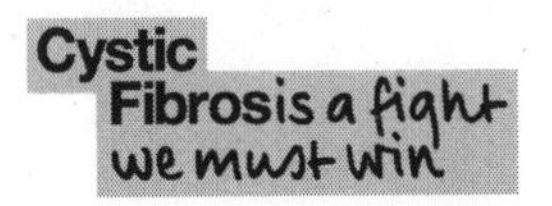

ISBN:
ISBN-13:

Typesetting and Design by
Mark Heslington Ltd, Scarborough, North Yorkshire

Contents

This book is dedicated to all those battling against Cystic Fibrosis and Cancer and to the wonderful people fighting to find a cure for these life-shattering illnesses, in support of which this anthology was written. Most of all this book is dedicated to two very special boys –

For Stephen Sutton – an exceptional young man who stirred the hearts and minds of millions, including the contributors to this anthology.

And for Thomas – a gorgeous and cheeky little chap in equal measure – and the thousands like him, who deserve the right to a long and healthy life.

Our inspirations...

Introduction

It's an honour to introduce this lovely collection of short stories by some of my favourite people.

I like hats, which is a good thing because today I'm wearing two of them. As a writer, I got to know the writers and bloggers at The Write Romantics soon after my own novel, *One Night at the Jacaranda*, came out in 2013. They're a talented lot, and you're going to be seeing a lot more of their creative output in the years to come.

For now, let me assure you that within your hands is an anthology of stories that will make you feel good and keep you guessing. Yes, here within just a few thousand words you'll find plots with more twists than a bowl of spiral pasta (but far fewer calories).

As a doctor, I'm all too aware of the impact of serious diseases. It's shocking to realise that in the UK around seven young people aged 13 to 24 get a diagnosis of cancer every day. They develop some of the most aggressive and unexpected tumours, and they need expert treatment to give them the best outcome.

Because they're at a challenging stage in life, they also need support tailored to their needs. The Teenage Cancer Trust develops specialist units within NHS hospitals that do exactly this. They fund vital research too, and this is expensive. Survival rates have improved hugely since I first qualified, but more research could save many more lives and help these young people fulfil their dreams.

Although cystic fibrosis (CF) is also life-threatening, it's a very different challenge. Nobody catches or develops CF. It's an inherited disease caused by a faulty gene, and each week five babies are born with CF.

Thanks to improved care, those with CF can now live into middle age, but there's still no cure as such so there's a desperate need for more research. The CF Trust is committed to world-class research and innovation to help change the lives of those with the condition.

I'm sure you'll be pleased to know that sales of this anthology will support both these excellent charities. So sit yourself down and savour these wonderful stories. They'll bring a smile to your lips without leaving a trace on the hips.

Happy reading.
Carol Cooper

Carol Cooper is a doctor, journalist, author and The Sun newspaper's GP. She practises in London and also teaches at Imperial College Medical School.

If you'd like to find out more about Carol, here's how:

Twitter: @DrCarolCooper
Facebook: www.facebook.com/onenightatthejacaranda
Blog:http://pillsandpillowtalk.com
Website: www.drcarolcooper.com
Amazon Author Page: http://www.amazon.co.uk/Dr-Carol-Cooper/e/B005C2ZZ10/ref=ntt_dp_epwbk_0

One Night at the Jacaranda (2013) is Carol's racy romantic novel, available on Amazon. ISBN 1492803421

The Write Romantics would like to express their thanks and their gratitude to everyone who helped produce 'Winter Tales'.

We would like to thank our contributors for their willingness and enthusiasm to write the short stories that make up our anthology. We hope that the stories reach far and wide and raise money for our two nominated charities: Cystic Fibrosis Trust and Teenage Cancer Trust. Our thanks go to Rhoda Baxter, Zanna Mackenzie, Alison May, Holly Martin, Kerry Fisher, Sarah Painter, Jennifer Bohnet, Terri Nixon, Annie Lyons, Linda Huber, Sarah Lewis and Samantha Tonge.

A special mention also goes to Dr Carol Cooper for writing our introduction to 'Winter Tales' and to Liz Berry who came up with the title.

This has been a new learning experience for us and we couldn't have done it without advice and guidance from Ian Skillicorn, Mary Beavis and Tracy Irwin.

We really must thank The Romantic Novelists' Association (RNA) too because, without them, we'd never have met, this book wouldn't have been written, and there wouldn't be lots of money (hopefully) winging its way to two very worthy charities. So thank you, RNA, for running The New Writer's Scheme that gave ten aspiring writers the feedback and the belief that we could make it.

And finally our heartfelt thanks go to Mark Heslington for all his hard work supporting The Write Romantics. Mark came up with our fabulous logo, designed our cover, and typeset the book. He also designed a style for CreateSpace so that we could produce 'Winter Tales' as a paperback on demand as well as an eBook.

We hope that you all enjoy reading this wonderful collection of short stories as much as we loved writing them.

The Write Romantics

Not Just Another Winter's Tale

Jessica Redland

'He's coming!' Ben's chair fell to the floor with a clatter as he leapt to his feet, holding his mobile phone high in the air, his expression a mixture of jubilation and panic.

'Congratulations!' Our manager, Paul, rushed over to shake Ben's hand. 'You'd best get going, then. Enjoy your paternity leave.'

'Thanks, Paul.' Ben grabbed his coat and dived towards the door. 'I can't believe I'm going to be a dad at last!'

Whilst delighted for my colleague (I'd seen him crumble after three failed attempts at IVF), my heart sank as he pulled the door open. Ben had driven me to the team-building workshop. How was I going to get home? As if reading my mind, he paused in the open doorway. 'Oh! Emma. Lift.'

'Go!' ordered Paul. 'Or you'll miss the birth. We'll make sure Emma gets home safely.'

The door closed. I glanced around the room at my colleagues and did a mental count. Mike had four passengers already and Rachel only had two but her car was tiny and I remembered her saying it had taken five attempts to fit all their luggage in on Monday. Paul had come alone but I was sure he wasn't heading straight back. Which just left one possibility. Oh crap!

'I can take Emma,' he said. I didn't want to look at him because, if I looked, I'd have to pretend I was grateful when the thought of a two-hour drive with Troy Zimmerman actually brought me out in a cold sweat.

Paul had announced on Monday that a new team member would be joining us for the final day but had refused to give anything else away. When Troy walked through the door and smiled his dazzling smile, I'd have been less surprised if a unicorn had galloped into the room with Elvis on its back. It was just as well I'd been sitting down because my legs actually gave way beneath me and I had to take several big gulps of air to stop myself from passing out.

'Thank you, Troy,' Paul said. 'First day in the UK and already a team player. Now, where were we?'

I mouthed a reluctant 'thanks' across to Troy and squirmed as he smiled. Team player? Well, if the definition of "team player" was "completely untrustworthy and unreliable" then I guess he was an incredibly good team player.

As Paul continued to witter on about our team objectives for the year ahead, my mind drifted to the summer. It had all been Paul's fault. If he'd been watching where he'd been going instead of jabbering on his mobile as usual, he'd have seen the raised paving slab. He wouldn't have tripped. He wouldn't have broken his right arm and leg. He wouldn't have had to stay at home. As the only other team-member working on Project Phoenix, I wouldn't have taken his place during the US roll-out. And I wouldn't have met Troy bloody Zimmerman.

'Couldn't I just grab a lift home with you?' I whispered to Paul during the coffee break, hoping I'd misheard his plans.

'Sorry, Emma, but I'm not going back tonight. I've got family in Nottingham so I'm making a weekend of it while I'm in the area. Don't look so worried. You're in capable hands with Troy. Plus, you know him pretty well from the summer, don't you?'

I nodded and hoped he wouldn't notice my cheeks colouring. Yes, I knew Troy pretty well from the summer. A bit too well perhaps. And capable hands? Yes, he had very capable hands. I knew that too. Far too capable. A tingle ran down my spine as I recalled those hands running through my hair, down my arms and… Eek! He just touched me!

Troy steered me away from Paul. 'I have a conference call to The States after the workshop. I'll be about an hour. Hope you don't mind waiting.'

'Waiting for you? Been there, done that, got the t-shirt,' I muttered.

'I'm sorry.'

I sighed. 'I need a lift so I guess I don't have much choice, do I?'

'I'm sorry,' he said again. His hazel eyes pleaded with mine and, for a moment, I wondered if he was apologising for more than the delayed departure. I shook my head and walked away. Of course he wasn't. I was being stupid. He'd had plenty of opportunities to say sorry before now and he hadn't taken them. He was clearly unrepentant.

An hour later, my colleagues had left, Troy had disappeared back into the training room for his conference call, and the staff at the training centre were busy clearing up. I helped myself to a cup of tea then sank into one of the squashy armchairs in the large residents' lounge. I rummaged in my bag for my Kindle but I couldn't concentrate on reading. Every time I tried to focus on the words, all I could think about was the summer. And when I thought about the summer, I was back to those capable hands. And being kissed by that capable mouth.

I'd hated Troy instantly. Well, maybe not hated, but I'd disliked him intensely from the moment he'd asked his first question. I'd been terrified about stepping in at the last minute and briefing the project in an unfamiliar country to a bunch of strangers who were all at least two grades above me. The last thing I'd needed was his constant questions. Actually, questions I could have coped with but it was his challenges that I couldn't bear. Had we not considered x or y? Why had we developed the system this way instead of that way? Because we bloody well had! Get over it! I swear that first week in Texas had been the most stressful experience of my working life. Not just my working life; make that my life full stop.

After that, I was expected to stick around for another two months to make adjustments to the system to "meet the specific needs and cultural differences" of our US colleagues. Which would mean two more months of Troy Zimmerman. Absolutely hideous. Then, to top it all, I was expected to go on the Company Retreat just two weeks into my secondment. Aargh! A whole weekend surrounded by work colleagues who I barely knew, their families who I had no reason to get to know, and Troy.

I stood up and reached for my coat as Troy approached an hour later but the look on his face told me that my actions were premature.

'Sorry Ems.' The use of my pet name sent a tingle down my spine. 'It's not going as planned. We've broken for coffee but I could be another hour.'

I sighed as I sat down again. 'Just as well I hadn't made any plans this evening, then.'

'I really am sorry.' Once more, I got the feeling it wasn't just an apology for the ongoing delay. I averted my eyes and pretended to be gripped by the story on my Kindle until he walked away. I hoped he hadn't noticed it was upside down.

'Right team, this afternoon's activity is a treasure hunt,' the CEO, Will, had announced on day two of the retreat. 'Our very own Troy Zimmerman is going to hide out somewhere in these extensive grounds and the rest of you need to pull together as a team to solve clues to find him. But we can't leave him without company. Who shall we send with him?'

Will scanned the crowd and I knew in the pit of my stomach who he was going to pick. I tried to shrink back behind a couple of my taller colleagues but it was too late.

'I know! Let's do our bit for Anglo-US relations. Emma Chambers. Won't you come up here and join Troy?'

To cheers and claps, I was unceremoniously shoved forward, cursing under my breath. Hide and seek? With Troy? Urgh.

A backpack was thrust into my hands and a baseball cap dumped on my head.

'There's water, snacks, sunscreen and first aid supplies in the pack,' Will said. 'Troy knows where you're going. You should be there a good ninety minutes before anyone else so it's a great chance to really get to know each other.' He clapped us both on the back and beamed at me as though he'd bestowed some great honour on me.

'Ninety minutes before the others?' I didn't manage to keep the panic out of my voice.

Will laughed. 'You're in great company. Troy will keep you entertained, won't you Troy?'

'I'll do my best. Are you set, Ems?'

Snarling at his audacity at shortening my name, I trotted after him across the gardens and down the drive of the large ranch where we were staying.

'Where are we going?'

'Into the mountains,' he said.

'Are you going to elaborate on that?'

'Do you know the area?'

'No.'

'Then why would me elaborating on it make any difference?'

'Smart arse,' I muttered.

'What's that?'

'Nothing.'

I trailed behind him as he turned off the drive onto a pathway that meandered through the forest. What the heck were we going to talk about for ninety minutes when we got to wherever it was we were going?

We must have traipsed in silence for a good half an hour. I knew my face was the colour of beetroot, and the sensation of sweat trickling down my back and into my knickers made me squirm.

I removed my baseball cap and wiped the sweat off my brow. 'How much further?' I shouted up to him.

'Only about fifteen minutes.'

'But we'll have only been going for about forty-five minutes. I thought Will said it would be ninety minutes before they found us.'

'Mind the branch.' He passed a low hanging branch to me and I ducked under it. 'They have clues to solve and they won't come on a direct route so it will take them a lot longer than us to get there.'

'Where's there?'

'You'll find out in about fifteen minutes.'

I put my cap back on and swatted a couple of flies, imagining they were Troy. 'But…' But a low rumbling sound stopped me dead in my tracks. 'Was that thunder?'

'I didn't hear anything.' Troy kept walking. 'We checked the weather. We're not expecting a storm.'

'I'm sure it was thunder.' I cocked my head to one side, listening intently, but the moment had passed. I reluctantly ran after him up the steep track.

'What would happen if there was a storm?' I asked when I caught up with him.

'We'd need to run for shelter. Fast. When we get a storm here, the rain's so heavy that these tracks become like rivers of mud. It's not a safe place to be.'

My stomach lurched. 'Then why are we out here when it's thundering?'

Troy stopped, turned round and sighed. 'I've already told you, Ems, we've checked the weather. It's gonna be hot and sunny all day. Just like yesterday. Stop creating problems that don't exist.' He turned again and continued his ascent.

I strode after him. 'You're a fine one to talk.'

'What's that supposed to mean?'

'You've spent the last fortnight creating problems with the system that don't exist. It's been a nightmare trying to explain it to you with your constant aggressive challenges. I've never met anyone so confrontational and rude in my whole life. Do you know how difficult it's been for me to come out here on my own, last minute, and face all that criticism? It's been hell and I wish I'd never agreed to it.' I bit my lip. I hadn't meant to say all that. There had been some good bits and he hadn't been awful all the time. To be fair to him, he'd also given compliments and made some pretty good suggestions too but I wasn't going to tell him that.

He stopped but didn't turn round. I watched his shoulders tense. He had nice shoulders; very muscular. Nice legs too; tanned and strong. I had to tell myself to stop admiring his physique; it was just the wrapping on a rather unpleasant gift.

'Is that how I've come across to you?'

'Yes.'

He finally turned. His cheeks were red and his eyes were full of sorrow. 'That wasn't my intention, Ems. I was really impressed with the project. I'm sorry if that didn't come across in my questions. That's good feedback. I'm gonna learn from that. I'm really sorry I've made your time here so difficult. I just... Never mind. Definitely good feedback. Thanks for sharing.'

'I... er... you're welcome.' We stared at each other for a few moments. His hazel eyes had little flecks of green and gold in them that were really quite beautiful and mesmerising and...

His eyes widened as an unmistakably loud growl echoed through the forest.

'I told you I could hear thunder.' I couldn't resist the opportunity to gloat, yet my heart raced with fear as I saw the panic clearly etched across his face. 'Are we in danger?'

'Only if it starts to rain. Let's hurry.'

He set off at a pace with me scurrying along behind him. It wasn't long before a large drop of rain splashed on my forearm followed by another, then several more.

'Run!' Troy yelled.

My walking boots slipped in the mud as I scrambled up the track after him, heart thumping. I grabbed at nearby branches to pull myself up the track quicker. The branches cut into my palms but there was no time to worry about a few scrapes; the worry in Troy's eyes each time he glanced back told me we were in serious trouble.

'We're gonna reach the road in a minute,' he shouted over the rain. 'We need to run along it for a couple of minutes then turn off and scramble up a bank. Can you run, Ems?'

'Of course I can run.'

'I mean really run. Like fast.'

My stomach churned with fear. 'Yes. Really fast.' I actually hated running and fast was certainly not a word you'd apply to my efforts but I'd find some speed from somewhere. This was serious.

We reached the road. I say road but it was more like a river of mud. I felt sick.

'Troy?'

'I know. We can do this, Ems. It isn't far. Do you trust me?'

'Yes.' And, at that moment, I really did.

'My promise to you is that I'll get you to safety. If you trust me, you'll know it's true. Have you got your breath back? Can you run now?'

I wiped at the tears mingled with rain and nodded.

Thunder crashed, lightning lit the angry sky, the rain pounded my skin. It was like nothing I'd experienced before. The ground seemed to soften under my feet with every step. My boots were heavy with clods of clay and my body felt drained of energy with only my mind – and fear – to propel me forward.

Rivers of mud spurted down the mountains either side of us. *I'm not going to die today. Troy said he'd get me to safety and I trust him. I'm not going to die today.*

'Left,' he yelled, veering towards the side and scrambling up a bank.

He reached down and took hold of my hand to pull me up and for that brief moment with our hands held and eyes locked, a sizzle of something exciting passed through me. A crash of thunder quickly replaced that excitement with fear again and the moment was lost.

'Not far. Hold onto the branches.'

'I am,' I yelled. Did he think I was stupid? I hauled myself up, adding more cuts to my palms and arms. My feet slid out of control in the muddy waterfall cascading from high. My arms burned from the upper body strength required to stay upright.

'Emma! Look out!'

I glanced at my watch. Troy was seriously taking the mickey. Two hours had already passed. I stood up and stretched. My head ached. I reached up and rubbed my forehead. My fingers traced over the raised scar just below my hairline and a shiver ran through me as I thought of Troy's gentle touch when it was bleeding.

'Where am I?' The gloomy room smelt damp. I was laid on something too hard to be a mattress but too soft to be the floor. A camping roll perhaps?

'Emma? Thank God. I've been so worried about you.' His voice sounded thick with emotion.

I tried to sit up but my whole body screamed out in pain. I gasped as I lay back down.

'Don't try to move.' Troy crouched down beside me and took hold of my hand. 'You've had a nasty fall.'

I gripped his hand. 'Something hit me.' I reached up with my spare hand and rubbed my head. It felt sticky. I whimpered as I lowered my hand and saw the blood.

'Here. Let me.' I winced as Troy gently dabbed a wet cloth on my head. 'Sorry.' He lowered the cloth and gently pushed my hair away from my face. I nuzzled slightly into his hand. It felt warm and protective. It felt safe.

'The storm?'

'It's slowing.'

'Where…?'

'Where we're meant to be. The best way I can describe it is like a huge cavern made into a dwelling. It's the perfect shelter for storms like this. All the rain and mud washes over the roof while we're safe inside. It's got running water from an underground spring and a calor gas stove and lights. We could live here for weeks.'

'Weeks?'

Troy laughed. 'Don't panic, Ems. I said we *could* live here for weeks, not that we're *gonna* live here for weeks. If the storm subsides soon, they'll come for us tomorrow. Next day at the latest.'

'My head hurts.'

'I've got some aspirin. Would you like some?'

'Yes please.'

Troy leapt to his feet. I felt along my sides with my hands. Definitely a camping mat. Beneath my head was a pillow. I relaxed into the softness of it, pulled the blanket under my chin, and closed my eyes.

'Emma?' There was urgency in his voice. I flicked open my eyes. 'Thank God,' he said. 'I thought you'd lost consciousness again.'

He sat down on the floor next to me and carefully helped me into a sitting position. Keeping his arm round me, he supported me as I swallowed the tablets and sipped on some water.

'Thank you.' It felt comfortable resting against him. I stayed there. 'How did I get here?'

'After the log hit you, you fell down the slope but a tree broke your fall. I half-carried you and half-dragged you here. You're cut and bruised all over and covered in mud. I've tried to clean up the wounds but you've got a really bad bruise across your hip where you hit the tree.'

'How do you...?' I gasped as I realised I was naked under the blanket.

'I'm sorry. Your clothes were wet, muddy, and torn. I needed to get you out of them and I needed to clean you up. I tried not to look.'

I blushed at the thought of the man who'd been my adversary for the past fortnight seeing me naked and helpless.

'Nice tattoo by the way.'

My cheeks burned. My tattoo was just below my left breast. 'My mum died of breast cancer when I was twelve. She loved butterflies. I got it done on my sixteenth birthday to remember her.' My voice cracked as it usually did when I talked about her and I wiped at my ready tears. 'Not that I needed help remembering her. I'll never forget her. It's just...'

Troy pulled me closer. 'I know. My dad died when I was nine. Car crash. Believe it or not, I've got a tattoo to commemorate him too.'

'Really? What?'

'It's a Blue Jay. He loved birds.'

'Can I see it?'

'I'll have to lie you back down so I can show you.'

With the same tenderness one might handle a newborn baby, he lay me back down on the pillow then stood up and whipped off his t-shirt. My stomach did a somersault at his naked torso; tanned and toned but regular-guy toned as opposed to gym-obsessive-six-pack toned. He turned his back to me. Above his right shoulder-blade was a bird in the most magnificent shades of blue and turquoise. 'I know it's not exactly a manly bird of prey like an eagle but it was always his favourite. He said it reminded him of the summer sky even on a dull day and made him smile.'

'It's the same colours as my butterfly.'

'I know.' He pulled his t-shirt back on and turned to face me. 'We've got more in common than you might think.' He held my gaze and my stomach did somersaults again. 'I'm sorry if you think I was criticising you about the work you'd done on Project Phoenix, Ems. I should have found another way to get your attention.'

'My attention? What do you mean?'

'Do I have to spell it out for you? I like you Ems. A lot.'

'I thought you hated me.'

He lowered his eyes. 'Far from it. I–'

A loud rumble stopped him mid-sentence. The room darkened as it continued and sprinkles of soil dropped from the roof. I squealed. Troy dived towards me and protectively covered my body with his. Ignoring the pain, I curled myself into a ball and clung onto his legs.

Then it stopped.

'What was that?' I asked as he released me and sank back against the wall.

'Mudalanche.'

'What?'

'I may have made that word up. I'm pretty certain it was an avalanche of mud coming down the mountain.'

'Are we safe?'

'Very. This place has been here for centuries and it'll have seen hundreds, maybe thousands, of mudalanches in its time.'

'Mudalanche? It's a good word. If it isn't real, it should be.'

'Thank you.' Troy ran his fingers through his blonde hair and shook out some mud. 'You might want to do the same, Ems. Here, let me.' He helped me to a seated position and gently eased the bobble out of my dark hair then ran his fingers through it to knock out the soil. His hands brushed the side of my face in the process and those butterflies danced in my stomach again.

'You've got gorgeous hair, Ems. You should wear it down more often.'

I blushed. 'Thank you. Perhaps not when it's caked with mud though.'

'You look good even with the mud.'

We gazed into each other's eyes. *He's going to kiss me.* And I wasn't going to stop him. But he moved away and a wave of disappointment swept over me. Who knew?

'How's the head?' He stood up.

'Sore.'

'Can I get you something to eat?'

'No thanks.'

'Some more water? I think yours might have soil in it.'

'No thanks.'

'Is there anything you want?'

Yes. You. I shook my head, trying to dislodge the thought.

'Should I light some candles? Are you warm enough?'

'Will you sit down again, please, Troy.'

He hesitated then sat back down on the stone floor.

'I haven't said thank you.'

'What for?'

'For saving me. You could have been killed.'

'And you would have been if I'd left you and I couldn't–'

'You couldn't what?' Although I was pretty certain I knew.

He gently pushed my hair behind my ear. 'I couldn't live without you in my life.'

'Will your colleague be much longer, my duck?' I jumped at the sound of the cleaner's voice. 'It's just that I need to lock up and get home before the roads get blocked.'

'Blocked?'

She wrapped a scarf round her neck. 'Yes, blocked. From the snow.'

'It's snowing?' I leapt to my feet and span round to face the window then gasped. 'Oh my God!' How had I not noticed? Huge white flakes fell from a pink-tinged sky, thick and fast, joining the foot or so already on the ground.

I turned back to the cleaner. 'When did it start?'

'About an hour ago, my duck. Are you going far?'

'Yes. Oxford.'

She sucked in her breath. 'You should have set off a couple of hours ago. I wouldn't count on getting home tonight, my duck. You might want to book into a local B&B.'

The thought of being holed up in a B&B with Troy spurred me into action. I strode across the bar but, before I reached the conference room, the door opened.

'I'm done. I'm so sorry, Ems. That took way longer than expected.'

'Can we go now?'

'Of course.'

'Have you seen the snow?'

'What snow?'

I pointed towards the large windows. 'That snow.'

Troy clapped his hand over his mouth and stared for a moment. Then he removed his hand and smiled at me. 'What is it with the two of us and extreme weather, Ems?'

'I... erm... I'm just going to change into my boots.' Cheeks burning, I grabbed my hiking boots out of a carrier bag and tossed in the canvas shoes I'd been wearing. I rummaged in my large holdall for a pair of thick socks and a fleece then looked around for Troy as I pulled the socks and boots on.

He appeared a few minutes later with red cheeks and damp hair. 'It's pretty bad out there but I've got a 4x4 so we should be fine if the traffic's moving. What can I carry?'

'I can manage.' I hoisted my handbag onto one shoulder and my laptop bag onto the other but as I bent down to pick up my holdall, my laptop bag slipped off my shoulder. As I lifted it back up, the handbag slipped. Without a word, Troy picked up my holdall and the carrier containing my shoes and exited the building. Sighing, I trotted after him. It was going to be the longest journey of my life.

'You don't have to live without me,' I whispered, holding Troy's gaze.

'Do you mean…?'

I nodded. 'But we can't ignore the fact that I'm only here for another two months.'

'You could stay. There's a vacancy on the team.'

'I can't stay, Troy. I can't leave my dad. I'm all he's got. And you're–'

'–all that my mom's got. What a mess. I've tried so hard to resist you, Ems, but you've somehow gotten in here…' He tapped his head, 'and in here…' He tapped his heart. And at that moment, I realised he'd done exactly the same to me and I'd been oblivious to it.

I reached out and gently brushed a bit of dirt off his cheek. 'Two months is a pretty long time, though. We might hate each other by the end and be glad there's the Atlantic separating us.'

He closed his eyes and nuzzled into my touch, then gently kissed the palm of my hand. 'I'll never feel like that,' he said. 'But you're right. Two months is what we have and I don't think we should waste a minute of it, do you?'

And we didn't. Those two days in the cavern with Troy were the most incredible days of my life. We talked about anything and everything, we laughed, we cried over our parents taken from us too soon, we kissed, and we slept in each other's arms on two camping rolls and a pile of foisty blankets.

My body yearned for him. 'I wish we could… you know… but I'm not on the pill or anything and I don't imagine the first aid supplies include a box of condoms.'

Troy smiled and traced his hand lightly down my arm sending tingles of pleasure through me. 'I love that you blush when you talk about things like that. It's so English. The first aid box is a bit lacking in that department but I spotted a box in the cupboard.'

'Then why…? Don't you…' I pulled the blanket further up towards my chin.

'Oh my God, Ems, please don't ever think like that.' He shook his head. 'Believe me, I want nothing more but you're so badly bruised that I'm scared of causing you more pain.'

Relief flooded through me. 'We could try?'

'Ems, you have no idea how much I want to say yes to that but I can't do it to you. Not until you're healed. You don't hurt the ones you love.'

I nodded. Then his words registered with me. 'Did you just say…?'

He smiled tenderly. 'I love you, Ems. A great huge mudalanche of it.'

At that very moment, I knew I was in love too for the very first time.

I wiped at the tears flowing down my cheeks, hoping that Troy was too busy concentrating on the snow and the road to notice.

"You don't hurt the ones you love". Maybe not physically but, emotionally, Troy Zimmerman had hurt me more than the log that hit my head or the tree that caught my body. So why the hell had I managed to be trapped in a car with him going nowhere fast?

I'd actually been disappointed when we'd been rescued two days later. Squinting in the bright sunshine, I hobbled out of the cavern, supported by two men from mountain rescue. I asked them to pause in the doorway so I could look back at the place where I'd unexpectedly found love. I caught Troy doing the same and we smiled at each other.

The CEO, Will, couldn't do enough for us. He upgraded my hotel room, sent me on a shopping spree to replace the clothes I'd damaged and insisted I spent ten times the value of them, and gave Troy and me a week off to recover. We spent most of it together.

On the day before we were due back at work, I lay on a picnic blanket next to Troy in a meadow in the middle of nowhere. Blue Jays chirped round us and butterflies flitted from wildflower to wildflower. I propped myself up on my arm and gazed down at Troy. 'I think I might be healed,' I whispered.

He opened his eyes and smiled. 'It's only been a week, Ems. The doctor said it would take several.'

'What do doctors know?' I sat up, trying not to wince at the pain, lifted my t-shirt over my head and tossed it to one side.

Troy's eyes widened with desire. 'You promise you'll tell me if it hurts.'

'I promise.'

'Because you know I don't hurt the ones I love.'

'I know. And I love you for it. A great huge mudalanche amount.'

Troy smiled. 'That's my line.'

'It's a good one. So am I just going to sit here in my underwear or are you going to join me?'

'I'll join you.' Troy gently pulled me down on top of him and kissed me passionately. Pain seared through my side but it was worth it. Troy was worth it. And I'd thought I was too. So what happened? Why did he leave me in the restaurant all by myself on our final night together?

'It's getting heavier, isn't it?' The wiper blades could barely cope with the white onslaught.

'It seems to be. I know this isn't what you're gonna want to hear, Ems, but I think we should stop and find shelter.'

'With you? Remember how that worked out last time?' I bit my lip. The words had just tumbled out but it was what I felt; why keep quiet?

Troy kept his eyes on the road but I could tell from the movement of his jawline that he was grinding his teeth. He was either nervous or angry. Possibly both.

'I'm sure I saw a motel along here this morning.'

'I think you'll find it was a hotel, B&B, pub, or guest house,' I snapped. He frowned and my stomach churned. That had been childish and unnecessary. 'Sorry,' I said. 'I'm tired and I'm nervous.'

'Of the weather? Or of me?'

'Get over yourself. Of the weather, of course.' *And being less than a foot away from the only man I've ever loved.* 'I think I remember seeing somewhere too. It can't be far.'

'That was a nice slice of Meatloaf for you,' announced the presenter on the radio. *'The traffic report will follow in ten minutes but for any of you out there in this blizzard, here's David Essex with a wintery classic.'*

I scowled at the radio as *A Winter's Tale* started to play. I actually loved the song but it was all about failed love. Like Troy and me. Yes, we were just another winter's tale. A love that clearly wasn't meant to be. I couldn't listen to it. I jabbed at the "off" button and stared out of the window instead but there was nothing to see except a cloak of whiteness. Hedges were barely distinguishable from fields and where the fields ended and the sky began was anyone's guess.

I turned away from the window, shivered, then snuggled deeper into my soft fleece. Without a word, Troy flicked a switch and the temperature gauge on the dashboard rose two degrees. Damn him for being so considerate. It was the little things like that which had made me love him even more. So why had he been so inconsiderate that night? He could have phoned, texted, emailed, Tweeted or Facebooked me to tell me he wasn't coming. But he didn't do any of those things then. Or anytime in the months that followed. I, on the other hand, tried everything. Several times. No answer. In the end, I emailed one of his work colleagues, Suzy, to check he hadn't been run over by a bus or abducted by aliens. Apparently he was, "at work and absolutely swell". Swell? Without me? That was that then. So much for not hurting the ones he loved.

We passed a couple of cars abandoned by the side of the road but no moving vehicles. Nobody else was daft enough to be out in such treacherous conditions.

'I think I see the mo… er, pub, guest thing. On the right.'

I looked towards where Troy indicated. Yellow lights twinkled warm and inviting. Hopefully they had a couple of rooms left and I could sink into a hot bubble bath then snuggle under a thick duvet and watch some mindless TV. And not think about Troy Zimmerman.

Troy turned off the road and pulled up outside The Cavern Inn. Why did it have to be called that? I closed my eyes for a moment and willed myself not to think of the cavern where I'd fallen for Troy. *It's just a business name. It doesn't mean anything. Neither does Troy. Not anymore.*

He stopped the car. 'I don't know if I'm in a parking space or on their lawn. Hope they're not mad at me.'

I nearly said, 'If they are, they won't be the only ones,' but managed to stop myself. I didn't want to become the bitter, aggressive individual I was in danger of becoming around Troy. I just wanted to get inside, settle down for the night and hopefully wake up discovering it had all been a horrible dream and the man who'd abandoned me hadn't really moved to the UK where I'd have to work alongside him every day. I sighed. I wouldn't be able to do it. I loved my job but I'd have to leave. I couldn't torture myself by staying. And wondering. Yes, and hoping.

'I hope they've got some rooms.' I pressed the bell for attention on the small reception desk. 'The car park looked pretty full.'

'I'm sure they won't turn us away, Ems, even if they are full. Not in this weather.'

I hoped he was right.

A large matronly-like woman with grey curly hair appeared. 'You poor ducks out in this. I'm Maggie. I'm the landlady. Are you after a room for the night?'

'Two rooms please,' I said.

'Oh. You're not together?'

'Definitely not.' I couldn't bring myself to look at Troy.

'Slight problem, ducks,' Maggie said. 'Lots of folk sheltering from the storm and I've only got one room left.'

Crap. There was no way...

'Thank you,' Troy said. 'Emma will take the room. Do you have a lounge or bar area I can sleep in?' *Phew!* But then I felt guilty. He'd flown in from The States overnight. He had to be shattered. I couldn't offer to share, though. I just couldn't. Could I?

'Ooh, sorry my ducks but I can't allow that. You probably can't feel it with just coming in from outside but the heating's broken down thanks to the storm. It's too cold down here. I've got enough fan heaters for one per bedroom but no spares for down here. There's no hot water either.'

'I don't want to put any pressure on you, Ems. We can keep driving.'

Maggie cackled loudly. 'If I were you, my duck, I'd be counting my blessings. Gorgeous young man like that, no heating, one bed.' She gave me an exaggerated wink making me feel like I was on the set of a Carry On film. Carry On in a Cavern. Yep, been there, done that already!

'We'll stay.' I reached out for the key then turned to Troy. 'But you can sleep on the floor.'

He shrugged. 'Whatever you want, Ems.'

He trailed silently behind me as we made our way up two flights of stairs and along a corridor to room seventeen. *It'll be fine. I can do this. We'll put the telly on. We don't have to talk. Then we can sleep. Separately. Yes, I can do this.* But my hands shook and my stomach churned.

'Oh. It's a bit cosy.' A double bed was pushed against the window with the narrowest of gaps between it and the en-suite wall. There was no way he could sleep on the floor. A battered dressing table/drawer unit/wardrobe structure stood opposite the end of the bed but, again, left the narrowest of gaps. 'No wonder it was the last room to go.'

Troy peered over my shoulder. 'Sorry.' That word again. Uttered so many times but far too late. 'I'll sleep in the car.'

'Don't be daft. I wouldn't expect my worst enemy to do that.'

'I'm not your worst enemy, then?'

I stepped into the room and dropped my bag onto the dressing table. 'Maybe not the very top of the list. But we'll see how the evening goes. You could change that.'

He grinned. 'I'll try my best.'

'I meant you could move to the top of the list, not that you'd move down it.'

'Oh. I guess I deserve that.'

'I guess you do.'

I sat on the edge of my bed and removed my hiking boots while Troy hovered awkwardly in the doorway. 'You can come in, you know.'

'Thanks.' He put his bag and coat down on top of the drawer unit.

I bit my lip to stifle a laugh when he nearly went splat trying to remove his trainers whilst still standing. 'You can sit down on the bed too,' I said. 'I won't bite.'

Boots off, I grabbed the remote control, flicked the TV on, then sat against the headboard on the side closest to the gap. There was no way I was going to be pinned against the wall by him in the night and there was no way I was going to scramble over him if I needed the loo. I flicked through the channels but there were only the five basic ones and absolutely nothing on. I pretended I was engrossed in a documentary about hepatitis; anything to avoid speaking to Troy.

'I think I might nip down to the bar to get a beer if Maggie's serving.' Troy paused. 'Can I get you a drink?'

'No. I'm good thanks.'

I watched out of the corner of my eye as he struggled to pull his trainers on again before leaving the room. The moment he left, I released a long shaky breath. *This is going to be the hardest night of my life. I should have asked him for a drink. Might be the only way to get through it.* As soon as the thought popped into my head, I knew I wanted a drink. Medicinal purposes, of course. I'd ring him and ask him to bring me back a glass of Merlot.

I crawled across the bed and reached for my mobile. I'd never quite got round to deleting his number. I muted the sound on the TV and dialled his number then jumped as Elton John's, 'Sorry seems to be the hardest word' echoed round the room. It was coming from Troy's jacket. I lifted his coat up, reached into the inside pocket and took out his phone. My name flashed on the display over an image of us kissing. I looked at my mobile, then his, and disconnected the call. My heart thumped as the lyrics to the song circled round and round my mind. In the summer, he'd programmed his phone so that Van Morrison's 'Brown-eyed girl' played when I called. Why had he changed it? Was the Elton John song relevant?

I rummaged in my handbag for my work mobile and dialled Troy's number from it. A normal electronic ring-tone sounded. I called from my personal mobile again. Elton John sang. Did it mean something? Was it a message?

The sound of a key being inserted into the door startled me. I slipped Troy's phone back into his coat and dived across the bed, un-muting the volume just as he burst through the door.

'I know you said no but I thought you might change your mind so

I got you a bottle of Merlot. You don't have to drink it and, before you have a go, this isn't a ploy to get you drunk.' He placed the bottle and a glass beside my bag on the dressing table and took a swig of his bottle of lager.

'Thank you. I do quite fancy a glass.'

'Really?'

'Really.'

'You want me to pour you one?'

'If it's not too much trouble.'

Troy poured the wine and handed me a glass. 'May I?' He nodded towards the space beside me.

'You can hardly sit on the floor, can you?' I shuffled my legs round so he could get past.

As he clambered across the bed, his leg grazed mine and sent a fizz of electricity through me. The manly aqua scent of his deodorant made my heart beat faster. *Damn! Damn! Bollocks.* It was February. It had been over six months and I still hadn't got over him. Would I ever?

'Can we talk, Ems?'

'No.' My glass of wine was empty within ten minutes.

'Another?' he asked.

I nodded.

'I'd really like to talk, Ems.'

'I wouldn't.' Twenty minutes later, I'd drained my second glass. The stress of the scary journey had flowed from me but the stress of being so close to Troy was almost too much to bear. I put the glass down beside the bed. Another one would probably open up the floodgates and, if that happened, the tears might never stop.

I hadn't cried that night. I hadn't cried on the plane back to Heathrow. I hadn't cried when I unlocked the door to my empty flat or when I returned to work two days later. I hadn't cried because I'd believed him when he said he'd never hurt the ones he loved. I'd believed him when he said he couldn't live without me in his life. I'd believed him when he said he'd love me forever. And I'd genuinely believed that he'd jump on a plane with an apology and an amazing excuse for abandoning me. It was only when his colleague Suzy emailed me that he was at work and "swell" that I crumpled. Right there in the middle of the open-plan office. Paul had taken one look at my grief-stricken face and sent me home. I called in sick for the next two days. He never asked. I never confessed. To anyone. It was easier that way; I could pretend it hadn't happened. Almost. I'd have pulled it off if it wasn't for the ache in my heart and the scar on my forehead as a constant reminder of something brief but beautiful.

I grabbed for the remote control, flicked the TV off and turned to face him. 'Ok. Let's talk. Why are you here, Troy?'

'Because there's a storm outside and the heating's broken downstairs.'

'Don't be flippant. You know what I mean.'

He nodded. 'You wouldn't believe me if I told you.'

'Try me. I think you'll find I'm pretty gullible. I believed you when you spouted all that crap over the summer, didn't I?'

Troy grimaced. 'Ok. Here goes. You know how I said I never hurt the ones I love?'

'Vividly.' I folded my arms and glared at him.

'There are only two women I've ever loved...'

My heart sank. An ex girlfriend? They'd got back together? I should have known. We'd talked about exes in the cavern. He said he'd really cared about a couple of them but had never fallen in love. Had that been another lie?

'You. And my mom.' His mum? Ok. So no ex-girlfriend then. Phew!

He took a swig from his bottle and placed it on the window ledge. 'That night I was meant to meet you... our last night together... wasn't meant to be our last night together. I meant it when I said I couldn't live without you in my life and I knew that holidays together wouldn't have been enough for me...'

'We could have made it work.'

'I know we could but I didn't want to. That's not what I mean. I wanted us to work. I just didn't want a long distance relationship to be the solution. I knew you couldn't move to The States so I went to my mom's to ask for my grandmother's ring so I could propose to you and you'd know I was serious about moving to England to be with you as soon as I'd tied up loose ends back home.'

My jaw fell open and I stared at Troy, trying to make sense of what he'd just confessed. 'You were going to propose?'

He nodded.

'I don't believe you.' I actually did but it made no sense given that he didn't turn up. How could he have gone from proposal to no-show?

He clambered off the bed and rummaged in his coat pocket. I hoped he wouldn't notice I'd been playing with his phone. He turned round holding a small green velvet ring box. He eased open the lid revealing a stunning vintage ring of a very pale topaz-coloured stone surrounded by diamonds, with tiny diamonds either side on a wavy silver band. I gasped. It was the most beautiful and unusual ring I'd ever seen. I stared at it, mouth still open, then looked at Troy. He had tears in his eyes.

'I don't understand,' I whispered. 'You just left me there.'

He sat back down on the bed facing me and gently placed the open ring box on the duvet between us.

'I told mom all about you. She lectured me for not introducing you while I had the chance.' He shook his head. 'I don't know why I did that. I guess I just wanted you all to myself. Anyway, she gave me her blessing, gave me the ring and made me promise to visit as often as I could. I was twenty minutes from the restaurant when mom's neighbour rang. She'd collapsed while walking the dog.'

I clapped my hand across my mouth. 'Oh Troy, don't say she's...'

He smiled. 'No. She's fine. She had a heart attack. And before you panic, it wasn't because of my news about you. She'd been having chest pains all day and had ignored them assuming it was just the effect of an overly-strenuous pilates class.'

I instinctively reached for his hand and he held it tightly. 'She's really ok?'

'Plenty more years in her yet.'

'You could have called me. I get that you were preoccupied that night but the next day? Or when I got back to the UK? I left you loads of messages.'

'I know. I'm so sorry, Ems. I'm afraid I fell to pieces. She picked up a virus in the hospital so it was touch and go at first. I blamed myself. I thought I'd caused it and I realised that, in trying not to hurt the ones I loved, I'd hurt both of you. A month had already passed by the time she came home and I knew I'd failed you in every way possible. I knew I'd hurt you badly but I also knew that getting in touch with you again would mean hurting mom because I could see how much she'd needed me while she recovered. I figured best hurt one rather than two. Problem is, it hurt me doing that because, like I said at the start, I can't live without you in my life.'

'But Suzy said you were just "swell". I was worried something might have happened to you so I emailed to ask her if you were okay.'

Troy ran his hand through his hair. 'Oh Ems, anyone but Suzy would have told you the truth. Suzy and I went on one date and she wasn't for me. We never even shared a goodnight kiss but she's been a little obsessed with me ever since. I should have put two and two together before. She told me you'd emailed her to say you were relieved to be back in the UK and were dating some guy you met in a pub and were very happy with him. After that, I was sure I was too late to make it up to you.'

'There was no guy.'

'Really?'

'Really.' I realised I was still holding his hand and reluctantly released my grip. 'So I know what happened that night and why you didn't get in touch but why are you here now? Paul said it's a permanent position; not a secondment. Why my team?'

'Isn't it obvious?'

I shrugged but my heart banged out a rhythm of hope.

'I always spend Christmas Eve round my mom's house. My boss called round and said he had a Christmas bonus for me. I was confused because I'd already had a financial bonus. Mom said she also had something and I had to open her gift first then my boss's. Hers was the engagement ring which I'd returned when she got out of hospital. His was an envelope containing a job offer for a permanent role in the UK starting today. I told mom I couldn't leave her but she insisted I find the person who made my heart glow and if that person was in England, then that's where my heart must take me. So here I am. Trapped in a tiny dwelling with you again. During a storm again. And saying that I never stopped loving you. A whole big mudalanche of it.'

A crashing sound drew our eyes to the window just as an avalanche of snow cascaded from the roof.

'It seems we're back to where we started,' I said. 'But this time with a snowalanche instead of a mudalanche coming off the roof of our cavern dwelling. If you still want to ask me the question, the answer's yes.'

Troy's eyes widened and he glanced down at the ring then at my face, then back to the ring. 'Really?'

'You'll have to ask me.'

He clumsily grappled with the ring then got down on bended knee between the bed and the dressing table. 'Emma Chambers, will you forgive me for hurting you so badly and let me make it up to you for the rest of my life by doing me the honour of marrying me?'

Tears pricked my eyes and blurred my vision of the man I loved so deeply. 'Yes. Yes, I will. And thank you.'

'For what?'

'For understanding how important it is to me to be near my dad.'

Troy smiled. 'I have one problem, though. I want to kiss you but I think I may be wedged in this tiny gap.'

I giggled. 'Looks like it's my turn to rescue you.' I pulled on his arms and helped him to his feet then kneeled on the edge of the bed as he wrapped his arms round me and kissed me. I thought back to the song on the radio earlier. Clearly we were not just another winter's tale of failed love. Instead, ours was a winter's tale of found love. A great big mudalanche of it.

Author Details

If you've enjoyed this story and would like to find out more about Jessica Redland, here's how:

Twitter: @JessicaRedland
Facebook: *https://www.facebook.com/pages/Jessica-Redland-Writer/276002162588212?ref=bookmarks*
Blog: *http://jessicaredlandwriter.wordpress.com/*
Website: *www.jessicaredland.com*

Jessica's debut novel 'Searching for Steven' will be published by So Vain Books in June 2015

Reserved

Rhoda Baxter

Jenny was in the back, loading the returns trolley, when Merryweather, H came in. Her colleague, Kirsty, handed him his reserved journals and he left to find a seat.

Damn. She'd missed him. She should never have left the main desk at this time, no matter how bossy Kirsty was being. She could have kicked herself with her new sensible heels. This New Year's resolution thing was difficult.

She'd fallen in love with Merryweather, H the first time he walked into the library. He ordered journals from the stacks each day. Jenny had tried to talk to him, but she wasn't very good at that sort of thing, so all she'd ever managed was, 'That's reserved for you now,' and 'It should be here for you tomorrow morning after nine'.

Kirsty said, 'Can you take the desk, please? I need to get these upstairs.'

Jenny logged onto the computer behind the curving desk. From where she was sitting she could see Merryweather, H. She studied the profile that she knew so very well. It was a fine profile. She loved that profile. She loved his crystal blue eyes. She loved the way his cheeks went red whenever he spoke.

He looked up; caught her staring at him. They both looked away quickly.

She didn't know his first name. His library account just said H. What was it? Harry? Horace? Herbert? Humbert? She liked to think of him as Harry. Or just Merryweather, H.

When she looked up again, he was standing by the desk. She almost jumped.

He cleared his throat. 'Can I…?' He slid the request slip across the desk.

Now was her chance. She should ask him now. Something simple like, 'Would you like to go for coffee sometime?' Her throat closed up. All she managed was a nod.

Come on Jenny. This was the best chance. Do it. Do it. 'Uh.'

He looked up, eyebrows raised over the rims of his glasses.

She couldn't speak. She just smiled. Again.

His gaze flicked to the piece of paper in her hand, the screen, and back again. He moved his feet. Oh no. He was preparing to leave. She had to ask him. Now.

Suddenly, her heart was pounding inside her head. Her throat was dry. She couldn't do this. She was such a failure. She couldn't. She couldn't. 'Happy New Year?'

His face fell.'Thank you... uh...You too.' Another glance at the paper.

'Oh! Your journal.'

Kirsty returned. Jenny turned her attention to the request slip. She re-read the journal title on the paper. It wasn't a journal. It was a question. '*Would you like to go for coffee sometime? Henry M.*'

Henry Merryweather. She had failed in her new year's resolution to ask him out, but it didn't matter. He'd asked her instead. How wonderful. Her heart soared. She looked over at him. 'That's reserved for you. Be here for you by five thirty this evening,' she said.

His smile lit up the entire reading room.

Author Details
If you've enjoyed this story and would like to find out more about Rhoda Baxter, here's how:

Twitter: @rhodabaxter
Facebook: *https://www.facebook.com/RhodaBaxterAuthor*
Blog: *www.rhodabaxter.com*

Rhoda's current book 'Doctor January' (published by Choc Lit) is available now.

Seasonal Encounters of the Café Kind

Zanna Mackenzie

'He's here again.' Faith sets a stack of heavy plates down on the counter and raises her eyebrows questioningly at me. 'That's every day this week. Will you go and serve him or shall I?'

'I'll go.' I reach for my notepad and pen. 'He'll only ask for me if I don't.'

It might be only a week until Christmas and outside flakes of snow are swirling past the windows but inside The Coffee Pot it's sweltering. I wipe the back of my hand over my forehead. I tell myself it's hot because the café is packed with tourists who visit Carleton for the seasonal festivities and because the fire is flickering away in the log burner in the corner. It has nothing to do with the fact he's here.

Again.

Having Steve turn up as a customer definitely isn't helping matters though...

Pulling my pen down from its perch behind my ear I make my way through the tables towards where he's sitting. All alone.

His hair is shorter now. It suits him.

I clear my throat when I arrive at his table. 'What can I get you?'

'Liz.' He sets the newspaper he's reading down on the beech table top and smiles up at me. 'Gorgeous weather, isn't it?'

He loves snow. Memories of the skiing holiday we took together flash through my mind at warp speed.

Good memories.

I nod in agreement. 'Yes, lovely. Very festive. What would you like?'

Inwardly I curse myself for saying something he could take in a provocative way and quickly add, 'To eat, I mean. My recommendation would be the apple pie. Made by Faith, the woman who runs this place. It's legendary. People come from miles around for a slice.'

'Great. If that's what you recommend then that's good enough for me.'

'Vanilla ice cream or pouring cream with that?' I ask, trying to stay in waitress mode.

He shrugs. 'You choose.'

Scribbling his order down on the pad I turn to make my escape but am not quite quick enough.

He reaches out, lightly placing a hand on my arm. 'What time is your break? Can we go somewhere and talk?' Leaning forward he fixes mischievous blue eyes on me in an intense gaze. A gaze that, despite the circumstances, still has the strangest effect on me. Don't go there, I chastise myself. There's no point.

'I'm not having a break today. We're too busy and Sue is off sick.'

'Oh I'm sorry to hear that. Is she going to be OK?' he asks; concern in his voice even though he doesn't know Sue.

'She's pregnant. Suffering badly with morning sickness which seems to last all day. She'll be fine, though. Said this happened last time. Once she gets to the three-month mark it clears up apparently.' Why am I standing here chatting with him like this? I shouldn't be, and not just because we're so busy. Being around Steve is painful and confusing and it's all because of me.

All my own fault.

A group of teenagers arrive, bickering between themselves loudly, and set about trying to commandeer single unused chairs from other tables so they can all crowd round together. Glancing towards them I say, 'I'd better go.'

He gets to his feet, looking questioningly at me before nodding towards the boisterous recent arrivals. 'Will they be trouble? If you want I can go and turf them out for you.'

I shake my head. 'No, it's fine, they come in here often. They're OK.'

Pushing at the swing door to the kitchen I almost collide with Faith who's on her way back out to replenish the delicious cake supplies in the café's glass counter.

She pauses to whisper, 'Are you OK? Did he ask again?'

'Yes to both.' I notice her concerned look.

Faith has become a good friend since I made Carleton my home a few months ago. Back when I decided I needed to change my future because I couldn't handle my past.

She peers at me more closely. 'Are you really OK?'

I nod.

'Guess what I've just heard?' she says. 'This might cheer you up a bit. Apparently Carrdale has been purchased. Don't know who the new owners are as yet but it's great that the place is still going to be run as an extreme sports centre, right? It brings in lots of people to the area which helps keep plenty of businesses afloat, including this place.'

Faith is the Chair of the local tourism association and I know she's been worried about what might happen with Carrdale.

'That's fantastic news,' I say and I am genuinely pleased for my boss, my friend, and for this village I now call home. Carrdale is a thriving outdoor extreme sports centre just outside Carleton. It's been for sale for a little while now, not because of business or financial problems, but because the owners want to move to Canada. For a moment an uneasy feeling creeps up on me and I wonder if Steve might be involved in the sale. He's a businessman with his name on a number of projects. Surely he wouldn't buy Carrdale, would he? 'Best get on with his order,' I say, remembering the hungry customers in the café and turn to head for the kitchen.

I assemble the plate for Steve. Apple pie. Generous portion. Napkin. Spoon. Now, ice cream or pouring cream? A simple enough thing to decide but my mind is all over the place. I put a double scoop of homemade vanilla ice cream on the plate and then pour a serving of double cream over the pie as well.

Peering over my shoulder Faith pulls a face.

'No wonder he comes in here so much if you give him extra portions.'

Nudging me playfully she adds, 'Carry on like that and you'll be putting us out of business.'

'Sorry, I didn't mean to…' I blush.

'Hey, it's OK, I was joking.' Faith gulps down her now cold coffee then slips a hand across my shoulders before saying, 'But I do wonder if the lady doth protest a tad too much about him calling in so frequently of late. He seems lovely, not to mention he rates pretty near the top on the whole attraction scale. Steve's been quite chatty with me. Keen to know more about the area and all the different events we've got going on leading up to Christmas. Are you sure you and him…?'

'Yes, I'm sure.' I move to the sink to splash my flushed cheeks with cold water, partly in an attempt to cool myself down and partly to get away from her inquisitive stare.

'You're absolutely sure there's nothing between you?' Faith asks again.

'It's over,' I reply in a voice I realise is laced with sadness.

Faith shrugs, looking unconvinced. 'If you say so.'

'One apple pie.' I set the plate down on the table in front of him.

Ignoring it he stands up and places a hand over mine. It's warm, comforting, familiar. 'Won't you join me? Please?'

'I'm too busy, Steve.' Glancing around I lower my voice so none of the other customers can hear. 'I don't know why you insist on coming here all the time.'

'You do know why.'

'After what happened between us? You're either a glutton for punishment or…'

'Very much in love,' he highjacks my sentence, ending it himself. I feel a flicker of something – hope perhaps? – rise up inside of me. He still loves me?

'Steve, this is crazy. Why can't you just accept the facts?' I pull out a chair and sit down. It's safer if I sit; my legs feel all wobbly. Whether it's due to the heat in here or something more complicated than that, I don't want to think about it right now.

'You know me.' He looks faintly embarrassed. 'Too persistent for my own good.'

What's he saying? Does he mean…?

'Eat your pie,' I say, confused emotions swirling inside of me.

'Remember when we ate at that little restaurant on holiday?' he asks with a twinkle in his eyes. 'Remember what we did when we got back to the hotel afterwards?'

I remember and feel myself blush. It had been an amazing few days. Time spent with Steve had always been skin-tinglingly good.

Then I'd let fear take over and it had ruined everything.

He reaches for his spoon and sets about demolishing the apple pie. He always had a good appetite.

Faith scurries out of the kitchen armed with more plates of food and grins over at us, almost as though finding me sitting at Steve's table means she's been proved right and there's still a chance for something to be revived between us.

Hours later, I'm curled up and comfy on the sofa with a good book and a glass of wine when my mobile rings. I have it set to play Jingle Bells of all things. I'm trying to get into the Christmas spirit.

'Major problem!' Faith shrieks at me down the phone. 'Can you get round to the café pronto? I need your help. Some pipes have burst.'

I fling on plenty of layers of clothes and race round there. I live in a tiny rented cottage up the hill from The Coffee Pot. The village is pretty; a real tourist haven all year round. People come to this part of Derbyshire for the scenery, the endless walking opportunities and the vertigo-inducing climbing. In December they also come to see the town all lit up and take part in the various Christmas festivities.

As I hurry along the High Street, hands stuffed into my pockets because I forgot my gloves, I notice how deep the snow is now underfoot, though it actually stopped snowing a few hours ago. Outside each building on the High Street there's a single seven foot tall real Christmas tree, each of them decorated in the same way with simple traditional white lights. I love this village. Everyone has been so friendly since I arrived here after – well let's just say I needed to try and make a new start.

I arrive at the café through the staff entrance at the rear, accessed via a narrow arch and stone alley. When I fling the door open I find a bone-dry kitchen and instantly know something fishy is going on. There's no sign of burst pipes. The kitchen, as always, looks pristine.

I look at Faith. 'Where's all the water then? What's going on?'

'Little white lie,' she admits, smiling, grabbing at my arm and then hauling me through the swing door into the Coffee Pot.

'I hope I did the right thing agreeing to this,' she whispers as she pushes me forward.

I stop dead in my tracks as I take in the scene before me.

The fire is lit and provides the only light in the room except for two strings of white fairy lights decorating the walls and the Christmas tree in the corner.

Steve is sitting by the fire. He looks heart-stoppingly handsome. He also looks extremely nervous.

Before I can speak, he gets to his feet and holds up his hands to silence me. 'OK, so you panicked and ran out on our wedding six months ago and it's taken me an age to track you down since then but that's all history. I know why you left. I understand. I've found you again and I'm not leaving here until you tell me what I, and most people who know you, suspect to still be the truth.'

I draw in a breath, preparing myself, knowing what he's going to ask and knowing I can't lie to him.

'Do you still love me?' he asks. There's more than a hint of a tremble in his voice.

'Yes.' No hesitation at all. It's the truth. Even now, it's still the truth – for what good it is to either of us. 'But I let you down.'

'All forgotten.' He shakes his head. 'Doesn't matter. I don't care about that.'

'But I don't deserve you, not after walking out...'

'Liz, you deserve to be happy, to love, to be loved, you need to believe that.' He enfolds my hands in his. 'Promise me you'll let yourself start to believe that. Let me help. You got scared, I know that now. You warned me it was probably too soon. Look, I promise I won't ask you to marry me again.' Steve smiles at me, that lovely lop-sided smile which always makes my heart beat a little faster.

'You weren't ready. I rushed things before. I'm so sorry. This time,' he releases my hands and reaches for two glasses of wine. 'This time I'll wait for you to propose to me. No matter how long it takes, I promise. Deal?'

I take the glass he offers me, our fingers briefly touching again as I do so, sending a spark of energy, love and reassurance zinging through me. Can I do this? Do I dare?

'Deal,' I say, smiling up at him, clinking my glass against his, allowing myself a glimmer of excitement at the prospect of a second chance – a future – with or without marriage, with Steve, the man who tempted me to risk letting love into my life again.

When I'd married Kev, I'd been young, rebellious, had chosen to ignore the warning signs about his temper, his drinking. Five years later, it had all ended in a divorce court. My heart broken, confidence gone, trust shattered.

Eighteen months on Steve had shown me love still existed, encouraged me to believe, to hope. I'd wanted to marry him so much but memories had crowded in and I'd fled with only the briefest of explanations and a huge heartfelt apology. I'd convinced myself Steve was better off without me.

Steve obviously thought otherwise, though. Amazingly he'd forgiven me, wanted to try again, to take it slowly this time. He would be patient he said, he would wait for me to propose to him.... Could I see a future with Steve?

Yes, and maybe one day I would find the courage to propose to the man standing before me, the man I loved and who, despite all my insecurities, fears and doubts, loved me right back.

One day.

You can catch up with Faith and her chance to find love as well as discover who the new owners of the Carrdale Outdoor Extreme Sports Centre are in Zanna's novel *If You Only Knew*.....

Author Details

If you've enjoyed this story and would like to find out more about Zanna Mackenzie, here's how:

Twitter: @ZannaMacKenzie
Facebook: www.facebook.com/zanna.mackenzie
Website/Blog: www.zannamackenzie.blogspot.co.uk
Amazon Author Page:
http://www.amazon.co.uk/Zanna-Mackenzie/e/B00BKY1A18/ref=sr_ntt_srch_lnk_1?qid=1409828150&sr=1-1

'If You Only Knew' is out now from Crooked Cat Publishing

In All The Wrong Places

Jo Barlett

'How about putting, *easy-going thirty something seeks no-strings fun*?' Dom looked hopeful and couldn't be deterred, even when Jamie shook his head. 'Come on, mate, you need to keep it upbeat! You don't want to come off sounding like a sob story. One of those ads you see in the classifieds for a wedding dress that's never been worn, that sort of thing.'

'The truth is, Dom, I probably am the human equivalent of that.' Jamie tapped the side of his chair. 'And I can hardly advertise no-strings fun sitting in this thing.'

'You might be having a good week when you arrange a date and not be in the chair.' His best friend's irrepressible optimism was usually something Jamie valued but, on this occasion, it was making him a prime candidate for a punch in the nuts.

'Yeah and I might be writhing around in agony and losing control of my bodily functions. Maybe it's all just a stupid idea anyway. Whatever I say I can't get away from the fact they'll be signing up for *this.'* He ran his hands in parallel down the sides of his body. 'And if Natalie couldn't hang around after the diagnosis, then how can I expect a total stranger to?'

'Natalie was a self-centred cow. I always thought so.' Dom grinned. 'In fact we all did. We just didn't think it was the done thing to say so when you were married to her.'

'I wish someone had.' Jamie sighed. He couldn't hate Natalie, only what she'd done to him; or more accurately how it had made him *feel* – like a piece of rubbish only fit to be discarded.

'The good news is that only nice girls are going to go for you like this.' Dom laughed, ducking out of the way as Jamie moved to grab him.

'At least I can rely on you to tell it like it is.' It was true. Dom was the one person in the world he could laugh with about the MS. Everyone else just skirted around the issue, pretending that nothing had changed, while all the time acting so differently towards him that it might as well have been written across the sky.

'What we need is a female perspective and maybe a beer or two to help get the muse flowing.' Dom disappeared in the direction of the kitchen, and his voice was muffled as he called back, as though he was busy rooting through the fridge. 'Sophia's coming over with Poppy for lunch. She'll give us a hand. After all, she's had more bad dates than anyone in the Western hemisphere, so she'll tell us exactly what to avoid saying!'

'I'm sure your sister would be thrilled to hear herself described as an expert on dating disasters.' Jamie scrolled down the web page again, while he waited for Dom. All these women smiling back at him from their profile pictures. On paper he sounded okay; a well-paid job working mainly from home as a business development consultant, nice house, only one previous *not-so-careful* owner. Hell, he even had his own set of wheels; but would any of them still be smiling if he pulled up for a date in his chair? It was a good make, lightweight and fast, and he could do handbrake-style turns that would put a boy racer to shame. Still, he was hardly a knight on a white stallion, was he?

'Chloe should be home soon, too. She must have emptied the shops of stuff by now.' Dom was back, balancing a six-pack of beers on a tray with some pretzels and a tube of crisps; his idea of a balanced diet.

'She'll kill you if she sees that lot!' Jamie couldn't suppress a grin. He'd been best man at their wedding two years before and Chloe had kept a careful watch on everything Dom ate and drank in the past six months, since they'd decided to try for a baby. 'And I hope to God you're not sporting any tighty-whiteys – although I'm not about to check.'

'For your information, my friend,' Dom expertly popped the metal caps off two of the beers as he spoke, 'my balls are no longer the subject of a steward's inquiry. As it turns out, they work perfectly well!'

'You mean?' Jamie didn't even get to finish the sentence before Dom grabbed him in such a forceful hug that he almost upended the wheelchair.

'Yep, don't tell Chloe I told you without her, I was supposed to wait, but we're having a baby, mate! How awesome is that?' They clinked their bottles against one another and Jamie forced a smile so stiff it hurt his face. It wasn't that he wasn't thrilled. Of course he was. They'd make the greatest parents in the world. It was just that he wanted it so badly too. He'd had a wife and they'd been planning a family until the MS had struck and she'd slipped away; his dreams packed up forever with the rest of her stuff. And now it felt like he was being left even further behind.

By the time Chloe had arrived back from town, with so much Christmas shopping that Dom had immediately ordered her to put her feet up while he unloaded the car, Jamie had got over himself. The smile when Chloe told him the news all over again was genuine and, when she got out a photo they'd had taken the day before at the twelve week scan, the go-ahead marker to share their news, the tears that welled up in his eyes were real too.

'This is the best Christmas present you guys could have given me.' Jamie looked at the photo again. He could just make out what most of the bits were supposed to be and even though it did look like something from an Alien movie, he already loved the baby, just as he loved its parents.

'Well that's good, because socks and a CD are about all else you've got to look forward to!' Dom grimaced as Chloe dug him sharply in the ribs. 'Sorry, was that supposed to be a surprise?' He was quicker the second time, just ducking out of the way before she got him again. 'Seriously, though, mate, you will be here for Christmas won't you?'

'I don't know, I should let you guys enjoy a last Christmas together as a couple before the little one comes along.' Jamie swallowed hard. He could always spend it with his family. His mother would treat him like the baby she somehow thought he'd reverted to and his father would pretend he hadn't noticed the chair, just so he didn't have to talk about feelings or anything more meaningful than the football scores. He could handle that for a few days; it wouldn't be that bad – if you used hell as a measurement.

'You'll do no such thing!' Chloe shook her head so vehemently that her hair whipped across her face. 'A godfather's place is with his unborn godchild to be!' She clapped a hand over her own mouth. 'You two are lethal together!' She looked from Jamie to Dom and back again. '*That* was supposed to be the surprise Christmas announcement, that we wanted you for the top job, and now you've gone and made me blurt it out.'

'You've got me in so much trouble, mate!' Dom was grinning again, though. 'So don't even think about going elsewhere, or I'll take the battery out of your wheelchair.'

'When you put it as sensitively as that, how could I turn down the offer?' Jamie felt the relief flood through his body. He hadn't realised he'd been holding himself so tense, just at the thought of a few days trapped back at home with his folks.

'That's settled then.' Chloe got to her feet as the doorbell rang and Jamie relaxed. If he was facing another Christmas alone, at least he wouldn't be lonely.

Sophia swept into the room, her brown hair just as curly and untamed as it had been all those years before when they were at school. Jamie remembered her wearing it in plaits that were tightly woven together by her mother when they got on the school bus in the mornings, but by the time she trundled after him and Dom to catch the school bus home, with her brother always trying to shake her off, the plaits were invariably unravelled and the curls that had escaped were doing their own thing.

'Uncle Jamie!' Poppy, Sophia's six-year-old daughter, whose hair was oddly as poker-straight and neat as her mother's was wild, threw herself into his arms. Like Dom, Poppy seemed to have absolutely no regard for the fact that Jamie was sometimes in a wheelchair and she bowled into him with the force of small but determined hurricane.

'Hello gorgeous.' He ruffled her hair, which immediately fell back into place and he found himself wondering for the millionth time how her so-called father could fail to turn up for his contact visits so often. Sophia was a counsellor for couples in crisis, which might have been funny given that it was so ironic. Only it wasn't funny; not when it involved one of his oldest friends.

'Alright, faker?' Sophia bent down to kiss his cheek and her hair swept along his collarbone.

'It's why I love coming here,' Jamie tried and failed to keep a straight face, 'because the Henderson family are so sympathetic to my plight.'

'Sorry, Tiny Tim!' She dropped him a casual wink and her brown eyes sparkled with humour. It was easy being with Sophia, just like it was with Dom. Somehow they'd become more of a family to him than his own over the past two years.

'Who's Tiny Tim?' Poppy looked around the room, as if expecting to see a little boy somewhere, furrowing her brow with confusion.

'It's just a joke. It's a character from a Christmas story and your mum is teasing me, that's all.'

'We're doing the Christmas story at school and I'm going to be in it.' Poppy wrinkled her brow again. 'It's a nateeveetee.'

'The Nativity?' Jamie smiled, as she nodded her head. 'And are you Mary, by any chance?'

Poppy shook her head vigorously, but didn't venture any other information.

'Am I guessing?' Poppy nodded in response to his question. 'One of the three wise men?' He raised an eyebrow and Poppy shook her head again. 'I know! A shepherd?'

'No, but you're getting warmer.' Poppy, whose absolute favourite game was hide and seek, gave him an encouraging smile.

'Err, the innkeeper?'

'Of course, not silly, I'm the main sheep!' Poppy grinned, as though she'd just landed the lead role in a Hollywood blockbuster.

'There are *main* sheep?' Jamie struggled not to laugh, but Dom's niece was taking it all very seriously.

'Yes and I got the part, even though Maisie wanted it!'

'Have you got any lines?'

'Three. And I get to sing a bit of one of the songs on my own.' Poppy was leaping up and down on his lap, her excitement unstoppable. A talking and, more to the point, *singing* sheep in the nativity; it was certainly different.

'But that's fabulous. So can I come and watch?' Jamie looked at Poppy whose face was suddenly very solemn.

'We only get four tickets and Mummy got one for her and Daddy and Uncle Dom and Auntie Chloe.' Her bottom lip quivered, tears threatening, and he could feel the excitement draining out of her.

'I forgot I'm busy that night anyway.' Jamie forced a smile for the second time that day. 'But I'm sure your mum will video it for me and we can watch it together then.'

'That's a brilliant idea.' Sophia moved to sit in the chair closest to Jamie. 'And we can make a real night of it, we'll have popcorn and milkshakes and everything. Why don't you ask Auntie Chloe for a glass of milk now, she's out in the kitchen.'

Poppy nodded and hopped off his lap, looking much happier than she had a moment or two before.

'I'm sorry about that.' Sophia gave him a rueful smile. 'She's about as excited as it's possible to be that Christmas is just around the corner and, since getting the part, her excitement's gone into overdrive.'

'Well a singing sheep is commonly regarded as the pivotal role in the nativity.' He laughed and caught her eye for a second. There was something different there, something he couldn't quite put his finger on.

'And what about you? What would make your Christmas complete?' Sophia gave him a knowing look. If Dom hadn't already spilt the beans he'd eat the wheels on his chair.

'What apart from a miraculous cure, you mean?' He tried to keep his voice light, but despite himself it cracked a bit and Sophia placed a hand on his arm. She didn't say anything. Like Dom, she'd known him long enough to know when to make a joke and when to just listen. 'Okay, well if I can't have that and I can't go and see Poppy as the singing sheep, then I guess a kiss under the mistletoe would be a good start.'

'Dom said you wanted to try online dating?' When he nodded, she let out a little sigh. A kind of *been there, done that, got the tee-shirt* sort of sound. He braced himself to ask a question he wasn't sure he wanted an answer to. 'Don't you think it's a good idea?'

'It's not that, but I just wonder if it wouldn't be better for you to meet someone face-to-face.' She hesitated for a moment, as though she wanted to say something else but she didn't.

'Because of the chair?'

'Because I don't want you to get hurt.' Her warm, brown eyes crinkled in the corner and he knew she meant it. The girl who'd been hurt a hundred times herself and mostly by the same man.

'Okay, but I've given *waiting for things to happen naturally* a try for a year and the closest I've got to intimacy was a bed bath during my last relapse.' He attempted a smile but it went a bit wobbly.

'How about speed dating? That way you're in a room full of people who you know are looking for a relationship, but they also get to see you face-to-face from the outset. So there's none of that using fifteen-year-old photographs trick or being confronted by appalling personal hygiene...'

'Or a guy in a wheelchair?'

'Or that. They'll see you for who you are and if they can't see past the chair then they're idiots, but at least you'll know and you won't waste any time on arseholes.'

'I don't know, it sounds a bit,' he desperately wanted to say the word *scary*, but men weren't supposed to say that sort of stuff.

'*Forced*?' She gave him a get-out-of-jail-free card and he nodded. 'Well I suppose it is in a way, but it's focussed too and we've only got a week if you want to get a snog under the mistletoe by Christmas Eve. I'll come with you.'

'Great.' He meant it. It would be much easier with Sophia at his side and they could always get drunk together afterwards if it all went horribly wrong. 'Are you sure you don't mind?'

'It'll be a laugh and the pressure's off for me now I'm not looking for Mr Right anymore.' Their eyes met again and that look was back, a sort of glow. She was in love. It was the only explanation but he couldn't bring himself to ask. If she was back with Simon, Poppy's dad, he might not be responsible for his actions – wheelchair or no wheelchair. Sophia pulled a flyer out of her bag and passed it to him. 'There's a speed-dating event at the Old Tavern tomorrow night.'

'Tomorrow?' Nerves suddenly gripped him again, the flyer shaking along with his hand. 'I think it's too soon, they probably won't be able to fit us in anyway. Maybe we should wait until the New Year.'

'Too late, it's all booked.' Sophia planted another kiss on his cheek, the smell of her perfume stirring his senses. 'You can thank Dom later.'

'Oh I will, don't worry.' Jamie took a swig of beer. That punch in the nuts for Dom was well over-due.

The Old Tavern had a function room, separate from the two bars, and it was this that had been set aside for the speed dating. Jamie had tried to cancel, but Sophia was having none of it. Chloe and Dom were babysitting, it was all sorted and he was going whether he liked it or not. He didn't like it. He'd at least wanted to arrive early, slip in unnoticed so that his chair wasn't a massive issue, but Sophia had other plans. It was far better for everyone to see the chair from the get-go, she said. Easy for her to say; she wasn't the one sitting in it.

'Everyone's looking.' Jamie negotiated his way through the chairs and tables in the bar and across to the function room. He'd hoped that the relapsing and remitting MS might decide to remit overnight and that he'd be able to walk into the room. That sort of luck was for other people, though.

'They're not and if they are, then I told you it's better we know from the outset. Take if from someone who's wasted far too much time on people who weren't worth it. It's through here.' She stepped through the heavy oak door, holding it back on its hinges, so he could manoeuvre the chair through.

'Welcome, welcome.' A middle-aged woman with skin like alabaster and bright red lipstick, who was clutching a clipboard, greeted them with a smile that the Joker might have thought sinister. If this was a horror movie, she was letting no-one leave until they were all paired up. 'Get yourself a drink and we'll get going.' She smiled again, but she was dead behind the eyes, like a shark. 'We normally have the ladies doing the sitting and the gentlemen moving from table to table, but we thought we'd vary things for tonight.' Her eyes flickered down towards the wheelchair and she forced them back up again.

'Don't change things on my account.' If Jamie thought he could out-run, or rather out-wheel, Sophia, he'd have made a break for it there and then.

'Nonsense!' Clipboard Woman smiled again and disappeared into the group behind her.

'Here.' Sophia thrust a beer into his hand. 'Neck this and try to enjoy yourself. If nothing else, we can compare notes after and have a laugh.'

Jamie barely got the beer bottle to his lips before Clipboard Woman rang a bell. 'Take your places, gentlemen, your table numbers are on the board over there.' She gestured towards a whiteboard, propped against a chair at eye level if you were sitting down, almost certainly for Jamie's benefit. 'This is your lucky night. The ladies will be coming to you, so make the most of it!' She laughed, but there was still something totally humourless about her face. Jamie felt a dig in his shoulder and turned to see Sophia urging him on. He might as well get it over with. After all, how bad could it be?

In the end, it wasn't too bad at all. He had four reasonable conversations with girls who weren't completely tongue-tied by the fact that he was in a wheelchair and he even had one match. The system required you to mark a card with the people you were interested in seeing again and, if someone that you ticked picked you too, then email details would be exchanged. Jamie had ticked two girls' numbers and one of them had ticked him back. Of course he hadn't counted Sophia in that. They'd spent their three minute speed dating session giggling about everyone else around them and, of course, he'd see her again; just not like that. If there'd been a box for friends he never wanted to lose, she'd have got the biggest tick going, but she hadn't done so badly herself anyway.

'You alright?' Jamie addressed Sophia as they sat in another pub, down the road from the Old Tavern, for a post-match analysis. Neither of them wanting to sit in the Old Tavern and risk bumping into people they'd ticked, or who'd ticked them and it hadn't been reciprocated. Clipboard Woman was nothing if not efficient and, by the time Sophia was at the bar ordering their drinks, they'd both had an email come through on their phones detailing their matches.

'Yep, I'm fine.' She set the drinks down on the table. 'Did you get an email?'

'I've got a match! Maddie, you know the smiley one with the wavy blonde hair?' Jamie tried to keep the excitement out of his voice; he was at risk of sounding like Poppy, eulogising about her role as the singing sheep.

'That's great.' Sophia took a long drink from her wine glass, the rest of the bottle next to it on the table, indicating that she expected the post-match analysis to go into some detail.

'What about you, any matches?'

'I had eight expressions of interest, apparently, but not from anyone I'd ticked.' Sophia's voice was flat. 'Maybe that's what Clipboard Woman says to everyone who doesn't get a match.'

Jamie picked up her phone from the table and opened the email from *speedmeet.com*. 'I somehow doubt it. She's asking you whether you want to reconsider anyone that you didn't tick to see if you can get some matches. It says here that you are narrowing your options by only ticking one person. Who was he anyway? That fireman with biceps bigger than my thighs?'

'I told you, I'm not looking for Mr Right anymore. I just ticked one guy to see if I'd read the connection right, but I probably wouldn't have contacted him either, even if we'd been a match.' She was still talking about her quest for romance being over, but the glow that had been there the day before seemed to have been extinguished. It had to be Simon back on the scene; he was the only one who'd ever sent

Sophia swinging between happiness and misery like this. It was on the tip of Jamie's tongue to tell her to steer clear, but he didn't. If Sophia still loved Simon, there was nothing he or anyone else could do about that. Even Sophia wouldn't be able to stop it. He should know. He'd spent ten years loving a woman who'd never really loved him back and he still hadn't been able to let her go. Not until she'd forced him to.

'So what are you going to do about your match then?' Sophia was already topping her wine up as she spoke. His fingers itched to ring Simon's neck. Maybe he should speak to Dom before he said anything, work out a way between them to talk some sense into her before she fell into the trap again. He hoped she could help herself, he really did.

'I suppose I'll email Maddie.' His mouth formed a funny shape when he said her name, it was so unfamiliar. For so long it had been Natalie, Nat, and it seemed wrong, even after her decision to leave, to have someone else's name on his lips.

'You should do that.' Sophia set her wine down, looking unnaturally animated, as though she was forcing her worries about Simon to one side. 'Strike while the iron's hot. Email her on your phone and set a date.'

'Now?' His heart thudded against his ribcage at the thought. Still, he knew himself well enough to know it would only get worse if he procrastinated. 'Why not?' He took out his phone and looked up at Sophia as she responded.

'Why not, indeed.' There was a slight intonation at the end of the sentence, as though it were a question rather than a statement and an unreadable expression crossed her face. Melancholy and having Simon back in her life clearly went hand-in-hand. One thing at a time, though. He'd email Maddie first and then text Dom later and agree how they could help Sophia. They all deserved to be happy and maybe tonight really was the first step.

The first date with Maddie had gone well. So well in fact that they'd set another, for Christmas Eve. All morning, Jamie had felt the anticipation. He hadn't wanted to rush things and try to kiss her on their first date. It was awkward when you were in a wheelchair; you couldn't just lean in for a kiss when the woman towered over you. Not many first dates that ended with an uninvited lunge below the waistline went well – or at least he doubted they did. It would be easier second time around. He could take her hand while they sat at the table and kiss her then. They'd be more comfortable, less awkward. The fact that she'd agreed to a second date was sign enough of her interest after all.

He'd started getting ready, hours earlier than he really needed to, when his phone pinged announcing the arrival of a text. It was probably Sophia. He'd texted earlier to wish Poppy good luck for her big night. The school were performing their nativity play in the tiny church hall on Christmas Eve, hence the limited number of tickets available. Most teachers would have long disappeared on their own Christmas break by that point, but it was a tradition at Kettleworth Junior School, one which stretched right back to the days when he'd been a pupil there with Dom, and Sophia had been two classes below them.

Only it wasn't Sophia, it was Maddie. A bald little text, which said a hundred times more than the length of words accounted for. *'Sorry. Don't think this will work for me. I need to be the one taken care of. I thought it would be okay, but I can't get my head around it. Good luck, I'm sure you'll find someone special'*. It was followed by a smiley face and a kiss of all things. There should be an emoticon for a kick in the balls, because it would have been far more apt for a text like that.

He dialled Sophia's number before he even realised. He hadn't meant to, but he wanted to talk to someone. Someone who might convince him that he was worth more than a brush-off text, even while he was convincing himself that he never would be. Not anymore. The number just rang, she was probably somewhere with Simon and Poppy, getting ready for the nativity play. After all, other people had a life. They weren't just sitting by their phones, waiting for them to ring.

'Did you call?' Within a minute of him disconnecting, his phone had rung. Sophia was on the other end, her voice anxious.

'Yes, I'm sorry. I forgot that you'd be busy now. It doesn't matter, I'll call later.' He was about to put the phone down, when she cut through.

'It does matter and don't you *dare* put the phone down on me. Something's wrong, I can hear it in your voice. Is it Maddie?'

'That obvious that she'd dump me, eh?' He tried and failed to think of something funny to say.

'She's not good enough for you.'

'Apparently, no-one is.' His attempt at laughter was bitter and it caught in his throat.

'Bullshit! Come out with me instead.' For a moment he thought she meant on an actual date and he wasn't sure how he felt. 'It's why I wasn't answering my phone. I've been screening my calls. Simon, the arsehole, has let Poppy down again and I didn't want to hear him make a load more whinging excuses. Apparently the girls in his office have organised a drinks party tonight and he won't get there for the start if he goes to the nativity play first. Arsehole.' She said the word again, even though it was unnecessary and didn't even begin to convey how big an idiot he was.

'Well I've got nothing else to do.' He hesitated for a moment and checked himself. It was more than that. 'Actually, I'd love to.'

'It's a date then. At the church hall, 5 pm?' She didn't ask him if he was okay to get there or if he was sure he could manage and he was all the more grateful because of it.

The church hall was decked out in fairy lights. It was silly to think that a dusty old building, with peeling paint and an air of having seen better days was magical, but it really was. Almost all of the children were draped in brightly coloured tinsel, some of the girls with baubles hooked over their ears like jewellery, and the music teacher was wearing a flashing badge that bore the message 'Merry Christmas'. Something weird had happened to Jamie since Maddie's text. He'd been idly flicking through the channels to kill the time between the conversation with Sophia and the start of the play and there'd been one of those wedding reality shows on. This one featured a same-sex couple, who were twenty years apart in age and at least 100 pounds apart in girth and their wedding was completely joyful. So much so that he'd had to wipe away a tear. Gender didn't matter, neither did age or physical appearance and anyone who thought so didn't know love. Maybe most people never knew real love, but suddenly Jamie was sure he did. It wasn't about any physical act either; it was about a shared past, present and future. Something he had with Dom, Chloe and his unborn godchild, something that Sophia and Poppy were part of too. He'd been looking for love in all the wrong places, when he'd had it at his fingertips all along. He loved them all and they loved him. It was all he'd asked for and, watching a cheesy wedding reality show, he knew he'd got his Christmas wish.

'Remember when you were Joseph and you kept hitting that girl playing Mary with your staff?' Dom giggled and Chloe shot him a look, as Jamie nodded.

'Let's hope Poppy is better behaved than I was.' The lights in the hall dimmed and the singing sheep was first on the stage, her pure clear voice filling the room as she sung about Christmas saving all lost souls. Jamie turned to the side and saw Sophia's eyes shining, her hand finding his without even turning to look at him. Whether she'd done it consciously or not, he didn't know. All he knew was that it felt right.

'She was brilliant!' Jamie turned to look at Sophia as the lights in the hall came back on and this time she turned to face him, her hand still resting in his.

'She was, wasn't she? Simon doesn't know what he's missing.'

'He doesn't.' Sod devising a strategy with Dom, he owed it to Sophia to be straight with her. 'And I'm not just talking about Poppy.'

'What?' Creasing her brow, for a moment she looked at him and then she laughed 'You didn't think I was back with him did you?'

'No, well, yes, if I'm honest. It was just you said you weren't looking for love anymore and I thought...' It seemed stupid now. She'd called Simon 'The Arsehole' for years, but he'd been so sure that she'd relented. Maybe seen their shared parentage of Poppy and wanted that to mean more to Simon than it apparently did.

'It isn't about Simon, it hasn't been for years. In fact, looking back, I'm not sure if ever was.' Sophia was still holding his hand and, for once in his life, Dom seemed to have found an ounce of diplomacy from somewhere and had borne Chloe off to get some tea and cake, whilst they waited for Poppy to get changed. Jamie looked up briefly and Dom was smiling in a way that might have given Clipboard Woman a run for her money.

'I don't understand.' Even as he said the words, he realised he did. This love he felt for Dom and for Chloe and for Poppy and the unborn baby... it was different with Sophia. There was something else there, that indefinable something more that he hadn't been able to put his finger on for weeks, months even; if he was honest with himself, maybe it was years. He'd hated Simon before he'd ever put a foot wrong. Had it really been about Sophia all along?

'I think you understand perfectly. I've had a crush on you since I was your best mate's kid sister at primary school and I deliberately let you catch me in every game of kiss chase we ever had, but you just ruffled my hair and sent me packing. I didn't say anything before in case it made it awkward.' She was smiling now, but tears were swimming close to the surface and he knew how much she was laying on the line to say these things.

'And what about now?' He wanted to kiss her and it didn't feel awkward at all, despite years of friendship, but he had to be a hundred percent sure before he did.

'Now? Now you're the only guy whose box I ticked at a speed dating event and who didn't tick mine.' Colour swept across her cheeks. 'I can't pretend how I feel about you anymore, life's too short. So I wondered if you might want to take Clipboard Woman's advice and consider ticking one more box to widen your matches.'

He didn't answer, just leant forward to kiss her, not noticing the bunch of mistletoe hanging above his head. He had love, real love and it was more than most people would ever know. The MS didn't define him – love did – and all his Christmases had come at once.

Author Details

If you've enjoyed this story and would like to find out more about Jay Bartlett, here's how:

Twitter: @J_B_Writer
Facebook: https://www.facebook.com/jobartlettwriter
Website: jobartlettauthor.com
Blog: https://jobartlettauthor.wordpress.com

'The Gift Of Christmas Yet To Come' (novella) published by Fabrian Books will be available through Amazon in November 2014. 'Among A Thousand Stars' will be published by So Vain Books in June 2015.

Winter Melody

Harriet James

The freezing air punches me hard in the chest and folds up my breath as I clang the gate shut and set off down our road. I put my head down and concentrate on walking, trying not to think about my stinging ears, and it's not until I reach the bottom of the hill and start to cross the road that I spot Ryan. He must be going to school early too, except right now he isn't going anywhere. He's just standing there by the phone box where the road slopes upwards, past the woods. Even at this distance I can tell his eyes are on me.

When Ryan is with his mates they shout out stupid things like: 'Speccy Four-eyes!' and 'Ginger nut!' and once one of them – it might have been Ryan – threw a stone and scored a direct hit on one of my lenses, cracked it right across. I didn't let on. I said it happened during hockey because there's no point in inviting trouble. It isn't that I'm scared of Ryan and the other two he hangs around with. I find them dead irritating, that's all.

It feels different today, though, with Ryan standing there quietly on his own. My heart beats a little bit faster.

I'm close to him now and there's nothing to stop me walking straight past, yet my feet slow down as if they've got minds of their own. Ryan is in the year above and he's a head taller than me, but thinner. His thick grey hoody is zipped up past his chin and his hands are pushed deep inside the pockets, making two grey lumps like rocks. His rucksack hangs off one shoulder, the way he always carries it, and his trainers are white instead of black, which is just about number one on the list of uniform crimes but somehow Ryan gets away with it, like he gets away with most things.

'What've you got there, then, Jamie? Violin is it?' He nods towards the black case I'm carrying with the initials of the school in shiny white paint on the side.

I stop. The cold strikes through the pavement and bites my feet as if it's telling them to get a shift on but they stay right where they are. 'Yes, it's a violin.'

'Go on then. Play it. Give us a tune.' Ryan squares his shoulders and looks me in the eye. The challenge spears the air like a hot metal rod.

'What, here?' I do a kind of double-take.

'Yeah, why not?'

'I can't. Not in the street.'

Ryan gives a kind of snort. 'Bet you can't even play it.'

'I can. I don't want to be late, that's all.'

'There's ages yet.'

'I've got orchestra practice. We're playing in assembly.'

And still I don't walk on, even though he isn't actually stopping me. Our breath puffs out like cigarette smoke. Behind us, the woods drip into the silence. Somehow I manage to peel my feet from where they're stuck and take a couple of steps forward but Ryan darts sideways. He's only half blocking my path but the pavement seems to shrink, leaving me nowhere to go.

'I don't think you've got a grasp of the situation here,' he says, lowering his voice. 'You're not going anywhere. Not until you've played that thing.'

He points at the violin. His eyes, boring into me from under the hood, are icy blue, like the scrap of sky that's started to clear above the trees. I can tell he's deadly serious and even though I tell myself I have a choice, it doesn't feel as if I have, so I figure I might as well get on with it.

I fling Ryan a look that says he's being a total nuisance, shrug off my rucksack and let it drop to the ground. Then I pull my scarf away a bit, peel off my gloves and stuff them in my pockets. I put the case down, open it and take out the bow and violin, and all the while Ryan is watching me.

Lifting the violin to my chin, I start to play a piece called 'Morning' from Peer Gynt. I should be able to manage it without the book – I practised it about a million times last night in case I mess it up when we play in assembly. We aren't allowed to play hymns any more. According to Mum it's the thin end of the wedge. She says she's going to write to the *Daily Mail.* I wouldn't put it past her.

It's a bit shaky at the beginning because my fingers are already numb and it feels really weird playing in the middle of the street. I'm half expecting no sound to come out at all, that the notes will freeze on the strings, but no, they rise one after the other, pure and clean, into the air, as if they can't wait to be let out. The melody flows perfectly and it's the best I've played in my whole life. I forget about Ryan and for a while it's as if everything else is peeled away and there is only me, the music and the January morning.

I reach the end and look at Ryan. His face, the little I can see of it, looks kind of blurry and, if I'm not mistaken, he's crying a bit. I concentrate on fitting the violin and bow into their green felt compartments, fiddling with the catch on the case for longer than necessary. Then I re-tie my shoe-laces and pull up my socks. Eventually, I slot my arms through the straps of my rucksack and stand up. Ryan is lifting his hands, still in their pockets, to his eyes. He sees me looking and drops them again, fast. He looks dead annoyed, but somehow I get the feeling it's himself he's annoyed with.

'My dad used to play the violin,' he says, after a moment. 'Really good, he was. The best. He could play anything, any tune you could name.'

'Doesn't he play now, then?' I'm wondering where this is leading.

'He died, end of last year. Been ill for ages.'

'Oh,' I say, uselessly. My face heats up a bit. 'That must have been, well... not easy.'

Ryan shrugs, and crunches a piece of ice with his foot. 'You could say.'

There's a little silence, then Ryan pulls down the zip on his top and shakes his head so the hood falls partly away. 'It's my mum,' he says. 'She's kind of frozen up, as if she's... somewhere else, like, all the time, you know?'

I don't know but I give a little nod anyway.

'Look, Jamie...' Ryan moves a bit closer. I can smell chewing gum on his breath. His eyes aren't icy any more. They're just, well, sad. 'Will you come to my house after school, with the violin?'

Another double-take. 'What, actually play it? At your house?'

'That's about the size of it, yeah. Look, what's it to be, a yes or a no?' Something of the old Ryan kicks in at this point.

'Suppose it's a yes, then,' I say, wondering what on earth I've let myself in for.

Playing the violin in Ryan's front room feels even weirder than it did in the street, especially as I haven't a clue what I'm doing here and what madness made me agree to it in the first place. Ryan was waiting for me at the gate after school and when we got here he went to the kitchen to fetch us a couple of Cokes and I heard him tell his mum I needed somewhere quiet to practise.

I start off with 'Morning', then I prop the book up on the mantelpiece and have a crack at the old standards – 'Greensleeves', 'The Ash Grove', that kind of thing – and I'm wondering how long I'm supposed to keep this up when Ryan's mum appears in the doorway leading from the kitchen. Ryan is standing behind her with a funny look on his face and he's pulling at his collar, as if he's really nervous or something. I try not to look at him and go on playing from the book, then after a while I move on to some folksy stuff that I know by heart, improvising a bit as I go.

I'm just thinking that Ryan's mum is starting to look a bit teary when she lets out a little sob, turns round to Ryan and gathers him up, and the way she's hugging him, all kind of fierce, it's as if she never wants to let him go. She's crying properly now, making the shoulder of his school shirt all damp. Ryan is just about managing to hold it together but I can see there's a bit of a struggle going on there. It's all a bit embarrassing, to be honest.

Eventually, Ryan's mum quietens down but she's still clinging to him, and the two of them stand there, kind of rocking in each other's arms. Suddenly, a tiny blob of understanding slides down and pools inside me and I know that my job's done.

I take the book off the mantelpiece, pack the violin away, and shrug into my coat. As I wind my scarf around I glance at Ryan and his mum and there's daylight between them. There's something else too, something new and fragile. It swells and fills the room and I feel as if I could reach out and touch it, but I know that if I did it would melt away like a snowflake.

Ryan's mum comes further into the room and I notice how much she and Ryan look alike, with the same blue eyes and everything. She gives me a smile that has a thousand words behind it. I nod and smile back, then head for the front door, quietly, not saying anything. Just as I open it, Ryan comes up behind me and puts a hand on my shoulder. He doesn't speak either but he doesn't need to.

I get as far as the gate when he comes bounding down the path behind me.

'See you in the morning, then, by the phone box?'

'If you like,' I say, all sort of nonchalant.

'About half past?'

'OK. About half past.'

'Just don't bring that thing.' Ryan cocks his head towards the violin case. 'Can't stand it. Sounds like someone trod on the cat.'

I shoot Ryan a smile. 'Got you,' I say.

Then I head off home.

Author Details

If you've enjoyed this story and would like to find out more about Harriet James, here's how:

Twitter: @HJames_writer
Facebook: *https://www.facebook.com/HarrietJamesWriter*

Harriet's novel 'Remarkable Things' will be published by Crooked Cat in 2015

The Handsome Stranger

Alison May

'Well Clare's single. She can go.' Of course. That was always the way when there was a family crisis. Clare didn't have adorable little triplets like her sister, Susie, or an important job doing never-quite specified important things like her brother, Olly. Clare was 'a free-spirit,' a polite family euphemism that saved her siblings and parents from dwelling on unsavoury notions like 'broken engagements' and 'unemployment.'

So it was Clare that hauled her holdall up the hill from the tiny railway station in her great aunt's village. In fairness, she had no reason to be annoyed. The family's insistence that she could go and spend the festive season babysitting Great Aunt Aggie had got her out of the usual trial by one-upmanship of Christmas dinner at her parent's home. It had also meant that, for the first time since she'd broken up with Nick the stockbroker, she'd merited a mention in her parents' Christmas round-robin letter where the great deeds of their children and grandchildren were catalogued for the appreciation and envy of their social circle. Admittedly she'd been at the bottom of the billing under her nephew's prodigy-like performance at the junior school swimming gala, but her mother's note that 'Of course, Aunt Agatha's illness piqued Clare's caring nature so she won't be joining us for Christmas this year' was the nearest to praise she'd received from either parent since her father had, rather prematurely, complimented her on making such a good match with Nick.

Aggie's house was a tiny cottage at the very top of the hill, nestled between the churchyard and the village pub. Clare definitely thought of herself as a spiritual person but, even at Christmas, the village church was likely to be a bit old ladyish for her tastes so she could guess which of the two would get more of her attention over the festive week. She knocked loudly on her Aunt's door and waited. Voices and footsteps moved along the hallway towards her before the door swung open.

'Hello.' The woman holding the door was blonde-haired and perfectly groomed. Pristine French-tipped nails, hair swept into an elegant chignon, tailored dress that landed just half an inch above the knee to reveal shapely calves beneath. She flashed a flawlessly lip-lined smile.

Clare pulled her worn duffle coat around her and shifted her feet to hide her scuffed boots. She tried to return the stranger's smile. 'Er... hi. I'm Clare. Aggie's niece. I'm here to look after her.'

The woman laughed a perfect melodic scale of a laugh. 'Oh. Agatha is very well looked after.' She paused. 'But I'm sure she'll be delighted to see you. Come in. Come in.'

Clare followed the stranger into the cottage and through to the downstairs bedroom where Aunt Aggie was sitting up in bed with a tray of food on her lap. Three more perfectly turned out women were fussing around her. Clare stopped in the doorway.

'Excuse me, my dear.'

Another woman squeezed past her carrying a huge vase of flowers that she set about arranging on the dresser.

Aunt Aggie looked up and grinned at her niece. 'Clare!'

Clare pushed her way past the Stepford carers and leant across the bed to hug her aunt. Aggie was her father's father's sister and had always been Clare's favourite relative by far. Unpretentious, not at all concerned about appearances, and never averse to a little tot of something naughty, Aggie was the only member of the family that reassured Clare that she was somehow of the same genetic stock and not the result of some sort of administrative error at the maternity ward. Clare bent her head to her aunt's ear. 'Who are all these people?'

Aggie rolled her eyes and whispered back. 'Ladies from church. I don't think they're really here for me.' She grinned at Clare and raised her voice. 'I'm so glad you're here darling. It's lovely to have another visitor. I had the new vicar around this morning, you know.'

The air in the room shifted. The door answering stranger, Stepford carer number 1 as Clare now thought of her, turned her head. 'The vicar came this morning?'

Aggie nodded.

The woman's eyes narrowed. 'I thought you said he was coming later.'

Aggie shrugged her shoulders, a blank innocent look spreading across her face. 'Did I? I'm sorry. Since I had the fall, I'm very confused.'

The Stepford carers spontaneously and entirely independently each discovered the need to urgently be somewhere else. Clare closed the door behind the last of them, who paused on the step, pressing a paper into Clare's hand. 'These are my details. If he comes back, call me first. It'll be worth your while.'

Clare frowned and glanced down. In her hand she had the woman's card and a neatly folded twenty pound note. She had no idea what was going on, but twenty pounds was twenty pounds. She nodded. 'Sure.'

She mooched back to her Aunt's bedroom. 'What did you mean about being confused?'

Aggie was still wearing her most innocent expression. 'What do you mean?'

'You said you were confused. Dad just said you'd broken your ankle. He said you were abseiling down the side of the town hall trying to unfurl a banner protesting the plight of the Tibetan people.'

'Just my excuse for my little white lie.' Aggie smiled. 'They wouldn't have stayed if they knew he'd already been. And they're so handy to have around. Yesterday one of them offered to re-grout my bathroom.'

Clare plonked herself down. 'So all these beautiful, apparently capable women are hanging around here in the hope of bumping into the local vicar?'

Aggie nodded. 'He's new. Single. Quite dishy.'

Clare could picture the Stepford carers' idea of dishy. It wasn't unlike the piece of crap formally known as Nick the stockbroker. Well turned out. Smartly suited. Sufficient charm to make up for the lack of anything much between the ears. More fool them, she thought. She grinned at her aunt. 'So what are we going to do this evening?'

Aggie folded her arms. '*We're* not going to do anything. *You* are. It's Christmas Eve. You're not spending the evening cooped up here with an old woman. Get yourself to the pub.'

Clare shook her head. 'I came to here to see you and to make myself useful.' She glanced at the clock. 'I probably ought to go to the shop before everywhere closes. So, what do I need to do for Christmas dinner?'

'Apply heat.' Aggie grinned. 'You saw the army that have been looking after me. There's enough Christmas food in the kitchen to feed half the village. All we need to do tomorrow is warm it through.'

Clare frowned. A drink might be nice, but it didn't seem right to leave her aunt all alone.

Aggie patted her arm. 'I've had a long day. I'm more than happy here with my book. You get yourself to the pub, love. There's bound to be somebody you know around.'

Clare paused again. Aggie was probably right. She'd been a regular visitor to her aunt's village since she was eighteen. She knew enough of the local old boys to be able to find someone to pass an evening with, and she did have an unexpected twenty pounds in her pocket. 'Are you sure?'

Her aunt nodded vigorously. 'You go have fun. Take the key off the sill and latch the door when you go out. I'll be fine.'

'All right.' Clare wrapped her coat tight around her and walked the twenty yards to The Green Man next door. The fug of warmth and beer that greeted her felt friendly. A couple of farmers from the next village down raised their glasses to her from the bar. Clare bought herself a pint of proper ale and sipped, relieved to be in a proper pub rather than a champagne bar with a crowd of leery bankers. She glanced around the busy room. The old boys at the bar were deep in conversation and she didn't want to intrude. Apart from that, she didn't see anyone she recognised. No matter. A pint and half an hour on her own would be just as good. She carried her glass to the back of the bar and scanned for a place to sit. In the darkest farthest recess there was a corner bench cut into the window sill. There was a man drinking alone leaning back against the wall. Clare squeezed her way over to him and gestured at the empty end of the bench. 'Is this seat taken?'

He glanced up, and she met his eyes.

Oh.

Brilliant bright blue oceans of eyes, inviting the unwary to dive right in and float away. Clare shot her gaze away from his eyes and swallowed hard. Her eye settled on his chin. That was better. Nobody ever passed out from gazing too long at a well-proportioned chin now, did they? Even if the chin had angles so fine they might have been sculpted by Michelangelo himself. Clare shifted her gaze again. The floor. The floor was perfectly fine. She would just look at the floor.

'I said, it's fine.' The man was raising his voice. Of course, he must have answered her questions some time ago, during all the eye staring and chin business. Clare paused. Now she had to sit down, didn't she? If she just nodded and walked away, she would look like a mad person, or possibly some sort of pub seating monitor. That could work. She could walk away and he would just assume she was the official seating monitor. Clare shook her head and sat down. Pub seating monitors weren't a thing.

The man was staring at her face. 'You're not from the village, are you?'

Clare focussed all her energy on rediscovering the power of speech. 'No.' That was good. Not effusive, but functional, and she'd stopped before she'd declared her eternal love and disclosed her sudden but unshakeable belief that they were meant to spend the rest of their lives together.

The man nodded. 'Good.'

Right. Ok. So they were having a conversation then? Clare could do this. She'd had conversations before, frequently without finding herself stroking the perfect cheek of the person she was talking to. Admittedly she'd never seen a cheek this perfect. She'd been in relationships. She'd been engaged, but even before Nick the piece of crap stockbroker had ruined last Christmas with his work party dalliance with Jessica from public relations, she'd never felt like this about him, not even during the first flush of romance. She'd quite fancied Nick, but this...? This was something else. She swallowed, and forced her attention back to her pint. 'So you're not getting on with the locals?'

The man rolled his eyes. 'I wouldn't say that. I just...' He raised his gaze. 'Just look around.'

Clare did as instructed.

'What do you see?'

She shrugged.

'A pub. People drinking.'

He shook his head. 'Look again. Who do you see drinking?'

Clare scanned the busy bar. Everyone looked happy. Everyone was in good Christmas Eve spirits. And then she saw it. 'Men. Old men.' It was true. Looking around the whole room, there was precisely two people under forty and precisely four women, three of whom where here on the arms of septuagenarian husbands.

The stranger nodded. 'So, I guess, if you're a younger woman living somewhere like this, there aren't that many options.'

Clare scanned her eyes over her companion. Dishevelled dark brown hair, those bright blue eyes, perfect jawline, black leather jacket – she risked a glance down – messed-up jeans and heavy boots. Beautiful, but not really the type the women round here would go for. Clare shook her head. 'I think you're safe.' She remembered the scene that had greeted her at Aunt Aggie's house. 'From what I can tell, all the single women in this town are obsessed with the new vicar.'

The man took a sip from his pint. 'But not you?'

Clare shrugged. 'I'm not sure I'm the vicar's wife sort.'

He smiled. 'So what sort are you?'

'I'm more the leaving disarray in my wake sort than the flower arranging sort.'

'Fair enough. So what does the disarray sort do for work?'

Clare closed her eyes. 'I'm unemployed. I was a nursery nurse, but the owner retired and I got made redundant.'

She waited for the reaction. It could go one of two ways – barely concealed disappointment or rabid sympathy. 'Bummer.'

Clare laughed. That was a first. 'Yup.'

'There's a pre-school that meets in the church hall here, you know. I think they're looking for a new manager.'

Clare shook her head. 'Move to a town with only one eligible single man?'

'You mean the mysterious new vicar?'

'Of course. The new vicar, who we've already established isn't likely to be my type.'

'Of course.' Was that a hint of disappointment in his voice? Clare didn't dare to hope. But maybe, just maybe, he was wishing she saw him as an eligible single man.

They fell into silence. Clare gulped from her pint. Conversation. That was what they needed. She should ask him a question. She took a breath. This was fine. She could totally manage a conversation. 'So I'm an unemployed nursery school teacher. What about you?'

His jaw clenched for a fraction of a second before he relaxed. 'Well I've just moved here. I like motorbikes. I play rugby.'

Clare took a gulp of beer and tried to stop picturing rugby-player thighs under the thin layer of denim. The beer was starting to relax her. 'Something else. Something personal.'

He sighed. 'Ok. Well I'm a terrible disappointment to my parents.'

Clare clapped her hands together. 'Me too!'

He grinned. 'I think mine pictured me doing something ridiculously well paid and high powered. Like banking or the stock market.'

Clare shook her head. 'Not the stock market. I was engaged to a stockbroker for a bit. He was a tosser.'

'Well I'm glad I didn't do that then.' He stopped. 'Can I ask what went wrong?'

Clare shrugged. 'He cheated on me which, according to my mother, could have been avoided if I'd made more of an effort.'

The man leaned ever so slightly forward. 'I'm sorry, but if he cheated on you it was a lucky escape. I have no idea how anyone could do that to someone as…'

'As what?'

He stared down at his pint. 'I was going to say 'as beautiful as you.' That's probably way, way over some line, isn't it?'

It probably was, but Clare didn't care. To be quite honest, she'd vaulted over the line and dived headlong into the smitten category the second she'd sat down. Her reply came out in a squeak. 'It's fine. It's nice.'

'Ok.' The man downed the rest of his pint. 'Ok. Then I think you're beautiful, and I'm struggling to stop myself leaning across this table and snogging your face off in front of a whole pub full of people.'

Clare opened her mouth and then closed it again. She must have misheard. She lifted her head and met his gaze. Clear, intense, completely focussed on her. Maybe she hadn't misheard. Very slowly she leant across the table into the dark of the corner where her companion was sitting and pressed her lips against his. Straight away she felt him respond. Mouth pressing back against her own, fingers drifting to the side of her face. She lingered for just a second before she pulled back. It took a moment to remember how to speak, and when she did her voice was hoarse. 'Like that?'

He nodded. 'Something like that.' His eyes remained fixed on hers and he was grinning, a big wide-open grin that lit his whole face. From the glow in her cheeks, she realised, she must be doing the same. Time passed. Ice ages came and went. All around them people enjoyed their Christmas drinks. Eventually he looked away. 'I should probably at least buy you a drink now.'

Clare giggled. They seemed to have got their first date etiquette back to front, but she held her empty glass towards him and accepted his offer of the same again. While she waited at their table, she tried to pull herself back down to earth. It was a tipsy Christmas Eve snog. It wasn't the start of anything. This wasn't the story she'd be telling her grandchildren. Her head battled to pull her off her cloud and back down to reality. Her heart refused to comply.

He put a second pint in front of her and a lemonade in front of himself.

'You're not drinking anymore?'

He shook his head. 'Actually, I should probably tell you, I have to go to work later.'

Work? On Christmas Eve. Clare took a gulp from her pint. He hadn't even had the grace to come up with a plausible excuse to get away. Nobody worked on Christmas Eve. She nodded. 'That's fine. I'll just drink this and then we can get off. Or you can go if you need to. You don't have to wait for me.'

It was a single kiss. There was no reason to weep or wail. He wanted out. She wouldn't give him the satisfaction of seeing her upset.

He shook his head. 'No. No. I've got time.'

Clare shrugged. 'Whatever.'

'Hey.' His fingertips brushed the back of her hand. 'What's up?'

Clare swallowed her disappointment. 'Nothing.' He hadn't promised her anything. He'd bought her a drink, and technically, she'd kissed him. No harm. No foul. She forced a smile, which contradicted the ice in the pit of her stomach, to her lips. There was no reason not to be civil. 'So you're into bikes?'

They passed the rest of the evening in conversation and laughter. Asides from being intoxicatingly handsome, the guy was funny, and a breath of fresh air compared with Clare's uptight family and arrogant ex-fiancé. Despite her disappointment, she relaxed. She told him stories about the kids at nursery and listened to him reminisce about riding dirt bikes as a kid. At quarter past eleven, he shot a glance to his watch. 'I'm sorry. I really have to go.'

Clare nodded. 'That's fine. I should get back to my aunt.'

She followed him out of the pub and was surprised to see him turn left towards Aggie's house. There was only the church beyond her aunt's cottage. 'Where are you going?'

He stopped under the streetlight outside the pub. 'I told you. I've got to go to work.'

Clare furrowed her brow. 'I thought that was just a line to get rid of me.'

He gasped. 'No. Absolutely not. Definitely not. I....' His voice tailed off. 'I should have mentioned this earlier.' Very slowly he reached to his neck and unzipped his leather jacket to reveal the distinctive white flash of a vicar's collar.

'Oh.'

'Yes.'

'So I have to go and do the midnight service.'

'You're the new vicar?'

He nodded.

Clare reeled. She'd snogged a vicar. Not just snogged him. Some seriously impure thoughts had snuck in there too. 'I'm going to hell, aren't I?'

'What for?'

'I snogged a vicar.'

He laughed. 'It's allowed. Seriously, I have exes I can call, if you like, make sure none of them have been unexpectedly smote.'

Something else filtered into Clare's brain. 'So you weren't trying to get rid of me?'

'No.' He took a step towards her. 'Nothing would upset me more.'

She matched his single step. 'Really?'

He nodded. 'Look. I don't believe in love at first sight.'

Neither did Clare. She believed in compromise and making the best of things. That was how relationships worked. That was how she'd tried to make it work with Nick.

He reached his fingertips to the back of her hand. 'But I do believe in Christmas and I do believe that sometimes, when you really don't expect it, God puts exactly the thing we need right in front of us.'

Clare took another step forward. Making the best of things with Nick hadn't got her very far. Maybe divine intervention was a better option. He bent towards her and rested his forehead on her hair. His hand drifted to the side of her body. 'I really do have to go to work.'

Clare rested one hand on the leather of his belt. Neither of them moved away. 'And I should go and check on my aunt.'

'Your aunt?' He stepped back and glanced at the cottage. 'Aggie is your aunt?'

Clare nodded.

The vicar laughed. 'And did she, by any chance, suggest that you come to the pub tonight?'

Clare nodded again. 'Why?'

He shook his head. 'Guess who was the only person I told where I'd be tonight?'

Clare groaned. That interfering old woman. That fabulous, brilliant, interfering old woman. 'So God moves in mysterious ways?'

'But your Aunt Aggie is much more obvious.'

He flicked his eyes back to his watch. 'I really have to go.'

'So you keep saying.' And yet he still hadn't gone.

'But maybe tomorrow?' He stopped and sighed. 'Christmas Day. You must have plans.'

Clare remembered the overstocked kitchen. 'Come for lunch. We've got plenty.'

He paused. 'My grandma used to say that if you share Christmas lunch, you're part of each other's lives for the coming year.'

Clare smiled. She could live with that. 'Come for lunch.'

'Ok.' One giant step back towards her to drop a final fleeting kiss on her lips. 'Tomorrow then.'

'Tomorrow.' Clare turned up the path to her aunt's house and paused. 'Goodnight vicar.'

'Goodnight beautiful.'

Author Details

If you've enjoyed this story and would like to find out more about Alison May, here's how:

Twitter: @MsAlisonMay
Facebook: *www.facebook.com/pages/Alison-May/310212092342136*
Website: *www.alison-may.co.uk*

Alison's debut novel, 'Sweet Nothing', and her other Christmas stories are available now for Kindle.

Loving Mr Perfect

Holly Martin

I stared down at my swimming costume in horror. I'd been at the ski lodge spa for three hours, had chatted with the woman who hands out towels and a waiter, plus smiled sweetly at several other customers as I walked between the hot tub, the pool and the steam rooms and I'd never noticed that there was a big tear in the breast of my costume like some slutty peephole bra.

I looked around to see if anyone was looking in my direction. The man on the next sun lounger was facing towards me, but he appeared to be asleep.

I grabbed the material and tried to wrestle it closed over the gap, but as I pulled at the bottom of the hole my whole boob plopped out the top. Embarrassed, I pushed it back in and tugged my thick towelling robe out from under me, in an attempt to make myself semi-presentable before I ran back to my log cabin to change. The robe was caught on one of the legs of the sun lounger and as I gave it one hard yank, the sun lounger flipped backwards and deposited me, legs akimbo, on the cool tiled floor.

I blinked up at the sky through the huge skylight and tried to ignore the supressed laughter coming from the man next to me.

Sam, or the Smug Annoying Man as I had called him, had been the bane of my life since I had landed in Calgary that morning. As I had staggered out the airport with my overloaded suitcase, one of the wheels had broken and as the case rolled onto its side, the handle snapped off.

Smug Annoying Man had helped me to fix it, taking an inordinate amount of pleasure in doing so. To him I was obviously the little woman who needed saving, much to my disgust. He offered me a lift in his flash hire car, but I declined. I was quite capable of getting myself to the ski resort. Four hours and a sweaty bus ride later, I arrived at the hotel to find Smug Annoying Man already settled in the spa with a hot mulled wine in his hand.

He stood over me now, offering me his hand to help me up.

'I don't need rescuing, thank you,' I said, scrambling to my feet in the most inelegant and ungraceful manner possible. Smug Annoying Man just shrugged as he lay back down and picked up his book.

I grabbed my sarong and tied it round my chest.

'Aw don't cover it up, I was enjoying the show.' He peered over his book at me, his eyes alight with mischief.

I stared at him. 'You saw it?'

It. As if my breast had now suddenly taken on a life of its own.

His eyes travelled down to my chest. 'I can still see it, that sarong is quite see-through.'

I clasped my hand to my breast as if I was fondling myself. I snatched up my robe and pulled it on, staring at him angrily. 'You saw my breast and you didn't think to let me know. You let me parade around in the spa, go for a swim, go in the outdoor hot tub, talk to people with my breast hanging out and you didn't tell me?'

'There are some things that it's not polite to mention to a complete stranger. Besides, you seem intent on not accepting any help.'

I snatched up my bag and flounced back to my log cabin, running as quickly as I could along the snow-lined paths that took me the short distance from the resort spa to my room.

It was petty, I knew that, not to accept his help. But that was the whole point of this holiday alone; to prove to my husband that I could cope without him.

In my professional life as an events co-ordinator, I organise weddings, parties and conferences for sometimes thousands of people, managing the different requests and complicated itineraries with military precision. But in my personal life, I'm scatty, clumsy, uncoordinated and very unlucky and I seem to traverse through my life ricocheting off one disaster to the next. My long-suffering husband always seems to be following after me, picking up the pieces.

After rescuing me from the hard shoulder with a flat tyre the week before, my poor stressed out husband had uttered the fateful comment that led me to here. 'Jude, how on earth would you cope without me? I can't leave you alone for one day without you ringing me up for one problem or another.'

I had obviously taken offence to that. I didn't need him. After leaving university I had lived alone for five years and coped fine. Of course there were disasters, there always were when I was around, and I had sorted them out. But his words had stung. Since we had married four years ago, I had become needier. He was my rock and I turned to him for everything.

So after several very cross words, a wager was declared. He didn't think I would cope on holiday without him. He thought I'd be on the next plane home after just a day. Either that or end up in hospital after the latest calamity. I was here to prove him wrong.

And what a place to do it. I looked out at the view as I stood on the balcony of my cabin. It was like a magical winter wonderland. Miles of snow-topped fir trees stretched out as far as the eye could see. The turquoise waters of the lake below me danced with the fading sunlight as if jewels were buried beneath the surface. Formidable mountains surrounded us, cocooning us from the outside world. Directly below my balcony, tiny white fairy lights started to appear like fireflies, lining the paths that drifted lazily between the log cabins and the restaurants, shops and the spa. The log cabins themselves were fresh from the set of some glorious cosy Christmas movie with roaring log fires, cosy sofas, the biggest bed I had ever seen in my life and a giant beautifully-decorated Christmas tree that stretched up across two floors. Garlands of leaves, berries and lights curled over the mantelpiece and up the stairs; it was just perfect. Nothing could go wrong here. The place was heaven.

'It's beautiful isn't it?'

I turned to see Smug Annoying Man on the next balcony staring out at the view too. I was embarrassed that I'd left my robe inside and was standing just in my swimming costume again, but he'd already seen me at my worst so there was no point in hiding from him.

'Are you stalking me?' I tried to calm down the note of outrage in my voice.

'Well you checked in after me so I should be asking you that. Clearly, you saw the proficient way I fixed your suitcase and you thought mmm, a big, strong man who will swoop in and save me whenever I need him, and so you engineered your cabin being next to mine. Well I'm flattered darling, but I'm a happily married man.'

I could see he was teasing me, but the audacity of the man was staggering. I let out a noise. I was going for something between disbelief and a scoff of indignation but what it sounded like was a big fart.

His eyebrows shot up.

'That wasn't me,' I said.

'Well I suppose it was better out than in.'

I flushed and scurried back towards the safety of my room, only to find my hasty departure was impeded somewhat by the sliding doors being stuck. I tugged, lifted, pulled and pushed, but the doors stayed resolutely closed.

'Problem?' asked Sam.

'Nothing I can't handle.'

Sam turned one of the chairs to face me and sat in it, ready to watch the show. He gestured with one of his hands. 'Please, go ahead, handle it.'

I pulled some more at the door, desperate to get away from his smug grin but it was clearly locked.

I looked over the balcony and Sam followed my gaze, whistling at the sheer thirty-feet drop.

'You going to climb down?'

'Maybe,' I said, safe in the knowledge that I would never dare.

I looked around desperately for an answer to my problem, but nothing leapt out at me. I glanced back to Sam who was giving me his undying attention. His soft, grey eyes were filled with amusement at my predicament. He looked impossibly relaxed considering the eight-hour flight, whereas I looked frazzled and stressed, my dark hair sticking out like a thick bush. Sam had travelled in first class though; I had seen him as I walked through to cattle class. He probably slept all the way whilst I had a child kicking the back of my seat for the entire flight.

'Right.' I swung one leg over the top of the low wall between our balconies.

'I think you'll find that's breaking and entering.'

'I don't care.' I toppled precariously for a moment as I sat astride the wall and brought my other leg over. The back of my oversized spa slipper got caught and I started to fall.

Strong arms were suddenly around me and I grabbed Sam to stop myself from hitting the floor. He shifted to get a better grip of my tangle of arms and legs, staggered back into his chair and I landed on top of him, straddling his lap.

We stared at each other for a moment. I could feel his heat, his strength beneath my hands. And he smelt amazing. I had a sudden overwhelming desire to kiss him, which I quickly suppressed.

'Well, this is new.' Sam ran his hands up my thighs, his eyebrow quirked up in a playful question.

I scrambled off his lap. 'Pervert.'

'Spoilsport.'

I stormed through his room towards the door, though I could hear him following me.

'Jude, wait. If you're going down to reception, you might want to wear this.' I turned as he threw his robe towards me. He deliberately looked down at my chest, his eyes dark with hunger. 'I can still see it.'

I pulled the robe over my slutty swimsuit and stomped out.

I lay in my bed the next morning, staring at the endless sea of green that stretched into the haze of the early morning mist. I could barely appreciate it, since I had lain awake for most of the night. I missed my husband. In four years of marriage we had never spent a night apart. Had I really become one of those women who couldn't sleep without their husband? I had always been so independent and now, I seemingly couldn't function without him.

Sam's comment the day before had niggled; the big, strong man sweeping in and saving me. That, of course, had been how I'd met my husband. He had been a guest at a medical conference I'd organised, along with five hundred other doctors and professionals.

I had been at the back of the room, moving the vases of flowers ready for the buffet, when a wasp had zoomed out of one of the buds and got tangled in my hair. I shrieked hysterically, knowing I was allergic to wasp stings, and started some weird dance, waving my arms in the air and shaking my head in an attempt to dislodge it, drawing all the eyes of the delegates down on me.

My husband-to-be literally swooped in, like a knight in shining Calvin Klein armour, freeing the wasp and gently leading me out of the room at the same time. As my heart stopped pounding and we stared at each other, I realised that his heroic attempts had been in vain. I could feel the tell-tale tingle of my lips going numb as they no doubt swelled to huge proportions. My husband quickly took control of the situation, swinging me up into his arms and ignoring the incredulous stares of my colleagues, he marched towards the row of offices.

'I presume you have an Epipen?'

I nodded as I directed him to my office. A few moments later he had injected me and called an ambulance, quite literally saving my life. Well almost. My allergy to stings wasn't that severe. I would most probably have walked around with huge fish lips for a few hours and a tongue that was too big for my mouth, but it was unlikely to have killed me. Still he insisted on escorting me to the hospital and back to my home a few hours later when I'd been given the all clear.

That set the precedent for our relationship, I'd get into trouble and he would swoop in and save me. As much as I hate to admit it, I loved it. Maybe it was because I'd spent years looking after other people and it was nice to be the one being looked after for a change, or maybe the child in me had some weird fairy tale complex, to be the princess rescued by the handsome prince.

But obviously the prince had grown weary of the continual mishaps that had befallen me, which explained why I was now lying in bed alone in one of the most beautiful, romantic places in the world.

I made myself a hot chocolate with added whipped cream and padded out onto the balcony, stubbing my toe and spilling half my drink down my bare legs. My yelp of distress brought the unwanted attention of Sam again as he peered round our adjoining wall.

'You ok?'

'I'm fine,' I said, as I quickly wiped off the hot chocolate with my spa towel. I walked closer to the low wall. 'I'm just tired. I miss my husband.'

'Then you shouldn't have come on holiday without him.'

I took a sip of the remainder of my hot chocolate and stared into the cup. 'I bet he's having a great time without me.'

'You strike me as a high maintenance kind of girl. I imagine, without you to look after, he's bored out of his mind.'

'I do not need looking after.'

His mouth twitched into a smile. He had found my sore spot and was deliberately rubbing salt into the wound.

'Oh I bet you're the kind of girl that faints a lot, just so your big, strong husband can catch you.'

I felt my mouth fall open. 'Is that what you think? That I engineer all these disasters just so I can be rescued?'

His mischievous smile fell off his face at my hurt expression. 'No of course not, I was just joking.'

'Let me tell you something pal.' I jabbed my finger into his chest. 'Firstly, I have never fainted in my life, metaphorically or literally.'

Sam looked down at my finger and tried to suppress his smile. 'And secondly?'

There was no secondly but now I quickly needed one.

'Secondly, my husband isn't big and strong, he's actually quite scrawny. He couldn't catch me if he had an oversized baseball mitt attached to his hand. So I certainly wouldn't rely on him if I did faint. He can't cook, he never remembers his Mum's birthday, and…'

'And?'

'And he's lousy in bed.'

Sam burst out laughing at this and I could still hear his laughter as I slammed the balcony door between us and stormed off to the shower.

It wasn't true of course. My husband was huge, he towered over me, making me feel so safe whenever I was with him, he was an amazing cook and brilliant in bed, something I had found out that first night when we had come back from the hospital. He did forget his Mum's birthday every year, but this was the only flaw in an otherwise perfect man.

Which begged the question, what on earth was he doing with me?

I sat on a bench and watched Sam whizz up and down on a snowmobile. I narrowed my eyes as the spaghetti thin blonde on the back of it wrapped herself tighter around him, shrieking and laughing as Sam skilfully raced across the glittering snow. She was the winter sports instructor and, dressed in a pink snowsuit that somehow looked incredibly sexy, she looked like Winter Barbie. I had seen her gathering people to play ice hockey the day before and helping countless men with their skis, snowboards and snowmobiles. There was practically a queue of men outside her little hut every day, hoping to be schooled by the proficient Barbie. Her snowsuit clung to her fabulous figure, the curve of her breasts was tantalizingly evident. Sam, it seemed, had noticed them as well.

Well two could play at that game. As Sam brought the snowmobile to a stop. I walked over to Barbie's male equivalent who was manning the hut while Barbie was playing. He was tall, dark and handsome in that rugged, woodcutter kind of way. I asked for the map of the nature trail, which he handed over, barely giving me a glance. His whole attention was on Barbie, or rather her assets as she walked across the snow towards us, laughing loudly at something Sam was saying.

Twirling my hair round my finger, I leaned over the counter, fluttering my eyelashes. 'And could you perhaps show me the way?'

He tore his eyes away from Barbie and looked at me as if I was stupid. He pointed to the huge archway right next to the hut that was daubed with the words 'Nature Trail' in big yellow letters and the well-defined path that led into the trees beyond it.

Embarrassed, I quickly took the map and as I turned away I collided with Sam.

'I can show you if you like.' His eyes were gentle, not mocking. 'I was just about to go myself.'

'Ooh Sam, there's a great route that leads down to the lake. It's very secluded. We could take the snowmobile and I could show you some of the wildlife,' Barbie said, playing with the zip of her snowsuit in a way that suggested it was more than just wildlife she wanted to show him.

'Thanks, but I think I'll stick round here,' Sam said, his eyes intent on me.

Barbie eyed me in disbelief.

'Oh, don't let me get in the way of your fun,' I said, stalking past him and heading down the path.

I rounded the corner and was swallowed by the tall trees. Snow glistened on the branches, sparkling on the leaves. It was quiet here, the sounds of children playing in the snow nearby being smothered by the trees. I rounded another corner and came face to face with a bear, towering above me. In the split second before I turned and ran, I registered the size of its claws in huge paws that could tear me apart and its mouth open in a snarl of rage. I didn't stop to think whether running was the right thing to do, I just tore from the trees, screaming as loud as I could. As I broke the trees and ran into the clearing screaming, heads snapped in my direction. There were children playing nearby, I had to warn them.

'BEAR,' I screamed. 'BEAR!'

Panic erupted in the clearing. They knew the horrifying dangers as well as I did. Parents swooped on their children, quickly removing them from the snow and running up stairs towards the safety of their cabins. I somehow managed to run straight into a snowdrift, trapping myself in three foot of snow. I was going to die; there was no doubt about it. But in the panic that was rapidly emptying the snowy glade, Sam was running towards me.

'No, Sam, get back.'

But he didn't. He ran straight to me, his strong hands on my arms, making me feel instantly safe, even though the threat was far from over. 'Are you hurt?'

I shook my head. 'Quick! Run!'

'Where is it?'

I pointed with a shaky finger. 'Back there.'

Sam glanced over my shoulder as I tried to push him away, but suddenly his face cleared in relief. 'Is that it?' He pointed through the trees and I stared at what was obviously a stuffed bear, not moving, not threatening at all. I felt my cheeks flush with embarrassment as I nodded.

He touched my arm. 'It must have been very frightening for you.'

I looked out onto the clearing. Crowds of people were lining the trees and the cabin balconies to see if we were both going to die a horrible and bloody death.

Sam looked at them too. 'How do you want to play this?'

'I suppose the right thing to do would be to go up and apologise,' I said.

'We could just tell them that it's gone, that your screaming scared it off.'

For a moment I was filled with fantasies of everyone buying me drinks, applauding my bravery and getting me to tell the story again of how I fought off a bear and survived. But then I realised that most people wouldn't go back in the trees or play in the glade if they thought a bear was terrorising the forests, and therefore I would have completely ruined their holiday.

He helped me out the drift and I stomped through the snow until I could address everyone in the clearing. I looked around at all the scared children and at the couples clinging to each other. I only hoped they would see the funny side.

I addressed the crowd. 'My mistake, I saw the stuffed bear back there and thought he was real.'

'But it's not even moving,' Barbie said, laughing.

There were groans of disbelief, people shaking their heads and rolling their eyes. I wanted the ground to swallow me up, or at the very least the bear to come to life and maul me to death, therefore proving I was right to scream in the first place.

'To be fair, if you weren't expecting to see it, most of you would be scared by it as well. Maybe there should be warning signs,' Sam said, as he stood by my side.

'What? Beware of the dead bear?' laughed Barbie's male twin.

The crowd dispersed with laughter and a few people giving fake screams. It was mortifying.

'I would have gone with the bear being scared away story,' Sam said. He looked at me with pity. 'Come on, let me buy you a hot chocolate.'

With adrenaline still pounding through my body, I was too weak to even argue.

I sat in the quiet of a wooded gazebo, the eaves of which were entwined with tiny twinkling fairy lights, with only a scraggly grey dog for company.

I had spotted him outside whilst I ate my lunch. He was a big, ugly thing with eyes like chocolate. He was in desperate need of a bath and a decent meal. Though I couldn't help with the bath, I could definitely help with the food. The ski resort had tonnes of it; different cuisines from all over the world, all deliciously presented as a heavenly party for the taste buds. I had smuggled some sausages into my handbag and when I went out into the gardens, the dog was already waiting for me, obviously having spotted the word 'mug' tattooed to my forehead.

I was a soft touch, I knew this. Our beloved dog Zara was a stray I had found in the park and she had been living with us now for the last three years. Smoky the donkey had come to us in the same way. He was being forced to give donkey rides to children that were way too big for him when I liberated him from a travelling fair for an exorbitant price. My husband didn't even bat an eyelid when he came home to find Smoky in the kitchen as I cleaned him down. Now he spent his days in our large back garden being fed carrots and apples. My husband called him Sir Smoky, on account of him being treated like royalty.

As I stroked my straggly grey friend, Sam came and sat with me, pulling the dog's ears affectionately.

'Are you hiding?'

'No, I'm just... Yes I am.'

'You just have to brazen it out.'

'Says you, Mr Perfect, I bet you never put a foot wrong.'

'Of course I do, all the time. Just last week, I said something careless to my wife and I ended up really hurting her. No matter what I say now, I can never take that back.'

The dog looked between the two of us like he was watching a tennis match.

‘I’m going snowboarding tomorrow, why don’t you come with me. Might cheer you up.’

‘Are you saying I’m a miserable cow?’

He sighed.

I knew I was behaving like a brat, which just made the situation worse. I opened my mouth to apologise just as Barbie walked past. She smiled and waved at Sam and he instinctively waved back.

I swallowed the apology on my tongue. ‘Why don’t you take Barbie instead?’

‘Maybe I will,’ Sam said, getting up and walking away.

I stayed in the coolness of the gazebo for a few minutes, tears stinging my eyes. There was only one way this situation was going to be resolved and it wasn’t sitting here with a stinky dog, feeling sorry for myself.

I stroked the dog as I stood up. ‘If you come by my cabin tonight, I’ll smuggle you out some Chinese.’

The dog wagged his tail and, knowing his free meal was over, pulled himself to his feet and lolloped off.

I sat on my sun lounger on the side of the indoor pool and watched Sam talking to one of the waiters. I looked down at my wedding ring, swallowing the huge lump in my throat.

I had been a complete cow to my husband over the last week after he said that comment about me being lost without him. He had apologised a hundred times, explained that the flat tyre had come after a very stressful day, but I had stupidly refused to forget it and move on. I hadn’t wanted to accept that I needed him, but the truth was I did. Not just for the manly stuff like changing a tyre or getting rid of spiders from the bath, or the large shoulder to lean on after a bad day at work. I needed him for the small stuff too, like holding my hand as we took Zara for a walk, or cuddling me in bed, the little touches, the warm looks, the amazing sex. I needed all of that. But was I too late? Had he grown bored of being there for me? Was my permanent sour face over the last week the final nail in the coffin?

A large shadow loomed over me as Sam settled himself down on the next sun lounger.

‘Missing your husband?’

‘Just thinking about why he married such a high maintenance, stubborn bitch.’

‘Because he loves you.’

‘I think my neediness has grown thin. I’m scared he doesn’t love me anymore.’

I could see him staring at me out the corner of my eye, but I couldn't look at him. He took my chin in his large hand and pulled my face gently in his direction.

'If your husband has made you feel, for one second, that he doesn't love you then the man is a complete and utter idiot. And if I see him, I'll tell him so myself.'

I smiled at this. 'Despite all my shortcomings?'

With his arm hooked round my waist he slid me across my sun lounger onto his so I was nestled against his chest. 'Because of them, because all your little traits are what make up you. You're kind, scatty, funny, stubborn.' He stroked my face, kissing my forehead. 'You're beautiful and I love you just the way you are. You make me so happy Jude, in every single way and I wouldn't change you for the world.'

I smiled as I fingered the buttons on his shirt. Sam started trailing kisses down my face.

'Let's have an affair,' he whispered as he reached my mouth.

'You'd better not mean with Barbie,' I said, wrapping my arms round his neck.

'No, I meant with you. Unless you want her to join us as well.'

I nudged him. 'Pervert.'

'Spoilsport.'

He brought my hand up to his mouth and kissed my wedding ring, just as he had done when he'd married me.

'So, your place or mine?' Sam said.

'Yours. I sort of managed to break my bed this morning.'

He smiled as he stood and scooped me up into his arms. 'How did you... Never mind, I really don't need to know.'

'It wasn't my fault.'

'I'm sure it wasn't.' He carried me out the pool and along the snow-lined paths.

'You see there was a spider...'

'A big one?'

'Huge. Well you see he lunged for me...'

'Did he have fangs too?'

'Yes.'

He laughed. 'Shall we see if we can break my bed as well?'

I curled my toes with delicious anticipation. 'Yes please.'

'Even though I'm lousy in bed?'

'Well, we can't all be perfect like me.'

Author Details

If you've enjoyed this story and would like to find out more about Holly Martin here's how:

Email: *hollymartin.writer@gmail.com*
Twitter: @hollymartin00
Blog: *http://hollymartinwriter.wordpress.com*

Holly's current eBook 'One Hundred Proposals' is available now and a short sequel 'One Hundred Christmas Proposals' is out soon

The Divorce Domino

Kerry Fisher

Kerry Fisher is the author of *The School Gate Survival Guide* (Avon, HarperCollins). The following extract is from her next novel, *The Divorce Domino*, which will be released in summer 2015, a story about how one woman's divorce blows apart her best friend's life.

Octavia

Jonathan usually loved choosing the Christmas tree. He would spend hours in the local garden centre, debating with the children until they found the perfect specimen, the one and only Norwegian Spruce that could grace our lounge. Then he'd haul it into the right place, the exact spot between the fireplace and the dresser. Immi and Polly would decorate it according to Jonathan's rigid spacing and ornament eking-out rules, with Charlie chucking the baubles on willy-nilly.

This year Jonathan had come up with 'I haven't got time/the girls don't want to go today/the trees will be cheaper nearer the day' until the one ritual I could delegate without guilt had plopped back onto my plate. The result was spindly and lacklustre. Sniping took the place of the usual argy-bargy over the fairy or the star on top and the divvying up of the glass reindeers. Resentment sliced into my fantasies of a cheery household floating about singing angelic bursts of *Once in Royal David's City* and lingered right through to Christmas Day itself.

Mum had arrived at eight o'clock that morning as though we would need five hours to prepare a roast lunch for six people. She stood in the kitchen hovering but not actually 'doing' until the hairs on my neck were quivering with irritation.

I managed to shoo her out to play Scrabble with Immi, which meant I could slosh industrial quantities of Chablis into my glass without copping the fourteen units a week speech. This year's project of knocking our lounge and dining room together to make one big living space was beginning to look like a mistake. Instead of being tucked away with the X-Box, Polly and Charlie were right under Mum's nose. As with every Christmas, Mum decided to deliver the 'Give a child a cardboard box and they'll be just as happy' speech.

Normally, Charlie would just laugh and say, 'Oh Nanna, get real,' but this year, a huge bellow of 'Jesus Christ, we're not in the 1950's,' came echoing through to the kitchen. A door slam followed.

I poked my head through the hatch and saw my mother rear up like a meerkat on its look-out mound, turning from Jonathan faffing about with the precise angle of the serviettes, to me, waiting to see how we were going to deal with – shock, horror – taking God's name in vain on Christmas Day.

Jonathan rolled his eyes and went back to straightening the knives and forks that Polly had thrown down in a slapdash manner. I tried Roberta's new age bollocks of visualising lying in a hammock in Barbados, but discovered that only a hiss at the husband would do.

'Jonathan, could you go and deal with Charlie, please, while I finish off lunch?' I probably sounded calm to the casual listener but seventeen years of marriage had taught him to recognise a meaningful '–CCCHHH' on the end of a sentence. With one last tweak of the table mats, he made his way upstairs.

I shouted through to Polly. 'Come and take through the cranberry sauce for me, love.'

No answer. I shouted again.

'In a minute.'

'No, now, we're nearly ready to sit down.'

'I'm just finishing this game.'

Immi came through instead. 'My tummy hurts. I don't want any lunch.'

'It'll make you feel better if you have something to eat. I've made your favourite cauliflower cheese.' I stroked her strawberry blonde curls.

'I'm not hungry. I already ate all my Selection Box. Do you want to know what I had? I had a Curly Wurly, a Mars Bar, a Milky Way, a Twix – I've got one stick of that left – and a packet of Jelly Babies.'

'I thought Dad said you could only have one thing.'

'He did, but then when I asked him if I could eat the rest, he just went 'hmm' and carried on reading his book, so I thought it was OK.'

I could feel a bit of a Jesus Christ incident coming on myself. I shook my head.

'I gave the Maltesers and Revels to Stan, though. I wasn't that greedy.'

'You shouldn't give chocolate to dogs. It's bad for them. Anyway, never mind.' Now the gravy had gone all lumpy.

I took a deep breath and called through to the front room. 'Mum, it's ready. Can I pass you these things through the hatch?'

Mum scurried over and busied herself with the food while I shouted up to Jonathan and Charlie.

Jonathan appeared at the top of the stairs. 'He won't come down.' There was something pathetic in his tone, a waiting for me to get it sorted.

The food was getting cold which made me want to have my own

tantrum. It was definitely early onset middle age – more bothered about chilly Brussels sprouts than my son having a Yuletide meltdown. Not for the first time, I mourned the era of spending every holiday backpacking on a diet of beer and crisps. I trudged up the stairs. 'Start serving.'

'Go away.' Charlie was nose down in his pillow.

'Please don't spoil the day, darling. I know Nanna's irritating. She irritates me as well and no doubt, when I'm old, you'll bin my false teeth so you can't hear what I'm saying.'

'I hate Christmas.'

'So do I.' And I really meant it.

That made Charlie sit up. 'How can you hate Christmas?'

'How can you?' I smiled, trying not to think of my gravy getting a skin on it. 'Come on, love, help me out here.'

He got to his feet, torn between wanting a hug and wanting to be bolshie. 'OK. Sorry.'

I squeezed his hand or rather the cuff of his sweatshirt. Charlie didn't seem to have hands any more. He scuffed down the stairs, still my little boy under that gangly mini-man.

In the dining room, I jollied everyone along, praying that Mum wouldn't choose right now to need an apology. 'Let's pull the crackers.' Polly snatched the fat end of the cracker from Immi, claiming ownership of her plastic purple earrings. Immi burst into tears and slid under the table, refusing to come out even when Polly handed them over.

As I slopped the chipolatas wrapped in bacon onto plates, I heard Stan throwing up in the kitchen. Season of festive fun, my worn out old arse.

I wondered when I'd last enjoyed Christmas.

An image of peeling off wetsuits, dragging a windsurf up a deserted beach, building a fire and huddling round with a couple of beers and some prawns on skewers rushed into my mind. I could almost smell the Mediterranean maquis that grew along the seashore. The age-old longing that I kept buried, occasionally bunging another layer of earth on top, caught me off guard.

I wondered if he ever thought about me.

Roberta

Christmas Day in the Green household was a day for singing twee Australian songs. This year, I clung to the ritual as proof that we were still a family, rooted in our customs and traditions. I closed my eyes as I sat in the passenger seat, marvelling at Scott, who was blasting out *Waltzing Matilda* as though he were off to Bondi Beach with no more on his mind than the state of the surf. Despite Alicia's entreaties, I couldn't join in.

When we arrived at the hotel, Scott strode in, making himself known to the staff, booming a big Happy Christmas to all. Alicia was right behind, light on her feet in her silver sandals, as wispy and delicate as Adele was stocky and stout. Granddaughter and grandmother linked arms together, pointing out the tree covered in glittery hearts and crimson ribbons. I glanced around at the other families and wondered if any of their smiles camouflaged upset so intense that they could feel it trembling in their chests.

Staff in black and white uniforms offered us Buck's Fizz at the door to the wood-panelled dining room. Scott picked two from the tray. As we sat down, he handed one to Alicia.

'She's under eighteen. She can't drink that in here,' I said.

'Lighten up. It's Christmas, for God's sake. Bloody British licensing laws. They're not going to chuck us out. It's only like a bit of lemonade and orange juice.'

Alicia looked at me, not knowing which way to jump. I didn't have the stomach for any more fighting. 'I'm sure Daddy's right. Just don't draw attention to it.' She glanced round and took a big gulp.

Adele was cooing over the log fire. 'In all these years I've never got used to Christmas in the sunshine.' Off she went on her usual discussion about what it would mean to move back from Sydney to Scotland now, but with all her brothers dead, and barely knowing her nieces and nephews, except that wee Caitlin who would keep coming out and staying for months on end...

Scott yawned and beckoned for some more drinks. Alicia started texting God knows who. I fixed my face in Adele's direction and nodded occasionally, bewildered by the family map. 'My cousin Archie is still in Aberdeen, but his wife, Siobhan, she passed away in 1999. No, let me think. Not 1999. It must have been 2000, because it was the year Sydney had the Olympics...'

My will to live was seeping away by the time the scallops on pea puree arrived. Scott raised his glass in a toast. Alicia's glass was empty and two bright spots had appeared in her cheeks. I ordered her an orange juice. We drifted in and out of conversation, with Alicia quizzing Adele about schools in Sydney while Scott quaffed the Châteauneuf he'd chosen.

Enormous platters of roast goose arrived. 'I wonder how Octavia's getting on cooking for her brood,' I said. 'It's such a luxury to have it all done for you.'

Scott looked over at me. 'She hasn't trained Jonathan right, has she? Unlike you, who's never cooked from day one.'

I put my mouth into a smile and kept my tone light. 'That's not true. I do cook, though I get a bit stressed if I'm catering for a lot of people or if it's your business colleagues.' Scott always liked to make out I was too idle to do anything myself, but the truth was he thought paying other people to clean, fix and garden was a sign that he'd arrived. He loved boasting that his wife didn't have time to work because 'managing the staff was a full-time job'. Cooking was the one area where I still retained a little control.

Adele was brewing up opposite me, no doubt ready with some comment about how she always makes double the amount and freezes half of it, but Scott hadn't finished.

'Come off it. When did you last cook a proper meal? Something that wasn't out the freezer or the microwave?' He stuck a whole potato in his mouth and sat back with his arms folded.

Alicia frowned and put her fork down. 'Dad, that's not true. Mum was cooking fish pie the other night when you called the police on her. And she'd made that asparagus quiche she'd seen in a magazine.'

I glanced at Adele who was all buzzy with interest. Everything in me tightened, ready for blast off. Before I had time to think of a cover up, if a cover up were possible, Scott turned on Alicia. Bits of potato flew out of his mouth, sticking to his wine glass. 'If you hadn't gone out dressed like a little trollop then I wouldn't have got angry with your mother.'

I put out a calming hand. 'Anyway, that's all over and done with. We were both a bit silly. Come on, let's not spoil Christmas Day.'

'I'm not spoiling it, Dad is. I wasn't dressed like a trollop, was I, Mum?' Alicia said.

'I'm not going to discuss any of this now,' I said, making a conscious effort to keep my voice low.

The Buck's Fizz had unleashed a bravery in Alicia I'd never seen before. 'There was nothing wrong with what I was wearing. It's called fashion, Dad. You're always ruining everything. Keira's mum saw the police taking Mum away on Thursday night. All my class were asking me how many years she'd got and pretending to put handcuffs on me.' Her bony shoulders were hunched up around her ears.

'Police station? What were you doing in the police station?' Adele was wide-eyed. 'Scotty? You didn't tell me Roberta was at the police station.'

I was just working out which words I was going to put together to form an explanation that wouldn't wreck the whole day when Scott slammed down his knife and fork with such force it made the glasses chink together.

Scott scraped back his chair but didn't get up. 'Mum, shut up. It's none of your bloody business.' I had my hand on his arm to quieten him down, but it was too late. 'Don't you dare shush me. If you weren't such a shit mother, I'd never have called the police in the first place.'

The silence in the dining room dominoed from table to table until the only noise was the laughing and banter from the customers by the window. I steeled myself to look round. The Maître d' was bristling his way over.

'Everything all right, sir?'

'Yes. Fine.' Scott didn't sound contrite or conciliatory.

The Maître d' didn't go away. I was aware of the woman at the next table telling her children to be quiet and turning their heads away from us. I closed my eyes. I wanted to smile and pretend everything was OK. I looked down at my plate and picked up my fork. My stomach wouldn't co-operate. It had shut down, closed over like a pair of lift doors. Alicia was huddled in her chair, tension radiating from every pore.

Adele stepped in. 'Sorry for the noise. My son is a very passionate man and I think I may have spoken out of turn. That's families for you. We know how to push each other's buttons, don't we, Scotty?'

Scott mumbled something and the Maître d' offered a crisp, 'Very well, Sir,' and clipped off again.

Nobody spoke. Not even Adele. Alicia sat opposite me with fat tears dropping onto her plate. I reached over for her hand. She gripped my fingers hard, like she used to when she was a toddler and a dog sniffed at her. 'I can't eat any more.'

Maybe it was the rasp in her voice. Or the whispers in the dining room. The heads craning round pretending to look for a waiter but having a jolly good stare at the wife with the atrocious husband instead. Alicia's humiliation was tangible, her whole body rigid. We were supposed to protect her, not invite ridicule. I looked at Scott. His jaw was set, that familiar look of self-justification clamped around his features. A hot rush of emotion coursed through me. Then a surge of release as though I'd removed a pair of crippling shoes.

Just because I wanted our marriage to work didn't mean I could make it work.

I was never going to make it right. Never. I got quietly to my feet, picked up my bag and held my hand out to Alicia. 'Just pop out to the car for a minute, darling.'

Alicia hated being the centre of attention and relief mingled with her confusion. She scuttled past Scott before he had time to argue. I looked at Adele, who was fiddling with her necklace and looking every one of her sixty-eight years. 'I'm sorry, Adele. We shouldn't have let you come over this year. We've had a bit of a tough time lately.'

I sucked myself in, clenching every muscle in my stomach in case I suddenly jellyfished onto the floor. There was only one chance to say this. I screwed up my eyes, then dived in. I forced out little more than a whisper.

'I'm leaving you.'

Scott sat back in his chair, hands in the air in disbelief. 'Don't be silly. Where are you going to go? Come and sit down.'

I couldn't say anything more. Too many eager faces were waiting for my next move. Enough of my life had been played out in public. I stared at Scott, the man I'd loved for so long.

Maybe I still loved him. Now I had to save myself. And Alicia.

He looked like he didn't believe me, somehow thought he had the magic word, the clever spell to bring foolish Roberta back in line. It was all over his face. My last glimpse of him was sitting there puzzled, as though he'd been showering me with compliments and I'd taken umbrage at nothing.

I turned round and concentrated all my energy on putting one foot in front of the other. I squeaked out a 'thank you' and a 'sorry' to the Maître d' at the door without stopping to hear his reply. Just a corridor to go. A courtyard with a Christmas tree. A patch of grass. Then the car. Alicia was standing by the passenger door as pale as an icicle in the sun. I pushed out the last words I could manage.

'I'm sorry, darling. I've left your father.'

Author Details

If you've enjoyed this extract and would like to find out more about Kerry Fisher, here's how:

Twitter: https://twitter.com/KerryFSwayne
Facebook: https://www.facebook.com/kerryfisherauthor
Website: http://www.kerryfisherauthor.com
Amazon Author Page: http://www.amazon.co.uk/Kerry-Fisher/e/B00AOAAXJ4

'The School Gate Survival Guide', a funny novel about school gate snobbery is available now - http://bit.ly/SchoolGate and 'The Divorce Domino' will be released in summer 2015.

The Other Side of Christmas

Sharon Booth

It's snowing. Well it would be wouldn't it? All afternoon people have been coming into the reception and announcing the fact as if we're not capable of looking out of a window and seeing for ourselves.

'Blowing a blizzard out there,' they tell us cheerfully. 'It'll be murder on the roads. Hope you haven't got far to go when you finish here.'

The older ones look worried, asking us to ring taxis for them after they've seen the doctor, but the children are delighted, staring out of the health centre windows as big fat flakes, stark white against the dark sky, shower onto the pavement as if someone's shaking a giant box of washing powder onto the world.

I'm only just starting to log off my computer when Penny appears at my side, all ready to leave. 'Hurry up, Katy. Let's get out of here. Can you believe it's snowing?'

Well yes, I can actually. In fact I'd have put money on it. The one year when Christmas is a total washout from my point of view, when I've made up my mind to ignore it to the best of my ability, and it has to go all Charles Dickens on me. Of course it does.

'Thank God that's over with,' she calls as I head into the cloakroom and collect my coat. 'So glad it's not our turn to stay till six this year. Why are you dawdling? Four o'clock finish today, remember? Or have you forgotten it's Christmas Eve?'

'Never! Is it really? No one mentioned it,' I say, pulling on my gloves and winding my scarf around my neck. I keep my head down so she doesn't see the tears that have suddenly appeared from nowhere. How embarrassing. I blink them away angrily and pull myself together. I'm thirty-one for God's sake. It's just one wretched day. I can cope with that.

'What time are your mum and dad expecting you?' she asks, as I stoop to get my handbag from under the desk, and blushes as I straighten up and catch her popping a mini sausage roll into her mouth. She shrugs and peers longingly at the plates of left-over sandwiches and quiche. She can't still be hungry, surely? She practically cleared the tables single-handedly. No one loves an office buffet like Penny.

'I told them to expect me when they see me,' I say casually. 'It's all very informal at our house. Dad will probably be asleep in front of the telly and Mum will be in the kitchen, helping herself to the advocaat and peeling three tons of potatoes. I don't have to clock on or anything.'

'Lucky you,' she says. 'It's going to be manic at ours tonight when the hordes arrive. How we're going to fit everyone in I don't know. Are you sure you don't mind Mike's mum taking your room?'

'It's hardly my room,' I point out. 'I've only been lodging there for a few weeks. Anyway, don't be so daft; you've had this arranged for months. Oh, and don't worry, I've hidden anything that may shock her.'

Penny's eyes widen and I sigh. 'I'm kidding. Stop worrying.'

'I just feel mean,' she says. 'It would have been lovely to have you for Christmas but there simply isn't the space for everyone. Mike's sister and brother-in-law will be in sleeping bags on the floor as it is.'

'You'll manage,' I say. There's no doubt about it. Penny and Mike go through the same performance every year. Their house is always chaotic and bursting at the seams with guests on Christmas Day, but they always enjoy it and invite everyone back for a repeat performance. I can hardly complain. They've been good enough to take me in and let me live in their spare room for the last seven weeks. The least I can do is make way for their guests without making them feel guilty about it.

We say goodbye and merry Christmas to the unfortunate girls whose turn it is to stay on duty till six o'clock, then head out of the health centre into an alien, white world. A silver Astra is parked in front of the door and Penny beams as Mike winds down his window and whistles at her. He has a Santa hat on his head and I can hear Wham's *Last Christmas* blaring out for what feels like the thousandth time this week.

'Bloody hell, he's actually on time. It really is Christmas,' Penny says. She hugs me and tells me to have a fabulous time, then climbs into the passenger seat.

'Happy Christmas,' calls Mike. 'Think of us when you're lounging around stuffing your face and watching telly in total peace. I'll be putting a doll's house together, trying to fathom out my mother's new phone and watching sodding Power Rangers' DVDs all day. Roll on seven o'clock and the *Doctor Who* special.'

'I knew you loved it really,' I laugh.

He pulls a face. 'You must be joking. I'll leave all that tosh to you. Point is, by the time it finishes it's time for the kids to go to bed and everyone else will be falling asleep. *Doctor Who* marks the end of all the Christmas palaver and I can settle down with a lager and look forward to normality resuming. Have a good one, Katy.'

They drive off and I wave until they turn the corner, then head to the staff car park at the back of the health centre. Whatever Mike says

I know perfectly well that they'll have a fabulous Christmas. They've been looking forward to it for weeks and it will run like clockwork, and even the chaos will add to their fun. Christmas was made for families like the Baxters if you ask me.

I clear the snow from the windscreen of my little Fiat and set off. I have to call at the supermarket before I head out of Hull. I need something for Christmas dinner and some general provisions. There'll be nothing at home. I should really have made a list, I think, hoping that by now the shopping frenzy will have died down.

I should have known better. After driving round and round for a full ten minutes, muttering and cursing as I'm out-manoeuvred by aggressive dads with reindeer antlers on their heads, and harassed mothers in tears, I manage to squeeze myself into a space at the far end of the wretched car park and crunch through the snow to the main entrance of the supermarket. I have to push my way into the store and sigh as I see what looks like the entire population of East Yorkshire dashing round the aisles with fully-laden trolleys and manic expressions on their faces. Here we go then, I think, picking up a basket.

The checkout girl looks a bit stunned as, forty-five minutes later, I dump my meagre amount of shopping on the conveyer belt and wipe the sweat from my fevered brow.

'These are buy two, get one free,' she informs me, waving the box of Quality Street at me and giving me a kindly smile.

'Thanks, but I only need one,' I say.

She looks quite put out by this and scans the chocolates, not even bothering to ask if I need any help with my packing, which I suppose isn't surprising given the tiny amount of shopping I've done. Behind me a queue of exhausted parents has built up. They lean on their trolleys, which are packed full to the brim with festive goodies, and mutter to each other about how ridiculous it all is for just one day. Above the relentless din of whining children and couples arguing about how much beer they'll really need and whether sprouts are truly essential, Band Aid are asking *Do They Know It's Christmas*? I think, with a distinct lack of seasonal spirit, that I wish I was somewhere right now where no one had a clue.

The checkout girl gives me a knowing look as she scans the toilet roll, soap, coffee, milk, bread and microwave turkey dinner for one. I see pity in her eyes as I stuff the shopping into two carrier bags and take out my credit card. For a brief moment I wish I was still wearing my engagement ring, just to show her I'm not some sad, lonely loser. Unfortunately, I'd posted it back to Simon, determined to show him that I was getting on with my life and not in the slightest bit bothered about being heartlessly cast aside, so maybe I am some sad, lonely loser after all. For the first time I regret sending it back. God knows, it had taken me long enough to get the damn ring in the first place.

We'd been going out for four years before Simon finally popped the question. Even then, it wasn't exactly a romantic proposal, more like a business proposition. He'd pointed out that we'd been together a long time, his colleagues and parents were hinting that it was time we were married, his company was keen to foster a respectable, family image and it would probably be good for his career – hardly moonlight and roses. I'd suggested a date in September, but then Simon had announced that he wanted a big church wedding and said these things shouldn't be rushed; it would take a lot of organising and maybe we should start planning it later.

'Let's get this year over with first,' he'd said, even though it was only May. 'We'll start making plans on the other side of Christmas.'

The other side of Christmas seemed to be his favourite time of year. He was always going to do things then. The twenty-fifth of December seemed to be the major landmark in his life, with everything important scheduled to take place once it was out of the way.

I take the receipt and mumble, 'Thanks. You too,' as the shop assistant wishes me a merry Christmas. I've been in that place for nearly an hour, thanks to all the crazed shoppers who are practically having fist fights over the last packet of Paxo. I need to get a move on. It's gone five already.

Normally the drive from Hull to Weltringham takes around forty minutes, but with people heading home for the holidays, and the unexpected snow, it's well over an hour before I even get close to the coast. If I'd been going to my parents' house I'd have been home ages ago, I think, feeling very sorry for myself as I drive through little villages, seeing fairy lights twinkling in the windows of houses as I pass and thinking enviously of families in their living rooms, all cosy and snug and loved. I'm beginning to feel like *The Little Match Girl*.

Mum and Dad had booked the cruise just days before I was going to ask them about coming to them for Christmas. Serves me right for making assumptions, I suppose. It's the first time they've ever gone away for the festive season, which is sod's law. I don't want them to feel guilty about abandoning me so I never told them I was being brutally ejected onto the streets and they think I'm spending Christmas with Penny and Mike. I have a key to their house and I suppose I could go there, but the neighbours are very nosy and they'll no doubt be keeping an eye on the place while Mum and Dad are away, so there'll be no chance that I can stay there without them finding out as soon as they get home. They'd be so upset that I was there all alone. It's best all round if I stay away.

I drive slowly, in no hurry to reach home. Home. It hardly seems like that any more. Had it ever, really? We'd bought it when we were full of hope and it had all seemed like an amazing adventure.

Penny thought I was mad even then. 'Why would you want to live all the way out there? It's the back of beyond. There isn't even a Tesco. It will take you ages to get into work every morning and what if something goes wrong with your car?'

'We have two cars,' I'd reminded her, 'and if anything goes wrong with mine I'm sure Simon can give me a lift in his. He only works three streets away, for goodness' sake. And who cares about a Tesco? There's a cute little post office and general store. We can do our big shop on the way home after work anyway.'

'But it's so dreary,' she'd protested. 'Even the roads commit suicide round there.'

It was true that the Holderness coast was eroding fast and many roads had crumbled away into the sea, but the village of Weltringham was a fair way from the cliff edge and Bramble Cottage was in no danger. Well, not in my lifetime anyway.

It had taken a while for Simon to convince me that living there was what I wanted, but I'd totally come round to his way of thinking. Weltringham was surrounded on three sides by fields and farmland and when we'd first visited the village – to look at a car Simon was considering buying, though he eventually decided against it – it was early summer; the fields were a blaze of bright yellow oilseed rape and the verges were draped in frothy cow parsley. It was like a little piece of heaven on earth, so different from the concrete streets we lived and worked in. I don't know how anyone can go there and not fall in love with it, though living there had actually been all Simon's idea.

We'd started making wedding plans and had got as far as booking the church when he came home one evening in April and said he'd been thinking about our living arrangements. Apparently, simply everyone in his office lived in the country and commuted into the city for work and he felt we should too.

'But what's wrong with this place?' I'd demanded, looking round our little flat in bewilderment. It was in the centre of the city and very handy for all the shops, cinemas and bars. We weren't far from the marina and liked to stroll round there on warm evenings, gazing enviously at the yachts and sipping drinks as we soaked up the sun and planned our future.

'It's fine for a young couple,' said Simon, as if we were in our dotage, 'but once we're married things will be different. We should sell this place and buy somewhere in one of the villages. It's the done thing.'

'But can we afford to move, what with the wedding and everything?' I was doubtful. Simon's plans for the reception alone were stretching our finances. Mum and Dad were happy to chip in but I couldn't expect them to pay for it all. Not with the extravagant event Simon envisioned.

'I think the house is more important than the wedding,' he'd said firmly.

'Fine,' I agreed. 'So we scale back the reception? I'm happy with that. And we can halve the number of guests we invite. I don't know who most of the people on this list are, anyway.'

'Of course not!' He looked shocked at the very idea. 'I think we should put the wedding off for a while. We need to get the house sorted first. It's a question of priorities. We'll spend this year finding our new home and we'll start planning the wedding again on the other side of Christmas.'

I'd taken some persuading but Simon convinced me that we were doing the right thing. Having made up our minds, Weltringham was the obvious place to start looking, given how much we'd loved it when we'd visited the previous summer. Penny wasn't the only one who thought we were mad, but we were determined to live our dream. It wasn't easy to find somewhere for sale round there and the months dragged on, but eventually Bramble Cottage had come up for auction.

We'd taken Penny and Mike to view it with us and Mike was appalled. 'Have you any idea how much work it would take to even make this habitable?'

'It's a wreck,' wailed Penny. 'Please don't even think about buying it. You do know Yorkie Homes are building a new estate not twenty minutes from us? Why don't you take a look at their brochure?'

But there was no chance of that. Bramble Cottage, a red brick shell of a building in urgent need of restoration, had totally won our hearts.

'I bet that's where Lord Lucan's been hiding out,' said Penny, nodding towards the weeds which stood shoulder high in some parts of the garden which stretched for a quarter of an acre. 'You're mad, the pair of you.'

Maybe we had been. Ours had been the winning bid and by September Bramble Cottage belonged to us. We'd thought that, after that, it would be plain sailing. We hadn't realised how long it would take to find an architect, draw up plans, get planning permission. Oh, planning permission – the two most hated words in the dictionary. The battle for Bramble Cottage seemed to drag on longer than the War of the Roses. Another autumn came and went and it was pretty obvious that the wedding would have to remain on hold. Our new home drained all our spare time and also our finances.

'Never mind,' soothed Simon. 'We'll spend the next year getting the cottage just perfect and then we'll book the wedding on the other side of Christmas.'

Mike helped us find a reputable builder. 'He did a brilliant extension on my cousin's house. Doesn't live far from your place. Here's his number,' he said, handing me a business card for a company called LI Builders.

LI himself turned out to be Luke Ingledew, a quiet, dark-haired man in his early thirties. He'd sold his house and had moved back in with his parents who ran The Seagull Inn, just a fifteen minute walk from the cottage, while he looked round for another renovation project. He looked at our plans, negotiated terms and prices with Simon, and started work in late February.

Simon had decided we didn't need a project manager as he was more than capable of organising everything himself, even though he had no experience of renovating a property or of anything to do with property actually. He didn't particularly like Luke and I got the feeling it was mutual. There were lots of disagreements and a great deal of tension as they stamped around the cottage, and I knew Simon would have happily sacked him if he'd thought he could get anyone else for the same price. Things would have been done a lot quicker if they'd co-operated, but everything became a battle. You could practically smell the testosterone as they locked horns and fought for supremacy. Simon blocked everything Luke suggested and found fault in everything he did, delaying the work and making himself extremely unpopular with Luke's employees and the other workmen he'd sub-contracted. I couldn't help thinking that some of Luke's ideas were much better than ours. He seemed to have an instinctive feeling for the property and knew exactly what would work. I found myself arguing with Simon more and more about how the finished cottage should look.

After some rather tiresome weeks of travelling backwards and forwards to Weltringham, Simon decided that it was pointless paying for the little house we'd rented near work after selling our own flat. He duly borrowed a colleague's static caravan and had it towed to the front garden of the cottage. We moved in and he was a bit happier for a while, believing he could keep a closer eye on Luke and make sure that the work was being done to his taste and satisfaction. He and Luke clashed endlessly and I wasn't surprised when they decided to part company. It was the first thing they'd agreed on.

'Please don't go,' I begged Luke as he loaded up his van, his face grim. 'You understand this place so well and your ideas are perfect. Give it another chance.'

He shook his head and slammed the doors shut, then turned to me. I saw the expression in his eyes soften and he put his hand on my shoulder as I stood there, blinking back tears.

'I'm sorry, Katy,' he murmured. 'If I thought I could make a difference, if I thought for one moment that he'd listen...'

'I'll make him listen,' I said, though I had no idea how I planned to achieve that.

He looked down at the path for a moment, his teeth nipping his bottom lip. Eventually he looked up and I saw the sadness in his face.

'It's too hard,' he murmured. 'I'm sorry. I can't stay here any longer.'

So he'd gone, and it wasn't long before Simon was cursing his actions as it proved impossible to find someone at such short notice to continue with the work. The weeks dragged on and he eventually found someone who could take over, but at a vastly increased price and not until he'd finished another project. It was the beginning of the end really...

Driving through winding country lanes at night is bad enough, but in this kind of weather it's a scary process. I peer through the windscreen, my wipers moving rapidly to clear the glass as flurries of snow shower the car with alarming frequency. I shiver, thinking of the caravan. What fun it's going to be, tucked away in that tin can on wheels for a couple of days. There's a Calor gas fire in the living room, but the bedroom will be freezing.

I'd called Luke the week before to warn him that I was spending Christmas in Weltringham and to ask if he'd mind putting on the caravan light and the fire before I got there.

'What time will you be here?' he'd asked.

'Around half past five, I should think,' I'd said, somewhat optimistically as it turned out.

Weltringham looks so pretty as I arrive at the main street that it brings a lump to my throat. All Saints' Church dominates the village, standing on raised ground with a high cobbled wall surrounding it. In the spring the church yard is a mass of daffodils. Tonight, the gravestones are shrouded in snow but it still looks beautiful, light shining through the stained glass windows of the church as preparations continue for the carol concert that's due to take place any time now.

I can see people spilling out of The Seagull Inn, already looking the worse for wear. I wonder if Luke's in there. I hope he remembered to put the fire on for me. In all likelihood he'll be with his workmates now getting well and truly blotto. Well, I can't blame them. In other circumstances I'd be doing the same.

I wonder briefly what Simon's doing. Probably still working if I know him. Not that I do know him – not the way I'd thought anyway. The Simon I knew would never have called off our engagement, throwing all our plans and dreams away for the sake of promotion and the chance to move to London.

I mean, London! What happened to our vision of country life, of a cottage by the sea? When it came right down to it, Weltringham couldn't compete with a huge salary increase and a swish flat in the capital which he was going to share with some colleagues.

'Let's face it,' he'd said, trying to be as gentle as he could, 'things haven't been right for a long time. You must have felt it, too? We've drifted apart. I don't know, maybe it was just the pressure of this place. We took on too much, don't you think? It was a stupid dream.'

'But it was *our* dream,' I'd protested, choking on tears. 'We were going to make it beautiful again and live here and start a family.'

He shook his head. 'I'm sorry, Katy, honestly. I just don't think we thought it through properly. It was a mad idea. I've been so stressed and tired trying to make it work, but in the end I had to be honest with myself. When this promotion came up I knew what it was I really wanted.'

'And what about me?' I'd asked, knowing already that I wasn't what he wanted.

'I wouldn't dream of asking you to move to London,' he replied. 'I know you'd hate it. You'll find the right person one day and when you do, you'll find the right home, too.'

'So what about the cottage? What do I do about that now?'

'I emailed Ingledew. He's happy to come back now that he knows I'm out of here. No point paying the exorbitant prices of that other builder and we never signed anything. Once they've finished the work we'll sell it. I'll need all the cash I can get and we should make a good profit when it's done. It will give you some capital to invest in your own place, too. It will work out better for both of us. We'll put it on the market the other side of Christmas. House sales pick up then. It's for the best, you'll see.'

I failed to see how. Bramble Cottage was my dream home and now I was going to lose it before I'd even lived there.

I'd stayed on at the caravan for a few weeks, trying to stay cheerful, trying to remain positive. Luke returned and I told him to do whatever he wanted to the place. Obviously, we had to stay within the plans, but the fixtures and fittings were up to him. I saw no point in creating a dream home that I'd have to leave very soon.

He stared at me, apparently as shocked as I was that Simon had called off our engagement. 'I can't believe it. How could he bear to… he must be mad.'

'I know,' I said. 'Swapping Weltringham for London. I just don't understand it.'

He seemed about to say something but then shook his head,

looking up at the cottage and considering for a moment. 'I'm so sorry, Katy. I know how much this place means to you. It's a crying shame. It used to be so beautiful and it will be again, I promise you. I'll create the perfect home for you.'

'It doesn't really matter,' I'd sniffed. 'I've got to sell it anyway. Simon wants his share back and I can't afford to buy him out. I'll never live here now. It was all a waste of time.'

He half reached out to me but then changed his mind. His arm dropped to his side and he looked at me with sad, dark eyes. 'You would have been happy here, I know it. I've loved this house since I was a child. I wanted it myself, did you know that? As a home, I mean, not a project. You outbid me, sadly. I've loved working on it, though. It's been a privilege to bring new life to the place. Whatever happens, you can be proud that you've helped bring that about.'

I tried to be noble about it but all I could think was that I was going to lose the home that I loved so much already.

Living in that caravan all alone wasn't any fun either. The two-storey extension to the cottage was finished and there was a brand new roof on the original building, but there was still no electricity, we needed a new boiler and central heating system, and we were in the process of replacing the rotten windows. It was a long way from being ready to move into, thanks to all those weeks with no builders, and I was getting seriously depressed as the nights started to draw in and the weather turned colder.

Luke tried everything he could to cheer me up. He showed me the plans he had for the kitchen and started coming up with designs for the garden. Now that Simon wasn't on the scene to push him around and bark orders at him he was eager to show me what he'd visualised for the cottage when buying it had been his own dream. I loved his ideas. I could really picture the cottage looking beautiful when it was done. Simon had wanted a very modern, contemporary design and we'd argued many times as I thought a more traditional look would suit Bramble Cottage. Luke showed me pictures of pretty country kitchens and suggested a stable door instead of the double-glazed one that Simon had decided on, and a gorgeous range rather than the stainless steel built-in oven and hob that we'd circled in one of the manufacturers' catalogues.

He took me to The Seagull Inn a few times after work. I think he felt sorry for me. The nights were getting dark and the weather was on the turn. It was quite chilly in that tin can and the pub was warm and cosy with a welcoming atmosphere.

'You can't live on microwave meals,' he said, ignoring my protests and handing me a menu. The dining room was packed. The food was good. His parents were friendly and kind and wouldn't hear of accepting payment for the meals.

We sat together, our heads almost touching as we pored over the drawings he'd come up with for the garden. I imagined how it would look when it was finished and I wanted to cry. Luke saw my face and apologised immediately.

'I'm being very tactless. I'll put these away,' he said rolling up the drawings and securing them with an elastic band.

'It's okay. I can see the place means as much to you as it does to me. Why don't you put in an offer for it when it goes up for sale?' I asked, my spirits sinking as I realised that the day was coming when the estate agent's board would go up in the front garden and Bramble Cottage would be nothing to do with me any longer. Christmas cards had started to appear in the shops. All that lay on the other side of Christmas was a big, black hole, where all my hopes and dreams would be buried.

He gave a half-laugh. 'You must be joking! I won't be able to afford it when it's finished. It will be well out of my price range. My own fault, I'm making it far too desirable. I should start doing some dodgy work on the place, bring the price right down.'

I got the feeling he was almost as sad as I was about the forthcoming sale and found myself wishing that he'd outbid us after all. He deserved to own Bramble Cottage. He'd loved it for years and would have restored it sympathetically, lived in it happily, and never abandoned it for some swanky flat in London.

As October turned to November living in the caravan became unbearable. Luke watched me with worried eyes as I pulled into the drive one night, my shoulders hunched against the cold night air.

'What are you still doing here?' I asked him. He should have clocked off an hour ago.

'I'm taking you to the pub,' he replied. 'Mum's got a hot meal waiting for you and a big mug of hot chocolate with marshmallows that's got your name on it.'

I was too tired to protest and climbed into the van, leaning back in the seat and almost falling asleep as he drove me to The Seagull Inn.

Mrs Ingledew was all sympathy and enveloped me in a massive hug as I walked in.

'Tomato soup to start with,' she said, 'then a nice roast dinner. Then I think,' she added as Luke helped me out of my coat, 'we should talk about you staying here till the work's done on that cottage.'

I shook my head. 'It's very kind of you, honestly, but –'

'I won't have any arguments,' she said, holding up her hand to silence me. 'Luke's worried sick about you and I'm not having my boy worrying, not when I can do something to prevent it. We've got a spare room and you're more than welcome.'

'But really –'

'You can't argue with Mum,' laughed Luke. He took my hand and led me to a chair by the roaring fire. 'Sit down and eat your soup. Let us take care of you. It will be our pleasure.'

They were so kind. I had no idea why they were so good to me, especially given all the trouble Simon had caused for Luke, but they didn't understand.

'The thing is,' I explained, after a few mouthfuls of tomato soup had defrosted me enough to enable me to hold a proper conversation, 'I've already got somewhere to stay. My friend Penny has asked me to move in with her and her husband. They only live ten minutes from work so it's ideal. It's really good of you but, you see, there's no need to bother you at all. I'm sorted.'

Mrs Ingledew glanced across at Luke, who was standing quite still, staring into the fire.

'So, how often do you think you'll come back to the cottage?' he murmured eventually.

I swallowed a chunk of crusty bread and took a sip of my hot chocolate. 'Not often,' I admitted. He turned to look at me and I sighed. 'The truth is, it's too painful being there now that I know it's got to be sold. I don't really want to see it any more.'

'But we're so close,' he said, his eyes pleading. 'It won't be much longer. Surely you want to see how it all works out?'

'I trust your judgement,' I said wearily. 'Just get on with it the way you think best. Before you know it, it will be the other side of Christmas. I need to focus on the future. I'm sorry.'

We'd eaten our meal in silence and he'd driven me home to the caravan, lighting the fire for me and wishing me goodnight before driving off, leaving me with a lingering sense of guilt and a strange feeling of regret.

I'd moved to Penny's the next evening and hadn't been back to Weltringham since. I'd had a few stilted conversations with Luke on the telephone as he informed me of purchases made and work completed. He asked me how I was doing and if I'd heard from Simon, and I told him I was fine and that the only contact I'd had from Simon was a recommendation for an estate agent he knew, some friend of his who would do everything he could to ensure a quick sale. Luke was silent. There didn't seem much to say. I hadn't called again until the week before Christmas Eve when I informed him I was coming back.

I drive slowly down the main street, passing a group of men who are laughing and serenading the world with a disrespectful version of

While Shepherds Watched Their Flocks. I think they're on their way to the other pub in the village, The Queen's Head. I'm almost certain some of them are Luke's employees. I peer as closely as I can at them as I pass, but I can't see any sign of him. He's probably working behind the bar. It will be very busy in The Seagull Inn and he's the sort of person who'd offer to help out.

Children are coming out of the general store, their faces bright with excitement. I see them waving goodbye to Suman who runs the shop. There are crowds of villagers heading past me towards the church now and I realise the carol service must be starting very soon. I wonder briefly if I should attend, but all those happy souls singing carols may be too much for me to bear. The only way I'm going to get through the next two days is to lock myself in the caravan, eat lots of chocolate and immerse myself in my favourite television programmes. It will be over before I know it. Mike's right. The other side of Christmas is just a *Doctor Who* special away.

I feel panic rising as I realise that getting through Christmas is far from my biggest problem. It's what lies on the other side that frightens me the most. I feel cold with dread and as I turn down the lane that leads to Bramble Cottage I wonder if I should have bought a big fat bottle of whisky, too.

The cottage is in darkness but I know from Luke's updates that the electrical works are complete. The new boiler and central heating system will be installed in January. It's all coming together at last.

The caravan light isn't on. I step out of the car and fumble for my key, my fingers numb with cold. The caravan door swings open and I peer into the darkness. The fire isn't lit. Luke has obviously forgotten all about it. I feel ridiculously disappointed in him and close to tears. I'm about to flick the light switch when hands cover my eyes and I feel someone's breath on my neck. I almost scream but the recognition of his scent strangles the sound before it leaves my lips.

'Did you know it was me?' he says as I turn to face him. He's standing on the caravan steps, smiling at me, and I'm tempted to push him off.

'You forgot to put the fire on,' I say accusingly. I'm horrified to hear the catch in my voice. I blink away tears and stare at him, standing there all happy and handsome, not caring at all that I've had a journey from hell or that the highlight of my next forty-eight hours will be a frozen turkey platter and half a pound of Quality Street.

'No I didn't,' he says. 'Come with me.'

He takes my hand and leads me to the front door of the cottage. It's only as we walk along the drive that I notice for the first time that there is a wisp of smoke coming from the chimney. I stare at it for a moment, then at him. He shakes his head.

'You have to close your eyes,' he tells me as we reach the doorstep. I obey, hearing the rattle of his keys and the creak of the door as it opens. He leads me inside and warmth seeps through my bones as I stand in the hallway, hearing him close the door behind us. He takes my arm and we walk forward. I hear another door being pushed open, the crackle of flames.

'Okay. You can open them now,' he whispers in my ear.

I open my eyes and gasp. The once crumbling old fireplace has been fully restored, and logs are burning merrily in a brand new wood burning stove. In the corner of the room stands a big Christmas tree, beautifully decorated and lit with dozens of fairy lights. Cranberry-scented candles burn in little pots on the mantelpiece and the hearth. The television from the caravan is on a small table and there's a battered leather sofa by the side of the fire. I look at it enquiringly.

'It's mine, from my bedroom,' Luke explains. 'It's pretty old but it will do for now.'

He leads me into the kitchen, flicking on the light. The kettle, toaster and microwave from the caravan are standing on a white plastic garden table which has four matching chairs tucked under it. All around the edges of the room are huge boxes. I can see from the drawings on the front that I have a new dishwasher, range cooker, fridge freezer and washing machine. The shabby old door has been replaced with a gorgeous wooden stable door and there are beautiful slate tiles on the floor.

'The kitchen will be fitted by the middle of January,' Luke promises. 'It's all in hand. After that, there's only the painting left to do. Do you want to see the bathroom?'

I nod, unable to find the words, and he leads me upstairs to show me a large family bathroom that is completely unrecognisable. I stare at the new suite and gorgeous shower in awe. Then I look at him, puzzled.

'It's really warm up here. You said the central heating system was getting put in after Christmas.'

He smiles. 'I wanted to surprise you. As soon as I knew you were coming back for Christmas I called in a few favours. I couldn't have you staying in that wretched caravan. Come and look at your room.'

I'm trembling as I follow him across the landing. The bedroom walls are freshly-plastered and Luke has put a huge rug on the floor to cover the floorboards. I stare at the bed in the middle of the room and raise an eyebrow.

'Where did that come from?'

He looks embarrassed. 'It's mine. Don't worry,' he says, holding up his hands, 'Mum's got a spare single bed at home that I can use. I just wanted you to be comfortable while you were here. Do you like it?

The en-suite's all done, too. I'm sorry about the kitchen. I really wanted it to be ready for you but there was no way it could be done on time, but we can make hot drinks and toast, and you're invited to the pub for Christmas dinner. Don't even think about saying no. Mum and Dad insist. I insist.'

'Do you?' I stare up at him, wondering why he's gone to so much trouble for me. I know the cottage means a lot to him but there's no need for him to worry about making me comfortable. I'm not his concern. Am I?

He smiles down at me, his fingers gently brushing away a lock of my hair that's fallen across my face. I take hold of his hand and he pauses.

'Why?' I ask. 'Why would you do all this for me?'

He cups my face and lowers his lips to mine. For a moment time stops and I think maybe my heart has too. His kiss is gentle, tender, and doesn't last nearly long enough. He looks at me, his eyes questioning.

'Don't you know?' he asks, and I realise that I do know. I know all too well.

'If you still want to sell up that's fine,' he says. 'Just know this. Wherever you go, I'll be there too. If you want to stay in the city, I'll move to the city. I love this cottage but I love you more. I can't be without you, Katy. Tell me you feel the same.'

I tell him without having to use a single word. Vaguely it occurs to me that Luke can probably afford to buy Simon's half of the cottage, and half of the cottage is all he'll ever need. It also occurs to me that it would be awfully rude to expect him to sleep in a single bed when there's that lovely cosy double just standing there, practically inviting us in.

He picks me up and swings me round and I laugh and kiss him again. It will soon be the other side of Christmas. A glorious future is just a *Doctor Who* special away.

Author Details

If you've enjoyed this story and would like to find out more about Sharon Booth, here's how:

Twitter: @sharon_booth1
Facebook: *https://www.facebook.com/sharonbooth.writer*
Blog: *www.sharonbooth.com*

Sharon's debut novel 'There Must be an Angel' will be published by Fabrian Books in March 2015.

The Art of Giving

Sarah Painter

My mother was very proper. She wore stiff gowns and clean gloves and always knew exactly the right thing to say in any social situation. She would correct my manners with a gently reproving glance and, when I sat weeping and frustrated at having failed to keep my clothes clean for the hundredth time, she said: 'I know that you find it difficult, Iris, but we must be above reproach.'

'Because we're ladies?' I sniffed, lifting my sleeve to wipe my nose before remembering to pull the cotton handkerchief from my pocket.

'Because you are a young lady, yes,' Mother said, 'but also because you are my daughter. A Harper.'

I didn't understand what she meant. Our name wasn't Harper. We had Papa's name, of course.

The point of which is to say that I had no idea my mother was cursed until the day she spat out a wedding ring at breakfast.

'What is that?' I asked, looking at the golden band sitting in her hand.

'Somebody decided they no longer required it and so it came here,' Mother said. Her voice was very tight and she closed her fingers to hide the ring, her wet palm, and the flecks of blood.

'Things which are thrown away,' Papa said from behind his morning newspaper. 'Small things, thankfully.'

Mother got up from the table, signalling an end to the conversation, but over time I grasped the essentials about her curse: She never coughed up ticket stubs or used tea leaves, but things which had been invested with emotion. Important things. When people threw those things away, sometimes they found their way to our house, where they tumbled out of my mother's mouth in a fountain of spit.

She always carried a handkerchief and I realised that all the times I'd seen her hold it delicately to her lips weren't an affectation; she was hiding whatever had popped into her mouth.

In my mother's room, there were patterned china bowls filled with jewellery. Engagement rings set with emeralds and sapphires, plain gold wedding bands of varying thickness, and the occasional watch. There was a silver tie pin in the shape of a fox and a pair of earrings, encrusted with finely cut diamonds, that must have cost a small fortune.

Mother never wore any of it. They just sat there, unused trophies from hundreds of unknown lives and loves. I was allowed to play with the treasure, as long as I was careful to put it all back afterwards.

Mother explained, in a flat tone as if she was discussing the correct way to eat soup, that if I lost a piece it would reappear in her mouth and she'd prefer not to have 'any more than was strictly necessary'.

I knew that we didn't speak of Mother's curse in company. I don't remember her telling me that it was a secret but it was clearly not a topic for polite conversation.

When I turned fourteen, however, I began to battle a secret of my own. I started to feel strange compulsions, wicked notions that I could not suppress. I took milk from the jug in the pantry and poured it out for the tramps who knocked at the back door, even though I was expressly forbidden from giving anything except hot water and, perhaps, a little tea.

I took my best dress, the one that Mother had bought from Liberty's in London, and gave it to a friend. I couldn't explain, even while in the most dreadful trouble, why I had done it. Only that I'd felt a itching all over my body that I somehow knew wouldn't go away until I'd given the dress to Catherine.

These compulsions grew stranger and more numerous until I spent from morning till night fulfilling them. Mother wasn't any help; she refused to speak about such things. I asked her, in desperation, whether it would get better and she replied that it was a matter of controlling oneself. Then she coughed for five minutes before managing to remove an ugly peacock brooch from her throat.

For the next few years, while my school work suffered and friends fell away, I carried out my strange tasks, realising that I seemed to give people things that they needed, even if they did not know that they needed them. I did become better at controlling my compulsions, but I felt very alone and I grew more resentful of Mother's silence. I vowed that if I ever had a child (not that I had any intention of doing such a thing), I would never leave them in the dark this way. I would help. I would, I decided, write clear instructions, like the handwritten recipes our housekeeper consulted.

I suppose I ought to be grateful, as if I hadn't been taking nettle soup over to Old Man Bailey's house, I wouldn't have tripped on that loose cobblestone and sprained my ankle. Not that I'm grateful for the sprain, you understand – that ankle still hurts when the weather is cold – but the young man who stopped to help me; I'll always be grateful for him. Despite the way things turned out.

He was called James and he was twenty years old. I was seventeen and – now that I am very old I can see this clearly – quite lovely.

'Are you all right, miss?' he said, helping me to stand and catching me when I stumbled. The pain from my ankle shot through my body, making me dizzy.

'No,' he said, his brow furrowing. 'You're not. May I?' He mimed picking me up and I demurred. I was frightened I would be too heavy for him; he was tall but rather narrow.

'I would like to lean on you, though, if I may?' I said, trying to hop a few steps. My forehead prickled with a cold perspiration and I felt sick.

'Not a chance,' he said, and scooped me off my feet. He carried me through the streets like a babe in arms. 'I'm James Farrier,' he said, looking at me as if I was something precious.

'Iris,' I said. My arms had snaked around his neck and were locked there. I never, ever wanted to let him go. The pain in my ankle suddenly felt like a blessing.

Once I was being courted by James Farrier, I thought that life could not become sweeter. If at times he seemed a little cold, the air soon warmed between us. If I glimpsed a shadow crossing his face or witnessed him using a harsh tone with his household's maid, I pushed away my misgivings. He was unfailingly gentle with me. He was intelligent and charming, and appeared so delighted with my every word that I felt newly discovered. Like secret treasure from an ancient tomb, brought into the light where it could shine.

James came from a good family and was polite, but Mother surprised me by remaining reserved. 'You'll have to tell him,' she said, finally. 'About your affliction. He will find out sooner or later.' I could see the fear on her face and read her worries as if they were written there; that James would run from me and my strange ability or, worse still, that he would spread rumours about town and ruin our family's reputation.

'But father understood your-' I hesitated, unsure of how to refer to it.

'Your father is an exceptional man,' she said, her eyes soft.

'So is James!' I was incensed by her mistrust. And, if I felt misgivings of my own, I didn't let them fester. James loved me. I would tell him the truth and all would be well.

She just looked at me sadly. 'People fear what they do not understand.'

'James isn't frightened of anything,' I said, not realising that this was not necessarily a good quality.

Mother just shook her head. 'I hope you are right but, whatever the outcome, you mustn't feel ashamed. We can't help the way we are made and we must trust God's purpose.' The moment the words were out of her mouth, her lace handkerchief was back in front of it again, concealing the latest item to come tumbling out. She was a fine one to talk about not being ashamed, I thought.

When James proposed, presenting me with a beautiful diamond solitaire ring, I told him that while my heart was singing 'yes', I had to tell him something first and that he might not want to marry me once he'd heard it.

He became serious and still, but listened while I explained my affliction without interrupting. At the end, I felt a profound sense of relief when his features broke into a smile.

'You silly goose,' he said. 'Why would that stop me wanting to marry you? Your good heart is part of why I love you.'

I wanted to explain that he'd misunderstood, that I didn't give people things they needed from any sense of duty or inherent goodness, but because I had no choice in the matter. The words stuck in my throat. He looked so pleased with me, his whole face was lit up, and I felt myself grow taller under his gaze.

It was a balm to the confusion and anger I so often inspired. Just that morning I had tramped through the winter snow to deliver a layette of baby clothes to Mrs Compton. Her children were almost grown and her face was a picture of misery when she saw what was inside the bundle. She sagged against the wall, her face pale. 'You can't be here. I know what you do.' She held her hands up in front of her face, as if she was warding off evil. 'Take them away. Please.'

'I can't,' I had said. She looked so upset that I wanted to cry. I didn't know why baby clothes were so terrible a gift to an old married woman. She already had children, what was one more?

Mrs Compton refused to touch the clothes, so I put them on the floor in front of her, like an offering to an old God and she shut the door in my face.

'What should I have done?' I asked Mother, even though I had no great hope she would answer. Sure enough, she shook her head, mute, and then coughed delicately, spitting out a door key and putting it into her pocket.

James wanted to get married as soon as possible. I pictured a spring day, with white blossom and yellow daffodils, but the date was set for December. 'It's my present to you,' James said, and he looked so pleased that I hadn't the heart to argue.

The day before our wedding was the midwinter solstice, that day of near-endless dark. I was awake very early and I kept as still as possible, not wanting to move and allow any cold air to seep into the warm cocoon of my bedding. Finally, when I realised that I wasn't going to fall back asleep, I braved the icy air to reach out for the ring sitting on my bedside table. I traced my fingertips over the bevelled surface and imagined my new life as Mrs Iris Farrier. There was a small house on Silver Street to start us off and James had a good job with the family business.

I loved him, I was certain of that, but even more than love I felt relief. I had fulfilled my destiny as a lady and this was my reward. The wife of James Farrier was a safe and respectable thing to be. I could see that James was a strong man and, under his guidance, I might even be able to resist my affliction, to keep it securely locked away with all other childish things.

At least I wasn't like my mother, I reasoned, spitting out jewellery all hours of the day. I had, at least, some measure of control. No sooner had I completed that disloyal thought when I felt the familiar prickling sensation of my affliction. I knew immediately that I had to fetch something warm and take it to James's house. Not for him, but for his sister, Roberta. A shy girl with light brown hair and a lisp. I hadn't exchanged more than a handful of words with Roberta and I didn't relish the prospect of the meeting. I was worried that James would be embarrassed by my strange behaviour, but I knew as the pricking sensation grew stronger and my head began to swim, that I didn't have any choice in the matter.

I dressed warmly with thick boots and a wool coat, and collected the oldest blanket I could find in the linen cupboard. My auburn hair, down to my waist when loose, took valuable minutes to wind up and secure into a bun on the back of my head and there was no time left to curl my fringe or add rouge.

The air outside hit me like a slap. Suddenly, blush seemed beside the point. I knew that I'd have glowing, ruddy cheeks by the time I'd made it to the Farrier's big house and, probably, a red nose to match.

The snow crunched under my feet, loud in the blanketed quiet. It was early and so cold that anyone with any sense was indoors next to a fire or tucked up in bed. I envied them, but after a few minutes of hard walking, I'd warmed a little and my mind strayed to more pleasant thoughts: How pleased James would be to see me, how his face lit up when we talked, and how that made me feel.

By the time I arrived at James's home, my heart was stuttering with expectant delight and I'd quite forgotten the reason for my visit. My head was filled with images of my beloved and my new life.

The Farrier's house was a large detached affair with a high wall around its extensive garden. I unlatched the gate but couldn't push it open because the path was still thick with snow. The prickling sensation was stronger than ever, though, and I knew it wouldn't stop until I'd delivered the blanket. I threw my bundle over the gate, hitched my skirt and climbed after it.

I had taken less than three steps when I saw the dark shape, hunched on the path next to the front door. I knew that it was Roberta immediately, some dark part of my mind supplying the information before I'd crouched down beside her and lifted her head.

Her face was white, her lips were blue, and her light brown hair was coated with frost that sparkled in the first rays of sunlight creeping over the trees. I wrapped the blanket around her and held her tightly, calling her name softly.

I will say it now. I thought she was dead. I thought that I was too late. That the minutes I'd spent fussing with my hair had meant the difference between a girl's life and the end of it. I sent up prayers to whomever might be listening that I would never, ever, dally again. That I would heed my curse immediately. Obey without question. Deliver whatever to whomever, if only Roberta would open her eyes.

Which she did.

'It's all right,' I said, the relief washing through me. 'I've got you.' I wrapped myself around Roberta and felt my warmth seep into her.

At that moment, the front door opened. I heard his voice before I saw him. 'You can come in, now if you've learned your lesson,' he said, the words dying when he saw that his sister wasn't alone.

'Hello, James,' I said, half-carrying Roberta into the house. I pretended I was strong, even though my future had just scattered like jewels emptied from a china bowl. 'I had to bring Roberta this,' I indicated the brown blanket wrapped around the shivering form of his sister.

'You can't just barge in,' he blustered. 'It's not done. It's not normal. When you're my wife, you won't be able to carry on like this.'

I didn't reply. I found the kitchen and, ignoring the maid who tried to stop me, I boiled water for tea. I put lots of sugar into the cup and took it to Roberta. Only once her lips had lost their blue-ish tinge and she was well enough to speak in her quiet lisp did I leave her side.

'It was a game we were playing,' James was saying. 'Tell her, Roberta. Tell her it was just a game.'

I took my ring off and left it on the dining table. I was shaking with the realisation of how close I had come to walking down the aisle and into the icy arms of James Farrier. I wanted to throw the ring into the river, to make some sort of grand gesture, but I didn't want Mother to have it to spit it out later that week.

It occurred to me that this was what being a Harper truly meant; it wasn't about being cursed or gifted, it was about consequences. It meant knowing that what was tossed aside could come back in unexpected ways, and that getting what you needed was sometimes a bitter medicine. I also knew this; my gift didn't save Roberta that day, it saved me.

Author Details

If you've enjoyed this story and would like to find out more about Sarah Painter, here's how:

Twitter: @SarahRPainter
Facebook: www.facebook.com/sarahpainterbooks
Blog: www.sarah-painter.com

Sarah's current book/eBook 'The Secrets of Ghosts' is available now

All I want for Christmas

Jackie Ladbury

Christmas is hurling towards us faster than a speeding snowball and normally I can't wait, but this year – my first Christmas with Luke – the enthusiasm is quickly waning. It's only a few days away now, although my Deluxe American Spruce tree has been up for so long the poor thing is almost bald. Every morning I'm greeted by another little pile of pine needles on the floor as its thinning branches droop a bit further under the weight of glass baubles and defeat. It's also probably a bit too close to the radiator, so that won't be helping, but then everything is a bit close to the radiator in my tiny flat.

Anyway, Luke, instead of getting in a Christmassy mood with me – knocking back the Bailey's and eating mince pies until we felt sick – was notable only by his absence and his lack of embracing anything Christmassy. In fact these days he wasn't even embracing me, which was a bit worrying considering we hadn't hit our first year anniversary yet. He disappeared once again first thing this morning after swigging tea and scoffing a sausage sandwich made by my own loving hands, mumbling something about overtime before legging it out of the door. I didn't even get the chance to arrange myself temptingly across the bed in my new silk nightie before he left; it was all rather hopeless.

I decided I would just have to get on with the festivities in my own way and tried not to think about the ominous change in Luke. I knew Santa was visiting my local garden centre in his Grotto, so I called around to my sister's and begged my niece Tabitha to come with me. She's a sceptical and cynical nine year old who would rather watch University Challenge than stand in a queue staring at dancing dwarves and juggling clowns, but the promise of a brilliant present from Santa swayed her.

The grotto was suitably decked out in fake snow and plastic reindeer, and a couple of Christmas angels flitted around rather fetchingly, although the one chewing gum looked as if she'd confused her outfit with a late 1980's Punk Rocker. But hey, who said angels couldn't sport facial hardware and a bicycle chain instead of wings and a halo?

I was listening to Tabitha quiz Santa on how ecologically friendly his workshop was and whether his reindeer had appropriate rest breaks on the journey from Lapland, when an elf tapped me on the shoulder and asked if I wanted a 'lucky dip' at a fiver a go.

'Nah, all I want for Christmas is the perfect man,' I said craning my neck to look up at the elf. I think he'd been at the Tomorite fertiliser 'cos he was about six foot tall and bright green with a shock of carrot top hair sprouting through a Noddy hat that jingled as he moved.

I didn't really mean it about the 'wanting the perfect man' thing, but I guess it must have been on my mind that Luke was rather letting me down on the perfection front.

Tabitha brought me back from my thoughts, tugging at my arm and squinting suspiciously at Santa who had already lost the will to, 'Ho, ho, ho,' after her interrogation. He dug into his sack, with undue haste I thought, and pushed a square parcel wrapped up in sparkly paper at her. 'Take it- take it!' he urged, but she folded her arms mutinously.

'It's okay, you are allowed to accept it, just this once; Santa isn't exactly a stranger,' I said pushing her towards Santa's outstretched arm.

'He might not be to you, but I've never seen this man before,' she retorted before snatching the gift and giving Santa a 'you may think you've got away with it but I'm not fooled,' look. I wondered how she'd feel when she opened it to find it was not the iPad mini she'd been banking on.

'Thanks *Santa,*' she said, her voice dripping with sarcasm, as she tore off the paper. Her interest plummeted to zero when she clocked the colouring book and stuffed it back into the ripped paper, looking for a bin to dump it in.

Her present reminded me of Luke a bit; the overall package looked good, but what was on the inside didn't quite live up to the hype. But Tabitha, being nine going on thirty had learned early on that stoicism often paid off. She swiftly overcame her disappointment and moved on. 'Why,' she demanded, 'is Jesus a baby in a manger surrounded by camels, when at Easter, only eight months earlier, he was a fully-grown man about to be crucified for eating too many Easter eggs?'

I know. You try working that one out.

Anyway, Elfman stuck his green thumb in the air and gave me a broad smile before disappearing rather suddenly in a puff of glitter, which I thought was rather clever. I quickly forgot about him though, once I'd dropped Tabitha back with my sister and realised I had another lonely afternoon ahead of me. I had nothing waiting for me back at my flat unless you counted a wilting Christmas tree, so I headed for a much needed coffee, intending to make the most of the Christmas atmosphere before sloping back to my solitary evening of sulking without Luke.

The best bit about my local coffee shop is the free chocolate you get with your coffee, but it still wasn't enough for me. I was in two minds whether to go back for a piece of cake when an impeccably suited man arched a groomed eyebrow and touched the back of the chair opposite.

I waved my hand to show it was okay for him to share my table, my mouth being incapacitated by Praline Delight at the time.

I was a bit put out to be honest; I mean the place was practically deserted. Most people were rushing around like ants before a storm doing their last minute shopping and I'd wanted to count my remaining funds without feeling all Scrooge-like about it. I glanced over at Mr Handsome who was stirring a no calorie espresso, a smug smile playing around his mouth. I'll bet he didn't have to count his pennies; he looked as if he could buy an aeroplane without his wallet breaking into a sweat.

He glanced at me and, without saying a word, slid a napkin over to my side of the table with his complimentary chocolate sitting on it. A tiny sliver of crystallised violet perched on top of its velvety chocolate exterior like a cherry on a perfectly iced cake. Violet Crème; my favourite.

'Really? For me?' My eyes lit up and my hand reached across of its own accord so quick was I to bag it. 'I mean, no thank you, I couldn't possibly.' I let my hand drop away, suddenly feeling like the fattest girl in the class all over again.

But he nodded towards it once more as if it was a done deal and I picked it up. 'You're welcome,' he said in a voice sounding itself like rich, smooth chocolate.

His over-familiarity was admittedly a little bit weird, but I could run with it for a Violet Crème.

He fixed me with a blue-eyed stare as I took a bite of the chocolate and closed my eyes in ecstasy as sweet, unctuous crème liquefied in my mouth. He was still staring when I opened my eyes. I stared back wondering what was so interesting about my rather plain face and wishing I'd stopped by the mirror and slapped on a bit of mascara earlier. Feeling self-conscious under the scrutiny of his unwavering stare, I stopped chewing suddenly aware of the silence between us. Violet crème gunk started to trickle down my throat, warm and sticky. It kind of took away the pleasure, to be honest, and made me want to cough.

I tried to think of something to say but where's the common ground when all you have between you is one Violet Crème? Funny really, because I was always getting ratty with Luke for prattling on about some invention or other; I could never get a word in with him. Take his model boat making hobby for example. He belongs to a club of weirdo, miniature boat-building people (the boats are miniature; not the people) and he spends hours and hours putting his together, only for it to crash every time he takes it on the pond. Never-ending circle of share and repair, that one.

And I won't even start on the 1950's toy robot he bought from eBay and is re-assembling using parts from an old computer motherboard. He's a real gadget freak. I suppose it can be handy sometimes, like when the zapper for the telly breaks and stuff like that. He's quite handy at making cupboards too, I suppose... but anyway, I digress. Just saying I would be quite happy for him to have been here to fill in the gaps right now and break the silence.

I decided to down my coffee and go; Mr Handsome was beginning to freak me out. Decision made, I took a swig realising too late that it was scalding hot. I started coughing and my eyes streamed with the shock of it. Mr Handsome flicked his napkin open in one slick movement and passed it to me and I blew my nose inelegantly.

'Here, let me get you another. You were obviously thirsty.'

Woah! Way past the call of duty. What did I tell you? He was seriously strange. 'No, you're okay, thanks, I have to go.'

'Go? But you can't, we're on our perfect date.'

'We're what?'

'You wished for the perfect man, so here I am. On our date.' Then he smiled. I've seen some pretty good smiles in my day, even if they are cosmetically enhanced in one way or the other, but this was the most dazzling I'd ever come across.

Luke's smile was nice, but he did have one tooth that stuck out a tiny bit more than the others, giving him a goofy look at a certain angle. My heart sank when I thought of how grumpy I'd been with him recently. Maybe he'd be pleased to get me off his hands. Possibly the appearance of Mr Handsome was what we both needed to move on.

As if he knew I'd succumbed, Mr Handsome leaned towards me with both hands raised and I blinked, not knowing what he was about to do. He smelled of lavender and mountain trees, unlike Luke who mostly smelled of glue and wood shavings, and I'll admit I felt a bit dizzy with the intoxication of this stranger and his overall perfectness. He lifted his soft, beautifully manicured hands, enclosed my cheeks in his palms and looked deep into my eyes. It could have been 'A Moment' but the trouble was, all I could think about was that joke. You know, where you push your cheeks together and say, 'Can somebody open the lift doors, please?' I snorted unattractively, but Mr Handsome didn't appear to even notice.

'You have beautiful eyes.'

Yeah, if your preference is for the colour sludge, I thought, but this was our perfect date so I was prepared to believe him, unlikely as it all was.

I heard a tinkle and swivelled around. Elfman was sitting cross-legged right behind me, on top of the coffee table looking greener and glossier than a sprig of holly, his bell jingling the hell out of me. He beamed and gave me the thumbs up once again.

'What's going on?' I hissed.

'You said you wanted to meet the perfect man. Well, here he is.'

'How did you do that?'

'I don't know.' He shrugged. 'It's just what we do.'

'Well, don't,' I hissed again. 'It's too unsettling.'

He shrugged again. 'Too late. You're stuck with him; at least until midnight.'

'Midnight?'

'Ermm, yeah, there's a reason for that. He's Charming.'

'What's charming about it?'

'It's his name; Charming.'

I sighed. So I was stuck with someone called Charming. My brain suddenly whirred. 'Please don't tell me he's a Prince.'

Elfman squirmed a bit.

'He is, isn't he?'

'He's always around at Christmas and who else could I have got at such short notice? I could have tried for the Little Drummer Boy, he's permanently available – on account of him being two foot tall, I guess.' He sniffed and muttered 'Ungrateful or what?' Then he rallied. 'Anyway, you'll have fun. What else were you going to do tonight?'

He had a point – watch a re-run of The Grinch and lose the good fight against drinking a bottle of red wine, probably. I tried a smile. 'So I have to spend the evening with Prince Charming at a Ball?'

'Not looking like that, you don't.'

'Oh, charming.'

'No, not you!' we both shouted as Prince Charming rose from his seat and bowed. But I warmed to the idea of Elfman transforming my winter garb into silk and chiffon and my hair into golden tresses. I closed my eyes waiting, but when I opened them I was still in my jeans, and my hair still hung damply around my ears. I patted the top of my head. Nope, no tiara. I quirked an eyebrow at Elfman, although obviously it wasn't a patch on Prince Charming's eyebrow quirk.

'What? Babe, I'm an elf not a bloody magician.' He looked slightly put out. 'You can't make a silk purse out of a sow's ear, that's all,' he mumbled, knowing he'd pushed it a bit too far.

Bloody cheek.

Prince Charming watched this carry on in silence and smiled his flawless smile, which to be honest was becoming a tad grating in its pearly white perfection.

So no Ball, then.

I swivelled back to my date, determined to be positive. At least he was here with me, being attentive and interested, not in some furniture factory curling wood shavings like Luke. 'Okay, what shall we do on our date, Prince Charming?'

'Whatever you want to do and, please, just call me Charming.'

'Okay, err, Charming. We could go to the cinema. What sort of films do you like to watch?'

'Whatever film *you* want to watch.'

I smiled uneasily. It normally took Luke and me ages to agree on what to do although, sometimes, that was half the fun. This was one easy date. Maybe a bit *too* easy. I didn't want him to have to sit through something he wouldn't enjoy though, so I said, 'How about going for something to eat, instead?'

'If that's what you would like.'

Good God, I thought, hasn't this man got an opinion of his own? 'Great. Perfect. Follow me.'

We headed for Bella Pasta down the road and Charming rushed to open the door for me, nearly taking my eye out as it swung into my face. Then he tussled with Mario the waiter in his determination to pull my chair out as we sat down. He flourished a napkin on to my lap and straightened my knife and fork before sitting down, earning some sniggers from the gaggle of open-mouthed teenagers.

Mario, bless him, merely raised his eyebrows when Charming ordered a glass of water, after he'd listened to me order enough to sink the Titanic.

'Are we sharing, then?' I asked as Mario gave up trying to tempt him with the nightly specials, before throwing his hands in the air, muttering something about precious bloody upper classes and retreating back to the kitchen.

Charming barely noticed; just shook his blond curls and patted his stomach. 'Perfection takes a lot of will- power, but I shall enjoy watching you eat.'

Cheers for that then, I thought, glumly, as I imagined spaghetti snaking out of my mouth and slapping tomato sauce down my chin.

'So what do you, you know, *do* all day?' I was dredging the depths now on the conversational front.

He quirked an eyebrow.

Question too hard? I wanted to ask. I drummed my fingers on the table as I dredged my mind for some genial banter, but received no feedback whatsoever. So I switched to serious conversation, even going down the politics and religion line that no one should cross at the dinner table. But he either appeared puzzled by my questions or agreed with everything I said, throwing me that infuriating, pointless, big smile until I imagined what his full, sensual lips would look like thumped. I knew when I was beaten. I've had more interesting conversations with Siri on my iPad.

Finally the one-sided eat and talkfest was over and once we'd got over the embarrassment of him attempting to pay the bill with Disney coins, we headed outside to be greeted by a flurry of snow. Charming tried flagging down a taxi by walking in front of it and answered the taxi driver's two-fingered salute pleasantly, with a Prince-like wave.

I was beginning to realise the only thing he knew how to be was charming (yes, I know the clue should have been in his name) and that he was a disaster on two legs (albeit a handsome one.) So I walked as far away from him as possible in case he saw fit to wipe my brow or blow my nose for me, and readied myself to catch him as he fell over his feet and bumped into people by bowing and waving at every turn.

The thin flurry of snow changed quickly into a full-blown storm and white soft flakes fell heavily, covering our clothes and the pavement prettily. Charming, however, looked horrified and pulled his jacket close to his chest, while I twirled around catching as many snowflakes as I could, lifting my face up to the dark sky. 'Don't you like the snow, I love it?' I twirled some more and waved my arms about.

'I didn't realise it was wet.' His lips turned down distastefully. 'It's never wet where I live.'

'Oh, where do you live?' Finally, something interesting coming from him.

'Not sure really, but I know the temperature is always just right. I never get wet, I never get cold and I never have to make *really hard conversation*.' I caught the beginning of a sob as he uttered the last word and his smile wobbled. I felt sorry for him, until he looked at his watch surreptitiously and his smile brightened once more. But then, I too had been clock watching, so I guess we were both on the wrong side of having fun.

I messed about in the snow for a little while until I saw Charming was shivering and looked like a bedraggled puppy, his curls finally giving up the bounce as they stuck to his head. I almost wished Luke were here with me; he knew how to have fun and he understood my childish love of snow. But it was clear Charming hated it so we headed back to my flat in silence.

I wondered if I'd have to invite him in for coffee as we neared my front door, when I saw we were no longer alone. 'Oh, hello. What are you doing here, this late in the evening?' My heart lurched with unexpected happiness to see my errant boyfriend sitting on the step, hunched inside his ancient charity shop coat. 'I saw the snow and I wanted to share it with you, so I came over, but you weren't in. I was worried, when you didn't answer your mobile, but I can see why you didn't.' He stood up stiffly. 'I won't hang around, don't worry, it's just that I had a present I wanted to give you and it seemed the perfect moment, with it snowing and all.'

Luke knew I loved English winters because I never saw snow until I was a teenager and I never spent Christmas with my family as I was mostly at boarding school, abroad. It's complicated; to do with step-parents and stuff and having a mother who lives in Australia. I was so looking forward to spending this Christmas with Luke. It was as if I was starting my own family here in England and I thought he'd understood how special it was for me. That's why it hurt so much when he kept disappearing, but it didn't matter anymore; he was here.

'It's a snow-themed present?' I asked as the cogs in my mind slowly whirred. With suppressed excitement, I suddenly remembered the travel brochures I'd found stuffed in a drawer in Luke's flat and it all clicked. I knew why he'd been doing so much overtime. It was to earn money to take me skiing – or maybe to Lapland. Yes! That's where we were going! 'Oh my God, oh my God!' I ran around like a demented Troll flapping my arms. Luke knew that going to Lapland was on my bucket list of things to do and he was going to take me there.

Prince Charming's bland face took on a pained expression as the wind whipped open his jacket, showing, it had to be said, an admirably toned body, but you know, it's really not all about the package. I heard him counting the seconds down to midnight and figured he'd probably had as miserable a time as me, poor lamb. 'Do you need to be somewhere, Charming?'

'Yes, I have someone waiting for me, someone who is rather pretty. We always have fun playing find the glass slipper at this time of night – or something like that.' He trailed off unsure, his brow furrowing. A jingling noise made me glance up warily and, before my eyes, Charming was engulfed in a puff of glitter. He blew me a theatrical kiss and waved his hand in a final flourish, fading before my eyes.

Elfman sniffed. 'Always was a bit camp, that one, I blame it on too many Pantomimes.' He turned to me, a self-satisfied grin on his smug green face. 'Finally realised that you had what you wanted all along, have you, hmm?' He swung his legs as he perched on top of the shed, his bobbing hat jingling away.

'Elfman, Charming was really boring, how could he be the perfect date?'

'Really? Surely a perfect man should look wonderful, agree with everything you say, ensure you needs are met and...'

'Yes, thank you. I realise what you were trying to do and I now appreciate that Luke was my perfect man, all along. You can shove your Prince Charming up your... well you know. Luke's taking me to Lapland because he loves me.'

He sniggered. 'Lapland? You think? Good luck with that idea, Babe.' God, he always had to have the last word, that elf. He stuck his irritating green thumb in the air once more and disappeared.

Luke took my hand. 'Come with me.' He smiled and that little sticky out tooth had never seemed more adorable. Everyone needs a little flaw to make them interesting, don't you think?

'Close your eyes.' He led me around the back of the flat to my tiny back garden and into my even smaller shed. I narrowly missed taking my eyes out on the whirly gig washing line and vaguely wondered why he felt it necessary to surprise me in the shed. That sounds ruder than it was meant, by the way.

'Luke, I'm so sorry, I didn't realise you were saving up for such a treat, you should have said.'

'Aww, it's nothing. I love you, Ellie, and I want to make our first Christmas together one to remember. You can open your eyes now.'

I peeled my hands away from my face not knowing quite what to expect, but what I saw certainly wasn't enough for me to do my demented Troll dance again.

'It's a sledge,' I said, rather unnecessarily; we both knew what it was. Had I escaped Cinderella just to walk into the set of Narnia? 'Is it *just* a sledge?' I checked, still hoping to see two tickets to Lapland stuck to it somewhere.

'No it's not just a sledge…'

I held my breath.

'It's a hand-made wooden sledge,' he added proudly. 'I copied it from a magazine and made it all on my own – by hand.'

Disappointment washed over me and I just about refrained from asking how else he could have made if he hadn't used his hands.

'It has a steering wheel for when the snow is too thin to sledge on, and reins for if you wanted to tether Huskies to it.'

Yeah, 'cos there are loads of Huskies wandering around the streets of Hampstead at the moment, I thought uncharitably.

'I hand polished it, too. So much better than varnishing, it will just mellow with age. Who knows; maybe our kids can use it one day.' He ran his hand along the rounded edges of the polished wood, his eyes pleading for me to like it. And suddenly I did. It was the best present in the world that anyone could receive. I saw how much love and care had gone into making it and nothing I was ever given again would be quite as wonderful as this. I ran my own hand over the smooth wood until I met his hand and we entwined our fingers.

I sighed with happiness as he folded me in his strong arms and kissed me. I loved his smell; aged pine with a faint smell of creosote; so addictive. And he was all mine. My own perfect boyfriend who had spent weeks designing and building my very first sledge to show how much he loved me.

He released me from his embrace, excitement in his eyes. 'The park will be covered with snow by now. Come on, let's take it for a spin; it could become a new hobby for both of us. What do you think?'

'I think I love you, Luke Horan.' And I realised I did. I loved his enthusiasm, his optimism, his half-built robot, his crashed model boat, and the beautiful sledge he had made, for our children and us. Who cared about impeccable manners and handsome features, when everything I wanted in a man was right here.

'I love you too, Ellie, and I promise that as long as I live, I'll make every Christmas the best one you ever had,' he said.

I kissed him once again as the snow fell enticingly around us both, until we could wait no longer. 'Let's do it,' Luke said.

'Yes, let's,' I agreed.

He grabbed the reins of the sledge and pulled it out of the garden.

'Race you to the park,' I laughed, and we were off. Our first perfect Christmas had just begun.

Author Details

If you've enjoyed this story and would like to find out more about Jackie Ladbury, here's how:

Twitter: @lackyjadbury
Facebook: *https://www.facebook.com/jackie.ladbury*

The Bookshop of Dreams

Helen Phifer

Martha Potter locked the front door of her cottage and tugged her scarf tight around her neck. It was colder outside than she'd thought. The snow which had dusted the ground overnight glistened through the filtered sunlight. She grinned, hoping she'd find a kid to throw some snow balls at. Even at twenty-nine she loved nothing more than a good old snowball fight in the village square. The postman pulled up in his red van and wound the window down, 'Morning Martha, just the one letter today.'

He handed the big brown envelope to her and she thanked him, at the same time feeling her heart sink to the bottom of her feet. Bugger another rejection to add to her list. The van drove away and she crossed the deserted street whilst sliding her finger under the flap to open and read her letter. She made it to the other side but didn't see the black ice which had formed on the pavement outside her shop and, as she stepped onto it, her arms went into the air and she managed to flail around keeping her balance until she landed against a man she had never seen before. A really gorgeous man to make it even worse. He shouted out in surprise but managed to catch hold of her before she knocked them both into her coffee shop window.

'Oh my, I'm so sorry. Are you okay?'

He laughed and released his grip on her arm, 'I'm fine, I hope you are. That must be a pretty interesting letter.'

'I wish it was but unfortunately it's just another standard thanks but no thanks. I'm fine, well apart from my bruised ego, that is.'

'Well I'm sure whoever sent it is very misguided. If they saw you in person, they wouldn't be able to resist.'

Martha felt her cheeks turn the same shade as her flame-coloured hair. Unsure of how to reply she laughed.

He held out his hand. 'I'm Matthew.'

Martha took it, 'I'm Martha and I'm just on my way to work.'

'Sorry, don't let me hold you up. I wouldn't want your boss to be mad at you.'

'Oh you're not, I'm already here.' She pointed to the shop behind her. 'And the boss isn't so bad.' She took the key from her coat pocket and winked at him.

'Ah so this is your lovely shop? I've been admiring it from afar. I'm looking forward to having a browse of the books and a decent cup of coffee. I'm a total book and caffeine addict.'

'Me too as you can tell.'

'Well I best let you get on. It was a pleasure to meet you Martha.'

She watched him walk away and wondered what had brought such a handsome stranger to the small village of Dalton.

The morning passed by in a blur with just about every villager coming into the shop for coffee and some of Martha's famous Victoria Sponge Cake. They were all excited about the New Year's Eve party tomorrow night that the new owners of the Manor had invited the entire village to. At eleven, her writing group turned up so it was another round of coffee and cakes. They were too busy gossiping to actually put pen to paper but Martha didn't mind. She was too busy thinking about Matthew. Just before closing time and after the pots had all been washed and stacked, Martha sent her assistant Claire home so she could spend some time alone. She made herself a mug of coffee and took her notebook out of her bag to write up the days happenings. One day she would write a novel about her life, if something exciting ever happened. There was a knock on the window which made her jump and she lifted her head to see Matthew waving at her. Her heart skipped a beat. He walked to the door and opened it.

'Am I too late? Have you shut up shop for the night?'

'Sort of but you can come in, I'm just having ten minutes to myself. Can I help you?'

'I just wanted to check that you were going to the party tomorrow night.'

'I don't think so. I'm not really a party person and to be honest I don't care one little bit who has bought the manor. If they can afford to live in that rambling old house then let them get on with it.'

'Oh that's a shame, I was going to say that I'm pretty new here so it would have been nice to know a friendly face but if you're not going then I might not bother. I hate social gatherings as well.'

'You'll be just fine. Ten minutes and my writing group will be swarming around you wanting to know everything from your address to your shoe size.'

He laughed. 'You run a writing group as well? I'm seriously impressed. Do you write then?'

'I do. I love it.'

'Have you written anything that's been published?'

'Ah, the dreaded question all writers hate. Yes and no. I have a bi-monthly column in the parish newsletter and my monthly blog. And yes I've written a novel which unfortunately no agent in England seems remotely interested in so that's not published – yet.'

'Really? That's a shame. It's tough getting an agent, but well done you. Writing a novel is a huge achievement. Maybe we could talk about it at the party. I'd love to know more about it.'

'That's blackmail, Matthew.'

'I know but has it worked?'

'I'll think about it, but it's a fair distance to the manor and my car died two days ago.'

'I'll pick you up. Where do you live?'

'Apple tree cottage. It's easy to find. It's the one on the corner of the village square which is covered in white fairy lights. I'm a sucker for fairy lights.'

'What time would you like me to come for you?'

'Well seeing as how my fairy godmother packed her bags and left six months ago, could you make it eight o'clock so I have time to get ready?'

'Your wish is my command.' He turned to leave then picked up the latest best seller which was on display by the door. 'Have you read this yet?'

'No, it's on my huge to read list.'

'It's good. I read it ages ago. I know the author; he's a really nice guy. I'll take this please.'

'You can have it. Payment for the lift tomorrow.'

'Thank you, that's very kind, but I'm pretty sure it's difficult enough trying to earn a living running a book shop without giving your stock away.' He handed over a ten pound note and told her to put the change in the charity box. Then he turned to leave and Martha felt her heart skip a beat again. Was it possible that someone so good looking could be interested in her or was he just clutching onto her because he was new and didn't know anyone. To be honest, she didn't care. She'd often looked at famous men who were as handsome as Matthew and wondered what it would be like to wake up to see someone so gorgeous lying next to you in bed. How would you keep your hands to yourself? She chuckled then began turning out the lights. Picking her notebook up, she tucked it into her handbag and decided that today had been a really great day.

The next night, Matthew drove to the village square. He saw the cottage at the end which was lit up like something from a fairy tale and smiled. He'd never really appreciated just how pretty fairy lights could be until now. He parked up and strolled up the small path to the front door which still had an evergreen, sparkly wreath hanging from it. He knocked and a window opened above his head.

'Sorry. I'm running a little late. Crisis at the shop earlier. Please come in and sit in the kitchen. It's the warmest room in the house. Help yourself to a glass of wine.'

He walked in closing the front door behind him. A row of flickering candles lit the way to the kitchen. The air smelt of apple and cinnamon and it was cosy. He walked along the narrow corridor, one wall lined with bookshelves crammed full with every kind of book from the Famous Five to Stephen King and he nodded his head in appreciation. He loved books just as much if not more than Martha clearly did. He found the kitchen and smiled at the uncorked bottle of red wine and two glasses. One was a quarter full. He poured a small amount into the other glass and looked around. There was a brown envelope and letter on the side from yesterday and it had his company logo at the top. He almost dropped his glass. He wouldn't normally do this but he had to know if it was the letter which she had been reading yesterday when they met. He walked over and began to read the standard rejection letter that his assistant sent out at least ten times a week to budding novelists. He pulled out his phone and rang Amy his assistant. Her phone rang and rang but he kept on until she answered in a breathless voice.

'Yes Matthew, what do you want?'

'Did you read a submission from a Martha Potter this week?'

'I don't know. Why?'

'I need to know Amy, as soon as possible.'

'It may have slipped your mind but it's New Years Eve and I've already drunk a bottle of champagne and I intend to drink lots more. I'll tell you tomorrow.'

'No you won't, you'll tell me tonight. It's very important and I need to know as soon as possible. If you don't, you can forget about having an extra week off.'

'That's mean Matthew and why are you whispering?'

'I know it is, but please, you have no idea how important it is Amy.'

'Bloody hell, you might be my boss but you are a huge pain. I'll get back to you soon; I'll go and check my computer and you'll owe me more than a week off for ruining my social life.'

'Thank you and yes I will.'

He disconnected the call and took his glass of wine to the kitchen chair furthest away from the worktop and that awful letter.

Martha walked into the kitchen smelling of Chanel perfume she looked stunning in a simple black dress, her hair swept up and piled loosely on top of her head, exposing matching diamante earrings and necklace.

'You look amazing.'

She laughed. 'Really? That's very nice of you to say. It's just an old dress I've had for years.'

'Well regardless of its age, you do look lovely.'

'Thank you, you're not too bad yourself. Shall we go and get this over with?'

'I suppose we better had, otherwise I'll be tempted to finish that bottle and stay here in your very cosy kitchen all night.' He followed her as she walked along blowing out each candle in turn.

'I hope you make a wish when you do that.'

'I always do, but I can't say that any of them have ever come true.'

'I'm sure they will very soon. Just keep on believing. Come on, Cinders, let's get you to the ball.'

They arrived at the huge gates to The Manor and Martha wondered what it would be like to drive up to a house like this knowing that it was yours. How amazing must that feel? She got a warm glow thinking about her cottage. It may be small but she'd worked hard for it and it was all hers.

'A penny for your thoughts?'

'Oh I'm just being soppy. So where are you staying in the village. Did you rent one of the holiday cottages?'

'Sort of, but I'm only here until the day after tomorrow. Work calls I'm afraid. I have a lot on so I'll be back up to London.'

As he drove along the long drive, the house came into view and Martha sighed. 'Oh it's beautiful.' Every window was lit up and there was a huge Christmas tree in front of the house with even more white fairy lights than her own front garden.

'It is rather impressive isn't it?'

Martha nodded. She could feel at least three different stories beginning to form in her mind.

He parked his car behind her neighbour Wanda's bright red Fiat and they got out. He ran around and opened the door for her and she smiled. 'Such a gentleman. You know there are very few of you around.'

'I was taught well. My mother is very strict. No messing around and good manners or a clip around the ear it was.' He offered his arm and she took it. Martha was naturally quite shy but if he was off back to London in a couple of days, she was determined to make the most of this evening. He probably wouldn't give her a second thought once he was away from here.

'So do you know the mysterious son who lives here?'

'I do. In fact I know him really well.'

They walked in and immediately the women from her writing group flocked towards her, several of them making a beeline for Matthew who excused himself to go and get some drinks. They asked her a million questions and she laughed, 'Ladies, I have no idea who he is except that he's called Matthew, he likes to read, and he's very gorgeous.'

There was a lot of high pitched laughter and Matthew returned with two very full glasses of champagne. 'Should we see if we can find our hosts and introduce ourselves?'

Martha ignored the squeals of laughter from her friends and followed Matthew who led her from the main hall and dining room towards another room. She never thought to question him and ask how he knew his way around so well; she just assumed that he was hoping for the best. They reached another huge room and this time Martha's mouth dropped open. Now she was impressed. It was the biggest library she'd ever seen inside a private home. There were wall to wall books and she felt her eyes light up at the sight of them all. 'Oh, I think I've just died and gone to heaven.'

'It's pretty amazing isn't it? I love how you love books so much.'

Martha grinned at him. 'I'll let you into a secret. I've never understood anyone who doesn't read. My first three boyfriends hated reading and as soon as I found out, I dumped them. I have no time in my life for anyone who doesn't realise how magical opening a book can be.'

In the corner were an older couple who looked very distinguished and Martha didn't have to ask if they were the owners of The Manor; they looked as if they were meant to be here. They were busy talking to the local vicar and his sidekick Miss Walker who Martha was sure was more than the woman who cleaned the vicarage twice a week but it was none of her business. Matthew led her towards them and the woman smiled at her, she held out her hand.

'I'm Sophie and this is my husband Steven and you are?'

'Martha, I own the local bookshop and run the writing group.'

'Well it's a pleasure to meet you, Martha. It's a gorgeous shop and café you have there. I was admiring it yesterday when I nipped into the village. Unfortunately I was too busy to call in but I'm looking forward to it.'

Martha grinned. 'Thank you.'

Matthew's phone began to ring and he excused himself and walked as far away as he could from the crowds of people and to the office at the opposite side of the house. 'What have you got for me, Amy?'

'Well I've just had a quick scan of the submission and the synopsis is pretty crap which is probably why I sent out a rejection slip. But I've just read the first chapter and it's good. Really good. I think you'll love it. Its right up your street. There's a murder on the first page and it just keeps getting better.'

'Thanks Amy, make sure you send it to my email and flag it as important and when you get a minute I want a letter sending out to Ms Potter. I owe you big time.'

'Yes boss, and yes you do owe me big time. Now can I go back to my party or do you want me to check every other submission we've had this year?'

'No thank you, just that one. Have a lovely evening Amy.'

Martha and Sophie had both watched as Matthew disappeared. 'You'll have to forgive my son, sometimes I think he's glued to that phone of his. He gets so involved in his work, he forgets how to act in public.'

Martha felt her throat begin to burn. Of course! No wonder Matthew was so at home. He lived here. Her cheeks flushed red and she laughed to hide her discomfort. 'Ah, he never actually told me that he lived here. In fact, he hasn't really told me anything about himself at all. Sorry.'

'Don't you apologise. He takes after his Dad. He did exactly the same to me a long time ago. I think it's some kind of genetic man thing or being embarrassed about having money.'

Martha found herself chatting away to Sophie until the local councillors moved in for the kill. Sophie shrugged her shoulders and Martha left to go and find her writing group. She didn't care if she didn't see Matthew again. He'd made her look like an idiot. Her friends were stood in a semi-circle around the bar and she went across to join them. She spotted Matthew out of the corner of her eye but she turned her back on him and consumed several glasses of champagne followed by four double vodkas. When the room began to swim, she realised it was time to try and find someone to take her home. Matthew had been over three times to talk to her and she'd made some polite conversation with him but that was it. He was obviously not interested one bit if he could let her think he was staying in a cottage in the village. Wanda had decided to call it a night so Martha grabbed onto her elbow and followed her out.

'I'm so drunk,' she said as she tripped going down the steps and almost fell flat onto her face into the snow-crusted pea gravel. Wanda giggled and held onto her arm.

'Yes you are. Where's Mr Handsome? You looked like such a great couple when you walked in and the next minute you're sinking champagne like it's going out of fashion and he's nowhere to be seen.'

'Ah well, there's a reason for that. You know that bachelor boy who lives here?'

'No.'

'You know the one. Everyone has been speculating about him for weeks now.'

Wanda shook her head.

'Well Matthew is him or he is Matthew. Whichever it is, he's him and he didn't have the courtesy to tell me. So I'm me and I'm going home to be sick in my tiny bathroom. That's if I make it.'

Wanda pushed her into the front seat and pulled her seat belt across.

'Well, well. Yes you are drunk so don't be sick in my car or you're walking home. That's a good thing isn't it if he likes you?'

Martha screeched and started to laugh. 'How is it good. Poor – and I mean poor – old me has nothing in common with rich old Matthew.'

Wanda didn't say anything. She just began to drive to try and get Martha home before she was sick all over the place. She pulled up outside Martha's cottage and helped her out of the car. 'Come on you.'

Martha let her lead her out of the car and into her house.

'Will you be okay now?'

'Yes thanks, I'll be fine. Night Wanda.'

'Night Martha, lock your door and drink plenty of water.'

Martha shut her front door behind her and locked it. She kicked off her shoes and stumbled into the kitchen to get a big glass of water. The room was spinning and she felt ill. Why had she drunk so much? She forced herself to drink her water and took herself off to bed, dangling the washing up bowl by her side just in case she couldn't make it to the bathroom in time.

Martha opened her eyes and squinted, wondering if she'd been in some kind of car accident. The pain in her head was horrendous and her mouth felt dry and furry. Urgh. She shut her eyes again and remembered the party, Matthew, and her acting like a spoilt brat getting drunk. She wanted to kick herself if only she could move her body enough to do so. She didn't drink more than two or three glasses of wine at a time ever, so what had she been doing? Looking across at the clock on the wall she couldn't believe it was almost one in the afternoon. It was a good job it was New Year's Day and she didn't have to open the shop. What a way to start the New Year. Her number one resolution was to avoid champagne at all costs. Just the thought of it made her mouth fill with water. There was a loud knock on her front door and she couldn't move to open it if she had wanted to. Instead she whispered, 'Go away,' and went back to sleep.

Sometime later she dragged herself from her bed and stumbled along the hallway to the bathroom where she took one look at herself and groaned. Splashing her face with cold water and brushing her teeth she felt a little better. Taking two painkillers from the cabinet she swallowed them with a large glass of water then made her way downstairs to make some toast. By the front door was an envelope. It didn't look like a belated Christmas card so she made herself walk down to get it. As she bent down, the room began to spin and she picked it up, swearing loudly. She was definitely not drinking alcohol for a long, long time. She didn't recognise the elegant handwriting but she knew instinctively that it was from Matthew. Why had she been so mean to him when he hadn't done anything wrong? Tucking it into her pyjama pocket she went into the kitchen in search of food and ended up eating a massive chunk of Christmas cake, a bar of chocolate, and three mince pies. Feeling slightly better, she took a large bottle of water from the fridge and went back upstairs to crawl back into bed and read the letter.

> Dear Martha,
>
> I'm sorry if I upset you last night; it was never my intention. I should have introduced myself better but I find it all a bit embarrassing to be honest.
>
> Anyway I hope you are not too hung over after the vodkas. Matthew x

Bugger! What had she been thinking? He was a nice guy. She wished she had his phone number so she could phone him and grovel. At least he was still interested which was amazing considering how rude she'd been. She fell asleep clutching the letter.

The next morning when Martha opened her eyes, she felt surprisingly normal. She could move her head and got out of bed to get ready for work. She saw the crumpled letter and picked it up, placing it on her bedside table. He would have gone by now, back to whatever it was he did in London. She left her cottage, glad to be out in the fresh, frosty air. She turned the corner and saw him standing outside her shop, hands in his pockets, pacing up and down. He turned and she tried her best not to grin at him.

'Hi, how are you feeling today?' he said.

'I'm fine thank you. You?'

'I'm fine, look I couldn't go until I'd apologised. I'm sorry I didn't tell you who I was but you have to look at it from my side. It's a bit embarrassing saying, 'I'm the son of those rich people who bought the manor' to everyone I meet. Please don't be mad at me.'

'I'm not mad at you. I'm embarrassed because I should have known who you were and I made an idiot of myself.'

'How exactly? I don't remember you making a fool of yourself at all.'

'Did I not? Oh well that's good then.' She turned her back on him and unlocked the door. He followed her inside. 'I need to get sorted out. Did you need anything?'

'Sorry, a cappuccino would be nice.'

'Café doesn't open till ten.'

'Oh. What about a bog standard mug of coffee then?'

Martha was infuriated with him and with herself, but she wouldn't tell him to leave because she didn't want him to so she nodded and went to turn on the kettle whilst he began to browse the books. He picked up three books then sat down and drank his coffee.

'So where do you work Matthew? You seem to know everything about me.'

'Oh just some office in London. Nothing exciting really I have to read a lot of reports and stuff.'

'Do you enjoy it?'

'Yes, I love it although I would love to run a shop like this even more. Do you ever get authors to come and do book signings?'

'I do occasionally but they're normally local writers and it turns into another excuse for free cake and wine for the village. I don't think anyone famous would want to come here and do a talk.'

'How about if I ask my author friend, the one whose book I bought the other day? I'm pretty sure he would be up for it. He feels the same way as I do about supporting independent book shops.'

'Well you could ask him and that would be amazing but I won't get my hopes up.'

'Leave it with me. How about a drink in the pub when you close?'

Martha wanted more than anything to say yes but tonight she had promised the writing group that they could come around for belated Christmas drinks and she couldn't let them down because they would still be around long after Mr Handsome was gone. 'I'm sorry, I can't make it tonight.'

'Oh okay. How about tomorrow? I'll meet you here at five.' He stood up and tucked his brown paper bag with his books inside under his arm then strode across and kissed her on the cheek. He left her standing there with her heart racing and her face burning.

The next day went by in a blur with deliveries and a busy café all day. Martha didn't have much time to dream about Matthew but when she looked at the clock and saw it was almost five o'clock, her heart began to beat faster. It got to half past five and she felt sick. He wasn't coming. What if he'd changed his mind? She gave him until six then shut up the shop and walked home. The village was quiet and everyone had taken down their Christmas lights. It all looked very bare. She kept telling herself it was never meant to be. She'd go home to watch some black and white films and feel sorry for herself. Martha checked her phone and then realised that she'd never even given him her number. How stupid was she?

The next morning she decided she wasn't going to think about Matthew; she was going to concentrate on everything but him. She opened the shop and it was relatively dead until a man walked in who she recognised. He went to sit down in the café and looked at the menu, Martha walked over to him and he smiled.

'Now then, I'd like a hot chocolate with the full works and a toasted teacake. I've also come to apologise on behalf of Matthew for not letting you know he couldn't meet you last night.'

Martha laughed. 'Really, there's no need. You don't have to. I understand.'

'No. I need to explain this to you or he'll go mad. He made me promise. He got an urgent phone call from the office. One of his clients went into… Now what was that word he said before he left?' He paused for a moment, 'Oh yes, I remember now. They went into meltdown.'

'Honestly, please tell him its fine next time you speak to him.'

'Ah but it's not fine, letting a pretty young thing like you down without an explanation. But he did say that he'll make it up to you as soon as he can.'

Martha walked away and he finished his drink and teacake then stood up, tucking a ten pound note underneath the bell on the counter. When she realised she ran out into the street after him but Steven was nowhere to be seen. She turned to Claire, 'What do I do with this, I can't accept it.'

'I bloody can. He can afford it. Did you see their house and all that champagne?'

Martha had because she drunk her fair share of the stuff. 'I'll put it in the charity box for the hospice.'

'All right. If you insist.'

Martha popped it into the plastic container then went back to the book shop and began checking off the delivery that had arrived just before Steven. There was a carton of books that she knew she hadn't ordered. She ripped off the tape and opened it. Tucked down one side of it was a note. 'Thought I'd better stock up for you. My famous writer friend said yes and the locals will be clambering all over to get to him for his autograph, Matthew x.'

Martha laughed. Well who'd have thought: a celebrity author coming to her little old book shop? She hoped he drank cheap wine because that was all she could afford. She sat down with her notebook. She was a big believer in making plans and was so busy writing that she didn't notice Jim the postman standing in front of her until he coughed and she jumped.

'Sorry.'

He handed her a letter. 'You need to sign for that.' Then he held out the small terminal so she could scrawl her name on the screen.

It was a crisp white, envelope and felt very expensive. Her first thought was that she was being summoned to court so she took a deep breath and opened it. Pulling the letter out she had to read it three times before the words sank in.

> Dear Ms Potter,
>
> I'm glad to tell you that I have made a huge mistake and got your submission mixed up with another one. I would like to take this opportunity to tell you how much I enjoyed your first three chapters. I cannot apologise enough for the mix up but I would be very interested to meet you tomorrow if you can make it to my office. The address is on the top of the letter. Should we say four o'clock to give you the chance to travel to London? I'm very much looking forward to seeing you and I truly hope that you can make it so we can discuss your brilliant novel and your future career as a published author. If there are any problems please contact my assistant who will only be too pleased to help you.
>
> Yours truly
>
> Matt Ashworth.

Martha let out a scream and thrust the letter into Claire's hands, hugging her. 'Can you cover tomorrow for me, please?'

Claire laughed. 'Of course I can. Wow! How exciting. You might finally be able to sell your own book.'

Martha sent Claire home and then set about closing the shop for the day; she had too much to do. She needed to go over the rest of the manuscript before she could let him read it. This was what she had been dreaming about for the last six years. She couldn't believe it.

When Martha finally stepped off the train at Euston station, she smiled. It had been a long time since she'd been to London. She made her way to the taxi rank and got into a black cab, showing him the address on the top of her letter. She felt sick and hoped that this Matt was some kind person who wouldn't judge her on her nerves. Finally the taxi pulled up outside a huge white building. She passed him a twenty pound note and told him to keep the change.

As she made her way into the reception area, she actually considered turning around and leaving. She was so nervous but she managed to force herself to sit on the brown leather sofa.

'Mr Ashworth won't be too long. Can I get you a drink?'

'No thank you.' She was terrified of spilling anything down the front of her blouse. A tall, blonde haired woman came out of the lift and spoke her name. Martha stood up. She followed the woman into the lift and along a corridor to an office at the end. Her hands were shaking and she hoped she would be able to grip his hand properly. The woman opened the door and she followed her inside. Matt was standing with his back towards her talking on his phone but she recognised his voice and when he turned around to face her, he grinned from ear to ear.

'I'm so glad you could make it, I didn't know if you would turn up.'

The assistant left them alone, closing the door behind her. Matt walked over and kissed her on the cheek. Martha's mouth dropped open as her cheeks began to burn.

'Now Ms Potter, we need to talk business. Do you know that your synopsis is terrible? It doesn't sell your story at all. But luckily for you my assistant took a look at the first chapter and absolutely loved it. I read it myself two days ago and I love it. I can't wait to read the rest of it. Have you brought it with you?'

'Yes, I have.'

'Brilliant. Now I'm taking you out for a bite to eat where we can discuss some finer points and then if you're interested, I'd like to sign you up. Today.'

Martha who was speechless for the first time in her life nodded her head. This time she wasn't going to mess it up and she might even break her New Year's resolution and drink champagne.

Author Details
If you've enjoyed this story and would like to find out more about Helen Phifer, here's how:

Twitter: @helenphiferl
Facebook: https://www.facebook.com/Helenphiferl
Blog: Helenphiferblog@wordpress.com

Helen Phifer's current eBooks The Ghost House and The Secrets of the Shadows are available to buy now

---

Muriel's Christmas Surprise

Jennifer Bohnet

Feisty is the word that best describes my mother-in-law. Muriel Morgan's a forthright lady and she doesn't hold back when she thinks she's right about something.

I've lost count of the number of good causes she's championed. This year it's her local animal shelter.

'It's disgraceful the way some people treat their animals. Even when they're prosecuted they just get a slapped wrist. They should lock them in a room with no food and water for days on end and see how they like it!'

Tom, my husband, says she's always been a fighter. She certainly fought to bring him up after his dad left when he was five. She's also always been very independent and Tom can't remember her ever having boyfriends while he was at home.

I don't think she has any special male friends even now. Once, when I plucked up the courage to tackle her about it, she just shrugged.

'Not lucky in that department,' she said. 'And now I don't think I could be bothered. I've got more important things to do.'

She's spending Christmas and New Year with us. It'll be her first visit to this house, so she's sure to have a lot to say about all the renovations it needs.

William from next door is joining us for Christmas Day lunch. Not that I've told Muriel about him yet.

William's a poppet. He adores the twins – plays cricket with them, takes them swimming. He's even bought himself a computer so he can keep up to date with the games they play.

At first I worried the boys were being a nuisance but when I said this to him, William just laughed.

'Those boys of yours are a lifeline for me. Don't know how I'd have coped with retirement without them.'

Apparently William had retired a couple of weeks before we moved in and had been finding his life a bit empty with nothing to do. His wife died about five years ago and they'd never had any children.

I have tried to warn him about Muriel and I have my fingers firmly crossed that she will be on her best behaviour over Christmas.

When Muriel arrived on the twentieth, the boys were next door with William and I was up to my elbows in pastry and mince-pies.

Not expecting her until late afternoon, I ignored the urgent blast of a car horn after lunchtime. Seeing a red sports car parked outside the gate, I still didn't twig that Muriel had arrived early.

Last time we saw her she'd had an elderly estate car, but this was a lethal machine. With a huge dog in the passenger seat.

Muriel waved at me.

'There you are – at last! Take this and I'll get Jeeves.'

Jeeves?

Dazed I took the suitcase and the large cardboard box she handed me. Muriel was clearly still as bossy as ever.

She followed me into the kitchen, trying to stop the dog from wrapping his lead around her legs. An Old English sheepdog, Jeeves seemed to be desperately in need of a crash course in acceptable canine behaviour – and a bath. He smelt terrible!

'How long have you had him?'

'Picked him up this morning,' Muriel replied. 'Literally saved him from death row. He'd been in the refuge a year and that's their cut-off time. Didn't bear thinking about.'

The smell didn't bear thinking about, either. Even Muriel acknowledged that.

'He rolled in something when I let him have a run in the park before we left.'

'What are you going to do with him?'

'Keep him of course. Unless you'd like him for the boys…'

The horrified look on my face must have given her an instant answer.

'No? Well, he'll be company for me then. Where are my grandsons?'

'Next door with William. What's happened to your old car?'

'Scrapyard,' Muriel said cheerfully. 'My Premium Bond came up so I treated myself to the red goddess. I've always wanted a sports car, and it goes like stink.'

I was afraid of that. Before I could say anything, the kitchen door flew open and the boys fell upon their grandmother.

'Can we have a ride? What's the dog's name? Can we take him for a walk?'

'His name is Jeeves and yes you can take him for a walk, but only after he's had a bath.' I couldn't stand one more minute of that awful smell.

Twenty minutes and much hilarity later, a fluffy, sweet-smelling Jeeves emerged from under one of my best towels and the boys took him and Muriel off to meet William.

The next few days passed in a whirl of all the usual pre-Christmas activities – last minute shopping, cooking, present buying and frantic wrapping.

A lot of time too, was spent with Jeeves, trying to instil some obedience into him. It was quite a sight to see the boys running after

Jeeves on his long trainer lead, with Muriel in her flowing purple cape, waving and shouting at them to slow down.

I noticed that William was spending a lot of time helping with the training, too. Muriel's abrasive attitude to life seemed to amuse him.

Muriel duly took the twins for a spin in the red goddess (with strict instructions from me not to break the speed limit and to be back within ten minutes). When William casually said he wouldn't mind a ride, she told him to hop in.

The last I saw of William, he was hanging on for dear life as the car took the corner at the bottom of our road at breakneck speed. They were gone for ages and I was getting seriously worried, but then the red goddess turned sedately into our road.

To my amazement, William was driving and judging by the smile on his face, enjoying himself immensely. Muriel was sitting in the passenger seat looking subdued.

When she got out, she simply shrugged her shoulders and said, 'Men!' before she vanished indoors.

There was one genuinely sticky moment and that was in our nearest town on Christmas Eve, when it looked as if the red goddess was about to be given a parking ticket.

'Don't even think about booking me, young lady,' Muriel shouted at the traffic warden.

'Two minutes, that's all I was, getting something for this poor abandoned dog here. Where's your Christmas spirit?'

The traffic warden backed away without writing a word.

'Muriel, Muriel,' William said, shaking his head. 'The poor woman's only doing her job. And you really shouldn't have parked there. It does say deliveries only.'

I held my breath, waiting for the usual sarcastic retort from Muriel but to my surprise, she simply shrugged.

'Suppose you're right.'

Turning, she yelled at the retreating back of the traffic warden.

'Merry Christmas, love.'

I looked at William in amazement. He'd got away with telling Muriel off – and lived to tell the tale.

The six of us were a happy bunch as we walked to church for midnight mass on Christmas Eve. William had a twin on each hand and Muriel had Jeeves on his lead, having flatly refused to leave him behind.

'He'll think he's been abandoned again if we all disappear.'

I didn't have any real objections, but the priest did when we arrived at church.

'What do you mean I can't bring him into the church?' Muriel demanded truculently. 'It's Christmas and he's one of God's creatures.'

'Animals are not allowed in the church,' the priest said. 'I'm sorry but I don't want him upsetting other people.'

'Well you're certainly no Francis of Assisi, are you?' Muriel said rudely. 'Denying a dumb animal.'

She would clearly have said more, but William interrupted.

'Would you object to us sitting in the porch with Jeeves, rather than going home and missing out on the service altogether?'

The priest, who knew William as a regular churchgoer, shook his head.

'No objections to that. But any barking and you must leave immediately.'

So that was what happened. Tom and I took the boys into church and William, Muriel and Jeeves stayed in the porch.

Christmas Day was great – a real family day. There were lots of presents under the tree for everyone.

Muriel was delighted with the earrings William had bought her – small silver witches sitting on gold broomsticks in a gold hoop – and immediately fixed them to her ears.

Muriel, William and the boys took Jeeves for a long walk after lunch. Tom and I did the clearing up and then had a peaceful hour to ourselves. Or it would have been peaceful if Tom hadn't wanted to talk.

'What are we going to do about Mum?'

'What d'you mean? She's fine – happier than I've ever known her. She's having fun with both her new car and Jeeves.'

'Whatever possessed her to buy the red goddess?'

'Probably because she could. You admitted you enjoyed driving it yesterday morning and I know William certainly did.'

'Oh, it's a nice car. Lovely to drive. It's just not a suitable car for Mum. She's not exactly the best driver in the world. I'm going to have a word with her and tell her she's got to sell it.'

'Best of luck, Tom. I'll be waiting to pick up the pieces when she demolishes you.'

But Tom never did say anything to Muriel about getting rid of her car. She got rid of it herself. To our amazement she sold it to William.

'He made me an offer I couldn't refuse,' was all she said when I expressed surprise. 'Now, we're all seeing in the New Year at his place, aren't we? I thought I'd make one of my special cakes for the occasion. I'll use his kitchen and give him a hand getting everything else ready. I'll see you later.'

Later that evening, when Tom and I took the boys next door, a smiling William greeted us.

'Come in, come in. Muriel's in the kitchen, just putting the finishing touches to things. She'll be through in a moment.'

'William!'

He raised his eyebrows. 'She who must be obeyed calls. Go on through and make yourselves at home. I'll be back in a moment.'

Tom and I settled ourselves in the sitting-room, where Jeeves was already ensconced in front of a roaring log fire, looking completely at home. The twins made straight for William's computer.

William and Muriel returned to the sitting room together with a bottle of champagne.

'Half an hour to go before midnight,' Tom said, checking his watch. 'You're a bit early, William.'

'Oh, there's another bottle on ice for then,' William said popping the cork. 'We have something else to celebrate before then.'

He went and stood next to Muriel and put his arm around her.

'Muriel and I are getting married by Special Licence in two days' time.'

Tom was the first up to congratulate his mother. He was genuinely thrilled that she'd finally found someone as nice as William to care for her. 'You deserve every happiness,' he said, kissing her.

'You don't think we're rushing things?' Muriel asked, sounding uncharacteristically anxious. 'At our age it seems silly to wait.'

I couldn't stop grinning.

'I think it's brilliant. Just so long as William realises what he's taking on. His quiet life will be over.'

'I think I'll cope,' William said, giving Muriel a loving look.

'Where are you getting married?' I asked.

'Local church. Luckily Muriel's forgiven the priest for Christmas Eve.'

It was a lovely wedding. Muriel looked radiant in a long cream-coloured dress with a short scarlet cape thrown over her shoulders.

Watching William and Muriel getting into the red goddess to set off on honeymoon, I remembered her saying that William had made her an offer for the car she couldn't refuse. Helping Muriel brush the rose petals from her cape, I asked her what the offer had been.

'Oh, he said he'd only marry me if I sold him the car. So what could I do?'

Author Details

If you've enjoyed this story and would like to find out more about Jennifer Bohnet, here's how:

Twitter: @jenniewriter
Facebook: *http://tinyurl.com/oopne9b*
Website: *http://www.jenniferbohnet.com/*

Jennifer's current eBook, 'You Had Me At Bonjour' is available now.

Wherever I'll Be

Harriet James

I make a sympathetic face across the grey stone font at Roberta, my elder sister, as she wrestles with the sizeable squirming bundle in her arms, and wonder why she's bothering. She makes a face back, nudges George, her husband, and passes the bundle to him as if it's a sack of potatoes. The white crocheted shawl loosens in the process and one of my nephew's chubby legs emerges to thrash the air. A loud squawk follows, and George crooks his forefinger and puts the knuckle to the baby's mouth to forestall a full-blown yelling session.

'It's a family tradition,' Roberta said when she rang, after I'd pointed out that none of us goes to church as a rule and she wasn't even married in one. 'We were both christened at Saint Peter's, and Mum says a baby doesn't have its name properly until it's done. So you'll be godmother then?' It wasn't really a question.

This is the only reason I'm home, the christening, no matter what Mum thinks. As soon as it's over I'm back to Bristol and heading off for Christmas in Tenerife with the gang from uni. I can hardly wait. I have told Mum I'm going and it's not my problem that she doesn't believe me. It's handy being home, though; I can pick up my bikini and some summer clothes.

'I said that shawl wouldn't suit,' Nan whispers loudly, leaning up to my shoulder. 'It's meant for a neat little baby like you were, not a great lump like him.'

I giggle, and Mum glares at the pair of us. Nan isn't finished. 'Why are they calling him Robert? Daft, if you ask me. The boy should have his own name, not his mother's with the end chopped off.'

I'm inclined to agree but I can't help thinking that Robbie Williams has a part to play in it somewhere.

The godfathers, George's younger brother, John, and Malcolm, our cousin, are thumbing the service sheets, Malcolm adjusting his glasses in an attempt to focus in the failing light. I look down at my own sheet. Our bit is coming up in a minute. I mark the relevant place with my finger and let my gaze wander.

We're arranged in a loose semi-circle at the back of the church, an obedient gathering, coated and booted against the chill of the day. Around us, several hastily repositioned candles join forces with spasmodically dimming overhead lights in the struggle to hold back the gloom, the rows of empty pews marching down the nave receding into near darkness. (Something's gone wrong with the wiring; the vicar greeted us with this news the moment we arrived.) Triumphant arrangements of glowing white lilies, Christmas roses and trailing ivy rest on pillars at the top of the aisle and the saints, shadowy in their niches, have bunches of greenery tied with red ribbon at their feet in keeping with the season.

It's a timeless scene with no relevance to the world beyond these walls. A romantic one, too, in a Gothic sort of way. I'm thinking about this, letting my mind drift vaguely through the possibilities, when something happens that snaps me back to the present.

The light alone announces his arrival, a sudden burst of brightness from the sky that strikes through the glass robes of Saint Peter and casts a theatrical glow on our little party; there's no sound, other than the vicar's undulating voice. Shamelessly revealed, he stands a few feet away from us; thinner than the last time I saw him, his hair shorter and the beard gone, but unmistakeably, Oscar. A second's hesitation and he steps forward and merges seamlessly into the group.

'Hello Louise,' he whispers, and touches me lightly on my left shoulder. I half turn, making my face a deliberate blank, then turn back and concentrate on my service sheet.

The rest of the proceedings pass in a blur. The only clear thing is the look of satisfaction on my mother's face as I catch her eye. At least she has the grace to look slightly guilty too.

As well she might.

The sky has darkened again and there's a sensation of snow in the air as we file back to our house like a band of nomads crossing the Russian Steppes, the all-terrain buggy leading the way. Nan fastens herself to my arm, providing a buffer between me and Oscar. Thwarted in his attempt to walk with me, he drops back.

'Sorry I was late,' I'd heard him say to my mother outside the church. 'I thought you said quarter past.'

Typical, I thought; he never was on time. Mum used to excuse him, saying it was because his mind was on higher things. As it turned out, it was exactly the opposite.

'What's he doing here?' I demand once we're home and I corner Mum in the kitchen where she's shoving a tray of sausage rolls into the oven, still wearing her coat and hat.

'I told you, Alison,' Dad says, taking the Prosecco from the fridge and feeling the bottle to test the temperature. 'I said she wouldn't like it.'

'Too right I don't. Robert's christening isn't anything to do with him. This is a family occasion. Anyway, I don't want him here. Whatever made you think I would?'

'Now don't make a fuss, Louise,' Mum says. 'Oscar's here because I heard he was home for Christmas and I invited him. He did come to Roberta's wedding, after all.'

'That was two years ago, when we were together,' I say.

'Yes, well perhaps it's time you put all that behind you and stopped sulking. Just have a little chat with him, ask him if he's working on any interesting experiments or something.' Mum flaps a tea towel as if she's starting a race. 'He works for a major pharmaceutical company now, you know. He's done very well to get where he is, very well indeed.'

Buried in this remark is Mum's opinion that science is a worthy career whereas reading a lot of books is not. It doesn't help my cause that I have no idea what I want to do when I finish my masters in classical and contemporary literature next summer.

'I don't care if he's invented the elixir of life. I'm not talking to him, and that's that.'

'Well, it wouldn't hurt you to be civil. Extend the hand of friendship. It is Christmas, after all.' There's the tiniest hint of defeat in Mum's sniff. She fills the kettle and switches it on. 'Somebody might like tea instead of wine. Louise, don't just stand there. Take the clingfilm off of those sandwiches.'

The thing about Mum is that once she's made up her mind about a person, nothing short of a tsunami will get her to change it, and she made up her mind about Oscar the first time I brought him home. He was intelligent, well brought up and – this was the big one – he was going to *make something of himself.* He also had, Mum asserted, a genuine look about him. Whatever that meant.

'She's only doing what she thinks is best, Lou,' Dad says, once Mum's gone through to the hall to take her coat off. He polishes a glass and holds it up to the light to inspect it. 'Maybe she's right and you should let bygones be bygones, eh?' He grins hopefully and I can't help smiling back.

'I'll be polite and that's all she's getting but if she's got any ideas about me and Oscar, well…'

My voice catches in my throat. I'm shocked at the strength of feeling bubbling up inside me, feelings I thought I'd rid myself of long ago. I'm angry too, at Mum for bringing my ex-fiancé into our home when I swore I would never set eyes on him again, let alone speak to him, and angry at myself for reacting like this. I shouldn't be too hard on Mum, though. Dad's right, she acts with the best intentions, even if they are misplaced at times. Besides, she doesn't know the full story.

Most people assumed it was the months we spent apart that finally broke us. Some, my family included, also knew that Oscar went out with another girl at the start of his second year and lied about it for ages, even though I heard the truth from a friend of a friend who was at the same university as him.

After a Christmas spent in tears – mine, mostly – followed by weeks of recrimination, conducted mostly by phone since we were back at uni by then, I decided I loved Oscar too much to let him go over one mistake, and at Easter we got engaged. I don't think we'd ever spoken about marriage up until that point but after what happened we felt we needed to do something to mark our renewed commitment to each other, so Oscar proposed and I said yes and that was that.

I wasn't even twenty. What was I thinking, getting engaged when there so much I wanted to do, places I wanted to see? Deep down I knew it was madness but I swept all the doubts to one side because I loved Oscar, loved him so much that I cried for days each time we parted and could hardly breathe until we were together again.

The dining chairs have been arranged against the wall and Oscar is trapped on one between Nan and Auntie Margaret as they lean across him, nattering away. I see him look up at me as I sway past with the plates of sandwiches. It's a complicated look, one I don't want to analyse. I don't want to analyse my responses either. They're unexpected, and almost frightening. My stomach curls involuntarily at the sight of those deep-set hazel eyes, the curve of his mouth, the glimpse of pale, soft skin where his shirt collar dips to one side. All the old familiar sensations creep up on me and I need them to go away before I do something I'll definitely regret.

George is leaning in the doorway, jiggling a squalling Robert in his arms. I put the sandwiches on the table and go across.

'Roberta's heating up his bottle,' George says, nodding towards the kitchen.

'Shall I take him for a minute?' I say. I hold my arms out, trying not to look at the finger of drool that's escaping down the baby's chin. A respite is a respite, after all.

'No, you're all right.' George looks over my shoulder. 'I think your boyfriend needs rescuing. Sorry, *ex*-boyfriend,' he adds, seeing my face.

George is right. I can't ignore Oscar any longer. I virtually manhandle him out of his seat, across the room full of chatter and out to the conservatory. If we must have a conversation it's better we have it in private.

It's fine at first. We make small-talk – his job, my course, people we know.

'I like the new look,' I say truthfully. 'Great haircut, and... everything.'

Oscar smiles and rubs his clean-shaven chin. 'I thought it was time to ditch the student vibe.'

'Well, it suits you.' I drop my gaze, feeling suddenly shy.

'You're home for Christmas, then, like me,' Oscar says. Unfairly, the assumption annoys me.

'No, I'm only staying tonight.'

I tell him about Tenerife, the cheap flights we got through someone whose father works for the airline, the apartment that six of us have rented overlooking the beach and how I'm looking forward to spending Christmas in the sun for a change.

I don't tell him about Dillon.

Dillon has been trying to persuade me to go out with him for weeks. We flirt a lot, josh around with one another, but we've only kissed once, after he'd insisted on walking me home from a party – he's old-fashioned like that, chivalrous. It's one of the many things I find attractive about him. The kiss was nothing short of spectacular. But the last thing I need is to fall in love and have my life messed up again. Even so, now I know he's coming to Tenerife too, I can't help feeling that fate has taken a hand.

'Louise,' Oscar says, his eyes serious. *Here it comes.* Why else would he be here?

'What?'

He looks down at the floor then back at me. 'It's so good to see you. You look... beautiful.' He smiles, or tries to. I can see he's struggling. A part of me melts inside.

'I don't think so, but thanks anyway.' I pat my midriff. 'Too much studying, not enough exercise.' I laugh but it comes out wrong. He ignores it anyway.

'I shouldn't have come today but when your mum invited me all I could think about was seeing you again and how much I wanted that. Selfish, I know, but still...'

I don't reply. Oscar continues.

'I'm so sorry I hurt you. If it's any consolation I've paid the price because I've missed you so much, every day since. I think about you all the time. I'm still in love with you, Louise. I always will be.' He gives an elaborate shrug, facing his palms upwards, as if he's stated his case and he's putting himself entirely in my hands.

'Oh, Oscar.' I give him a long look, and for a moment I really want to tell him that I still love him too.

I'm saved by Roberta opening the door to tell us they're about to the cut the cake.

All through my father's little speech, the cutting of the cake, the pouring of the Prosecco and the toast to my nephew, I feel Oscar's eyes on me and I don't look. I won't look, in case he sees the aching doubt I'm trying hard to suppress, the feeling of longing that threatens to ambush me and turn my resolve to dust.

Later on, when everyone else has gone, we're sitting in front of the telly; me, Mum, Dad, and Nan, who's staying the night too. Dad's finishing off the dregs of a bottle of wine along with some left-over sausage rolls. Nan is snoring gently. It's only six o'clock but beyond the window the darkness of the frozen night is complete.

'But you love Christmas at home, you know you do,' Mum says, after I've looked up the temperature in Tenerife on my phone and found it a satisfying twenty degrees.

Mum's right, I do love our Christmas with the tree always in the same corner, the same wobbly fairy lights in the porch, the same meals served up from Christmas Eve through to Boxing Day and the endless card games played without the Ace of Hearts which Roberta hid one year while cheating and then forgot where she'd put it. But it will all go on just the same, wherever I'll be.

'I know,' I say, 'but it's all arranged now. You don't really mind if I give it a miss this year, do you?'

'You go, love,' Dad joins in. 'Have a smashing time.'

'No, of course we don't mind,' Mum says. And then she gives me one of her sideways look and adds: 'As long as you're sure.'

If only she hadn't said that. If only. Because the truth is I'm not sure, not any more, and not just about Christmas, although the two decisions seem inextricably bound together.

Christmas at home, and Oscar. Christmas in Tenerife, and Dillon.

Mentally I curse my sister for making me godmother, my mother for meddling, myself for being so easily swayed, and Oscar himself for... well, for being Oscar, the boy I fell in love with at seventeen. How arrogant we were, the two of us, believing love would last for ever! It wasn't as if I hadn't read enough books to know that the opposite was the most likely.

Oscar and I meet up again the following day for a lunchtime drink in The Fox – his idea. I'm catching the one-forty train. I'm all packed and ready to leave, I've said my goodbyes and Happy Christmases to Mum and Dad, Nan and Roberta, and now all I have to do is get through this. It's not going to be easy, on either of us.

Surprisingly, he's already there when I arrive five minutes early – I wouldn't let him pick me up from home. He stands up and waves me over to the corner where he's commandeered a sagging leather sofa next to an artificial, optically-lit Christmas tree. There's a vodka-tonic – lemon but no ice – waiting on the table, next to his bottle of lager. Again I smart at his bald assumptions, firstly that I'll turn up and secondly that vodka-tonic is still my drink of choice, which it is, but it would be nice to be asked. I drop my rucksack down beside the sofa with a thump.

Somehow I manage to relax and we chat easily, laughing over incidents from our shared past, like the Christmas afternoon at

Oscar's when we sneaked down the garden to the icy cold summerhouse for a snogging session and his kid sister locked us in for a joke and then lost the key. I go along with the reminiscences for a while, and then something in me gives a sharp twist and I realise that this is no longer small talk. It's a deliberate ploy on Oscar's part to remind me of how we used to be.

I freeze. Oscar notices. 'What's wrong?'

'As if you didn't know.' I work my arms into my coat and stand up. 'This was a bad idea. I shouldn't have come.'

'Please don't go.' Oscar gets up too, making the table wobble in his haste. 'We need to be together, Lou. It just doesn't work otherwise. I'll move, get another job so we can be near each other. We can start again...'

'You don't know where I'll be. Even I don't know that.'

Somehow, we're sitting down again. I still have my coat on.

'I have to go soon,' I say. 'I don't want to miss the train.'

Oscar lifts his arm and rolls back his cuff to check his watch. It's the one I gave him for his eighteenth birthday. I'm surprised he hasn't upgraded, and then I think that he probably has, and he's only wearing it as another reminder of us.

He puts a hand on my shoulder. 'Don't get the train. Let's have another drink.'

I sigh, and shrug him off. 'I must. The next one's too late and I don't want to leave it till the morning. I've got things to do in Bristol, then we're flying out tomorrow night.'

'No, I mean, don't go at all. Stay home for Christmas. We can talk properly.'

Oscar leans towards me and I think he's going to kiss me but he doesn't and I don't know how I feel about that. He sits back and glances at his watch again.

And then my mind sends me back to that night. It's our engagement party and all I've done since we arrived at the restaurant is check my watch, over and over. I check my phone, too, but no message arrives. We wait round the table – my family, Oscar's family and a few of our friends – as the minutes tick by until they reach fifteen, then twenty, then thirty, and still he doesn't come. Eventually my father stops pretending to inspect the menu and slaps it down.

'Well, where is he then?' he says, looking round at us all as if one us has Oscar secreted away beneath the table.

Oscar's parents start to apologise on his behalf although it's clear they have no idea what's happened. Mum, bless her, tries to laugh it off and I sit there with the embarrassed murmur of conversation around me and want to die because I know exactly why Oscar's late, and who he's with. I've been told often enough by well-meaning friends but I chose not to believe it. Oscar loved me. We were getting engaged. There must be some mistake.

But when he finally arrives, forty minutes late for his own engagement party, I know there's no mistake. As he takes his seat next to me, muttering meaningless apologies, and kisses me on the cheek, I smell perfume that isn't mine, and for the rest of the evening, he can't look me in the eye.

I went along with it all for the sake of my parents and Oscar's. I don't know how I managed it but I got through that evening, and the days that followed, and the weeks that followed after that. End-of-year exams were coming up and I threw myself into my studies. In July I came home and quietly posted the ring through Oscar's door in an envelope. No note, just the ring. I didn't need to explain because he already knew why. Nobody else did, those that hadn't guessed anyway, and I didn't enlighten them. It was too painful to talk about.

'No,' I say firmly, standing up again and zipping up my coat. 'We can't go back. Too much has happened. Bye, Oscar. Have a good Christmas.' I kiss him briefly on the cheek.

My eyes are stinging as I leave the pub and walk to the bus stop.

At the station I study the information board, willing the platform number to flash up, but it's too early. I think about Mum running through her endless shopping list in case something vital has been overlooked, like the box of dates that nobody wants but she buys anyway, and Dad casting an eye over the bottles at the bottom of the larder like an army captain inspecting the troops. I think about Roberta and George wrapping presents for their son's first Christmas. And I think about Oscar walking home from The Fox with his hands in his pockets and a heart full of regret.

Other travellers are traipsing past me towards the trains, laden down with luggage and armfuls of presents, going home for Christmas. Suddenly it feels all wrong to be heading in the opposite direction, away from home, away from Oscar. All I have to do is turn around and go back.

But even as I think this, I know it's too late. The platform's displayed now. The train is in. I hitch up my rucksack, and then I hear my name being called and I turn to see Oscar racing across the concourse towards me. He stops before he reaches me, and waits. I can see his chest pumping with the effort of running. I meet his gaze, but before I can start towards him my mobile stutters in my pocket and automatically I pull it out. It's Dillon. He's sent a photo of himself posing in huge, joke sunglasses and miniscule Speedos, also a joke – at least I hope they are. 'Will I do?' reads the message.

The phone still in my hand, I walk over to Oscar and put my arms around him and as we hold each other I remember that of all the things he's said, the one thing he hasn't done is promise he won't betray me again, probably because he can't, and I know I'll never be able to trust him.

I break away. 'I'm sorry,' I say.

Then I turn and walk towards the turnstile.

Author Details

If you've enjoyed this story and would like to find out more about Harriet James, here's how:

Twitter: @HJames_writer
Facebook: *https://www.facebook.com/HarrietJamesWriter*

Harriet's novel 'Remarkable Things' will be published by Crooked Cat in 2015

Christmas in July

Helen J Rolfe

Annie Harper had a real handle on family values. So when her ninety-year-old, Irish-born neighbour, Eleanor, invited her to celebrate Christmas in July at a glamorous hotel in Sydney's Upper Blue Mountains, there was no way that Annie was going to let her down.

The engine in Annie's little blue car churned out the heat as it crept its way towards the quaint town of Butterworth. Annie had been friends with Eleanor ever since she bought the townhouse next door to the little old lady and, despite their age gap of sixty years, the pair had bonded over their mutual frustration at junk mail being shoved into their unsuspecting letterboxes. Before long they were meeting regularly over tea and scones in either townhouse courtyard. Annie helped Eleanor with her weekly shop, and when Eleanor made family-sized cakes and biscuits she brought the leftovers for Annie and her friends. Annie's own grandmother died five years ago but they had been close right up until the end, and Annie was determined that, even though Eleanor's own family appeared to have forgotten about her, she could step in and see that she was well looked after. What Eleanor lacked in family, she certainly made up for in friends.

Annie took the turning off the main road towards Butterworth and the further she climbed into the mountains, the more the location held a promise of a magical day. The trees were tipped with frost and almost covered by low lying cloud, and the surrounding fields were flecked with white where the lack of sun had failed to warm the earth on a winter's morning.

In all the time that Annie had known Eleanor, she had never once seen a family member show their face; never heard about a visit or even an impending one. Eleanor mentioned them, in particular her grandson Jack, but Annie suspected that it was through the proverbial rose-tinted glasses.

As the road narrowed and Annie began to think that she was going to have to pull over and check the map, Butterworth Manor came into view. The gravel crunched beneath her tyres as she drove through the gates and followed the crescent driveway around to the car park, and when she climbed out of the car her breath plumed against the cold air as she made her way to the grand entrance of the hotel.

'Annie!' Eleanor was waiting in reception as Annie pushed open the enormous wooden door with the wrought-iron knocker and a holly wreath with ruby red berries.

Annie hugged Eleanor tightly. 'Let me check in, and then I can relax.'

The twinkle in Eleanor's eyes competed with the lights strung across reception and the tree off to the left which stood as tall as the ceiling. Eleanor waited impatiently for Annie to go through the formalities, get a key to her room, and pass the porter her overnight bag.

'Come, let me introduce you to everyone,' said Eleanor. Her close-knit group of friends, all of whom Annie had met at various times since she'd known Eleanor, looked as excited as each other. It was a joy to see and even though their ages were much closer to Eleanor's than Annie's own thirty years, their sense of fun seemed timeless.

'This place is gorgeous.' Annie stood beside the tree and her eyes followed the shiny baubles, twinkly lights, and white frosted ornaments all the way to the top. 'It's just like –'

'Christmas,' Eleanor finished for her.

Annie grinned. Born and bred in the Southern Hemisphere where winter fell in June and July, this expat tradition of Christmas-themed celebrations held mid-year was something she'd never seen before. But it was truly magical.

She looked across at Eleanor. 'You look beautiful today.'

With a wave of her hand Eleanor dismissed the compliment. Glowing, in a royal blue dress with her curly hair pulled away from her face with bobby pins, she said, 'You're the one who's beautiful, Annie Harper.'

Annie's strawberry blonde hair was swept away from her face in an elegant chignon and instructed to dress for the festivities she wore an emerald green, crushed-velvet dress which flattered her curves.

'And you're wearing the necklace,' Eleanor gushed.

Annie ran her fingers across the pear-cut emerald pendant that hung on a silver chain around her neck. Eleanor had given it to her last month on her thirtieth birthday and although Annie hadn't wanted to accept such an exquisite gift from her at first – it hadn't felt right – Eleanor had been most insistent and told her that at her age she could do whatever she wanted with her money.

With the scent of pine hanging in the air, Annie spotted a cluster of mistletoe tied above the doorway to the room. 'I hope you've got someone in mind for that.'

'Cheeky devil,' Eleanor giggled. 'I plan to live vicariously through you of course!'

'You'll be lucky,' Annie giggled. The average age in the room had to be at least eighty-five.

'Come on, it looks as though Millie's starting up.' Eleanor nodded to the lady sitting at the baby grand piano in the centre of the room.

'Let's enjoy it while we can. She'll only be able to play for thirty minutes or so, then her arthritis will get the better of her and she'll need to take a break.'

Millie's hands cantered across the keys, belting out Christmas songs old and new and spreading a blanket of joy over everyone. Eleanor stood, arm in arm with Annie as they listened, singing when they knew the words.

'If she gets too tired, we'll put my iPod on. It's full of Christmas music thanks to Jack,' said Eleanor proudly.

Annie wondered whether the old lady was as enamoured as she made out, or whether she would've preferred Jack to spend the money on a plane ticket to come and see her, rather than downloading Christmas tunes.

'Why do you keep looking out the window?' Annie asked Eleanor who seemed unusually distracted.

'No reason.'

Annie clasped both hands against her chest and feigned hurt. 'Have you been cheating on me and found another thirty year old friend? Are they coming here today?'

'Oh stop it!' Eleanor giggled. They'd always had an easy repartee, both able to effortlessly coax a smile out of the other one.

'You're smiling like you've got something up your sleeve,' Annie persisted.

'What nonsense.'

'Then why do you keep looking outside?'

The increasing volume of the piano and voices belting out *We Wish You a Merry Christmas* put pay to any further inquisition, and as the singing continued, Annie's eyes were drawn to the window. She leaned closer to Eleanor and whispered in her ear. 'Did you arrange this?'

'Arrange what?' Eleanor was gearing herself up for the next song now.

'Take a look out of the window.'

Eleanor's voice caught. 'It's snowing.' Her eyes held a sheen and Annie wondered for a moment whether she should help her over to a chair.

'I thought you'd be pleased, Eleanor; it's a white Christmas in July.'

Eleanor's gaze was transfixed to the first flakes of snow that Butterworth had seen this winter. One by one the snowflakes drifted down as though someone was standing on a gigantic ladder outside and sifting them over the crescent driveway of the Manor.

'I am pleased,' said Eleanor. 'I wish for this every year. Sorry, Annie, I'm just a little overwhelmed.'

Annie squeezed Eleanor's shoulder.

'There's one more thing that would make today extra perfect,' Eleanor smiled.

'Are Santa and his reindeer about to make an appearance?'

Eleanor grinned. 'Actually, there are two things...' She led the way over to a table on the far wall. From a silver-plated punch bowl she ladled out two servings of mulled wine and handed one to Annie. 'That's number one...'

Annie took the glass and asked, 'What's the other one?'

Eleanor weaved her way back over to the window so that they could watch the snow, and Annie sipped the mulled wine letting the warm liquid ooze down to her tummy.

Eleanor nodded towards the car pulling up in the car park. 'There... That's the second thing that could make today extra perfect.'

Through the white flakes and the low lying cloud Annie saw a sleek, midnight blue Mercedes pull in to view. It fitted right in with the grandeur of the place.

'You've bought yourself a new car?' Annie joked.

'I'm going to have to do something about that sense of humour of yours, Annie.'

'Sorry, I'll stop it now.'

Eleanor grinned as the door to the Mercedes opened. 'It's Jack, my grandson.'

Annie's love life had taken a serious nosedive right before she met Eleanor for the first time, so it was no secret that she was single. In fact, it had been the topic of discussion over many a cup of tea and cake. But Annie had always thought that she was safe from any matchmaking by Eleanor, because neither Jack nor any other male member of her family had ever shown his face.

Annie had always pictured Jack as a middle-aged man with a paunch, balding, and with a mobile phone stuck to his ear so that he could do his international deals on the fly. He definitely didn't sound like someone who understood the value of family, and as far as Annie was concerned, that was a deal-breaker for her. But the man striding across the car park towards the entrance to the hotel now was the polar opposite of all those things.

Annie stepped out of their line of vision when Eleanor scampered off to greet Jack in reception, but she could see him in the reflection of the mirror behind the grand teak desk as you stepped into the entrance hall. Instead of a paunch he looked to have a toned body beneath a black dress shirt when he took of his coat; instead of poor-fitting scruffy jeans he had a smart, dark denim pair; and instead of losing his hair he had lustrous, jet black hair that Annie noticed was a little longer on top. As the door shut behind him, Annie watched his ringers ruffle his hair to get rid of any lingering snowflakes.

Eleanor didn't waste any time dragging her grandson in to meet everyone and Annie hovered beside the mantelpiece pretending to be mesmerised by the miniature wooden nativity scene.

Eleanor's voice was soon behind her. 'Annie, love, I'd like you to meet Jack.'

She had to hand it to her; Eleanor had played this set-up perfectly. She had had no idea that she would be introduced to Jack today, and judging by the look on his face, he had only expected a room of oldies too.

Annie turned round clutching her glass of mulled wine. Why was it always the good-looking ones who broke hearts?

When he spoke, Jack's voice was as warm as the flames beside them. 'It's lovely to meet you.'

'Likewise,' Annie replied. 'I've heard a lot about you.'

'All good things I hope?'

Of course it was good, which was more than could be said for Annie's own opinion.

'I'm so glad you're both here.' Eleanor grinned.

She wasn't fooling Annie; Annie knew exactly the sort of matchmaking plan on the old lady's mind, and it wasn't going to work.

Jack looked around him at the flickering lights on the Christmas tree, the nativity on the mantelpiece, the holly and ivy arrangement in the vase beside the piano. 'You've certainly gone all out this year, Gran.'

'I have, haven't I?'

'It makes a change to have it in a hotel too, and it means that you'll get spoiled for a change.' Jack gave Eleanor's shoulders a squeeze and planted a kiss on her cheek. 'Talking of spoiling you...' Jack let a small, white box tied with a red satin bow drop out of his sleeve, and handed it to Eleanor. 'Merry Christmas, Gran.'

'Oh Jack –'

'Don't tell me I shouldn't have, because I wanted to.'

'Can I open it now?'

'Of course you can, although you do realise that it's five months too early.'

Eleanor turned to Annie. 'He never understood the need to have Christmas in July.' And then she nodded over to the room on the opposite side of the reception where children were congregating around the big man himself. 'If Santa over there hears you saying that, you'll never get what you want for Christmas young man.'

Annie leaned closer to Eleanor and whispered, 'I didn't realise we were exchanging gifts.'

'Don't worry,' Eleanor replied, not bothering to hide her response from her grandson, 'the rest of us aren't giving presents. This is Jack's attempt to buy his way into my heart.'

Well that sounded about right.

Eleanor pulled the box open. 'Jack... it's... I don't know what to say.'

He smiled. 'It's a beautiful brooch, for a beautiful person.'

Eleanor held his gaze for a moment. 'Is it... is it the...?'

He nodded and Annie felt strangely excluded from the moment. She watched Jack pin the brooch carefully to Eleanor's dress and as a subtle wave of manly aftershave came her way – a smell she could've almost predicted when the man was as impeccably dressed and well-groomed as Jack – Annie leaned in to admire the brooch.

'It's gorgeous, Eleanor,' said Annie, gazing at the diamonds set around an iridescent blue stone that appeared to change colour depending on the light. She turned to Jack. 'You've got good taste.'

'I certainly have.'

She looked away from the marine-blue eyes that had caused a zip of electricity in her tummy when he held her stare. She needed to fight every instinct to tell Jack that one visit and an expensive brooch didn't make up for how little time he gave his grandmother. But this was Eleanor's celebration and it was to be a happy one. Jack was here for the day and that's what she needed to remember, and after today, well, Eleanor would have her on hand to pick up the pieces when once again her family deserted her.

'Jack, I'll get you a glass of this wonderful mulled wine.' Eleanor left them alone and Annie had no doubt that she would take her time getting the drink.

When Eleanor was out of earshot Annie said, 'I assumed that you'd be off travelling the globe; that's what Eleanor told me last week when I asked who was coming to her Christmas in July party.'

'I cut my trip short to surprise her.' He seemed amused by her obvious cynicism. 'There's no way I'd miss this. I think she loves this day as much as Christmas itself.'

'You don't share her enthusiasm?' She hid behind her glass of cinnamon-infused mulled wine.

'Actually I quite enjoy it. It's like Christmas but without the pressure.'

Eleanor had never divulged much about her family and Annie wondered what 'pressure' he was referring too. Eleanor talked about Jack a lot: how he was a successful businessman flitting from one country to the next, but she had never really spoken about anyone else in her family. Perhaps she was too proud; perhaps it was too upsetting to talk about.

'You don't see much of her, do you?' Annie's question was out before she had a chance to remind herself that they were here for Eleanor, not to throw around accusations and demand explanations. She partially blamed the mulled wine for the fire in her belly.

'What's that supposed to mean?' he asked.

'It's not supposed to mean anything.'

'No, come on, if you have something to say, please, feel free.'

'She's on her own a lot, that's all.' Annie wished she'd never opened her mouth.

'I make sure she's well looked after.'

Annie looked over to Eleanor standing next to Millie with no extra glass of mulled wine in sight. Her tone softened slightly. 'She may be healthy, physically, but don't you think she gets lonely?' Annie hated to think of her ageing parents, one day being all alone. Her own grandmother never was and she was proud that that had been the case.

'She has lots of friends, and I'm only a phone call away,' said Jack.

By now Eleanor had seen them looking over and she scurried off towards the punch bowl filled with mulled wine to fulfil the task she was supposed to.

Jack kept his voice low. 'Now, if you've finished interrogating me I'd like to enjoy the day. Or do I need your permission for that, Annie?'

The sound of her name on his lips had her for a moment as he casually leaned against the table and said, 'Some people might say that you're only visiting my grandmother because you're after her money.'

'What?'

Shrugging he added, 'Maybe you're hoping she'll include you in her will if you become close enough.'

Hand on hips she hissed at him, 'I don't believe this!'

He seemed amused and calmly added, 'It's about as accurate as you suggesting that I neglect my grandmother, and it's based on about as much evidence.'

Point two to Jack.

His assessment was spot on but it didn't make it any less hurtful. Annie lowered her voice as Eleanor made her way slowly towards them, a fresh glass of mulled wine cupped between her hands. 'I resent the insinuation that I'm friendly with your grandmother for any other reason than I enjoy her company.'

Eleanor's reappearance put pay to any further rebuke and as though the conversation had never happened, Jack noticed Annie's empty glass and asked, 'Can I get you another?'

Determined not to ruin this day for Eleanor, she replied, 'Yes please, that'd be lovely.'

'I assume you're staying overnight?' he asked.

What did that have to do with anything?

'I'd get you a soft drink otherwise,' he explained, with a hint of a smile as though he knew he'd momentarily surprised her at the reference to staying the night in the same hotel as he was.

Cursing her sudden attack of the nerves, Annie cleared her throat. 'Yes, that's right. I'll be staying here tonight.' Why did it feel as though he could undress her with his eyes?

When Jack reached out for her glass, his fingers brushed along the back of her hand. Her cheeks coloured against her strawberry blonde hair and Annie felt sure that Eleanor hadn't missed the moment. She hid her embarrassment by focusing on Millie, who was underway with her second stint on the baby grand piano, this time belting out one of the liveliest renditions of *Away in a Manger* that Annie had ever heard. So much for the arthritic hands – the woman had barely stopped playing since Annie arrived.

Jack did the honours with the drinks and Eleanor stood beside Annie, giving her the odd sideways glance. To Annie's relief the piano was too loud to be grilled about the way she had reacted to Jack just now. But the second Jack returned brandishing the refilled glasses, Eleanor made a quick getaway.

Annie watched Eleanor singing her heart out alongside Millie and Josephine. She couldn't help noticing that when Jack looked their way, all three ladies beamed back at him, eyes dancing.

Did he have that effect on all women?

'Millie used to teach the piano,' said Jack. 'If I ever get more time she's said that she'll teach me too.'

'Really?' asked Annie.

'Don't look so surprised. I've wanted to learn for a long time.'

'You don't strike me as the type to want to play music.'

He turned his attention towards Annie. 'There's a lot about me and my family that you don't know, Annie Harper.' He reached out to the food table and took a cracker topped with brie and pear. 'Contrary to what you might believe, I do talk with my grandmother. Granted, I'm not physically present much in her life, but believe me when I say that I'm always there.'

Annie wondered whether he'd rehearsed that speech as he ladled out the mulled wine.

Millie launched into a bittersweet rendition of *White Christmas* and just as Annie was about to ask more about Jack's family, he abruptly left her side. In a split second he was across the room with Eleanor. One arm circled his Grandmother's waist and with the other he held her hand in the air as they swayed to the music.

In an effort not to stare at them, Annie turned away as she tried to work out what had just happened. Eleanor had gone from laughter and frivolity to looking as though the weight of the world was on her shoulders, and in that moment, Jack had been there to catch her. How much did she really know about Eleanor and her family? Before today, she would've said she knew Eleanor pretty well, and even Jack whom she had never met.

Annie watched the pair dance as though the rest of the room didn't exist. Cracks in her opinions, particularly of Jack, had begun to appear and the more she watched him, the more they grew. Here he was, proving her wrong: Tall and strong, dark and annoyingly handsome, and more importantly, there by his grandmother's side.

As the tune came to an end, Jack's gaze found Annie. But she couldn't look at him. She moved over to the Christmas tree and watched the scene unfolding outside the bay window. The cold snap had blanketed the gravel driveway outside in snow, and the parked cars sat like individual Christmas cakes covered in the traditional white frosting. She reached a finger up to the window and, unable to resist, wrote her name in the condensation.

'I wanted to do that too,' Jack's voice startled her and she couldn't help but smile. 'I used to do that in the mirrors at home when I was little, after bath time,' he continued. 'It annoyed Mum no end because she claimed it left smears in the glass, but Gran thought it funny.'

'I can imagine.' Annie rubbed her wet finger against the palm of her hand to warm it up. 'Did you enjoy your dance?'

Before Jack had a chance to answer, Eleanor appeared beside them. 'He's a fabulous dancer,' she said, never one to miss a moment.

Annie couldn't help but admire her tenacity but anxious to deflect from her nerves around Jack, she asked, 'What's the stone?' and pointed to Eleanor's brooch.

Eleanor's fingers rested on the jewel and she looked at Jack and then back at Annie. 'It's a moonstone in the middle, diamonds around the outside.'

Annie hoped that Jack didn't assume that admiring the jewellery was all part of the ruse to befriend Eleanor and burrow her way into the old lady's bank account. Could he really have formed as low an opinion of her as she had of him, without knowing all the facts?

'Jack designed it himself.' Eleanor took a deep breath and said, 'The moonstone has a very special meaning in my life.' And with that she patted Annie's hand before she rose and went to mingle with the other guests again.

Jack got straight to the point. 'Why do I get the feeling that you've decided not to like me?'

'I've done no such thing,' she said defensively. 'You're being paranoid.'

He stood close enough now that she noticed the tiny nick in the skin just above his lip where he must've cut himself shaving. 'I noticed how swiftly you changed the subject when Eleanor told you that I was a good dancer,' he said.

'I did nothing of the sort.' Another sip of mulled wine and Annie changed the subject. 'What's the significance of the moonstone?'

He leaned against the windowsill right next to where she had written her name with her finger and his eyes levelled with hers. 'Eleanor was only ever in love once,' he began, 'and when my grandfather proposed, they couldn't afford a flashy ring. He had found a moonstone – don't ask me where – and put it in a box lined with cotton wool, which he showed to her when he was down on one knee. He promised Eleanor there and then that one day he would have it made into something beautiful, just like her.'

'That's incredibly romantic.'

Jack looked over at Eleanor and smiled. 'My grandfather proposed on Christmas Eve when the snow was falling outside and *White Christmas* played in the background. So yes, he was incredibly romantic.'

Annie gasped. 'Was that why -?'

'As soon as Millie started playing *White Christmas* on the piano, I saw my Grandmother's face change. It caught her quite off-guard.' He looked around at the grandeur of the hotel from the snow outside and the roaring fire at one end of the room, to the Christmas tree that could mesmerise even the most hardened person to the joys of Christmas.

Annie felt a sudden rush of admiration that when Eleanor really needed him, Jack had actually been there.

'Christmas was always a huge celebration in my family,' he continued, 'and when my grandfather died, Eleanor couldn't bear anything to do with the season.'

Annie sat on the windowsill next to him. 'I can't imagine that.'

'It's true. She put Christmas on hold for three years: no roast dinner at lunchtime, no music, no gifts and no marking the day in any way. I was old enough to remember it and I know that Dad found it upsetting, but he had no idea how to handle the situation – emotions weren't exactly his forte.'

Annie wanted to ask Jack more about this family that seemed to have so many layers beneath the surface. His demeanour was softer than when he first arrived at the party, but then perhaps that was because Annie could see him as a real person now, rather than somebody she had built up in her own mind, in her own way.

Jack raised a hand to wave at Eleanor when she sneaked another glance their way. 'We're close, Eleanor and I.'

'I realise that now.'

'Between you and me though,' he nudged Annie, 'I think her emotions may be heightened by too much of this stuff.' He indicated his glass filled with a good measure of mulled wine.

Annie looked over at Eleanor who stood chatting to one of her friends, and her eyes fell on the jewel in Eleanor's brooch. It was giving off a purple shade as she stood next to the twinkly lights of the tree.

'What happened to the moonstone that your grandfather gave Eleanor?' Annie asked Jack.

Jack kept his eyes fixed on the brooch too. 'You're looking right at it. We thought she'd lost it when she moved house a couple of years ago – she was so upset at the time – but I found it earlier this year amongst a box filled with board games; it'd fallen loose, out of its box. It took a lot of willpower to keep that quiet, let me tell you.'

'I'll bet,' said Annie. 'And you had it made into a beautiful brooch as a surprise?'

Jack nodded and Annie waited for him to say something else, but he didn't. She wondered whether she had been wrong about him or whether she was simply caught up in the magic of the day.

Their conversation was interrupted by the announcement that lunch was about to be served in the dining room, but the move to another place didn't disappoint. An enormous square window at the end of the room looked out over fields that were slowly being blanketed with a layer of snow, and another, smaller, Christmas tree stood in the corner of the room. A rich, mahogany table stretched down the centre and on top were silver-plated bowls and pots and white place settings with an elegant gold rim.

Jack sat on one side of Eleanor, Annie on the other, and the sumptuous feast began. Crackers were pulled, the tacky gifts inside were giggled over, and laughter erupted as the jokes were reeled off one by one. When lunch was over, Jack took Eleanor back to the main room and settled her into a chair looking out of the window at the snow that was still falling. Millie sidled up next to Annie now that the chair beside her was empty.

'Jack was all set to be an investment banker,' Millie whispered without preamble. Annie knew then that she had been sprung staring at him, again.

'He landed a top job overseas, in London,' Millie continued.

Annie smiled and turned in her chair. Millie obviously liked to gossip when she wasn't playing the piano, and Annie wanted to make the most of the opportunity to find out more about this family. 'So what happened?' she asked.

Millie shuffled closer still and kept her voice low. 'Eleanor's late husband started a jewellery business before they were married and then when he died, Eleanor handed it down to her son, Dale.'

'Is Dale Jack's father?'

Millie nodded. 'Dale got into all sorts of trouble, financially, and his dishonesty about the business created an enormous family rift that never healed.'

'That's sad.' Annie's own father was head of the local art group, member of the chess club; an honest, truly nice man. She couldn't imagine having a Dad who was anything but.

'I don't think Eleanor or Jack have seen or heard from Dale in years,' said Millie.

'That must be hard on them both.'

Millie nodded over towards Jack as he draped a blanket across a sleeping Eleanor's lap and kissed her gently on the forehead. 'It is very sad, but the bond between Eleanor and Jack will never break. Just look at them.' Annie did exactly that. 'Jack stepped in at the right time, and I think that it was the making of him; it didn't just save the jewellery business.'

'What makes you say that?'

'I met Jack years ago. Back then he was all about making money, having the best of everything, fast cars. Mind you,' Millie giggled, 'he still likes a good set of wheels.'

Annie smiled as she thought about the posh Mercedes parked outside not far from her own little car.

'The jewellery business softened him,' said Millie, 'and not in a bad way.'

Annie lifted her glass of wine to her lips and with her sip came the realisation of what Millie's words actually meant. 'So what exactly is Jack's role in the business?' Annie wanted to be abundantly clear about this family from now on. 'Does he manage the accounts? Buy in jewellery?'

Millie giggled. 'Oh no dear, he's far too talented for that. No, Jack *makes* the jewellery, with his own fair hands. Didn't you see the brooch he made for Eleanor?'

Millie's voice trailed off and Annie couldn't hear a word she was saying anymore, because she was too busy coming to grips with the revelation that Jack was so very different to the man she'd assumed him to be. She'd assumed that he had paid to have that moonstone made into something beautiful; she'd never for one second imagined that he could be the man behind something as intricate and as personal as that brooch; something that spoke of beauty and heart.

Millie took to the piano once again and Annie felt the need to move with all that food layering her stomach. She stood beside the fireplace and watched as the flames licked at the logs, sending glowing dots onto the hearth when it crackled.

When Jack joined her she nodded towards a sleeping Eleanor and said, 'You must have the magic touch.'

Millie tinkled *Have Yourself a Merry Little Christmas* in the background and, looking thoughtful, Jack said, 'I'm sorry if I was rude to you earlier.'

'When were you rude?'

'When I suggested that your friendship with my grandmother was anything but genuine.'

'Oh, that.'

'Yes, that. And it was incredibly rude of me.' He nodded humbly. 'I apologise.'

'Apology accepted.'

'Thank you.'

They moved over to the doorway, away from the festivities. Focusing on the twinkly lights of the Christmas tree, Annie asked, 'So you don't think that I'm after an old lady's money anymore?'

His lips curved into an irresistible smile when he realised that she was teasing him, and only now did Annie see the family resemblance to Eleanor. They both had the same marine-blue eyes, the eyebrows that knitted together when they were trying to figure something out.

'I know my grandmother pretty well,' he explained, leaning against the door jamb. 'She may look like a naïve ninety-year-old but if she had any inkling that you were up to no good then she wouldn't adore you as much as she tells me she does.'

Annie blushed. 'She's generous with her friendship and I'd never take advantage of that.'

'I know that now.'

She wished he wouldn't stare quite so intensely. She had no glass of wine to hide behind now and she wished she hadn't left it back in the dining room.

'The necklace suits you by the way.' He nodded to the emerald cluster hanging around her neck.

'I didn't want to accept it.'

He held up a hand. 'No need to be defensive. Eleanor's a persistent old thing when she wants to be. So do you like it?'

'Are you kidding?' Annie's fingers ran across the emerald. 'It's beautiful.'

He focused on the stone. 'Eleanor was quite insistent on the colour for you, and I can see why.'

He was staring again as Annie began to realise what he was saying. 'So you designed this, and made it?'

'With my own fair hand,' he shrugged. 'And after many lengthy phone calls might I add. I was in the UK at the time and the time difference meant she had me working on it at all hours.'

Annie didn't know what to say. His eyes held hers and she could feel the necklace against her collarbone as though his hands were resting there too, still teasing the beautiful jewellery into the perfect shape.

'The international side of the business is thriving,' he explained, moving a step closer.

She cleared her throat. 'That's great.'

'It means that I'll be around a lot more.'

He moved even closer still and she held her breath when he reached out and lifted the emerald pendant. 'My father left Eleanor with no money, only debt,' he explained, so close that his aftershave wreaked havoc with her senses. 'It's taken many years to get her straight, set her up with a place to live, not allow the jewellery business to fall apart. Travelling the world was the solution to our problems and it was something I had to do.'

'It was wrong for me to judge you,' Annie breathed. 'I assumed that you cared more about your career than anything, or anyone else.'

His laughter caught her off guard. 'Ten years ago you would've been exactly right. I expect Eleanor will tell you the whole story one day, but let's just say that she, and circumstances, changed me. And for the better, I might add.'

Annie had no problem with being proven wrong. She took a step back and looked over at Eleanor asleep in the chair. 'Do you think we should help her up to her room?'

'Are you kidding? She'd be devastated to miss the rest of the day. No, this is a power nap and then she'll be raring to go again.'

'Maybe no more mulled wine for her though,' Annie giggled.

His eyes lingered on her and she looked up at him when he asked, 'Do you think that maybe we could start again, Annie? I think that we got off to a bad start.' He held out his hand. 'Allow me to introduce myself. I'm Jack Falmer, business man and maker of fine jewellery.'

Annie grinned. 'Annie Harper.' She took his hand and the feel of skin on skin set every nerve ending in her body alight. 'Media Officer at the children's hospital, and lover of exquisite jewellery.'

His smile reached his eyes now. 'See, that's better.' Instead of dropping her hand he held onto it. 'I feel like we know each other better already.' Still he didn't let go. His eyes sparkled with mischief when he glanced upwards. 'You know what this means, don't you?'

Her heart thumped at a million miles an hour when she realised that they were standing directly below the mistletoe. Their bodies slowly moved closer and Jack gently reached out to touch her cheek, tilting her face up towards his.

The feel of Jack's lips warmed Annie right through and when they pulled apart he put his arms around her and held her close.

'You know I really admire you, Annie.'

She gulped as the back of his hand brushed lightly against her cheek. 'Why?'

'You care about people. Not many people would adopt a gran like you have.'

She shrugged. 'I've always been close to my own family and I'd hate to think of any of them being alone. And besides, Eleanor is pretty easy to like. And she makes a mean chocolate mud cake!'

'Ah, the real reason behind your friendship with my grandmother comes out now,' he laughed. 'So tell me, Annie. Will your family approve of me?'

'I guess you'll have to meet them and we'll see,' she teased.

'I can do that, no problem.'

When he moved to kiss her again she said. 'There's just one thing.'

'Oh?'

'You'll have to be approved by my siblings if we want to start seeing each other properly.'

'That's fine by me.' He moved in again. 'Do you have a grandmother I can impress the way you've impressed mine?'

His lips almost on hers she said, 'No, but I do have four brothers.'

'Four?'

'Don't look so nervous.'

'I'm not.'

She was enjoying this. When he'd first walked in to the hotel she would've bet that he couldn't be rattled by much. But the idea of four brothers had certainly done that. Giggling she looked over at the Christmas tree, at the star that glowed at the top heralding the celebration. And then she noticed that instead of snoozing in the chair where Jack had left her, Eleanor had pulled on her coat, scarf and gloves and was outside the hotel.

'What's she up to?' Jack had noticed the same thing.

'I haven't a clue.'

Hand in hand they braved the outside, through the vast entrance door to Butterworth Manor. The cold snap sent goose pimples shooting up Annie's arms and across her chest, but Jack's arm warmed her enough as they walked over to where Eleanor stood, a stick in her hand leaning over to write something in the snow.

'What on earth are you doing?' Jack asked. 'You'll freeze out here.'

Jack and Annie looked down at the snow beneath the window where Annie had written her own name in the condensation. Using a stick, Eleanor had written the names: Annie & Jack.

Jack grinned. 'This looks like fun.' He took the stick from his Grandmother's hand.

Annie snuggled in close to Jack as she watched him etch a giant heart around their names.

'Let's go back inside,' Jack smiled. 'I owe you a dance, Annie Harper.'

Annie grinned and as Eleanor led the way, the snow began to fall more heavily and wrapped Butterworth Manor in the magic that was Christmas in July.

Author Details

If you've enjoyed this story and would like to find out more about Helen J Rolfe, here's how:

Twitter: @HjRolfe
Facebook: helenjrolfe

Helen's debut novel, 'The Friendship Tree,' will be published by Crooked Cat in early to mid 2015

A Pistol For Propriety

Alys West

Harriet Hardy took her pistol from her reticule and flipped open the barrel. Unlocking her desk drawer she took a small, shiny bullet from a cardboard box and slid it into the missing space. Clicking the barrel shut, she returned the gun to her bag, added two sets of keys and snapped it shut.

Standing, she smoothed the creases from her charcoal grey skirt and put on her coat. On the back of her office door hung a mirror. She shoved a couple of pins more firmly into her dark brown hair before positioning her wide-brimmed hat at the exact angle that fashion required.

In the outer office, Mr Jowett, the chief clerk turned away from the calculating machine and looked at her over his half-moon glasses. 'I do wish, Miss Hardy, that you'd let me take this appointment. We know nothing about this man.'

'We know he's in Debretts and Viscount Ripley, I mean, Lord Ripley–' Harriet corrected herself having earlier ascertained the correct form of address from that estimable volume '–asked for me personally in his letter. We cannot afford to offend the aristocracy. Not even the Irish ones.' From Debretts she'd also learned that the Viscount was heir to an estate in County Carlow. 'Especially–' Harriet added, smoothing on her gloves '–when they want to rent one of our best properties for two weeks in December.'

'If you'd let John–' Mr Jowett gestured at the office boy who'd just brought in a bundle of files '–escort you to The Crescent I would be happier.'

Harriet fiddled with the clasp on her bag. Sometimes Mr Jowett was more of a mother hen than her own mama. But then he actually knew what she got up to during office hours. Harriet was very careful to make sure that Mrs Hardy thought that she did nothing more strenuous than book-keeping.

Yet, after what had happened yesterday, perhaps Mr Jowett did have a point.

'Oh, very well,' she said gesturing to John who dumped the files with alacrity, pulled his cap from his pocket and followed her. Outside the office the brass plaque that read '**Hardy & Sons – Whitby**' shone in the weak November sunlight. The Hardy in question was her great uncle, Humphrey, who'd started the firm and acquired a number of properties while land in Whitby was cheap. When the place became a popular resort he'd started acting as agent for other property owners who wanted to rent out their houses.

With John trailing two steps behind her, Harriet walked briskly up West Terrace towards The Crescent. Hardy & Co owned two of the elegant Regency houses and she fully intended to rent one of them to Lord Ripley at very profitable rates.

Hearing the sound of the omnibus puffing up the hill behind her, her feet slowed. Waiting for it to pass before she crossed the road, she turned her head to avoid the steam billowing behind it. The North Sea was its usual winter grey, the waves tipped with flecks of white as they hurtled towards the cliffs. The harbour was busy with trawlers leaving on the high tide. Red roofed houses climbed up the steep slope to St Mary's Church and the abbey; both newly famous from the adventures of Count Dracula.

Crossing the road, Harriet proceeded along The Crescent to number five. Taking the keys from her bag, she opened the door. Not having been inhabited for over a month the house smelled musty and unlived in. John came in behind her and hovered uncertainly.

'Open a few windows in the back of the house,' she told him. He scurried away and she moved into the drawing room and slid the sash window up half an inch letting in a blast of brisk sea air.

As she turned the bell rang. She counted to five and then went to answer it. On the doorstep was a man dressed in a tan leather flying jacket that buttoned up the left side of his broad chest. His brown trousers, marked with streaks of soot across the thighs, were tucked into heavy boots that fastened with brass buckles. He was tall, well over six foot with dark hair that was brushed back from his forehead in the latest style and a neat, fashionable beard.

'Miss Hardy, I presume?' he enquired. His deep, soft voice triggered a distant memory that she couldn't place.

Harriet blinked at him. 'And you are?'

'Lord Ripley. We have an appointment. I must apologise for my attire. I flew to Scarborough and there were some difficulties with the landing which meant I had to come straight here by steam automobile and I haven't had the opportunity to change into something more–' his hand moved to take in his clothes and Harriet saw that he held a leather cap and brass goggles '–conventional for our meeting.'

'Forgive me but I was expecting someone older. According to Debretts Lord Ripley was born in 1845 which you, sir, were not.'

The man appeared slightly discomposed by her directness. 'You're right of course but I'm afraid events have overtaken Debretts. That entry refers to my uncle who was indeed born in 1845. However, he is now the Earl of Carlow. The former earl sadly died in January.' He gestured to the black band around his upper arm. Taking in the width of his arm highlighted by the tightness of his leather jacket Harriet hastily returned her eyes to his face. 'I appear–' the man patted his jacket pockets '–to have left my cards in my coat but I assure you I am Lord Ripley. If you prefer I can return later with my cards and a letter of introduction.'

Harriet hesitated. Leaving aside the man's unconventional appearance, if he was who he said he was then securing him as a tenant would be a big coup for the firm. She could easily imagine how other prospective tenants would react when she dropped into conversation that Lord Ripley had rented one of their properties. For that kind of prestige she was prepared to dispense with a few formalities.

'No that will not be necessary, my Lord,' she said, holding the door open for him and gesturing for him to enter. He dropped his cap and goggles on the carved walnut table and looked around him. 'I see you have steam heating and gas lighting. Is that all over the house?'

'Indeed. The house was updated a few years ago. I personally oversaw the renovations and I can promise you that all modern conveniences were installed. This is now one of the most up to date and luxurious properties in Whitby.' Harriet gestured for him to follow her. 'There are three reception rooms,' she said. 'Dining room, library and this drawing room which as you can see is very elegantly proportioned and appointed in the latest fashion.' Her sweeping hand movement took in the sofas, chairs and occasional tables that she'd chosen from Leak & Thorp in York. They were all at least eight years old and therefore could hardly be called the latest fashion but Lord Ripley didn't look like a man who was well versed in interior design.

The Viscount strode past her into the room. 'You can spare me the patter, Miss Hardy. I can see for myself.' He grinned at her over his shoulder which not only took the sting from his words but made Harriet's heart beat a little faster.

Moving over to the piano, she stared at his back. He stood, long strong legs planted squarely on the Axminster carpet, staring out of the window, apparently more interested in the view than the décor. What was it about the way he spoke which took her back to those last lazy days in York? Careless, summer afternoons of tennis parties and glorious evenings dancing in the elegant Assembly Rooms. The young men she'd known then had that same casual confidence, same easy charm.

She shook her head slightly. No point dwelling on the past.

'Is there any information you would like to know?' she asked. Her tone was more pointed than she'd intended. 'My lord,' she added, more quietly.

'You can stop tripping over the title for one thing.' He turned to give her a quick glance over his shoulder. 'I've only had it for a few months and as I've never been one to stand on ceremony it's been hard to get used to.'

'If you wish,' Harriet said carefully. She'd not had many dealings with the nobility but this kind of behaviour seemed as unconventional as his clothes.

'I'll be visiting with my mother and two younger sisters. Amelia's been ill and mother thinks some sea air will do her good. As they're mad for this Dracula book they wouldn't consider going anywhere else.'

'Mr Stoker's book has caused quite a sensation in London I understand. Your sisters are not the only ones who want to see the places they've read about.'

'I'm just grateful they haven't taken it into their heads to want to go to Transylvania,' Lord Ripley said a little grumpily.

'May I enquire as to the ages of your sisters?' Harriet found herself drawn to join him at the window.

'Eighteen and twenty one.' As if he'd suddenly become aware of it, his hand rubbed at the soot marks on his trousers. 'I don't think they have a sensible thought between them from one day to the next.'

Harriet smiled. 'I'm sure I was no different at their age.'

Lord Ripley raised his eyebrows. 'That I cannot believe, Miss Hardy.'

His gaze held hers. She blinked and turned away. 'Shall we view the dining room?' she asked hastily. Not waiting for his reply Harriet swiftly returned to the hall and opened the door to the dining room.

Trailing her hand along the lengthy expanse of the mahogany table, Harriet felt a little flushed. It had been a very long time since a man had looked at her like that. Whitby society had long made it clear that her involvement in the business was considered improper and a major detriment to what few matrimonial prospects she might have. Once she'd let it be known, not long after Humphrey's death, that she was running Hardy & Co she'd been treated as an unmarriageable spinster.

Hearing Lord Ripley quietly enter the room behind her, Harriet quashed the urge to turn to look at him. At this point in a tour of the property, she'd usually point out the elegant corniced ceiling and the William Morris curtains. Having been silenced on those points she simply waited.

'Have you lived in Whitby for long?' Lord Ripley asked.

Startled by the question Harriet looked over her shoulder at him. 'Eight years.'

'And where did you live before that?'

'In York.'

'I see.' He nodded. 'And what brought you to Whitby?'

Frowning, Harriet turned. The full chilly expanse of the twelve foot mahogany table separated them. 'Family reasons.'

The Viscount walked a couple of steps towards her. 'I'm prying. I apologise. But I was in York eight years ago. Perhaps we met.'

Harriet moved back up the opposite side of the table. 'I don't think so, my Lord. I've never moved in those kinds of social circles.'

He laughed. 'Neither did I back then.' He leaned on a carved dining chair. 'Did you ever go to an Assembly Room ball?'

Harriet looked away. She had more than once. But for some reason she didn't want to admit it to this perplexing man. 'I am a woman who works for her living, Lord Ripley. I do not get invited to balls. Now if you've seen enough perhaps we can move on to the library.'

'Of course.'

'John?' she called when she reached the hall, wanting to make it clear that she was not alone in the house. The boy appeared from behind the door that led to the kitchens. Realising that she needed to find something for him to do, she said, 'Run upstairs and open the curtains and then wait there for me.'

Bedrooms, she'd found, were where gentlemen were most likely to forget themselves. And after yesterday there was a bullet hole just above the mantelpiece in the blue room to prove it.

'The library is well stocked and includes many modern novels.' Harriet swung open the door. 'There's even a copy of Dracula in case your sisters forget theirs.'

'Impressive.' Lord Ripley moved over to the book cases. 'Do you read much Miss Hardy?'

'Only account books.'

He laughed. It was a rich, infectious sound. Despite herself, Harriet found herself smiling. 'You're like me. I only read technical manuals. My sisters despair. But then I tell them what use is a novel to me when I'm flying at six hundred feet and a propeller gets stuck!'

Harriet blinked. She'd thought the jacket was just for show. 'You're a dirigible pilot?'

He grinned. 'Yes. With the Great Eastern Company.'

'Oh. I hadn't….' A blush crept up Harriet's cheeks as she realised that she couldn't possibly finish that sentence without insulting him.

'Thought I was one of the idle rich, did you?' The laugh came again.

Eyes fixed on the highly patterned carpet, Harriet blushed more deeply. The man was deeply provoking but he was potentially a very important client and if that meant she had to swallow her pride and apologise then she would. 'I….I'm sorry, my Lord. I should not have made assumptions.'

'Not unreasonable assumptions. Mother's always on at me to give it up. The previous two Viscount Ripleys died rather untimely deaths. She doesn't want me to be the third.'

There was a thread of emotion in his voice that made Harriet look up. 'Piloting dirigibles is dangerous, is it not?' she asked quietly.

'Yes but that's half the fun of it! Have you ever flown, Miss Hardy?'

Harriet shook her head. 'No. It's something I've wanted to do for a long time but...' Her father had promised a flight to London for her eighteenth birthday. Like so many other things it was a dream best forgotten.

'That's a shame. I think you'd enjoy it. If you want to give it a go, I'll take you up,' he said. 'Now that the company's opened the aerodrome at Seamer it's as easy as taking the train.'

Harriet smiled at his enthusiasm. Then she remembered she could never accept. 'Thank you, my Lord. That's a very kind offer'

'Which you won't take me up on?' he queried moving to stand closer to her.

'Regretfully I....' She blinked up at him, discomforted both by his sudden closeness and surprising ability to read the meaning behind her words. 'I think it's time I showed you the rest of the house.' She pushed past him to the door.

In the hall her hand moved to cradle her bag. The weight of her pistol was reassuring. Moving quickly to the stairs, she fell back on property particulars to fill the silence. 'There are four bedrooms. The two largest have sea views and the other two have views over the town. All of the rooms have gas lighting...'

She broke off when she heard whistling and glanced behind her. Lord Ripley's lips were puckered, his hand tapping a beat on the bannister. Recognising the tune, a lump rose to Harriet's throat as a memory filled her mind.

Dancing under the lights of a thousand candles, spinning between the marble pillars of the Assembly Rooms as the orchestra played 'After the Ball'. Charlie's arms around her. Her chest pressed against his scarlet coat. His dark eyes never leaving hers as they waltzed and waltzed.

Stepping onto the landing, Harriet shook her head and sucked in as deep a breath as her corset would allow. What was it about this man that made her remember that which was best forgotten?

Throwing open the nearest door, she gestured for the Viscount to go first. 'This is the blue bedroom.' Hovering by the open door her glance moved automatically to the mantelpiece where only one blue and white Chinese vase now stood. She was relieved to see him barely glance at the fireplace as he walked over to the four-poster bed and pressed on the mattress. 'This room would do for my mother. She likes these old-fashioned kind of beds.'

Harriet was about to assure him that there was nothing old-fashioned about that bed when the doorbell rang loudly and persistently.

'Who can that be?' Harriet frowned. 'Are you expecting anyone, my Lord?'

Shaking his head, Lord Ripley moved to the window and looked down. 'It's two policemen with a rather portly gentleman. Ugly little fellow but he looks a bit agitated.'

Harriet swallowed hard. The odious man wouldn't have returned here, would he? And with the police! Heart pounding she hurried to the window. After a quick glance, she shrank back. 'Oh no!'

'They're here to see you, Miss Hardy?'

'I fear so, my Lord.'

'Splendid!' His grin was sudden and utterly surprising. 'And to what do you owe the pleasure of a visit from The North Yorkshire constabulary?'

Harriet hesitated. She had no reason to trust him but she knew instinctively that only the truth would keep his respect and abruptly that mattered to her. Not for the business but for some other reason that she didn't have time to examine.

'The gentleman outside has formed the ridiculous idea that I tried to kill him.'

'Better and better.' Lord Ripley walked quickly to the door and called quietly, 'Boy?' When John appeared, he said, 'I believe the gentlemen outside are looking for Miss Hardy. Please tell them that we left ten minutes ago and that you heard me say I was taking her for tea at the Royal Hotel.' A coin changed hands.

'Right you are, sir. I mean, me Lord,' John said before darting away.

Lord Ripley silently slid the door shut and turned back to her. 'Now why on earth does that man think you tried to kill him?'

'Well, I did shoot in his direction. But I assure you I had no intention of actually hitting him.'

'I don't doubt it.' He stole quietly back to the window and angled himself so that he couldn't be seen by those outside. 'Do you shoot many clients or was his a special case?'

With a sigh Harriet dropped onto the chaise longue at the end of the bed. 'The gentleman made certain suggestions which no lady should be expected to hear. When I asked him to leave he refused–' Harriet fiddled with the clasp on her bag. She'd not spoken of this and it was surprisingly difficult to find the words '– and he…he…well, he made it pretty clear that he wasn't going to take no for an answer.

At that point I took my pistol from my bag and asked him again to leave. He laughed and said that... You don't need to know his exact words but he implied that I didn't know how to use a gun. I felt I had no option but to demonstrate that I can use it very well.' Pointing at the mantelpiece, she was disappointed to see that her hand shook slightly. 'If you look behind the Chinese vase you'll see the bullet hole. The gentleman was standing at least six inches away from it. There was no danger of me actually hitting him.'

'He was no gentleman.' Scowling, Lord Ripley picked up the vase and examined the hole in the wall. 'Do you carry a gun at all times, Miss Hardy?'

'I don't take it to church.'

He laughed softly. 'I'm pleased to hear it.'

Shouted words, muffled by the closed door, made them both turn their heads.

'I know she's in there,' a voice called in a pronounced Tyneside accent. 'I'm not leaving until I speak to her. The brazen harpy!'

'Perhaps we should continue this conversation elsewhere?' Lord Ripley said.

'Certainly.' Harriet opened the door to the dressing room. 'If you'll just follow me.'

Hurrying down the back stairs, Harriet felt her pulse racing. This was possibly the most insane thing she'd ever done and yet it was thrilling. To throw her lot in with a man she barely knew and make a run for it! She couldn't repress a grin as she tugged the kitchen door open and ran across the flagged floor. She'd not felt like this in years. It was the kind of excitement she used to get from riding too fast or dancing all night.

She unlocked the back door and eased it open. Daylight was fading, leaving the yard in shadow. Lord Ripley slid past her and stepped out first.

'All's clear, Miss Hardy,' he whispered.

The only way out of the yard was by half a dozen narrow steps that rose to street level. Climbing the steps after him Harriet's gaze rested momentarily on the trousers snuggly encasing his backside. Hurriedly, she glanced away. The movement unbalanced her and she wobbled.

A strong hand reached out and grabbed her arm. Held her until she reached the pavement and then lingered a moment longer than was necessary. 'Are you alright?'

'Yes, I...' Harriet glanced up and was surprised to see that his dark eyes were soft with concern. For a long moment they stood slightly too close in the dimly lit street. Then she looked down and shuffled her feet.

With a slight cough, he said, 'We need a cab. If you'll just wait here for a moment I'll see if I can flag one down.'

Harriet pointed him in the direction of West Terrace. Watching him walking quickly away, she leaned against the railings and tried to still her thoughts. Yesterday's experience had left her more shaken than she'd wanted to admit. After the loathsome man had finally left, she'd been shaking so much she could barely lock the door behind him. She'd made it as far as the kitchen before sinking into a chair. It had been a long time before she'd had the strength to even get a glass of water. Much longer before she'd felt ready to return to the office and pretend to Mr Jowett that all was well.

Heavy footsteps clattered along the pavement. Harriet's head whipped round. One of the policemen was striding towards her. Without thinking Harriet picked up her skirts and ran along the street in the direction that Lord Ripley had walked moments before. Her hat flew off but she kept going, bursting onto West Terrace and skidding inelegantly to a halt. She looked frantically around.

He was stood on the other side of the road, scanning the traffic for a cab. Harriet darted round a passing carriage. The piercing sound of a police whistle followed her.

'Cabs are in short supply. Can I make an alternative suggestion?' he asked as she reached him.

'Anything.' Harriet puffed out the word.

'This way then.' Grabbing her hand, he started to run down the hill towards the town centre. Sucking in a breath, Harriet struggled to keep up. Her corset wasn't tightly laced but it certainly wasn't designed for this kind of exertion. At the corner of John Street they slid to a halt. Lord Ripley raised his arm.

Harriet glanced behind. The policemen were converging on them. One was about to cross the road when the steam omnibus lumbered around the corner forcing him back. The other was charging down the hill behind them.

Tugging a little frantically on Lord Ripley's arm, she said, 'Why have we stopped?'

'Because our transport has arrived.' As he spoke the omnibus indicated and slowed down. 'Hop on.' Grasping her around the waist he lifted her on to the still moving platform at the rear of the vehicle and then jumped on himself.

Harriet slid into the back seat as they pulled away. She glanced behind in time to see the policeman, his face red with exertion, stagger to a halt and raise his hand to point after them.

'Oh my goodness!' Harriet's hand rose to her mouth. She turned to look at Lord Ripley in the seat next to her. 'They'll never believe me now. That man...

'The one who threatened you?'

'Yes. He's an alderman from Sunderland. They'll never take my word over his. And now I've run away from the police...This could... this could *ruin* me.'

'Then marry me?'

Harriet's eyes widened. 'What...?'

'Marry me.'

She blinked at him. 'Have you lost your mind, my Lord?'

'No. I've just been reunited with the girl I love.' He pushed his hand through his hair and it flopped forwards over his forehead. 'Unfortunately she doesn't seem to remember me. But then eight years is a long time. I shouldn't have expected...'

As his words sank in, Harriet stared into his eyes. The same familiar brown eyes. How had she not realised? Time slipped away until she was that girl dizzily in love with a young soldier. 'Charlie?' she whispered. 'Charlie Davenport?'

His smile was all the answer she needed. 'You do remember?'

'Of course. I...I mean, I can't believe it. You look so very different now.' She gestured rather confusedly at him. 'Much broader. And with the beard and your hair like that. Now it's falling in your eyes again you look much more like your old self.'

'You've not changed a bit. You're still the prettiest girl I've ever met.'

Eyes brimming, Harriet smiled a little ruefully. 'Still Charming Charlie!'

He laughed. 'I can't tell you how many times I've longed for you to call me that.' Gently he took her hand. 'You see, I'd planned... That is, you remember that last ball at the Assembly Rooms?'

'I'd forgotten it. I tried to forget everything about that time but then I heard you whistling 'After the Ball' earlier and it all came back to me.'

'Do you recall that I said I'd call on you when I got back from the visit to my aunt? That there was something in particular that I wanted to ask you?'

Harriet looked down. 'I remember.'

'I wanted to marry you, Harriet. When I got back to York I went straight to your house intending to ask for your hand. That was when I heard what had happened to your father.'

She glanced quickly up at him. 'Didn't that change your mind?' Her voice cracked but she pushed on. 'It should have done. I was the daughter of the man who'd defrauded half the city and then thrown himself in the river? No one else in the city wanted to know us.'

'It didn't change how I felt about you, Harriet. Nothing your father did could do that.'

'No one else saw it like that. Father's creditors took everything. There was barely enough money left for his funeral. Uncle Humphrey was one of the few people who came to it. He offered Mama and I a home with him in Whitby. He was father's uncle and he'd been fond of him when he was a boy. We had nowhere else to go.'

Charlie touched her hand. 'If only I'd spoken sooner you wouldn't have had to go through all of that.'

Harriet looked down, blinking back tears. She couldn't let him see how much his words were affecting her. She'd always thought that his regard for her had disappeared as soon as her father's crimes came to light. 'It's not been that bad. Uncle Humphrey was very kind to us. Mama's not been well since it all happened. He paid for her to see the best doctors. I started helping with the business as a way to repay him for his kindness to us. To begin with he'd only let me choose carpets and curtains and pick out furniture. Then he was ill one winter while we were renovating the house you've just seen. We had a booking for the season which meant we couldn't postpone the work so I took over. When he was better the tradesmen told him they preferred dealing with him because I drove too hard a bargain. Uncle Humphrey was delighted. After that he taught me everything about the business and when he died two years ago he left it to me.'

'I wish I could thank your Uncle for what he did when I could not.' His hand tightened on hers. 'I looked for you, Harriet. I searched everywhere I could think of. Even when I went back to my regiment I kept looking, writing to everyone who'd known you. No one knew where you'd gone.'

Her eyes met his. 'You did all that?'

'Yes. And then last week, I saw Hugh Armstrong at my club and he told me he'd seen you. That his family had stayed in Whitby in the summer and he'd seen you at church.'

'Hugh was here? I didn't know.'

'He couldn't wait to tell me how lovely you looked. First chance I got I flew up here to see if he was telling me the truth.'

'But why didn't you just come to see me? Why go through all that elaborate façade of telling me you're Viscount Ripley and that you want to rent a house?'

Charlie laughed. 'My dear girl, that not a lie. I am Lord Ripley!'

'No, you can't be! You…' Harriet shook her head, lost for words.

'I assure you it's the truth. The Earl of Carlow was a distant cousin of my father's. So distant in fact that I'd never met him and I certainly never had any expectations. But then his sons died, one in the Transvaal conflict, the other in a hunting accident. The Earl passed away in the spring and my uncle Albert inherited the title. As he has no sons I'm his heir.'

'You really are Viscount Ripley?'

'I've got a coat of arms at home that I can show you if that'll make you believe it?'

Harriet was silent for a long moment. 'You really have gone up in the world, Charlie. I'm so pleased for you. No one could deserve it more.'

'Then share it with me. Be Lady Ripley.'

Gently, Harriet pulled her hand from his. 'That's impossible.' Unable to look at him she stared out of the window. The omnibus was slowly crossing the swing bridge over the harbour.

Charlie leaned towards her, trying to make her look at him. 'Why is it impossible?'

'You're part of the aristocracy now. It matters who you marry. I am the daughter of a disgraced con man. I work for my living and I'm probably about to be arrested for shooting one of Sunderland's aldermen.'

'I have lawyers who will deal with the alderman. You should never have been put in that position. If I'd only found you sooner...'

'Don't be silly, Charlie!' Harriet said more sharply than she'd intended. What he was offering was wonderfully, amazingly tempting. She had to remember that there were so many reasons why it couldn't work. More calmly she added, 'I love working. I mean it has its hazards but when Uncle Humphrey left me the business I knew what I was doing. That's why I learnt to shoot. And yesterday was only the second time I'd even had to get my pistol out.'

'You always were a game girl.'

'You're just saying that because I always beat you at tennis!'

The omnibus slowed. Harriet glanced out of the window. In the narrow streets night was settling in. 'Let's get off. The policemen won't catch us now.'

Charlie rang the bell and the omnibus stopped. After helping her to climb down, he asked, 'Which way?'

Harriet hesitated. There were so many things she should be doing right now. Warning her mother, contacting her lawyer, putting in place arrangements for the business in case she were arrested. Only she didn't want to do any of them. She simply wanted to be with Charlie. She'd been convinced for so long that he'd forgotten her. To discover that not only had he looked for her but he still cared for her was like a dream come true. A dream that she would have to wake up from all too soon. For a little longer she wanted to pretend they were still the girl and boy who'd fallen in love all those years ago.

Pointing towards the steps, she said, 'There's one hundred and ninety nine to the church. I'll race you up them!' Then before he could reply she stamped hard on the toe of his right boot and darted past him.

'Of all the…!' she heard him say as she took the first steps at a run and she couldn't hold back a quick shout of laughter. Dear Charlie, he'd always fallen for the same trick!

She walked this way often and had made the climb in under four minutes last Sunday when she was late for church. But, she knew that encumbered by corset and skirt she couldn't possibly beat Charlie even with a head start.

When her legs started to burn she glanced behind. It was too early for the gas lanterns to be lit. Through the gathering dusk she saw that he was gaining on her. He wouldn't do the gentlemanly thing and let her win. He never had. She was over half way up when he passed her. She didn't slow her pace but kept running, her breath coming in puffs, her heart pounding.

Reaching the top, she leaned against the hand rail and looked around the churchyard. He'd not been that far ahead. Where had he gone?

'Charlie?'

A dim light shone from the windows of the church and threading her way along the path she headed towards it. In the twilight with the moon hanging over the sea, shadows hid behind the gravestones. Harriet shivered. Since she'd read Mr Stoker's book it was impossible to be here without thinking of Count Dracula.

The church door was slightly open. She called again, got no reply. Pushing the heavy door, she stepped into the gloomy interior of the church. The dark wood box pews sucked in the lights of the candles. She walked up the narrow aisle between them, her boots tapping out a beat on the stone flagged floor.

'Charlie?'

He stood by the altar. He didn't turn to her, didn't speak and she was suddenly nervous. 'What's wrong? Why are you in here?'

Tall candles burnt brightly on the altar. Their light cast shadows over his face, making him look older than his twenty-seven years.

Turning to her, he took her hand. 'Harriet, I have loved you for eight years. I thought I would never see you again and suddenly, miraculously, I have found you. I am not going to give you up because of what other people may think.' He dropped to one knee. 'Marry me. Not because of the trouble you may be in but because of the love we had and the love we will have. Marry me, not to be Lady Ripley but to be my wife. Marry me and spend your life with me.'

Harriet swallowed hard. She'd dreamt of him proposing. All those long years ago, she'd known what he intended to say. Had read it in his eyes at the ball. Then everything had changed and she'd quashed that memory along with all the rest. But she'd loved him then. She would have said yes without a moment's hesitation.

'I'm not the girl I was,' she said quietly.

'I can tell that. She didn't carry a pistol but she did stamp on my foot on a fairly regular basis.'

'And I won't give up the business.'

He hesitated for a moment. 'Alright if you promise not to ask me to give up flying?'

She nodded. 'Agreed. Maybe we both need a bit of excitement in our lives.'

'Is that a yes, Miss Hardy?'

'Yes.' Her smile started small and then grew until it filled her face. 'That's a yes, Lord Ripley.'

'Excellent! Then I can get up off this damned cold floor.' He stood and took both of her hands in his. 'A month, Harriet. A month and not a day longer before we stand at this altar and I make you my wife.'

Pulling away she walked backwards down the aisle, her laughing eyes fixed on his. 'Two months. Weddings take a lot of organisation. And I've got a business to run and my name to clear.'

He caught up with her before she got to the door. 'We'll clear your name together.' His hand reached around her waist and pulled her towards him. 'Six weeks and not a day longer.'

'Done!' Harriet smiled. And then he kissed her.

Author Details

If you've enjoyed this story and would like to find out more about Alys West, here's how:

Twitter: @alyswestyork
Blog www.*alyswest.wordpress.com*

Alys' debut novel, 'Beltane' will (hopefully!) be out in 2015. Please see Alys' blog for more details.

A Tooth for a Tooth

Terri Nixon

It had been doomed to failure from the start. I knew it, we all knew it. Then, when it all kicked off, guess who was the mug they called in to sort out the mess? Which was how I found myself, on Christmas Eve, hanging on for dear life by my fingertips, with sweat trickling into my eyes and the hands on the church clock across the road continuing their steady, ruthless march towards the twelve. I let out a groan; I wanted it to be exasperation, and it was, partly, but the bigger part was pure scaredy-cat whimper. Where the hell *was* she?

To take my mind off the enormous lump of nothing beneath my swinging feet, I allowed my mind to scamper back over the path that had led me here. I must have been mad to take the job on to start with, but I'd been desperate – why else would I have been stupid enough to sign up as Corporate Troubleshooter to a bunch of shiny-faced over-achievers like The Directors? They threw buzzwords around like confetti, and made all the proper, concerned noises about their Investment In People, but I'd lost count of the times they'd driven out the best qualified person and replaced them with one of their own inside contractors.

This case was a prime example: Tania Featherfly – even her initials suited the job – had been the best tooth fairy in the business, but, like so many other small franchises she'd had to increase her prices to maintain those high standards. I remembered the board meeting and hearing the words: 'Economic Downturn,' and 'Credit Crunch' bandied about, but all it really boiled down to was: 'My Lot Are Cheaper, You're Fired.' And bingo! Tooth fairying was farmed out to a pool of corporate suits with as much sense of tradition as a brick.

Tania had, quite rightly, been somewhat annoyed at being laid off so close to Christmas; from Hallowe'en trick-or-treating onwards it a lucrative time for the collection of enamel, so she'd decided to do something about it. But did she go to the administrators and offer to work at lower cost? No. Not her style. She thought it would be *far* more entertaining to follow the new contractor on his rounds, and start removing perfectly healthy teeth while they were still in the mouth.

And there was certainly no money being left in return for these filched fangs.

That was when I got the call. Luckily, the only person to wake during one of Tania's dubious 'extractions' had been the chairman of the board that had fired her, and only then because she'd really gone to town on him; quite the revenge-seeker is our sweet little Tania.

I still remember him trying to talk through a mouth that had only one tooth left in it. 'Joe, it's vital you get every single one of those teeth back where they belong, before midnight.'

I took a moment to decipher what he was saying, then asked, 'Why midnight?'

'Come on, you *know* this is a special night.'

'Christmas Eve, yeah. What difference does that make?'

The chairman sighed. 'Midnight GMT, Christmas Eve? Think about it.' With exaggerated patience, he quoted: 'If there be mischief abroad in The Netherworld at that time, all magic will cease to have effect." When I didn't answer, he growled, 'The guy in the red suit?'

'Ah.'

'Yes, 'Ah.' The Human World will be thrown into turmoil, there will be no belief in *anything* anymore. And that means?'

'Er, no teeth left out for collection?'

'The penny drops. Now get onto it. And, Joe?'

'Yeah?'

'I hardly need remind you which teeth are top priority.'

So I'd collected a copy of the evening's itinerary, and set out. First I had to find Tania and talk her into coming with me, which might be difficult. Not the finding her part; that was easy. I just started at the end of list and worked backwards through the as-yet unvisited kids, all sleeping happily with sugar plums dancing on their heads... or whatever. Never been any good at remembering poems.

Eventually I ran into the new operative. I didn't think there was any point telling him what was going on, he didn't look the type to cope well under pressure, so I just nodded as he sidled past on the window sill. He gave me a nervous look, obviously aware of my position within the company.

I smiled. 'Nothing to worry about, Brian, you're doing a great job.' I kept smiling and nodding while he slipped off into the night, looking over his shoulder, suspicion still furrowing his brow.

I glanced at my list. How far behind was Tania? Was it worth trying to beat her to the previous house or should I just wait here till she arrived? I didn't have to ponder long; she'd followed so closely on Brian's heels it was a miracle he hadn't seen her. Actually no, it wasn't: Tania was *good*.

I stepped into her path as she alighted on the sill. 'Hey, Tania. Thinking of pitching for the Santa franchise next year?'

She gave a helpless little squeal, then glared at me, dropping the pretence. 'Oh, it's you.'

'Nice to see you too. Look, you have to stop what you're doing.' I tried to sound understanding, but Tania's glare intensified, and she held up her pliers.

'Get out of my way, Joe, I'm busy.'

I dropped reasonable and launched into pleading. 'You have to help me put this right.'

'After what they did to me? They can kiss my fairy ass! Now move, I've got a lot to do tonight.'

'Look, it won't work. You'll just end up destroying us all!' I said, my voice rising in frustration. 'Please, Tania, we'll sort this and then go to the board together. Try to work something out.'

I gestured at the room beyond the window. A red and green woollen stocking lay draped across the foot of the bed, and the boy's face reflected that curious mixture of utter peace, yet enormous potential for mischief, that only a sleeping child can convey.

'Don't mess it up for them,' I said, and I knew I'd succeeded in chipping through her layer of betrayed fury. She hadn't become the best tooth fairy in history by accident; she genuinely liked her customers – under normal circumstances.

'We don't have time,' she said, and I was relieved to note a touch of regret in her voice.

'We will if we work together,' I said. 'Come on, we'll go back the way you came.'

And so, with Tania back on side, albeit accompanied by mutinous muttering, we'd started back along the path of destruction she had laid. In each room I prised open the child's mouth, while Tania consulted her own list then selected the proper tooth from her gilt-embroidered bag.

Some of the kids were awkward little sods. They'd turned over onto their fronts, making it nigh on impossible to get a good grip on their jaw, and one or two opened sleepy eyes and blinked a few times while Tania and I stood dead still, so tense we could hear each other's heartbeats.

In the fourth house we re-visited, I was holding open a little girl's lips while Tania shoved the tooth back into the socket, when the girl spoke in her sleep; 'Don't want no coal…'

I gave a yell and jumped out of the way just as the girl's hand flopped out of the covers to brush at her mouth. Her finger caught the back of my head and sent me tumbling onto the pillow, where I floundered in a mass of blonde curls.

'Well that's one kid with a new wobbly tooth tomorrow,' Tania said. 'I'm not going back up there to glue that one in place.'

'At least you can fly,' I grumbled.

We worked well together, in fact, and even managed to sort out the chairman's revolting teeth, and replace them in pretty good time. All purloined premolars were soon firmly back in their rightful mouths. When we got to the second-to-last house, I thought Tania looked a bit troubled.

'What's wrong?'

'Nothing. Come on, let's get this one done.' She caught at my arm to lift me into the room, where the boy lay flat on his back, his mouth obligingly wide open. I grinned at Tania, celebrating our luck, but she still didn't look pleased.

I chose not to say anything, and a glance at the bedside clock told me we'd better hurry to get the last house done in time. A sense of great achievement filled me; I'd done it again! Troubleshooter Extraordinaire saves the day! I might even get a pay rise out of this one.

We landed on the last window sill and I turned to Tania, rubbing my hands. 'Come on then,' I said. 'We've got a few minutes spare but let's not take it down to the wire.'

'Joe, there's a problem.'

'Problem?'

'There are no more teeth left in the bag.'

'What?' A cold feeling wormed its way through me and I could feel my grin dropping away like a shed skin. All my happy thoughts sank into my feet and started seeping out of my boots.

'I thought so at the last house, and now I'm sure; that was the last one.'

'But it can't be!' I grabbed the bag – it was one of those bizarre ones that has endless depths when it's full, but when it's empty, it's empty. 'There's nothing there,' I said dully, turning it inside out.

Tania bit her lip. 'No, there isn't.' Then her face lit up. 'Oh! I know where it is!'

Relief banished my scowl, but only until she spoke again. 'I threw it in the pond.'

'What?' I stared at her, incredulous. 'Tania, you –'

'I was angry, Joe! This was the first house I'd done, and I just threw it away when I came out of the room. I saw it land in the pond.'

'And this helps us *how*?' I snarled.

'I can get it back. There are water nymphs in that pond.' And without another word she jumped into the air and was gone – leaving me stranded on the windowsill of a fourth floor room, the church clock slowly ticking towards the destruction of everything.

I sat down. There was little point in wearing a path in the wood by pacing up and down, and at least if I kept my back to the night I wouldn't have to look at those mercilessly marching hands as midnight crept ever closer.

A sound made me look up hopefully. Tania back already? But it wasn't her. Instead there was a rushing of air and I closed my eyes against the dust and bits of leaves that blew into my face. When I opened them again I was just in time to see the current Santa Claus franchise holder leaping back into his sleigh. That guy was fast! I was lost in admiration for a moment, but as the sleigh took off again the downdraught hit and, suddenly numb with fright, I found myself sliding towards the edge of the window sill. There was enough breath left for me to yelp as my feet lost contact with the solid surface, and somehow I twisted and caught at the edge of the sill.

And that's how you found me. Hanging on, blinking sweat out of my eyes and almost able to hear that church clock ticking away my last hope.

'Tania!' I yelled. 'Hurry up!' My hands were slipping, and my heart pounded harder than it ever had before – it occurred to me I could actually die here. I felt sick and my arms started trembling with the effort of holding on, my fingertips burning against the rough wood.

Finally, blessedly, I heard her land on the sill. 'Got it!' she beamed, holding up the missing tooth. Then she gave me an impatient look. 'Well, come on, we haven't got all night.'

I managed a glower. It was quite a good one, considering my situation, and even as I put all the force of my fury into it I could appreciate the way it must have burned her. Or it would have, if she hadn't turned her back and ducked into the bedroom. I took a deep breath and tried to imagine I was doing pull-ups at the gym. I never went to the gym.

My fingers were slipping again, and this time I had no hope that Tania would swoop in and grab me at the last second, because she was already gone. Another slip, maybe half an inch but felt more like a foot, and my fingertips were on fire now.

'Tania!' I gasped, close to blind panic now. 'Hey!'

'Oh, for goodness sake,' she said, and swooped in to grab me at the last second.

I'd known she would.

Thinking it over, safe and warm in my bed on Christmas morning, I decided I'd been quite the action hero, and I allowed myself a smile of satisfaction. Tania would have some explaining to do, but we'd work something out – at least she'd helped put it right and I could relax again, knowing I'd saved the Netherworld from a terrible fate.

The phone rang. I picked up, still smiling. 'Merry Christmas!'

'Joe? We have a problem: we just had to fire Santa and he's not happy…'

Author Details

If you've enjoyed this story and would like to find out more about Terri Nixon, here's how:

Twitter: @TerriNixon
Facebook: www.facebook.com/terri.authorpage
Blog: http://terrinixon.wordpress.com/

Terri Nixon's current book/eBook 'A Rose in Flanders Fields' is available now

---

It's a Wonderful Life

Annie Lyons

'Only one more sleep 'til the big Ho, Ho, Ho *and* it's snowing!' shrieked Maisy, jumping on her slumbering parents.

'Watimeisit?' mumbled Cath, longing for more sleep.

'It's Christmas time!' yelled Maisy, jumping up and down on the bed whilst belting out a very enthusiastic verse of *Jingle Bells*.

'Six o'clock,' murmured Pete, 'on a Saturday.'

'At what age do children start to sleep in?' asked Cath wearily, trying to turn over and ignore the fact that her head was being violently bounced against the pillow.

'Well Jake's still asleep,' replied Pete, before he realised what he was saying.

'Jakey's not awakey!' cried Maisy, leaping from her trampoline and dashing down to her brother's room. Within moments, Maisy was back with her older brother in tow. Jake did a forward roll across the bed and flung open the curtains.

'That is totally awesome!' he declared, gazing out at the swirling flurries. He was right. It was still quite dark and fast-falling flakes made even the sickly light coming from the street-lamp look magical. Cath flung back the covers and pulled on her dressing-gown, her brain now buzzing with all the things she needed to do. Might as well start early.

'Right, who wants to help Mum make some gingerbread?'

'No thanks,' said Jake. 'I'm going to watch the snow.'

'Me too,' declared Maisy, nestling alongside her brother.

Pete grinned. 'Cheaper than paying for Sky I guess.'

Cath made her way downstairs and flicked on the kettle before finding some carols on the radio. By 8 o'clock she had made thirty gingerbread biscuits, twelve mince pies, and was just shoving a tray of sausage rolls into the oven. She walked over to the sink to start the washing-up and smiled as she spotted the snowman family that the kids had built with their father, even though the 'sprout eyes' gave them a slightly alien appearance.

'Mmmm those mince pies smell yummy,' said Maisy, flinging open the back door, leaving melting mounds of snow behind her as she strode into the kitchen.

'Boots off now!' yelled Cath.

Maisy frowned at her. 'You're not allowed to be cross at Christmas, Mummy. Father Christmas won't bring you any presents.'

'He never does,' sighed Cath,' but I'm hoping that as I've been really good this year, he'll deliver me Daniel Craig in a gift-wrapped box.'

'You're weird, Mummy,' declared her daughter.

At that moment a large snowball landed with a watery splat on the kitchen window. Cath frowned, ready to scold her son and spied her husband grinning sheepishly at her from the garden.

'Dad did it,' confirmed Jake as she opened the window.

'I'm going to make some breakfast before the shopping's delivered,' said Cath, waggling a finger at Pete.

'Aye, aye captain,' saluted her husband.

Cath was just on her second piece of toast when the phone rang.

' Isthatmissisthompson?'

'Yes.'

'Fing is Missis Thompson, cos of the snow, we've 'ad to cancel all our grocery deliveries this morning.'

'What?'

'Yeah see, fing is, we can't get out on the roads. Cos of the snow.'

'But surely it's not that bad,' said Cath, approaching the window and realising that actually it was quite bad.

'Nah fing is, we're not allowed to send the drivers out. Cos of the snow.'

'Yes I see that but what about my shopping? That's all my Christmas food! Will I be able to get another slot before Christmas?'

'Nah see, the fing is we're all booked up and if it carries on we'll have to cancel those as well. Cos of -'

'Yes, cos of the snow. I see.'

'But we'll send you a ten pound voucher as a good-will gesture, you know, cos of the snow.'

Cath replaced the handset, panic spreading through her body. She turned to Pete who was already doing his man-on-a-mission face.

'Don't worry my love. We'll walk into town with the sledge. It'll be an adventure. We'll pick up the turkey, get what we need. Bish bash bosh.'

'Now don't you go turning into Jamie Oliver,' said Cath. 'I've got enough to worry about.'

'It'll be fine, darling. Just go with the flow,' he said kissing her.

'Okay, I will. I'm going for a shower, you can clear up the kitchen,' she grinned, gesturing at the piles of baking trays, mixing bowls and breakfast things.

She was drying her hair when Pete appeared in the doorway. 'Mum just called. She and Dad aren't going to make it for Christmas. Apparently they've got six inches of snow up there.'

'Oh, that's a shame,' said Cath and meant it. Most of her friends hated their mothers-in-law but Cath's was actually quite a giggle and very partial to a drink or two at Christmas. She and her husband had become like surrogate parents to Cath since she lost her own mum and dad and she would miss having them around. She knew the kids would too. 'You'd better break it gently to Jake and Maisy,' she added.

Pete nodded. 'I think I'll pop round to see if Mrs Jarvis wants anything from the shops.'

'Who? The Duchess?'

'Stop it. She's on her own and it's Christmas Eve.'

'You're the one who said she was superior.'

'I just don't think she likes me.'

Pete shrugged. 'Whatever you think best, my sweet. Right, I'll go and talk to the kids and then we should head out.'

Cath knocked at number 15 and stood back. There was no festive wreath on the door and no obvious sign of life within. A voice trailed down the hall, old but fierce and strong.

'Who is it?'

'Er, it's just Cath from three doors down. I wanted to check if you were all right?'

'Oh.' Just one word laced with meaning. Cath contemplated doing a runner but knew she'd have to face her neighbour at a later date. She stood her ground and waited as the door was unbolted, unchained and unlocked.

A bad-tempered face with immaculate hair peered out at her. Cath took a deep breath. 'Hello Mrs Jarvis. Pete and I are just popping into town and wondered–'

'Don't stand on the doorstep letting all the cold in. Come inside!' Mrs Jarvis turned on her heel in a remarkably sprightly fashion and walked back down the hall. Unsure of what else to do, Cath went in, wiping her feet with care before removing her boots and wincing as the melting ice pooled onto Mrs Jarvis' spotless floor. She followed her into the living room, where the electric fire was emitting a furnace-like heat. A scattering of Christmas cards lined the mantelpiece and a glass of port stood on the occasional table next to a green wing-back armchair. A black and white film was showing on the television. Cath recognised it immediately as *It's a Wonderful Life*, her favourite film which she made Pete watch every Christmas without fail.

'Oh I love this film,' she enthused, smiling at her neighbour.

Mrs Jarvis regarded her with raised eyebrows. Did Cath spy an air of approval? 'I met him once,' said the old lady, looking back at the screen.

'Who?'

'James Stewart.'

'Really? Wow, how amazing! What was he like?'

'He was a gentleman. Now, what did you come round for?' Mrs Jarvis was not one to chat.

'Oh right, yes. Pete and I are just popping into town for our turkey and I wondered if there was anything you needed?'

'Actually there is, if you don't mind.'

'Not at all,' said Cath with an encouraging smile.

Mrs Jarvis reached into her handbag and pulled out a notebook. She licked her finger and leafed through the pages. When she found what she was looking for, she tore out the page and handed it to Cath. Cath glanced at the list. It was very long and quite specific. She bit her lip. 'The thing is, we're walking with the sledge and the kids, so I'm not sure how much we'll be able to carry.'

'Well if it's too much trouble,' said Mrs Jarvis sulkily, reaching for the list.

Cath was starting to feel hot in her coat. 'No, no, it's fine, I just don't know how much we'll be able to carry but we'll do our best.'

Mrs Jarvis nodded and sat back in her chair, returning her attention to the screen.

'Right, well I'll see myself out then,' said Cath.

'All right and if you wouldn't mind pulling the door to on your way out,' said the old lady without looking at her.

On her way back home, Cath had to keep telling herself that it was Christmas and it was important to show goodwill to your fellow men, even if they were demanding old women who didn't say thank you.

'He's beeeeeen!' squealed Maisy, flinging open her parents' bedroom door and dragging her stuffed stocking onto their bed.

Cath rolled over and reached out to turn on her bedside lamp. *Click*. The room stayed dark.

'Damn, the bulb must've gone.'

'S'ok, I've got it,' said Pete, reaching over to his side. *Click*. Darkness reigned. 'Hmmm, must be a fuse. I'll go and check.'

'Hurry Daddy!' implored Maisy.

Pete grabbed his dressing-gown and stumbled downstairs. Moments later he was back. 'Power's off.'

'Oh no!' cried Cath. 'It better come back on soon or we won't have any Christmas dinner.'

It didn't. Jake joined them and they opened their presents by the glow of the battery-operated fairy lights Cath had bought from the Pound Shop. They ate their bread and jam breakfast by candlelight, with Cath longing for a coffee. Pete phoned the electricity company on his mobile and was told that a power line had come down overnight in the snow and they were doing their best but couldn't promise when it would be fixed.

'How are we going to cook the turkey?' wailed Cath. 'I told you we should have got a gas oven!'

'We'll just have to cook it when it's back on,' said Pete. 'We can have cheese and crackers and mince pies.'

'And sausage rolls!' shouted Jake looking up from his new Lego.

'And chocolate buttons,' shouted Maisy looking up from her chocolate buttons.

'I suppose. It's just a shame,' said Cath sadly. 'It doesn't feel quite like Christmas without turkey.'

'Well you've got the most wonderful husband in the world and your children aren't bad either,' said Pete winking at Maisy and Jake. 'So you'll just have to settle with that.'

'I suppose,' repeated Cath, knowing he was right but not feeling quite ready to admit it. 'All I can say is thank goodness our central heating is gas-fired.' A sudden vision of Mrs Jarvis' electric fire leapt into her mind. 'I've got to just pop out for a minute,' she added, carrying her plate over to the sink.

'Are you going to play in the snow without us?' asked Maisy, suspicion etched on her face.

'No I'm just going to see someone.'

'Is it the Duchess?' asked Pete. He could read her like a book, damn him.

'She's only got an electric fire so she'll be freezing. I just want to check that she's okay.'

'She'll be fine. Why do you have to worry about everyone?'

'It's Christmas Pete. She's on her own.'

'Yeah Daddy, don't be so mean,' chimed Maisy. 'Can I come?'

'Er, I don't know-' said Cath panicking.

'I could sing her one of my Christmas carols.'

'I don't know if she'd like that.'

'Why not?'

Cath looked to Pete for help but he just shrugged. 'Well, some old people don't like a lot of noise,' said Cath carefully.

'I'll be quiet.'

Cath looked at her daughter and for a moment it was like looking in the mirror, such was the determination on her face. 'All right then.'

Cath and Maisy approached Mrs Jarvis' front door. Cath rapped at the knocker with false confidence.

'Who is it?' said Mrs Jarvis from deep within.

'It's us!' shouted Maisy. 'Merry Christmas!'

Moments later, Mrs Jarvis was standing before them, frowning. Cath glanced down at her daughter and noticed she was frowning too. 'Hello Mrs Jarvis, sorry to bother you,' said Cath. 'I just wondered if you were warm enough –'

'Well come in, come in, you're letting in a draught,' said Mrs Jarvis. They did as they were told, taking off their shoes just inside the door. Mrs Jarvis disappeared down the corridor towards the kitchen and Maisy followed, gesturing for her mother to do the same. They reached the kitchen where the oven was belching out heat. Candles were dotted on the table.

'Oh, you've got a gas cooker,' said Cath with a note of jealousy in her voice.

'Yes, gas cooker but electric heating, goodness knows why,' said Mrs Jarvis. 'Anyway, at least I can keep warm in here and heat up my dinner,' she added gesturing at the ready meal on the side.

'Well that's good,' said Cath, longing to ask the favour but knowing she never could.

'Can we use your oven please?' asked Maisy.

'I beg your pardon?'

'Your oven,' repeated Maisy in the loud voice she reserved for old people and those who were annoying her. 'We can't cook our turkey because our oven is electric and Mum's sad but probably too scared to ask you. We could share our dinner with you.'

Cath thought she saw a tiny spark of amusement in the old lady's face.

'Well I don't know,' said Mrs Jarvis.

'Oh come on, it's Christmas and everyone's supposed to get on at Christmas. I mean I know you don't like my Mum, and my Dad calls you the Duchess but they're quite nice once you get to know them.'

'Is that right?' said Mrs Jarvis, her lips twitching at the corner of her mouth.

'Yes, and actually being called a Duchess is quite nice isn't it? Sort of one step off being a princess or something. And if you come, I'll make you a Loom Band pouf-ball.'

'I have no idea what that means and it's very kind of you but I think it's up to your mother,' said Mrs Jarvis looking at Cath.

'Oh yes, of course,' gushed Cath with too much enthusiasm. 'I mean it makes sense. You have the oven, we have the heating. Do come. Please.'

Mrs Jarvis gave a small smile. 'Thank you. That is very kind.'

Five hours later, everyone declared they could eat no more. As they finished their meal, the power was restored and they all cheered. Pete volunteered to do the washing-up and Maisy and Jake settled down to watch the Christmas Day film.

Mrs Jarvis sipped a glass of port and glanced over at Cath. 'It's not true what your daughter said.'

'What's not true?'

'That I don't like you.' Mrs Jarvis shifted in her seat. 'To be honest, I've been on my own for so long now that I tend to keep myself to myself.'

'It's all right,' said Cath. 'You don't need to explain.'

Mrs Jarvis nodded. 'Well anyway, I've got something for you,' she said, 'a token of thanks.' She passed a brown board-backed envelope to Cath. Cath took it and pulled out a photo. It was a signed picture of James Stewart.

Cath was gob-smacked. 'You can't give me this. It's precious!'

Mrs Jarvis dismissed Cath's protestations with a wave of her hand. 'I would like you to have it. I know you'll look after it.'

'Thank you,' said Cath smiling at her. 'I'll treasure it. Merry Christmas Mrs Jarvis.'

'Please,' said Mrs Jarvis, 'call me Barbara.'

Author Details

If you've enjoyed this story and would like to find out more about Annie Lyons, here's how:

Twitter: @1AnnieLyons
Facebook: http://www.facebook.com/annielyonswriter
http://www.carinauk.com/annie-lyons

Annie's current eBook 'Dear Lizzie' is available now and 'Not Quite Perfect' is available in both paperback and as an eBook

---

Something Blue

Linda Huber

All I could do was stare at the ventilation grid on the ceiling. In the background I could hear the distant beat of music and voices from the party – my wedding reception – upstairs. All these people had come to help us celebrate, and now the entire thing was going to be ruined. My hands were shaking so much that my mobile slipped through my fingers and I only just caught it before it hit the floor. Another glance at the ceiling had me panicking. I flipped on my phone, punched out 999, and ran.

Rewind two months:

'No honeymoon! Oh Jeff!'

I had to laugh at the expression on Mum's face.

'We'll have a holiday in summer,' I told her. 'We want to visit Suze's family, but it seems daft to go all the way to Toronto in December. We've booked a nice cheap trip in June.'

My mother cast her eyes heavenwards. 'How very romantic.'

'Suze is as romantic as I am,' I said, grinning at the thought of my down-to-earth, humorous girlfriend planning anything even remotely related to romance. 'But here's some good news for you. We've booked Erbury Castle for the wedding. There's a little chapel for the ceremony, and the party'll be in the reception room on the first floor. Nothing fancy – just family and a few friends.'

'Hm,' said Mum. 'I'll have a word with Suze. Leave it to me.'

I wasn't quite sure what I was leaving to her, but it was easiest just to agree. All Suze and I wanted was something very laid-back here in Bedford, then a nice little party in Toronto for the family there. Suze's father's health prevented him from travelling to England so this seemed the best way to please everyone.

What we hadn't reckoned on was my mother hankering after top hats, bridal gowns and bridesmaids. But her way of thinking was that as mother of one child (me) she wasn't going to get another chance to organise her offspring's wedding, and she was determined to rise to the occasion.

Poor Suze had been congratulating herself on having avoided the whole mother-of-the-bride scenario. Like mine, her skills were more practical than artistic. We'd met at a training course our respective IT companies had sent us to in Derby a couple of years ago and it had been fun at first sight for both of us; we'd laughed our way through the entire weekend. When the chance of a job with her company in London came up the following spring, I leapt at it. We found a flat in Wimbledon and settled down to live happily ever after.

Getting married seemed like the logical next step, but we really hadn't planned on 'A Wedding'.

Enter Mum.

'Do you want me to help you choose a dress, dear?' she said to Suze that evening. (We were spending the weekend with my parents so that I could help Dad get the garden ready for winter.)

'I'm not wearing a dress,' said Suze cheerfully. 'It'll be much too cold in December. I found a lovely Indian silk trouser suit on the market a couple of weeks ago.'

Mum's face fell a mile. 'Is it whi– What colour is it?' she said hopefully.

'Yellow, with turquoise and green flowers and leaves,' said Suze. She leaned over and patted Mum's hand. She was kind, was Suze. 'We don't want a traditional wedding, Marion. We'll have our own special celebration and it'll be perfect.'

Mum gave up on the dress, but she persuaded Suze to agree to a bouquet and a posh car to drive her to the castle. She wasn't quite as happy with Suze's choice of lilies for the bouquet, but as Dad said, Suze's outfit was colourful enough already and at least white went with everything. I asked Mum for help choosing a new suit, so that made her happy too.

The wedding was to take place on the first Saturday in December, and the week before saw us visiting Mum and Dad again to make the final preparations. The ceremony itself was arranged, the caterers were booked, the forty friends and family had accepted, and my cousin Mark had volunteered to bring his disco equipment to give us music to dance to.

'Well, it's not very traditional, but I think it's going to be charming,' said Mum bravely. 'What about photos?'

'Craig's doing those. He did a course with his digital camera in the summer holidays,' said Suze.

'Good,' said Mum. 'Now all you need is something old, something new, something borrowed and something blue.'

Suze laughed. 'Okay. My outfit's new, I've never worn it. And as it's a winter wedding, I'll wear my old long-johns to keep me cosy so that's something old.'

'Too much information, dear,' said Mum, a determined expression on her face.

'The bracelet your Grandma gave you when you left school,' I suggested, nodding towards Suze's left wrist. It was a thin gold chain and she never took it off.

'Perfect,' said Mum. 'And you can borrow my white feather fascinator.' She ran upstairs and returned with the fascinator, which she fixed on Suze's short dark curls. Even Suze agreed it looked great, and being white it would match the lilies in the bouquet. Mum beamed. At last we were doing something traditional.

'Something blue, now?'

We all sat staring at each other. It was hard to imagine where anything blue would fit in with Suze's already multi-coloured outfit.

'We'll think of something,' said Suze, heading for the kitchen. 'I'll make coffee, shall I?'

My wedding day dawned cold and grey in spite of the optimistic weather report for the entire weekend. We were starting from Mum and Dad's for easy travelling to Erbury Castle, and we all had rooms in a hotel in Erbury for the night. Mum fussed around checking Dad's shirt and phoning the florist's to make sure the flowers would be here on time. I sat in the kitchen eating toast and watching as a stiff easterly wind chased the clouds away. By the time Suze emerged from the shower, the sun was attempting to melt the thick layer of frost over everything.

'It's windy,' announced Mum when she came in from the hairdresser's. 'Very cold, too.'

'That's okay,' said Suze. 'You're all wearing frost-free outfits, and I've got my long-johns and my–'

Mum gave her a look. 'Suze, dear, you really shouldn't see Jeff on the morning of the wedding. It's not traditional.'

My bride-to-be blinked at me over the rim of her coffee mug.

'Neither is Suze,' I said.

But she was more traditional than I'd thought. An hour or so later we were upstairs, putting the finishing touches to our wedding outfits (Mum had given up on 'the groom mustn't see the bride' by this time) when Suze started hunting round her handbag and then the floor.

'I can't find my stone,' she said, complete dismay in her voice.

I was a bit slow on the uptake. It was a long time since I'd tied a tie and my double Windsor was squint. 'What stone?'

'My blue stone – you know, the one I found on the beach at Brighton and I said it could be my something blue, and your mum was so pleased when I showed it to her.'

We searched around the floor and in both our suitcases, but the stone was nowhere to be found. Suze came to the conclusion that she'd either lost it or left it at home. It seemed best not to tell Mum, but when we went downstairs we realised that another problem had arisen.

'It's snowing,' said Dad, standing at the window watching as a few lazy flakes swirled by, followed by a few more and then more still until a positive blizzard had developed. The garden took on that fresh, crisp look you get when a fresh snowfall hides the scruffiness of winter.

'Trust us to get married on the coldest day of the year in the middle of a howling snowstorm,' I said, trying to put a smile on Mum's face.

'I do hope the castle's well-heated,' she said. 'You know how your Dad feels the cold.'

Fortunately, that wasn't a problem. We rolled up to Erbury Castle just ten minutes late; a minor miracle considering the state of the roads by that time. I could only admire the way the limo driver handled his vehicle on the narrow, now snow-covered track. The castle dated from the 12th century and was a forbidding grey stone structure with a lovely little courtyard and an enormous oak tree dominating the right hand side. Summer wedding parties often took place out here, but sadly this wasn't an option for us. Suze nipped inside quickly while Dad and I helped Mum across the few feet of cobblestones to the doorway.

Most of our guests were already seated in the small chapel leading off to the left of the huge entrance hall. I could hear the high-pitched, excited voices of the seven children amongst our guests as well as the more restrained buzz of talk from the adults.

'Over there, Suze dear,' said Mum, as she and Dad came in, brushing the snow from their wedding finery. Suze was opening doors on the other side of the entrance hall.

'I know. I just want to take off my long-johns,' she said. 'It's way too warm in here for ski underwear.' She disappeared into the ladies and emerged a moment or two later looking slimmer.

The ceremony was amazing. The chapel was tiny so our guests filled it up very nicely, and we had two huge flower arrangements on the table at the front. Suze and I stood there with the registrar, a tall lady with jet black hair and jade green earrings. We had poems, and Dad made a short speech before Suze and I exchanged rings. Craig took photos of everything, and Suze's friend Anita sang 'Love will keep us alive', after which Suze and I were back-slapped or kissed by everyone in the room. It was lovely. I saw Mum looking round the little chapel with such a happy look on her face, it brought tears to my eyes. Maybe the flowers were mostly lilies (we had a few red carnations too) and maybe Suze was providing more colour than a bride usually did, but we had all the love in the world at our wedding and I wouldn't have changed a single thing. We moved on upstairs to the reception room feeling very pleased with ourselves.

The only slight problem was the heat in the place; it was like walking into a sauna and most people immediately shed a layer or two of clothing. The owners had obviously been determined that we wouldn't feel chilly in our wedding finery. Dad went to the window and reported that there were about four inches of snow on the ground but it had stopped now and, as most of us were staying the night in the village, the weather didn't really matter anyway.

There was no kitchen in the castle, but a restaurant in the village proper provided the food for parties. As it was winter, we'd chosen leek and potato soup, followed by stuffed mushrooms on chicory salad, followed by saffron risotto with (or without, if you were a vegetarian) lamb chops, or chicken nuggets for the children, and amaretto ice cream for pudding. It was heavenly.

The disco began while we were having coffee, and Suze and I got up to do the bridal waltz. Mum and Dad were both beaming proudly as I twirled my wife round the floor.

'Well, we made it,' I whispered. 'Safely married in spite of the lack of something blue.'

Suze grinned. 'I've remembered where I put the stone,' she said. 'It's in my travelling jewellery case. You know; the little one. I didn't bring it because, apart from Granny's bracelet, I'm not wearing any other jewellery except my wedding ring, of course.' She looked at the white gold band on her wedding finger with what was almost a soppy expression on her face.

'Steady,' I said.

'Time to cut the cake,' said Mum, when we returned to our table after the first few dances.

I pulled at my collar. Getting married was hot work, especially when a place was as efficiently heated as this one.

'I'll just go and splash my face first,' I said.

The loos were on the ground floor. I ran the water cold, sloshed quite a lot over my face and neck, and was patting myself dry with a paper towel when I saw it. Smoke. A thin grey tendril was emerging from the ventilation grid high above me, growing thicker and greyer even as I watched. And couldn't I smell burning?

I'd never dialled 999 before, but they make it easy for you. 'Fire brigade – Erbury Castle!' was all I had to say, and I raced upstairs with the emergency operator assuring me that help was on its way.

'Fire! We have to leave the building!'

I stood there in the doorway yelling. For a couple of seconds people thought I was joking, then they realised that I was deadly serious. Fortunately no one except Craig's seven-year-old panicked, and we all hurried downstairs to the entrance area. You could smell smoke, but it was faint and there was no sign of an obvious fire.

'Into the courtyard, everyone,' I said, pushing Mum and Dad outside first. 'Craig, Mark and I will bring the coats out to you.' I nodded at my cousins then looked round for Suze. She was nowhere to be seen and I ran back inside. The smoke was more obvious now.

'Suze!'

She emerged from the ladies pulling at her tunic. 'Just putting my long-johns back on,' she said.

'Oh for goodness–' I stopped. It was a bit soon to have the first quarrel of our married lives.

Craig, Mark and I were still hurling coats through the cloakroom window when sirens became apparent in the distance. A minute or two later a large fire engine skidded into the snow-covered courtyard, followed by a smaller vehicle. The chief fireman jumped down.

'Is everyone accounted for?' he demanded.

'I'll check,' I said, feeling stupid that I hadn't thought to do this before.

Two firemen disappeared inside while the rest set up lights. My head count didn't work the first time because Craig was running around taking photos and I counted him twice, but we sorted ourselves out. Forty guests, Suze, me, Mum and Dad, plus five restaurant staff. We all stood watching the firemen and stamping our feet to keep warm.

The chief fireman re-emerged and shouted unintelligible instructions to the crews before turning to Dad and me.

'No actual flames. The boiler in the cellar has overheated, causing the smoke. It's fairly slight but we're going to blow it out of the building.'

We watched as they fed a large tube-like construction into the castle. The kids were all fascinated, of course, and Craig was still taking photos. A van appeared in the floodlit courtyard and a couple of men jumped down.

'Coffee's on the house!' called one, and I recognised the owner of the restaurant who'd provided the meal. They produced huge flasks and plastic cups and started to dispense coffee. The whole situation had taken on a completely unreal feeling – the odd snowflake floating down, the old castle, lit by the floodlights from the fire engines, the drone of the smoke pump, and happy children's voices as the kids ran around watching it all.

It was to become even more surreal. 'Cake!' shouted one of the firemen, as he and a colleague came out bearing our wedding cake.

Everyone cheered, and Suze and I stood there under the oak tree cutting our cake as if it was the middle of July and not December.

In the end, we abandoned Erbury Castle and adjourned to the restaurant for a final drink. Suze kissed all the firemen before we left and so did Mum, and the kids all had a turn at sitting in the big red fire engine and turning on the siren. What the people of Erbury thought about that I don't know, but there was a lot of good-natured laughter when we arrived at the restaurant, anyway.

'You know it's all your fault,' I said to Suze as we were walking along to our hotel an hour or so later. 'If you hadn't forgotten your something blue, we might have had better luck.'

She smiled at me, that mysterious Suze-smile when I couldn't tell at all what she was thinking.

'No,' she said at last. 'It was the most perfect wedding in the world and I wouldn't have changed a single minute.'

It was Christmas when the final part of our wedding day story came to light. Suze and I had decided to have our first Christmas Day at home together and then go up to Mum and Dad's on Boxing Day. We'd agreed with the family that we wouldn't do presents; it seemed silly when we'd had so many wedding gifts just a couple of weeks beforehand. So I was surprised to see a flat rectangular parcel under the tree when I came home from the gym on Christmas Eve.

'It's from Craig,' said Suze.

I looked at her. Craig had already made us a beautiful wedding album with an entertaining bunch of photos. As well as the usual ceremony/reception pics, we had gems like: the bride, the groom and the chief fireman; all the children perched along the fire engine; the mother of the groom handing out wedding cake to a team of burly firefighters. What on earth was going to be in this extra package?

'More photos?' I said. 'Or maybe he got the one with the kids enlarged for us.'

Suze started to open it. Inside the brown paper was a flat parcel wrapped in electric blue paper, and a note. 'Suze told me about Something Blue. Thought you might like this. Craig xx'.

We sat down on the sofa and opened it together. It was a photo, but it wasn't my cousins' children. There we were in the courtyard, me and Suze. I was standing with a plastic cup of coffee, and Suze was beside me chomping a piece of wedding cake. And behind us was the fire engine, blue light flashing, illuminating Suze's white fascinator just below. It really did look as if she was wearing a luminous blue halo.

Suze peered at it closely, then hi-fived me, grinning from ear to ear.

'That's it!' she said. 'Our most traditional wedding photo; look, you can even see my bracelet. We did it, Jeff – something old, something new, something borrowed and something blue!'

Author Details

If you've enjoyed this story and would like to find out more about Linda Huber, here's how:

Website: *www.lindahuber.net*
Twitter: @LindaHuber19
Facebook: *www.facebook.com/authorlindahuber*
Blog: *http://lindahuber.net/blog/*

Linda's current book/eBook 'The Cold Cold Sea' is available now at *http://www.amazon.co.uk/Linda-Huber/e/B00CN7BB0Q/ref=sr_ntt_srch_lnk_1?qid=1409919876&sr-1-1*

Ghosts of Christmas

Sarah Lewis

As the melody of George Michael singing 'Last Christmas' filtered through the stereo speakers, something flickered behind Mary's eyes. Memories of a time when her biggest dilemma in life was whether to wear black kohl or electric blue eyeliner pricked at her mind, as she cozied herself in nostalgia three decades old.

Mary tried to pinpoint why Christmas day 1984 held such a special place in her heart. After all, it had none of the pure, unadulterated enjoyment she had experienced during the first Christmas with her son or her daughter. Neither did it hold that childhood magic, recaptured by seeing the season through their wonder-filled infant eyes. The Christmas Eve ritual of reading 'The Night Before Christmas' snuggled together on the sofa, with both Zack and Grace silently mouthing the words, as Mary read from the book that had come to encapsulate Christmas for them. Waiting until the pair was fast asleep before filling the stockings they had hung upon their bedroom door handles, then sneaking down the creaky stairs, laden with beautifully wrapped presents that would transform the lounge into their very own Winter Wonderland.

Mary recalled how the trio had been fortunate enough to visit a very real Winter Wonderland, when they had travelled to Lapland for a long weekend. The image of how the kids' faces had lit up when they had met the 'real' Father Christmas would stay with Mary forever. So too, riding over a frozen lake in a reindeer-drawn sleigh, the spectacular sight of the Northern Lights, and the piercing shrieks of Grace's fake terror when she had ridden pillion, with Mary steering their snowmobile over every mound she could find in an attempt to emulate a James Bond chase!

Tears began to sting Mary's eyes at the thought of her now grown-up children and their absence this Christmas. It was the first Christmas she had ever spent apart from them. It was the first Christmas she had ever had without seeing any of her family. Mary had never felt so alone. How had it come to this?

'Crowded room, friends with tired eyes...' Wham!'s front man stopped Mary from wandering down the road to self-pity, and planted her back in 1984. It had been Mary's first Christmas as a teenager. Nothing particularly remarkable in that, but Mary had seen it as a step towards the independence she so craved, something she had since gained in bucket-loads. The irony of life was not lost on Mary. Thirty years ago, it had seemed that it would take nothing short of a

Christmas miracle to reach her goal. Life had since taught her that the only 'miracles' she would experience were those arising from her own hard work and bloody mindedness.

Mary mentally rebuked herself. This was no time for wallowing. She had always loved the festive season. The scent of pine needles every morning as she entered the lounge and saw the huge, elaborately decorated Christmas tree, which dominated the room. Baking aromas of cinnamon and nutmeg mingling with sherry and brandy, as batches of mince pies and a rich, dark Christmas cake arose from the confines of their tiny, dated kitchen. The candlelit carol service in the village church, during which Mary would sing with fervour, instilled at an early age during hours of hymn practice at primary school. Mary adored Christmas, and the message it brought. Just because this one had not turned out as she had planned, it was no reason to start behaving like a victim.

The mere thought of the word triggered her to recall Christmas 1983. Not because she had been a victim, but because it was a time when Culture Club's single, 'Victims', held prominence in the charts. 'Push aside those who whisper never,' thought Mary, instantaneously summoning the words Boy George had sung with such feeling. The way her mind worked amused Mary, but often drove her family to distraction. They told her it wasn't normal to spout lyrics at the drop of a hat. It was bad enough when they could see the connection to something that had happened or had been said, but often it would appear to them that Mary would quote a line from a song, or even worse start singing in public, for the most obscure reason. Mary had given up trying to explain herself, except to say that one day she planned on becoming the character in the Jenny Joseph's poem 'Warning', and they only needed to start worrying about her when she began to 'wear purple with a red hat which doesn't go, and doesn't suit me.'

Mary's propensity to quote or sing lyrics did not worry her, as she could always trace what had prompted her 'outbursts', even if sometimes it took her a while to work it out. Like the time she had spent a whole day trying to get the tune of Dave Dundas' 'Jeans On' out of her head. Mary had been perplexed. It wasn't a song she particularly liked, or even knew that well, but the lyric 'I put my blue jeans on' had rotated around her mind on a loop all day. It was only when she returned home from work, and went to retrieve the washing from the line (which included her own pair of blue jeans) that the quandary was solved, and the earworm stopped.

Despite such incidents, which she knew some would take to be a sure sign of insanity, Mary was neither disturbed nor surprised by them. Music had been the one constant in her life. During the ups and downs, happy times and sad, it had underlined her life and her feelings about it. It was an unstoppable force, over which she had no control, regardless of the painful emotions it would evoke on occasion. Even when the emotions had been almost by proxy, the pain had been very real. Take Christmas 1974, when Mud had topped the charts with 'Lonely This Christmas'. It had been the last Christmas a very young Mary had spent with her grandfather, before he succumbed to cancer weeks later.

Mary's memories of her grandfather were sketchy; visiting him in hospital, feeling the crispness of his cotton pyjamas as she hugged him goodbye. Yet, she only had to hear the opening bars of the song to be transported back in time and feel a very tangible grief. His loss had hit her whole family badly, but none more so than her nan, who never did remarry, despite only being in her late forties when he passed away. A soothing warmth enveloped Mary at the thought of her nan, and the Christmases they had spent together. As much as she enjoyed Christmas Day when she was younger, Mary had always looked forward to Boxing Day more. Her entire family – aunts, uncles and cousins, as well as her parents, nan and brother – would gather at the local social club to celebrate the day, consuming more alcohol in the space of a few hours than any of them would normally drink in a week.

Mary's nan would always be dressed to impress, her outfit topped off with a dark faux-fur coat. Her hair would be perfectly coiffured, held in place with a liberal spraying of Harmony hairspray. Her fingernails would be immaculately polished, one hand holding a cigarette, the other a glass of whisky and dry ginger. The only time she seemed to put either down was when she got up to dance, usually to Jeff Beck's 'Hi Ho Silver Lining' or Shakin' Stevens' 'Merry Christmas Everybody'. Mary's nan had always been the last to leave the dance floor. Where she got her energy from was anyone's guess. Mary wished she could summon some of that energy now. Her eyelids were feeling heavy, her battle to stay awake becoming futile.

Grace and Zack stood arguing as their grandparents entered the room.

'This bickering reminds me of when you two were little,' remarked Bill, placing himself in the middle of the warring siblings. 'You should be there for each other at a time like this, not at each other's throats.'

The pair were silenced immediately and, bowing their heads slightly, looked suitably reprimanded.

'I don't think anyone needs reminding how difficult this Christmas is,' said his wife pointedly.

'No, it's tough on all of us, Viv,' he replied. 'All the more reason for us to stick together.'

'I was just saying that I thought at least one of us ought to make the effort to go and see Mum today,' stated Grace. 'It is Christmas after all. Mum's always loved this time of year.'

'And I was just saying,' mimicked Zack. 'What a total waste of time it would be.' His voice became thick with emotion as he continued. 'It's not like she's been there recently for us, is it? It was her decision.'

'That's not fair, Zack. How can you say such a thing?' Grace was close to tears. Her pale blue eyes glistened with emotion.

'It's true,' countered her brother. 'She left. Even after I'd begged her not to, she left.'

Zack strode across the room. He looked out of the window, into the inky blackness of the night. The sky was clear, the night air chilled, as the first forming of frost spread across the lawn. Not like the early November evening when Mary had left, in spite of his protests. The cold, damp mists of that evening had clung to the smoke of bonfires and firework displays, creating a lingering, impenetrable smog. Zack had felt powerless, as he watched his mother disappear from sight merely feet from his front door, swallowed by the noxious fog.

Sensing his grandson's train of thought, Bill stepped forward and placed a weather-worn hand on Zack's shoulder. 'C'mon lad. It wasn't your fault. No one could've stopped her leaving. We all know what your mother's like when she's made up her mind.'

Zack's Adam's apple bobbed up and down, as he fought to hold back the tears, threatening to cascade at any second. He nodded his head, almost imperceptibly.

'Maybe we should pay her a visit,' the younger man conceded.

It was almost 10pm when the group arrived at Mary's temporary accommodation. They spoke in hushed tones, as the elder couple led the way. Vivian carried a potted Poinsettia, a gift she had given her daughter every year for as long as she could remember. There was no reason this year should be any different. Alongside, Bill walked in perfect synchronicity with his wife. His left hand rested gently in the small of her back, his right hand clutched a copy of Clement C. Moore's most famous poem. Mary's children had also brought her gifts.

Grace had raised her eyebrows at Zack's choice of gift; an orange, clove and cinnamon scented room spray. 'Mum always said it smelt like Christmas in a bottle,' he'd explained.

Grace's gift choice had seemed obvious; a compilation CD of all the cheesy Christmas songs Mary sang at full volume every year, as soon as the first of December arrived. Except Mary had not been around to sing them this year.

As the four hopeful visitors approached Mary's door, Grace glanced over towards the nurse's station. The ward sister was sat at a desk, the blue glow of the computer screen illuminating her face in the otherwise dimmed lighting. She beamed at them. 'Merry Christmas! I was beginning to think we weren't going to see you today.'

'I'm sorry we left it so late,' apologised Grace. 'Is it still okay to see her?'

'Of course. Just make sure you keep that music turned down. I'm not sure the other patients want to hear Adam & The Ants blasting out at this time of night,' the nurse chuckled.

'It's Christmas songs tonight,' smiled Grace. 'But don't worry, we won't disturb anyone.' Grace turned to enter Mary's room, then paused. She looked over her shoulder at the nurse, and asked the same question she had asked every day for the last seven weeks. 'Is there any improvement in her condition?'

The nurse shook her head sadly.

As Bill finished reading aloud to Mary, 'Merry Christmas to all, and to all a good night,' Jona Lewie sang softly in the background, about wanting to stop the cavalry. The Poinsettia stood proud on the bedside cabinet, and the smell of Christmas hung heavily in the air, thanks to Zack's over-zealous spraying.

Grace looked despondent as she took in their surroundings, her mother deathly still in the midst of it all, her shallow breathing barely audible. Mary had always nagged Grace about not driving in bad weather. The first bit of drizzle and she would be on the phone, telling Grace to take extra care. Grace found it hard to believe that her mother had driven in such treacherous weather conditions, especially when Zack had offered her his spare room. Grace remembered Mary once joking, 'Take my advice, I'm not using it!' Perhaps it wasn't so difficult to believe. Whatever Grace believed, the outcome was there for them all to see; her mother in a coma.

'A penny for them.' Vivian's subdued tones brought Grace back to the present.

'Oh, I don't know, Nan,' sighed Grace. 'I really thought we would have managed to bring her back by now. We've tried stimulating her senses, like the doctor said. We've held her hand and kissed her, read her favourite books and poems to her. We've even sprayed her favourite smells around her, but nothing seems to work. I really thought that if anything was going to work, the music would. She used to drive me and Zack mad with her singing and music trivia,' Grace sniffled. 'I pictured being here today, and Mum waking up in the middle of 'Fairytale of New York', just in time to sing the scumbag and maggot bit.' Grace was sobbing now.

Vivian embraced her granddaughter, gently stroking her soft, blonde hair, until the tears had subsided.

'I know that was her favourite Christmas song,' whispered Vivian, 'but she loved the video for the one that's playing now. It's Wham!, isn't it?'

Grace calmed her breathing, and pulled away slightly from her grandmother so she could better hear the track that was currently playing.

As the melody of George Michael singing 'Last Christmas' filtered through the stereo speakers, something flickered behind Mary's eyes...

Author Details

If you've enjoyed this story and would like to find out more about Sarah Lewis, here's how:

Twitter: @MyEighties
Facebook: www.facebook.com/pages/My-Eighties/230733090286040
Website/Blog: www.my-eighties.co.uk / myeighties.wordpress.com
Amazon Author Page: Kindle Singles

Sarah's book, 'My Eighties' is currently available

Meet Me at Midnight

Rachael Thomas

The winter wind was keener than the last few days as Sally rounded the bend in the lane. Each morning she'd done this walk the countryside had been quiet, but today calls of sheep filled the valley.

Sheep were preferable to traffic, and she paced on down the lane, her trainers making barely a sound on the tarmac. She tried to push aside thoughts of London and the past she'd left behind, the marriage which had failed miserably; part of a life which no longer belonged to her.

'Stop there.'

The gruff command drew her attention up sharp and she looked up the hill to see a farmer herding sheep down towards the field gate. What had she done? Or was it a case of what should she do?

He shouted again, this time in a bid to encourage the sheep to move forward. Then he pulled off his woolly hat, an obligatory item even she'd indulged in as protection against the December winds. With seemingly little effect, he shook it at the sheep.

Sally had to stifle a giggle as the sheep split up and began to move away from the gate, as if intent on mutiny. This was definitely going in one of her books – if she ever managed to put the time spent with Jake in the past, move forward, and start writing again.

A high pitched whistle broke through the cold air and, like a streak of black on the landscape, a border collie swiftly brought order to the moment of chaos. The sheep, bleating their protests, filed past her, across the lane and into the opposite field.

Their little hooves tapped like hundreds of drums as they passed, some sheep stopping to look at her with interest. Realising why the farmer may have shouted at her to stop, Sally preformed the task of human fence, happy to be of use.

As the last sheep trotted past she looked up at the farmer. Even with his woolly hat back in place he was attractive. In fact he was a lot more than attractive. He was gorgeous. Where had that thought come from? She hadn't looked at another man since the end of her marriage. She could have had the pick of many London businessmen who'd flirted shamelessly with her but, no, she had come to the Welsh countryside to hide herself away and had fallen for the first man she'd seen.

'Thanks.' Eyes so blue held hers as he stepped onto the road, his dog rushing off to the other field to finish the job.

'No problem,' she replied, not able to stop herself from looking at him. She guessed he was just a little older than her, about thirty, and he had a smile to die for. It lit up his face, making his eyes sparkle like the sea on a summer's day.

She shivered. Thoughts of summer reminding her she was standing on a hillside in Wales, in the middle of the winter.

'I think a cup of tea is in order.' His voice, with only the faintest hint of a Welsh accent warmed her more than any hot drink could. 'I'm Rob, by the way.'

'Sally,' she said and, for the first time in ages, shyness crept over her. That was something she thought she'd left behind in her teenage years.

'Sally.' He nodded as if in approval. 'What about that cup of tea then?'

She looked up at him and frowned, trying to hide her confusion at what was happening between them. Where was he going to find a cup of tea around here? She glanced briefly away; nothing but the road, twisting and turning its way against the hillside.

Strangely she didn't want the moment with this man to end. If she declined and walked on then it would be over, but if she accepted...

'A cup of tea?' She teased, her voice light, a complete contrast to how she actually felt. 'Where are you going to find that?'

He laughed softly and looked down the hillside in the direction the sheep had just gone. 'The farmhouse is just down there. About a ten minute walk.'

As she looked down the steep hillside she saw the rooftops of a farmhouse and barns, nestled against the green fields. 'I couldn't intrude.'

'Nonsense,' he said, took her gloved hand in a companionable way, and began walking.

If she'd been in London and a man she didn't know took her hand and started walking with her, she'd have done anything from scream to attack him with her bag. But this felt right, familiar in a strange sort of way. The Welsh air must be getting to her more than she knew.

'I'm not sure,' she hesitated and pulled back, causing them both to stop.

He smiled and summer shone from his eyes, warming her with thoughts of what could be. 'My sister won't mind.'

Sister. 'You live with your sister?' The words were out before she could stop them.

He whistled to his dog, which ran stealthily across the field towards them as they began to walk on again. 'She lives in our family home, after she took over the running of the farm whilst I was away.'

Her interest was piqued. 'Where did you go? When you went away, I mean.'

His long steps were hard to keep up with and the uneven ground they were crossing made it worse. Her trainers were far from suitable and already her toes were damp and cold. Longingly she looked at his wellingtons.

'I've been in London for the last two years.' The cold wind tried to snag each word from him.

'Small world,' she laughed, trying to image what she would have thought if she'd bumped into him in a London bar. Not that she would have been out; she'd been busy trying to salvage her marriage. 'I live in London.'

He paused and looked at her, his hand still holding hers, as if they'd known each other forever. 'Christmas holidays in Wales?'

'Something like that.' More like escape from the past, she thought as she looked down, suddenly not quite able to meet his gaze, wishing they were still walking through the field. The intensity in those blue eyes was too much and she wondered if he could see right into her soul and retrieve every secret she'd hidden. 'I decided last minute to get away from London.'

As far as she was concerned, she wasn't in a hurry to get back to the bustle of London and even though she'd only been in her little cottage for a week, she was glad she'd taken it for six months. If she hadn't got herself together by then, she probably never would.

His cold fingers lifted her chin, forcing her to look at him once more and the buzz of attraction she'd felt up on the road exploded into something much bigger. She was beginning to wish she had met him in a London bar. Suddenly going back to the bright lights seemed infinitely more attractive, especially if he was going to be there.

'I'm glad you did.' His eyes locked with hers, sending shivers of excitement down her spine.

She blinked, not believing what was happening and his hand dropped. Letting out a breath she'd had no idea she was holding, she stepped back away from him, acutely aware his other hand still held hers.

Something warm leant against her leg and she looked down as the somewhat bedraggled collie lolled against her, tongue hanging out. It was nice to think the dog trusted her enough to do that, but it also meant there wasn't any escape from Rob and the way he made her heart flutter. Something she thought it would never do again.

Rob couldn't take his eyes from Sally's face, the cold making her cheeks and nose red in a way that made him want to wrap her against him and keep her warm. Even greater was the need to prolong this chance encounter. He thanked the impending snow and the need to bring the sheep to lower fields for making sure he was on the hillside when she'd walked past.

'Right,' he said forcing his mind back to the present. 'Tea, before we both freeze to death.'

'It's gone much colder just since I left the cottage this morning.' She fell into step beside him, the companionship so natural it was as if they had made this journey many times before, with his faithful dog Toby, trotting alongside, as he was now.

'Are you just here for the holidays?' He hoped it was longer, but with New Year's Eve just days away he might at least be able to see her once or twice.

'I'm not sure. Maybe longer,' she said as they stopped at the gate, the warmth of the farmhouse much closer now.

He opened the gate, the metal catch clanking. Their eyes met again and the rush of attraction hurtled between them and he was sure it wasn't just him. 'Good.'

'What about you? Are you spending Christmas with your sister?' Her polite question brought back all she'd managed to make him forget with lightning speed.

'A bit more than that.' He couldn't keep the disappointment from his voice. Being back in Wales and running the farm had never been on his agenda. Megan had always been the farmer, even when they were kids. 'Anyway, less of that. A hot cuppa is needed.'

Toby led the way across the yard and towards the house and he followed, with his hand still around Sally's, almost reluctant to let it go. Now they were back at the farmhouse they would be warm, but he'd enjoyed the easy companionship.

'Oh, so warm,' she almost hummed the words as they stepped inside the porch. Her smile lit up her eyes and he couldn't help the amused laugh that escaped him.

He pulled off his hat and coat, hanging them with the array of other coats, and took hers from her. He had to stifle the gasp when she pulled off her hat and coat, revealing the most gorgeous auburn hair cascading down her back.

'Come through,' he said, aware his voice had become a little hoarse but, as he glanced at her, she was too busy taking in the jumble of life that was the farmhouse kitchen.

Further into the house he could hear his niece and nephew squealing, probably as they led his sister a merry dance. He still marvelled at how she and her husband had managed to keep the farm going after his father had gone into the home, especially after his brother-in-law's stay in hospital. But that thought took him back to the reason he was here, the duty he was expected to perform as the only son.

'This is nice.' Sally looked around her as the genuine words warmed him far more than the heat from the Aga.

'It's a bit lived in, but Megan is kept running from dawn to dusk with the twins.' He took the kettle from its trivet, placed it on the aga, and leant back against the warmth of it, watching his guest.

'Twins.' Her brows lifted in surprise and that warm smile spread across the lips he wanted nothing more than to kiss. Since when did women affect him so rapidly? Play it cool had always been his motto, especially after his fiancée had ended their engagement so suddenly.

'They're three.' Megan's voice startled him as she walked into the kitchen, carrying a bundle of washing. 'Hi, I'm Rob's sister Megan. So what brings you here?'

The curiosity on Megan's face was too much and he had to laugh, which earned him a sharp look from his sister and a confused half smile, half frown from Sally.

'I'm Sally and I guess I was in the wrong place at the right time.' She laughed, a light sound that made him think of the brook trickling over the rocks in the summer.

'Sheep?' Megan asked as she went through to the laundry room and dumped the washing before joining them. 'Rob always did like to get anyone passing involved.'

'Well, I'm glad he did.' She smiled across at him and he met her gaze unable to keep the smile from his lips. 'It's been a very inspiring morning.'

'Inspiring?' Megan asked and Rob was glad of her presence as he'd lost the ability to put words together.

'I'm a writer,' volunteered Sally and it was Rob's turn to be surprised. He hadn't considered what she might do for a living, but if he had, a writer wouldn't have been anywhere near the top of his list.

Was that surprise on Rob's face? Sally smiled at him teasingly. He really was very charming and attractive, but that had been a recipe for disaster previously. Her rational thought urged caution, but her heart was racing. She hadn't ever felt this spark before.

Enjoying the view, she watched as Rob turned his back and made the tea, his strong shoulders tense beneath the thick jumper. His brown hair, curling in an unruly and inviting way around his neck, drew her attention. Until she became aware of Megan watching, looking from one to the other.

'I'll just go and check on the twins,' she said and hastily walked back through the kitchen, her words trailing after her. 'When it goes this quiet, it always means trouble.'

Rob placed two steaming mugs of tea on the large pine table and gestured for her to sit. 'So, is that why you are here, seeking inspiration?'

'Partly,' she said and sat, gratefully hugging the mug with her hands. Her feet were still freezing, but the rest of her was quite warm, and it wasn't just from being inside. Each time Rob looked at her, heat simmered inside her. 'I got divorced last summer and I guess I just want some peace.'

'And I came along and hijacked it.' He looked so intently into her eyes she had to look away, but soon the temptation was too much and she met his gaze again.

'You can hijack my peace anytime.' After the divorce she thought she'd never be saying and wanting such things, but Rob seemed different. She didn't know how or why she thought that.

He laughed. An honest laugh. 'Your peace will be safe until the New Year. I'm busy here, preparing for lambing, then I'm babysitting those two rascals on New Year's Eve.'

'Until the New Year,' she said brightly, working hard to keep a smile on her lips and wondering if it was the brush off. 'I should get back. It soon gets very dark here. Without the help of streetlamps, I'm useless in the dark.'

'I'll drive you back to the village now,' he said finishing his tea in an impatient gesture. 'I need to get sheep feed.'

The old Land Rover looked tired and smelt of straw, dogs and sheep. Something else for my inspiration notebook, she thought as she climbed in. Sally tried hard to keep her eyes on the road ahead, but every now and then glanced at Rob, his profile set in concentration as he negotiated the bends on the way down to the village.

'When do you plan to go back to London?' She kept her voice light, as if chatting with friends, but the tension that suddenly infused the air warned her that this was far from a light subject.

'I don't think I can – at least not for the foreseeable future.' She saw his jaw clench, questions forming in her mind, questions she didn't feel able to ask.

They stopped at a junction and instead of turning to look for traffic he looked straight at her, his eyes sombre. 'My brother-in-law has been very ill and Megan can't do everything on her own. Farming's not my thing, I'd much rather be lost in the latest technology, but here I am.'

'When you go back to London, give me a call.' She pulled her purse from her coat pocket and handed him a business card. He looked at it then put it on the dashboard, as if discarding it.

'I'll be here for some time.' He thrust the gearstick forwards and the heavy Land Rover moved off and down the last hill towards the village.

If that wasn't a brush off she didn't know what was. Maybe it was just as well. Still fresh from her divorce it was probably best to have fun, enjoy life. Once she'd met her deadline, that was.

'This is where I'm staying,' Sally offered as her cottage came into view. 'I hope you have a good babysitting experience and see you in the New Year maybe.'

He nodded. 'Maybe.' She could feel his eyes on her as she slipped down from the Land Rover, but didn't miss the non-committal tone of his voice. 'Happy New Year Sally. May it bring all you want.'

'You too Rob, you too.'

She shut the door and watched the battered blue Land Rover drive on down the hill into the centre of the village, unable to shake the feeling that something had gone wrong. The sizzle that had instantly sparked between them had slowed to a faint glow, or had at least been stifled of oxygen.

Rob had mooched around for the next two days, sure it had just been a Londoner's presence that made him miss the bright lights and partying. He'd fended off Megan's enthusiastic questions and attempts at matchmaking, refusing to allow himself to think that it had been just a particular Londoner's presence. But he couldn't go there, not when she was only here for a short time. He didn't want a long distance relationship. What was he thinking? She was here for peace and quiet after her divorce.

Today was New Year's Eve and it had been so busy he'd hardly thought anymore about the woman who'd brightened his afternoon as he'd brought the remainder of the ewes down to the lower fields. She'd been like a ray of summer sunshine.

'This came for you,' Megan said as he came in for supper. 'The kids are in bed, but probably won't stay there. Are you sure you are going to be okay?'

'This is the first time you and David have been out since the twins were babies. Go and enjoy yourselves. It's New Year's Eve.'

He looked absently at the envelope, not recognising the handwriting, but deciding he'd open it later.

'Don't you want to go out?' Megan asked as she put the dishwasher on.

'No,' he laughed at her insistence. 'Neither do you by the sound of it.'

'Oh, I do.' She whirled round to face him. 'I've got a new dress to wear, but I thought maybe after our visitor the other day, you might have plans.'

'No, no plans. She'll be going back to London, so no point even starting anything, besides, there's more than enough to do here.' He kept his voice light and carefree. He wasn't about to let his sister know that the idea of spending time with Sally appealed to him. She'd be like a dog with a bone and he'd never hear the last of it.

Megan ruffled his hair as she stopped next to him. 'You're such a good brother, what would we do without you?'

'Go before I change my mind,' he teased and turned his attention to his meal.

As he heard the front door close, he put down his knife and fork and opened the letter.

Meet me at midnight. Village Square.

He read the line of flowing handwriting. No chance of that. His sister used to be a party animal. Whoever it was would be in the village square without him. That was for sure.

Rob looked again at the envelope. Could it be from Sally? There weren't any clues or hints as to who had sent it. But did it really matter? He'd already planned to watch the New Year's Eve festivities on the television with the twins tucked safely in bed. He hoped!

The story had been buzzing in Sally's head all day and she'd been tapping away at the keyboard for so long she hadn't noticed the time. She looked up from the circle of light she was sat in to see the rest of the room was in total darkness. That late.

New Year's Eve and she was on her own in a cottage in Wales. Exactly as she wanted. So why be downhearted?

The bright light of the kitchen made her blink as she turned it on then flicked on the kettle. From the kitchen corner where it was charging, her phone flashed, alerting her to a text. Good wishes from friends in London, she thought as she picked it up.

Meet me at midnight. Village Square.

Her heart pounded in her chest and her stomach felt like a thousand butterflies had all taken flight at once. It must be from Rob. She had given him her card after all. Quickly she glanced at the clock. Eleven thirty. How had the last hours of the year slipped by so anonymously?

Should she go? He hadn't seemed very keen, but then she hadn't told him she'd taken a long-term let on the cottage. She could, if she wanted, stay here until the summer.

'Okay, farmer Rob, you have obviously got out of your babysitting duties, so I will meet you at midnight,' she said aloud and dashed up the narrow stairs to quickly tidy herself. At least the village square was only a short walk away, but with the cold wind threatening snow, she'd need to bundle up.

Ten minutes later, wrapped up snuggly with her scarf and hat, she walked down towards the village square. There wasn't much there; just a disused phone kiosk that served as the community notice board and a bus stop sign. Opposite that there was a small bench outside probably one of the few remaining village shops in the country.

She looked at her watch. Ten minutes to midnight. She hoped he wouldn't keep her waiting too long. Hanging around in this cold wind, laced with its promise of snow, was not going to be pleasant.

The cold was biting, nipping at the toes and she stamped her feet and shoved her gloved hands deep into her pockets. Fireworks lit up the sky in the distance, their wild bangs marking the New Year. Sally shivered, despite her layers as the first flakes of snow fell, big fluffy white flakes which twirled like dancers to the floor, settling quickly around her feet.

This was silly. Alone, as snow fell on New Year's Eve. She could be inside, snuggled under her duvet watching the celebrations from London on her television. Instead she was chasing a dream.

'Thank goodness you're still here.'

She whirled round to see Rob heading her way and her heart skipped a beat. Beyond him she saw the Land Rover outside her cottage. She must have missed its arrival as the fireworks banged around her, but she certainly wasn't missing the driver's arrival.

'I'm so glad you text me,' she said stepping towards him, determined not to shy away from what she felt.

He stopped dead in his tracks, his brow furrowed into a frown. Around them the snow was falling faster and the road was becoming whiter. 'I didn't.'

Her heart sank. 'Then why are you here?'

'Megan,' he said and threw up his hands in exasperation. 'I should have known.'

Sally was totally confused. Did he want to see her or not? 'I don't understand.'

He stepped towards her, took her in his arms and pulled her close, his lips brushing over hers, sending skitters of excitement all through her. 'Happy New Year Sally,' he said as he pulled back from her and looked into her eyes. All around her snow was falling, but she was melting from the unveiled desire in his eyes.

'Happy New Year, Rob. I'm guessing we've got Megan to thank for this.' She reached up and kissed him, closing her eyes as the sensation of spinning around was intensified by the snowflakes playing their own games around them.

She stopped kissing him, opened her eyes, wondering if it was all a dream, one that would vanish. But he pulled her close, his warmth telling her he was real, that this was real.

'We have,' he said as he turned, pulling her against him and walked back towards her cottage, the Land Rover parked haphazardly outside. 'But for now, we'll just go inside and get warm. Megan can wait a while to see if her matchmaking has worked.'

'It's worked.' She snuggled against him as they walked through the thickly falling snow. 'This is the best New Year ever.'

Author Details

If you've enjoyed this story and would like to find out more about Rachael here's how:

Twitter: @rachaeldthomas
Facebook: *www.facebook.com/rachael.thomas.35977*
Website: *www.rachaelthomas.co.uk*

Rachael's next book, 'Claimed by the Sheikh', will be available from Harlequin Mills and Boon in February 2015

Into My Loving Arms

Lynne Pardoe

'Good Morning, Mrs Wilson. I'm Libby James, social worker, here to meet you and your grandson.'

She wasn't what I expected of a social worker. I thought she'd be a bit more scruffy. You know, long hair and shabby shoes, the sort that is vegetarian and only eats lentils. But there in front of me was a young, fresh faced young woman, dressed quite smartly and looking, well, rather pleasant.

'May I come in then?' she asked politely.

'Oh, yes, of course,' I said, forgetting myself and moving aside to make way for her. She walked in front of me, and stepped inside the sitting room. I pushed the front door closed and while she waited I saw her looking around the room, taking in every detail. I was glad I'd dusted every corner.

Baby Noah was asleep in his pram. She walked past him but didn't pay him any particular attention. Maybe his views didn't matter, but then again, I suppose he wasn't old enough to give them.

I'd washed and ironed the loose covers from the sofa and armchairs. Would she notice? I hoped so. The long pine dining table was bare except for the salt and pepper pots in the middle. Ron, my husband, said it always looked perfect anyway, and didn't need doing, but of course it did. How would he feel if Noah had to go and live somewhere else and I hadn't done my absolute best? I busied myself making two cups of tea, trying to stop my hands trembling, and filled the time by chatting about anything and everything. Yet I had to face the fact that she was here for a reason, and a very important reason at that.

We sat on two armchairs facing each other.

'Now Mrs....'

'Jo,' I interrupted, 'call me Jo,' I never did like being called anything formal.

'Okay then, Jo,' she smiled, putting some papers in her file in order.

I found it hard to smile back. This was a matter of life or death – no exaggeration. Noah's life depended on this woman's opinion, at least his life with us did, and it wasn't anything to be taken lightly.

'As you know, I've been asked by the family court to write a report on where Noah should live – is that Noah over there?' She pointed in the direction of the pram.

'Yes.' How many babies did she think I had in the house? I could hardly bear to look over at him. Just one look at that little nose, turned up just like his mother's, or that little fist clenched tight, showing that he wouldn't let go, and I'd be in floods of tears.

'He's very sweet.'

How did she know? She only looked at him for a few seconds. But I said nothing, only nodding in agreement.

'When you asked the court to make a special guardianship order so that you would have parental responsibility for Noah as well as his parents, they requested a social worker's report to guide the judges to a conclusion, and that's what I'm here to do. Is that okay?'

I didn't really have a choice, did I? As she'd probably guessed it wasn't on my top ten lists of things to do, but under the circumstances I knew I had to show willing. 'Yes, that's fine by me I replied.' The lie tripped off my tongue with surprising ease.

'Could we start by you telling me the situation, from your point of view?'

Oh crikey, this was it, the moment I'd been dreading, but it had to be done. 'It's Shona, my daughter – our daughter, she's...' Oh, how could I put it without bursting into tears? I took a deep breath. 'She's run off with a chap who isn't Noah's father. I don't know... we don't know who Noah's father is. We don't know where Shona is either.' There, that was it, done. What else could she want to know? Not a lot, surely. What else was there to say, after all?

The silver disco ball glittered as it spun brightly in the gloomy light. Loud pop music pulsed through the atmosphere, almost forcing people to move in harmony with the heavy bass beat of the sound.

Shona moved dreamily, her hair swinging across her face as she swayed to the sounds, her eyes shut tight as if she was in another world. From the side, a man watched her tirelessly. His face almost hurt as it tried to form an expression which echoed the mood of melancholy that seemed to surround her.

There was something about her that caught him, the way sorrow was etched on her face and the way she danced, as if she was trying to shut the world out. He watched and watched her, entranced. After a while, he downed the rest of his pint, crossed the few yards between them and began dancing in front of her.

His style wasn't as fluid as hers, he knew that and felt very uncomfortable, a frown wrinkling his forehead. Whichever way he moved, he always seemed out of tune with the music. But that didn't bother Shona. She didn't even seem to notice him.

'Hey babe,' he said eventually, 'how do you do that thing with your feet?'

She ignored him, oblivious. He tried again and still she ignored him. He tapped her on the arm. She opened her eyes and looked around, frowning as if disappointed to find herself back in the world.

'How d'you do that thing with your feet?' he repeated, jiggling his feet around as she did and making a mess of it.

'Oh,' she looked down and murmured, 'I dunno. It just kind of happens when the music starts.'

He looked at her and laughed at himself, then tried again, and again, but still couldn't get it right. She moved to his side, taking a lukewarm interest and showing him the motion of her feet.

'I give up!' he declared after a while. 'Why don't you come and sit with me?' He cupped his hand under her elbow without waiting for her reply and guided her to the table he'd been occupying. 'Let me get you a drink.'

He squeezed up close to her on the bench and they sat, Shona barely speaking, sometimes so troubled that a tear ran down her cheek, as he teased words out of her. He was so engrossed in her that he looked nowhere else, while she was so low that her gaze didn't lift from the floor.

Eventually he kissed her and she didn't protest. Wrapping his arm around her, he led her away with him; she went, willingly but not cheerfully. Happiness was beyond her at the moment and it wasn't his concern. It took all she had to exist, to stay in the world and keep breathing, but that was all he needed.

'What can you see, little baby? What can you see?' I jiggled Noah about, holding my grandson at the window. Holding him tight, relishing his baby smell of milk and honey, and the warmth from his body, as he snuggled close.

He looked out of the window, a cute expression of concentration lighting up his face as looked out. Cars were already coated white with frost and nothing, not even a solitary cat, was out. The town was steeped in silence, as if all had taken refuge from the winter chill.

'Put the child down, Jo, for heaven's sake.' My husband's voice growled from under the duvet. 'Can't you see I'm trying to sleep? I've got a busy day tomorrow.'

'Never mind that you can't sleep John. He can't sleep, I can't sleep. I keep wondering if he's missing his mother. Will he remember her, do you think?' I held the baby tighter still, trying to protect him from the world.

'You just feel guilty, you do.' John's words were blunt. 'It's not our fault. There's nothing we could have done to stop Shona. She's a big girl now and she's made her own choices in life.'

'Choices! You can say that again!' I had to leave the bedroom, had to escape from his version of the truth. It seemed like only yesterday that it was Shona's body hugging close to mine, when she was little and loving.

I put the baby down on the spare bed, the practicalities of motherhood guiding my actions. 'Let's see if this helps then.' He gurgled and chuckled as I changed his nappy as if he was having the time of his life, no matter that it was three in the morning. I'd almost forgotten about that, how babies ruled your world. 'Where is mummy then? Where is she now? Will she be alone this Christmas?' My words spilled into the emptiness in her old room. 'Where will Shona be?'

'What happened on the day Shona left?' Libby sat on the sofa, her fingers wrapped around a warm mug as she prepared to listen. 'I'll need to write it all in my report.'

The social worker was back. More questions. Questions, questions, questions. Please can someone give me answers? The words screamed inside my head but I forced a smile.

'Things weren't right from the moment the baby was born. He was beautiful, perfect. We all said so, but Shona just lay transfixed after the birth, exhausted and staring at the wall. She didn't seem to want to know Noah. The midwife said it happens sometimes, and I should just let her rest. It was the early hours of the morning and we were both tired, so the staff did all the night feeds and I did all the daytime ones.'

'You must both have been exhausted,' Libby sympathised giving me her whole attention. There was something very comforting in being listened to. She understood, I thought, she really does.

'Shona was much the same the next day, she could sleep for England. So we took her home, thinking she'd be better in her own room with her own things around her and that in a few days she'd bounce back. But she didn't. A few days later, I was downstairs with Noah making his bottle and I heard the front door click shut. By the time I'd gone up to her room and discovered she wasn't there, she would have been well away. That was way over four weeks ago now.' I stopped; I couldn't go on any more. It was as if my life had stopped dead in its tracks, right there too, I had such an ache in my heart.

'It must be very hard on you.'

'Thank you,' I nodded wiping a tear from my eye. 'It helps that you care.'

'I wish we could do more to bring her back,' Libby said. 'I have spoken to the police, and I know you have too.'

'They sent a family officer. She was very kind.'

'I'm glad to hear it.' Libby nodded and I knew her concern went beyond her official role. 'They said they were looking for her, that she was vulnerable, and I know they're doing their best. She may be suffering from post natal depression. It can make people act in ways that are totally alien. I'll finish my report now as I have as much information as I need. I'll be recommending that you and your husband bring Noah up because you're doing such a wonderful job here and he's clearly a very happy little lad. Courts aren't obliged to follow our recommendation, but in your case I can't see any reason why they wouldn't. Hopefully, though, it won't come to that and she'll be home way before Noah is much older.'

'I do so hope so,' I said, crossing every finger and toe that I had. With a smile and some more soothing comments, she was gone.

'Hi, Shona. It is you isn't it? Shona Scott from Kirkdale High?' A woman stood in front of the park bench where she was sitting, cutting off her only means of escape.

It was too late to hide. Shona looked up and recognised her straight away, those kindly eyes a dead give-away. Sally was standing right in front of her, dominating her view and smiling down at her. If she'd noticed Shona's haggard, careworn looks she didn't show it.

'Yeah, that's me.' Shona's voice was quiet, like a little mouse as she tried to rustle up a smile, but only the very corners of her mouth lifted up as she muttered an awkward 'Hi.'

'Hey, good to see you! I'm Sally Scott, remember me? Mind if I sit next to you?' Without waiting for the answer, Sally sat down and Shona shuffled along the bench to give her room. 'Great to see you! How are you, what you been doing honey?'

'Not much. You?' Shona replied, although it was an effort to speak.

'I bin doing just fine.' Sally chirped. 'I got myself a whole new job, just what I wanted so I'm well pleased. I ditched the latest boyfriend, could be doing better in the relationship department I realised.' She dipped her head towards Shona in a jaunty fashion. 'Been working in the Big Apple– New York – stayin' with family, but I don't start the new job until the beginning of the month, so I've got a bit of time to spare. Life's good, yeah, couldn't ask for more really.' Sally's gaze rested on Shona for a moment too long.

'Congratulations.' Shona couldn't manage enthusiasm, even though the sentiment was sincere. It was hard to be upbeat about anyone else's news, when your own life was just an existence.

'I worked hard for it. Stuck with a plonker of a boyfriend too long till the penny dropped. No change there then!' Sally elbowed her in the ribs lightly and laughed. Shona smiled weakly in reply.

'Hey, that's enough about me. Get me, being all me, me, me.' She threw her head back and laughed, 'My friends tell me off about it all the time, but do I ever learn? Uh uh!' Sally wagged her finger in the air to make her point. 'How about you honey? How've you been doing. Didn't I hear that you had a baby?'

Shona froze and reached into her pocket, pulling out a box of cigarettes. Reality wasn't supposed to come crashing in like this. Keeping her mind a blank was the only way. Her thin, pale fingers reached into the packet, her hand shaking. Just breathe, it was all she could do, all she had been doing.

Sally seemed to sense the change of tempo, the atmosphere that her question had evoked. She didn't speak again, but Shona sensed her watching. Sally wouldn't have missed the tremor that went right up Shona's arm. Her movements were tense, hesitant as she lit her cigarette. She had to concentrate so hard just to do this simple little task, everything about her uneasy, and she knew it must be showing on her face.

A deep purple bruise became exposed as Shona's sleeve slid back. Gasping, she covered it quickly, looking over at Sally, hoping she hadn't noticed, but it was obvious she had. Their gaze met and stayed locked for a few moments. Sally looked at her friend, really looked. She couldn't have failed to notice the bruise on Shona's cheek, even though it was old and turning ochre, and another newer one above her eye. For a moment Sally looked puzzled, her brow creased in surprise as she looked at Shona. But she said nothing, taking in all the evidence and clearly reaching a conclusion that was suddenly as obvious to Shona herself, as it must have been to her old friend.

The tone of Sally's voice lowered in sympathy and she put an arm around her shoulder. 'Things not been too good for you, eh?'

Shona looked down at the ground, a fine tremor enveloping her. 'No.' A tear ran down her cheek.

Sally watched silently, as if taking it all in. 'Hey, I got an idea right,' it was an announcement more than a question, 'let's go for a coffee? My treat. You'll be doing me a favour 'cos I'm at a loose end for a while.' She stood up, holding out her arm for Shona in a way that couldn't be ignored.

It was Christmas Eve, but how could I enjoy myself? A police liaison officer had been round in the morning to show me the latest 'Have You Seen?' posters they were putting out. The officer thought I'd have a better Christmas knowing that more was being done. But I just welled up with tears. The photo showed Shona looking happy and carefree, exactly as I knew she wouldn't be. She was right, though; it was good to know they were doing their best.

Later, when Noah was asleep and hubby was out at the pub in search of some festive cheer, I sat watching the telly. Snow was coming down in thick lumps again; it was a cold winter in more ways than one.

I thought I might be imagining things at first, the strange sound I heard; something like a wailing, a sort of low whimpering. I looked over at the cat but she was dozing on a cushion and I could see nothing was wrong with her; she came over to see me anyway. The sound kept on. It was very soft, you could just about hear it, but it hadn't stopped. I wasn't imagining it. Looking out of the window, it was as though someone had cut open a down-filled duvet above and the feathers were gently gliding down to earth, but there was nothing there that shouldn't be there.

Still the sound continued.

Then a thought struck me. The front door. It was near the front door. Slowly, carefully, I went towards it, barely letting myself breathe, then stopped. The sound definitely came from outside the door; I could hear it clearly above the distant chant of Christmas carols.

Not daring to hope, I opened the door inch by inch, so as not to scare whoever it was, and then, finally, I breathed. There, in front of my eyes was Shona, leaning against the door jamb, sobbing for all she was worth. I went to her and wrapped my arms around her, hugging her tightly to me, just as I'd done with her son in the weeks she'd been gone. She didn't say a word, her body shaking with tears. Neither of us moved for quite a few minutes despite the bitter winter chill.

Coming home hadn't been easy and somehow I knew that too much emotion might make Shona worse. So I just held her, a little frozen ice shard, like the babe in arms I held so long ago. Slowly she put her arms around me until she was hugging me back, just as tightly.

That's when I knew that everything was going to be alright.

Author Details

If you've enjoyed this story and would like to find out more about Lynne Pardoe, here's how:

Twitter: @spabbygirl
Website: www.lynnepardoe.com

Lynne's debut Pocketbook will be available in January 2015

An Early Christmas Present

Samantha Tonge

Ruth gazed around the three bedroom, semi-detached house and let out a sigh. At least they'd managed to find somewhere half-decent to rent, whilst they looked for a proper family home. The kitchen was a bit small and the wallpaper wasn't to their taste, but it was such a relief to get settled in over the October half-term holiday. Now Millie would be ready to start the second half of the autumn term in a new school.

How they had celebrated David's promotion to regional manager – until they'd discovered the region he was in charge of didn't include their address and they'd have to move. It was a wrench for Millie, leaving behind her friends. Plus Ruth would miss the neighbours and her flower-arranging club at the cathedral.

'But I heart this house, where we've always lived,' Millie had said in teen speak. Sometimes she spoke more like a text message from her phone. 'And what about my bezzie mates?'

Ruth had squeezed her daughter's arm. 'Thanks to the phone and internet, you can keep in touch. Before you know it, love, you'll make different friends'.

And sure enough, after a few nervous days, Millie began to enjoy her new school. By the time the end of November arrived, she'd been taken under the wing of a group of girls who, like her, were obsessed with the latest craze for novels about vampires and werewolves.

'I'm so glad Millie's fallen in with such sensible schoolmates,' Ruth said to David, one early December evening, as they sat in the lounge. 'Sensible, that is, apart from believing Dracula might be real and that it's dangerous to go out when there's a full moon!'

David nodded, one eye on the television. 'Am I driving them to the cinema this Saturday?'

Ruth nodded. 'Unless you want to do the weekly shop.'

They both grinned.

'Remember I've invited Dora and Jim, from next door, for lunch on Sunday,' she said. 'It's the least we can do after all the help they've given us these past weeks.'

'Yeah – Jim showing me where to turn off the water, quick-smart, saved a lot of damage when the washing machine leaked,' said David.

'Hmm, Dora's a real gem, introducing me to the flower-arranging club at her church. It's a pity she and Jim aren't our permanent new neighbours.' With the friendly retired couple next door, Ruth hadn't felt nearly as lonely during the day as she'd expected.

With a yawn, she put down the Christmas card she was writing, and gazed around. 'This living room's a decent size and would look even bigger without the lurid wallpaper – unlike that house we saw yesterday. Our two armchairs wouldn't have fitted in there, let alone our sofa.'

David switched off the telly and drained his cup of tea. 'I know you're impatient to find our own home, Ruth, but you know what the estate agent said about the housing market in December.'

"'It's an expensive enough time of year without people buying a property. Things will pick up in the New Year',' Ruth quoted, and sighed. 'I know – but it would have been nice to be in our own place for Christmas and get all our belongings out of storage. Still, this house feels quite homely now. Millie 'hearts' the built-in wardrobe in her bedroom.'

'Have to say the bathroom's my favourite part,' said David. 'That power shower is amazing and I love the grey and silver tiles.'

'I thought it was the shed you preferred?' Ruth said, a twinkle in her eye.

David chuckled. 'That's more like a mobile home. A man could lose himself for a month, in there.'

A scratching at the back patio windows disturbed them and Ruth got up.

'There's our little friend,' she said, as a pair of glinting eyes stared in from the darkness.

David joined her at the kitchen back door as she opened it. A raggedy black cat with a few whiskers missing, padded in.

'Still no collar,' said David as the creature sat down and washed its muddy paws.

The stray had visited them most evenings since Bonfire Night, when it had darted inside and hidden behind the kitchen bin. In fact 'visit' was the wrong word –Millie would giggle at how the cat now sauntered in, as if it owned the house. Ruth opened a can of cat food and scraped some into a saucer, which they placed on the floor. Just lately, the cat had let them stroke him afterwards. He'd even emitted a purr for Millie, after she'd spent a good five minutes scratching his ears. Tonight, meal finished, he curled up on the mat by the back door, eyes narrowed slightly as if to say, 'I'm not going to budge.'

'I don't like feeding someone else's cat, but he's so thin and doesn't look like he has a proper home,' said Ruth and ran a hand through her brunette curls.

David tickled under the creature's chin. 'We ought to give him a name, really.'

Ruth shrugged. 'I don't think it's fair on him to get too friendly. We could be gone in a couple of months.' Still, that didn't stop her letting him sleep on the mat until they went to bed. Well, it was frosty outside, she told herself.

'I heart that cat,' said Millie, a week or so later, in the middle of December. She and Ruth were eating breakfast in the small pine kitchen. 'Have you seen how long the hairs are, coming out of his big ears? He looks like a Gremlin.'

Ruth laughed.

'Mum?'

'Yes, darling?'

'Can we get a cat at our new place?'

'I don't see why not – in fact your dad suggested that, just the other day.' Ruth wiped her mouth with a napkin. 'Right. Off to school, Missy. I've got a viewing to get to. Something new has finally come on the market. Your dad couldn't get the time off work, so I'm under strict orders to take notes. Don't forget your gloves and scarf – sleet is forecast.'

Millie downed the rest of her orange juice and stood up. 'Okay Mum – and don't you forget, we're going to the school carol concert at seven tonight.'

They also attended the school's Christmas bingo evening and fair. Ruth decided it was a great time of year to meet people and make new friends. One of the mums told her about a dinner lady job that was going in the nearby junior school and they all sympathized with her disappointment that, so far, all the house viewings had come to nothing.

Christmas Eve arrived, Ruth having worked hard to arrange church flowers with Dora for the imminent festive services. Millie was doing last-minute shopping with friends, and David would come home from work at lunch time. Late morning, Ruth was just about to pop around to Jim and Dora's to invite them for Christmas drinks that evening when Mr Chapman, the estate agent, rang.

Ruth answered the call and listened intently. After several minutes her mouth drooped, she said goodbye and put the phone down. Then Ruth thought for a moment, her face suddenly brightened. With butterflies in her stomach, she picked up the receiver and, as quickly as she could, rang Mr Chapman back…

'Us viewing a house, *today*?' said Millie, just after lunch, a few hours later. Worn out from rushing around the precinct, she was now relaxing on the sofa. In awe, she'd been gazing at the Christmas tree – hardly an inch of branch was free from baubles or tinsel.

'I can't believe you agreed to that, Ruth,' said David and loosened his tie. 'It's Christmas Eve! Surely everyone is thinking less about work now and more about getting home to their families?'

'Not estate agents,' she said and smiled. 'Anyway, at first I didn't suggest we attend a viewing. When Mr Chapman rang to say the owner of this place was moving abroad, and would be putting this house on the market in January, I panicked. He went on to mention the low price of the property we're seeing, but I'd already switched off, in my head, and said goodbye.'

David nodded. 'It's not what we were expecting.'

'No, but the shock quickly passed when I did the sums and rang him back,' said Ruth. 'If we all agree on the house, it's a real bargain, and according to Mr Chapman the owner is desperate to sell quickly and said he'll accept the first offer that matches his asking price.'

David shrugged. 'Okay. I guess we can spare half-an-hour to look around this supposed bargain. Where is it?' He looked at his watch. It was two o'clock sharp. 'What time is the appointment?'

At that moment the doorbell rang. Millie answered the door and came back in, followed by the estate agent.

'Nice to see you again, Mr Brown,' he said to David and smiled at Ruth and Millie.

'Gosh, sorry, Mr Chapman, were we late meeting you?' said David and shook hands with the tall, blonde man.

The estate agent raised one eyebrow at Ruth, who beamed.

'Sorry – it's my surprise for the family, I haven't told them, yet,' she said to the estate agent. Ruth looked at David and Millie. 'Call it an early Christmas present.'

'What?' said Millie and stopped chewing her gum. David's brow furrowed.

'This place – it's the bargain property! Why view elsewhere, when it's gone up for sale? The location couldn't be better and the price is right within budget. In fact there would be a large enough amount left over to extend the kitchen. Dad likes the bathroom and shed, you love your bedroom... It's the obvious solution!'

David's jaw fell open. Millie gasped.

'Why don't I run over some details,' said Mr Chapman and grinned, as Ruth gave the thumbs up and went to put the kettle on. 'As Mrs Brown might have told you,' he continued, 'the owner is emigrating abroad and couldn't be more keen to accept an offer...'

By three o'clock the estate agent was gone and Ruth took out three clean cups and a Tupperware box of mince pies. David and Millie sat down at the kitchen table.

'Well?' she said.

David grinned. 'I think it's a brilliant idea, darling. This place is close to school and the church – plus in a lovely cul-de-sac. The more I think about it, the more it's the perfect solution.'

Millie clapped her hands. 'Can I decorate my bedroom? I fancy gothic reds and blacks...'

'We'll see,' said Ruth and smiled. 'I'm so glad we'll be staying next to Dora and Jim.' She lifted her handbag off one of the pine chairs and rummaged inside for a moment, before pulling out a small brown bag.

Millie opened it and her face lit up. 'A cat collar?'

'I called in at the vet's, just before lunch,' she said. 'He advised that we take our feline visitor in there, to check whether or not he's been micro-chipped. Apparently some people leave their cats behind when they move house. If an owner could do that, I doubt they'd have bothered getting him micro-chipped, so he'll be ours – if we want him.'

David and Millie beamed.

'I've made an appointment at the vet's for after Christmas – after speaking to Mr Chapman this morning, I felt so optimistic about us buying this house and felt sure you'd both agree it was a good idea.'

'So, he'll be ours if we want him?' said Millie and clapped her hands.

'Yes – although the vet's receptionist put me on the spot and asked what he was called.' Ruth's cheeks tinged pink. 'I'm afraid the only name I could come up with was 'Gremlin', so that's what he's been registered under.'

After a short silence, the three of them burst out laughing and Ruth's chest glowed. Against all the odds, they *had* moved into their new home, in time for Christmas.

Author Details

If you've enjoyed this story and would like to find out more about Samantha Tonge, here's how:

Twitter: @ SamTongeWriter
Facebook: https://www.facebook.com/SamanthaTongeAuthor
Website: http://samanthatonge.co.uk/

'Mistletoe Mansion' by Samantha Tonge is out 10th November 2014

Butterfly Nights

Harriet James

The car slinks around the square by itself, as if it knows what is required of it. Eyes shine out of the shadows and try to find mine. I stare ahead and increase speed like an ordinary driver passing through, but I fool no-one.

I don't like what I have become.

That building on the corner, chequered with lights, is where I used to work, until a signature on a form sent me away. From my seventh floor eyrie I would gaze down on traffic spooling in and out of the square, neon signs above doorways invisible by daylight, burger joints frilled with genderless teenagers, and painted girls emerging into the night like butterflies from chrysalises to hover by the railings or the shuttered newsagent's stand.

Watching the girls sucked up time, made sure I wasn't home before Evie carried the well-thumbed book of her despair to bed.

Now I spend my days fumbling around the margins of Evie's world, hoping to find a chink, a way in, but there is none, and at night I come here.

The air cuts in through the partly open window, stinging my skin. Above, the blue-black sky is star-clear, heralding frost. Slowing the car again, I glance round and am reassured by the sight of Freya's old parka with its peeling badges and scruff of fur around the hood.

I guide the car into a side-street where, half way along, a narrow passage splits a row of shops, its entrance lit by a solitary street-lamp. Sometimes there are girls here. At first I see no-one, and then three appear at once, as if the dank brickwork offers them up as a sacrifice. A cigarette lighter shoots a flame and gives me the face I am searching for. Her eyes flick towards the car. I lean across, open the door and wait. Taking her time, she draws on her cigarette then drops it, clicks over the pavement in her high heels and gets in. I catch the end of her seat-belt as she tugs it across and clip it into place, not looking at her, not speaking, and drive off.

We stop on rough ground behind the closed-down cinema, bumping over stones to reach our accustomed spot. The window purrs closed at a touch of a button. Reaching behind, I drag the parka from the back seat and she sits forward, allowing me to wrap it around her. Then I take her in my arms and hold her, warm and safe in her cocoon. I rest my head lightly on hers, breathing her in, sensing rather than hearing the rhythm of her heartbeat, until she tenses and I release her.

'Are you eating properly?'

She risks a pale smile. 'As always.'

'It's Christmas soon. In a week,' I say, keeping the emotion from my voice.

She doesn't answer but looks straight ahead. Bringing her hand to her mouth, she presses the thumbnail hard against her lower lip. After a minute I start the engine and we head back, Freya in her skimpy dress and jacket, the parka abandoned on the back seat.

Then, as we reach the square, something wonderful happens.

'Give my love to Mum,' Freya says, in a small, soft voice, and it's as much as I can do to nod.

Now I know the day will come when I will bring our daughter home, and on that day, Evie will come to life again and the light will return to her eyes.

Author Details

If you've enjoyed this story and would like to find out more about Harriet James, here's how:

Twitter: @HJames_writer
Facebook: *https://www.facebook.com/HarrietJamesWriter*

Harriet's novel 'Remarkable Things' will be published by Crooked Cat in 2015

Printed in Great Britain
by Amazon.co.uk, Ltd.,
Marston Gate.